STRAIN

AMELIA C. GORMLEY

ACG Publications
www.ameliacgormley.com

Cover art: Danielle Fine
Editor: Danielle Poiesz

ISBN: 978-1-62-622617-3
First Edition: February 2014
Second Edition: April 2018

In a world with little hope and no rules, the only thing they have to lose is themselves.

RHYS COOPER is a dead man. He's spent years hiding from the virus that wiped out most of the human race, but an act of futile heroism has him counting down his remaining days. The timely arrival of superhuman soldiers offers some feeble hope—but only if Rhys can reconcile himself to doing what is necessary to take advantage of it.

Sergeant Darius Murrell has seen too much death and too little tenderness, seeking out survivors only to put the infected out of their misery, or send the uninfected to a safe haven he and his fellow Juggernaut troops can never enjoy. Rhys's situation is different, though. Not only is there an improbable chance that Darius won't have to put a bullet in Rhys's head, but he has somehow managed to get under Darius's skin.

The virus Rhys must infect himself with is sexually transmitted, and optimizing his chance of exposure requires him to submit as often as possible to Darius—and the other soldiers. Though the boundaries of morality have shifted in this harsh new world, what they must do has them asking if their humanity is too high a price to pay for Rhys's survival.

READER DISCRETION ADVISED

Each reader is unique in their tolerance for graphic material. As such, please be aware that this novel may contain material or references which may be triggering for some readers. If you worry that this might be an issue, the author fondly encourages you take the time to read some of the reviews others have left at Goodreads and various ebook retailers to see if it contains subject matter you may find disturbing. Thank you.

To Paul and Tristan, for understanding when my muse gets more face time from me than they do;

To Tami Veldura, for beta reading; and to Jenny and Erin, whose input and encouragement through the whole process kept me sane.

1

PRIORITIES

Death smelled like old wooden pews whose varnish and cushions had become saturated with acrid layers of dust. It smelled like mildewing carpet rotting from rain that had leaked through a roof he'd never had the skill or resources to repair. The hymnals had long since been used for tinder, but the musty scent of old books—once so comforting but now vaguely nauseating —remained.

It was dim, too. The dust dancing in the speckled sunlight that filtered through the filthy stained glass windows could more accurately be described as sheets rather than motes. In the absence of any other light, it lent the room a dusky quality that would have been beautiful if Rhys hadn't despised it.

He took all this in during what he knew would be his final heartbeats. He brandished his useless shotgun like a baseball bat and scowled at the splintering door. A revenant started clawing through the hole, and Rhys used its struggle with the shattered timbers to strike the first blow. The moist, sickening *crunch* of the heavy stock smashing in the bones of the revenant's face was a sound he didn't think he'd forget, assuming he lived to remember. He wanted to puke all over the howling body that fell to the floor, its tangled hair streaming and its grime-caked breasts swinging. Even if it—*she*—was trying to eat him, she had once been a person.

He wondered if he should ask God for forgiveness while he bashed the still-struggling body into the aisle runner, which was so dark and dingy a red that, in the faint light, it looked like a river of dried blood flowing down the middle of the chapel. He hoped to snap the revenant's spine or pulverize the brain or at least blind it before the other revs that rampaged outside were attracted by the noise. If Father Maurice was to be believed, revenants weren't *actually* undead, despite the name. He'd said that rumor had only started because everyone had assumed the Rot to be fatal without exception. When the virus had mutated and began turning some of its victims into animals, people had panicked and made up wild claims about zombies. But no, the revs were alive, and if they were alive, they could be killed just about any way a living, breathing person could. They were just strong, insane, and impervious to pain.

Rhys was splattered with blood by the time the revenant stopped thrashing. A drop itched as it chilled and dried on his lip, its weight irritating.

Don't lick. Don't lick. Don't lick.

He supposed it didn't really matter. Even if he managed not to become dinner, he was still a dead man. He had been from the moment he'd breathed the same air as the revenant.

Knowing that made it easier, in a morbidly reassuring way. He had a small knife in his pocket, its faux-ebony handle cracked. It was useless as a weapon but enough to slit his wrists. If he managed to get out of here, he might still die a clean death. If he was smart, he'd do it now, before they got through the door.

But then they might still turn and go after Cadence and Caleb.

His chest heaved and his arms ached as he stared down with dispassionate curiosity at the caved-in face of the rev he'd killed. It was all about priorities. He could see that with a remarkable clarity he'd never had before. First, keep the revs from chasing his sister and nephew. Second, take them out and avoid being eaten. Third, kill himself before the Rot set in or he became a revenant. Knowing what to do had never been so easy.

Now, should he stay and wait, or try to bolt? It was taking the other revs longer than Rhys had anticipated to stampede in. He didn't feel like cowering in the chapel waiting to be eaten, though, so he tried to make a break for it.

It turned out to be a mistake. They caught him in the narrow stone corridor, where he didn't have as much room to swing his makeshift club as he'd had in the chapel. He sprinted down the hallway, gasping desperate breaths, trying to reach the outside door that would lead him to the courtyard between the building and the gates. Where he would go after that, he had no idea. The nearest town was a good ten miles away from the monastery nestled in the rolling hills that had once been the vineyards of the Willamette Valley wine country. Aside from a few scattered farmhouses and wineries, there was no place for him to hide.

It was a moot point, anyway. If the others were heading east toward Newberg, he'd have to go west, which meant it would be a lot farther than ten miles to another town. What had once been the city of McMinnville lay in that direction, if he remembered the old map correctly, but he didn't have a prayer of reaching it with revs on his tail, and he didn't dare try to meet up with the others until he lost them.

Besides, Father Maurice and Jacob probably wouldn't wait around to see if he could meet with them. After all, Father Maurice had forced Rhys's mother to give up on waiting for his father at their chosen rendezvous point, seven years ago when his dad had done the same thing Rhys was doing now: using himself as a lure to keep a pack of revs away from his family.

Rhys heard growling behind him and turned to face another pair of revenants. Hadn't there been more? Rhys could swear he'd seen at least four coming through the falling-down gate outside the monastery. These two had fresh blood on their faces, and he could only hope it was from Father Maurice or Jacob.

The pair snarled like rabid dogs and stank to high heaven. Their wild manes reeked of oil and dirt. The revs who had once been men had beards even more ragged than the facial hair that grew in haphazard patches around Rhys's jaw. Clearly hygiene wasn't high on the revenant list of priorities.

Rhys giggled madly. He was losing it. His senses were aflame, singing; his awareness of *everything* had sharpened to a keen point.

His heart raced, and his muscles quivered. In those moments before death, he felt more alive, more *vital*, than he had in the past seven years. He could almost thank the revenants for smelling so foul because it made his last breaths into something that actually had an impact.

For one instant, he considered not fighting. Let them kill him. Let his final moment of this *delicious* sensitivity be the excruciating pain of their teeth rending his flesh.

In the end, though, his survival instinct was too strong. He swung his useless shotgun-turned-cudgel with what limited momentum he could muster, knocking the first rev back as a spray of blood erupted from a cut on its brow. Its head snapped back toward him, its eyes narrowing in fury. So human and yet so lacking anything resembling humanity.

The other maddened creature charged him before he had a chance to draw the blood-smeared shotgun back for another blow. It knocked him to the stone floor, driving the breath from his lungs. The club flew out of his hands. He managed a lucky blow to its throat with his elbow, winning himself a moment more of existence as it recoiled, gagging. Then it pressed down on him again, yellowed teeth snapping.

The world exploded in a series of percussive blasts that bounced off the stone walls. A hot spray he thought must be his own blood washed over him. In the next second, everything was eerily silent except for the high-pitched ringing in his ears. The revenant above him was still, its weight crushing him until it was hauled away.

His first thought when he opened his eyes was that his final prayer had been answered. He'd died before the revs could begin to eat him. God appeared before him, stern and mighty enough to justify all the fuss people made about Him. His dark face was concerned in a detached sort of way. That made sense: Rhys had never seen any indication that God actually cared for him. He didn't know why God would be wearing camo fatigues or why He had His holy hair pulled back in a ponytail, but who was Rhys to question the Almighty? Instead, he accepted the proffered hand, and it pulled him to his feet as though he weighed nothing.

Then things got weird. God patted him down in brisk, hurried thumps as He mouthed something. He shouted, and Rhys could *almost* make out the words through the humming in his ears. It was like trying to listen to someone speak underwater. God ripped Rhys's blood-soaked shirt open. When Rhys stared mutely, unable to answer the questions he couldn't hear, God's expression turned grim and He frowned with merciless pity. He shook His head, and His nearly black eyes went cold. Then He turned away from Rhys to gesture to someone.

Rhys caught sight of the woman behind him, who held a shotgun in her hands. A startling streak of white threaded through the thick black braid that hung over her shoulder. Muffled and indistinct, as if from a great distance, the man's words pierced the ringing in Rhys's ears.

"He's not answering. He could already be going catatonic if this wasn't his first exposure. Put him out of his misery. We can't take him with us and risk exposing the others."

"No!" Rhys's shouted reply was muted in his own ears. "I'm not infected! At least I wasn't until—" He gestured to the corpses at his feet and the blood coating his skin.

"Call the others. Tell them to bring water! Soap!" the dark-skinned man shouted to his companion, then whirled on Rhys. "There's a wind pump outside. Is there running water here? Showers?"

Rhys began to sprint before he remembered to nod, dashing up the stairs to the communal bathroom. He didn't even bother to strip before he turned on the shower and stepped under the frigid spray. The man who'd saved him followed only a step behind, tearing away the remnants of Rhys's shirt with a wet snarl, then swiping the rivulets of crimson water away from his lips, which Rhys pressed closed.

"You have soap, son?" The man had to repeat it twice, louder the second time, for Rhys to hear.

Rhys shook his head and closed his eyes for good measure. They'd used the last of their supply of soap years ago. He inhaled only when the need for breath was undeniable, afraid of snorting some of the bloody water up his nose. The man began to scrub him with something harsh and pungent smelling. Rhys startled when unknown hands shredded his ratty jeans like they were tissue paper, not bothering to strip the tight, wet denim down his legs.

Only when someone shut off the water and pronounced him clean did he realize that he was naked in the presence of God knew how many people. Blind and still partially deafened, he'd hardly been aware of others coming into the bathroom.

"He's still been exposed," said a low, female voice behind him. Rhys blinked water out of his eyes to get a better look around. The man who'd washed him still stood in the shower stall with him. His fatigues were soaked, and water beaded on his ebony hair. His dark eyes were pitying. He patted Rhys down again, looking between Rhys's fingers and lifting his arms to peer underneath.

"Guess we'll wait and see, then," he said with an edge to his voice.

"Darius—"

He growled. "Don't, Xolani."

She sighed. "Well, there's no harm in taking him with us, at least until he starts to show symptoms. We can keep him isolated, hope for a miracle. There's nothing left here for him anyway."

Take him?

Rhys pulled away from the strange hands on his body, mustering every ounce of defiance he could, and scowled at the newcomers. "I'm not going anywhere with a bunch of strangers. Where's my sister?"

⋀ ⋀ ⋀

DARIUS HAD to hand it to the kid. With his shoulder blades visible beneath his skin, ribs jutting out like the bars of a xylophone, and his hazel eyes bulging with shock, he still had fight in him. No sooner had the question left his lips than he pushed past Darius.

"*Cady!* Cady, are you okay?"

Darius's stomach sank, and Xolani's normally stern expression softened with sympathy. The kid darted out the door before Darius thought to intercept him.

"Where is she? *Cady!*"

Shit.

"Keep searching the rooms." Darius stretched his neck to one side, then the other, trying not to growl. "Find me that last rev Jamie reported, and get him some damn clothes!" He took off after the survivor, his long strides carrying him down the stairs where he caught the naked, dripping young man almost out the door. He might as well have been trying to hold an angry badger. The survivor thrashed and flailed, and Darius finally had to push him away when he started scratching and biting. Last fucking thing he needed was for the kid to draw blood.

Not that it mattered.

Suddenly free, the survivor didn't pause but charged the final few steps to the door, against which Darius slammed him, chest first, to eliminate the hazard posed by the kid's teeth and nails.

"Settle down, son. There's still a rev on the loose, and we gotta find it. My scouts reported four. I'd hate to think you fended off those other ones just to run smack into the last."

"My *sister* might run into it!" The flurry of struggles renewed. "*Cady!*"

Darius growled to himself and tried to make his tone at least somewhat sympathetic. "There ain't anyone left alive out there."

The thrashing came to a shuddering halt.

"They got away?" The plaintive hope in the kid's voice probably made a whole host of angels somewhere burst into tears.

Darius was no angel, but he didn't want to be an asshole, either. "I'm sorry, son."

"But the revs were supposed to come after me. I was going to distract them." His voice cracked with desperate confusion. "They were supposed to get *me*!"

Oh fuck. This was why he hated dealing with survivors. Especially traumatized ones.

Futilely brave, fucking heroic traumatized ones.

"They probably heard the baby cry, and it was all over." As comfort went, Darius was pretty sure it fell short, but he didn't know what else to say. "Revs are predators, and like any predator, they know babies are easy prey. You couldn't have got their attention no matter what you tried."

To the kid's credit, he didn't cry. That would have put the perfect cap on Darius's afternoon. Instead, the boy drew a few quavering breaths and said almost calmly, "Let me go."

Darius sighed. "You don't want to see what's out there, son."

"Darius." Xolani spoke from behind him, and Darius almost jumped. Shit. He'd been so distracted by the kid, he wasn't even watching his six. "Kaleo and Gina are reporting the rev still at large isn't in the building or courtyard. Jamie says Titus is out on his bike. He suspects the last rev ran off from the pack, and Titus gave pursuit. We're still looking for clothes, but for now here's a blanket our survivor can wrap around himself."

Darius reached back to take the scratchy woolen blanket. "If you promise not to bolt, I'll let you loose so you can cover up."

The tips of the kid's ears turned red, and he gave a stiff nod. Darius eased his weight off him and stood back, proffering the blanket. Avoiding Darius's eyes, the survivor wrapped it around himself, then opened the door and dashed out.

"Fuck this noise." Darius threw up his hands in defeat. "It ain't my job to baby the civvies."

He heard Xolani sigh. "The profundity of your compassion makes me weep."

"They teach you those big words in med school?"

"Taught me a few short ones, too. The kind with four letters. Want to hear them?"

"Go saw some bones or something, and get off my ass."

She snorted and brushed past him, following the boy out the door. Growling, Darius went after her.

The survivor was standing before a row of four blood-soaked blankets lying over the victims Darius had seen in the weed-filled courtyard on his way into the monastery. One blanket-covered lump was the size of an adult. Another was only a foot and a half long, and from beneath a third trailed long, tawny hair that was nearly the exact shade of the kid's own. The fourth blanket lay over someone not much smaller than the girl.

For all his professed lack of compassion, Darius sent a mental thank-you to whichever of his people had thought to cover up the mangled bodies. That was probably Joe.

Xolani stopped a few feet from the survivor, giving him space. "You have a name, kid?"

The boy stared down at the lumps with an almost eerie lack of expression, as if he'd simply shut down. "Rhys Cooper." There was no inflection in his voice. He might as well have been a robot.

"Good to meet you, Rhys. I'm Xolani, and the big guy who was manhandling you is Darius."

The kid nodded, not speaking. He didn't even glance her way.

"She was your sister?" Darius wasn't sure what Xolani thought she was doing, prodding him to talk about it like that, but better her than Darius when the bawling began.

The young man nodded again.

Xolani's voice softened. "Was that her baby?"

Another wordless nod.

"Who was the father? The old man? There, under that one?" Xolani's question came a little cautiously. Darius grimaced, aware of what she was really asking. It wouldn't be the first time adolescent siblings cut off from the world had turned to each other when the impulses of puberty took over. It also wouldn't be the first time a patriarch had made a harem of the girls in his group.

Delta Company had pretty much seen it all.

The survivor shook his head. "No, it was—" He looked up from the bodies at last, glancing back and forth between them and Xolani. "Wait. If that's Father Maurice, where's Jacob?"

"These are all we found."

"He's Father Maurice's son. Late twenties? Tall, longish brown hair and beard?"

Xolani shook her head. "We'll keep searching." Her eyes flicked to Darius, and he nodded curtly. They couldn't leave an unaccounted-for—and possibly infected—survivor running around.

"I'll tell the rest of the squad to be on the lookout." Darius turned toward the building, glancing back over his shoulder. "We'll start gathering wood to burn the bodies. Two piles. One for the revs, the other for the casualties."

The boy turned his head, looking at Darius with that almost-empty expression. "There's wood in some of the damaged rooms.

Broken furniture. Old timbers that fell in the last earthquake when part of the roof collapsed. You can even use the pews from the chapel, if you can find a way to break them up. Just leave the orchard alone. Someone might come along and need it for food someday."

Darius couldn't help but be impressed with the kid's composure. Most survivors they found would have been hysterical by now. Of course, there was always the distinct possibility he'd melt down at any given moment, but so far he'd kept his head fairly well.

Fucking shame the boy was toast.

Darius nodded and went back inside. Encountering one of his men at the door, he paused. "Kaleo, do another scan of the whole building. We've got a civvie at large."

"On it, Big D."

Darius checked the rooms until he found the ones where the roof had collapsed and gathered up fallen beams and boards, easily snapping the ones that were too long before heading back out to the courtyard.

Would Xolani break the bad news, or was she going to make him do it?

As Darius emerged with his armful of wood, Titus came through the gates, on foot, hauling a blood-splattered civvie by the collar. His motorcycle was nowhere in evidence.

"Had to chase this pecker down." He spat into the dirt, flinging the guy away. Darius frowned. Titus didn't usually give a shit about most people enough to dislike anyone, much less handle a survivor so roughly. "That last rev went tearing after him. Would've caught him, too, if I hadn't taken it out in time. Now I gotta haul my happy ass a half mile back to get the corpse and my fucking bike from where I dropped it to save this dipshit."

"This the guy you said was missing?" Darius asked, trying to remember the kid's name. *Rhys Cooper. Right.* As if it mattered. It was never a good idea to get too familiar with the civvies, and especially not with one who was already exposed.

"Yeah." The kid sounded like he was chewing glass. Darius glanced at him to see his mouth twist in scorn as the newcomer got a look at the lumps beneath the bloody blankets. The man bent over, spewing his guts up.

"Whose blood is that on him, Titus?"

"Fucked if I know. Could be rev. He might've caught some splash when I blew a hole in the thing."

Shit. "Well, get him over to the pump, then."

With an irritated grimace, Titus dragged the civvie—who was still retching practically on top of the bodies—to the spigot at the base of the windmill-driven pump. These survivors had gotten lucky; they'd had indoor plumbing and showers, albeit cold ones. Titus dropped the guy onto the ground and opened the faucet while Darius jogged back inside for the soap he'd used on the kid. Just as he reached the doors on his way back out, he heard a reedy voice scream something and then shouts and the sounds of a fight.

Fuck. This day just kept getting better and better.

2

SAVIORS

Cadence and Caleb were dead, and Jacob had managed to live. Didn't that just suck? If the revs weren't going to chase and kill Rhys the way he'd intended, the least they could have done was gone after Jacob instead.

Rhys spared his so-called brother-in-law a disgusted look when he keeled over and began puking, then went back to contemplating what had been the last of his family. In a moment he'd start moving again. He'd help gather wood so he could do the proper thing and lay his sister and nephew to rest. The prevailing wisdom from back when the plague first began was that revs weren't above scavenging fresh graves, so cremation was the best way to spare a loved one the indignity of becoming carrion.

He heard the guy in charge, Darius, bark something about getting Jacob washed off, but Rhys couldn't be bothered to care. If the Rot took Jacob, Rhys wouldn't waste any tears. Jacob had agreed readily enough, after all, when Father Maurice had tagged Rhys to be bait, writing him off to save their asses.

"Don't know why we're bothering," he heard the grizzled guy over by the pump—had Darius called him Titus? What was with the Roman names, anyway? Was it a theme? Jesus, why couldn't he focus on a single thought?—grumble to the woman who'd introduced herself as Xolani. "More trouble than this shit stain's worth. It could just as easily be the girl's blood as the rev's. They were on her when the fucker ran off."

It took a moment for the words to make sense, and then everything went hot and cold all at once. Sweat prickled and chilled as it erupted from pores all over Rhys's skin. He could feel it running down his back to the crack of his butt. He clenched, like that flushed, crampy moment when your entire body seized up just before the first wave of a bad case of the runs. He whipped his head around to stare at Jacob.

"You *ran away*?" This was it, then. This was what it felt like to lose his mind. *Wow. You really* do *snap.* Rhys was pretty damn sure he felt something physically break inside him. "They were being attacked and you *left them*?"

Then he was flying at Jacob, the half-healed cracks on his knuckles breaking open as he swung his fists. He drove Jacob out of the pump's stream and into the muddy soil beneath it, screaming obscenities and trying to pummel him with far more rage than skill. Only Jacob's shock and the insane force of Rhys's anger gave him any advantage; he certainly didn't have the stature, weight, or skill to take down Jacob otherwise.

"Get off me, you cocksucker!"

"You left them!" Spittle flew from his lips, and he didn't care that he was screeching. His arms flailed, fists driving toward the body beneath him. He couldn't even *see* Jacob for the red rush of fury blinding him. "*I'll kill you! You left them!*"

Jacob managed to flip them, driving the breath from Rhys's lungs as he hit the ground. He didn't bother to throw a punch; he just grabbed Rhys's head and slammed it against one of the bolts on the thick steel pipe coming up from the well. Rhys saw stars, though he kept swinging blind punches toward Jacob as blood trickled down the side of his face and into the shredded, mud-churned bed of moss beneath him. He growled and snarled—sounding, he realized in some disconnected portion of his mind, like a revenant himself. His upper lip and chin were wet, and he wasn't sure if it was from the pump or if he really was foaming at the mouth. "*I'll kill you! I'll fucking kill you!*"

"What the fuck is going on here, Titus?"

He barely heard Darius's roar before Jacob bashed his head against the pipe again. Then everything went black.

⋀ ⋀ ⋀

HIS HEAD THROBBED, and his scalp stung above his left temple, followed by a gross rasp of something tugging on his skin. Rhys tried to bat it away, and someone grabbed his hands.

"Hold still, Rhys. I'm almost done suturing. You couldn't have stayed out of it a few more minutes, could you, kid?"

That was a woman's voice. For a mad moment, he thought it might be his mom. But no, it was that olive-skinned lady with the thick braid. Xolani.

"Did I kill him?" He blinked up at her, and she came into blurry focus. He lay on the floor surrounded by green tile. The bathroom. The light coming through the windows was too damn bright. It felt like daggers stabbing him in the eyeballs.

She snorted. "No, though not for lack of trying. I take it that guy's not a friend of yours?"

"Father Maurice made my sister marry him. If you can call it that. Said they needed to be fruitful and multiply, like the Bible commands."

"Ah." Another sting and a tug, and then something snipped. "There. All sewed up. You're gonna have a fucking wicked headache for a while. You're probably concussed."

He tried to lift his head, and it felt like it might fall off his shoulders. "Ow."

"Yeah, come on." Her arms slipped under his shoulders and helped sit him up as though he weighed nothing. "If you think you can stand, you can take a quick shower. Darius has sent Jamie and Titus back east to Newberg on their motorcycles to find some clothes for you. They shouldn't be long. I can get you another blanket in the meantime."

Rhys looked down and groaned. The sound made his head hurt worse. For the second time that day, he was naked in the presence of strangers, his skin covered in streaks of drying mud.

"How long was I passed out?"

"Maybe half an hour. We've got most of the wood gathered and have started burning the revs, but we decided to wait for you before we lit the fire for the others. We need to do it soon, though. It's almost evening, and we have to secure the gate before dark."

"Okay." Rhys swallowed and looked away until his eyes stopped stinging. His mouth tasted metallic, and if he'd had anything in his stomach, he might have puked.

"What happened to your knuckles? That's not all from trying to punch out that other guy."

Rhys looked down at his bloodied hand, red meat showing raw through cracked, bruised skin.

"Doesn't matter. Won't be happening again."

"Think you can stand? Otherwise, if you want to sit in the shower, I can turn it on for you while I go find a blanket."

"I can stand." With her help, he pushed himself to his feet and staggered into the shower. The shredded remains of his clothing still littered the bottom of it. Jesus, his jeans must have really been threadbare if they'd managed to rip wet denim off him like that. He leaned against the tile of the mildew-spotted wall and let Xolani turn on the cold spray.

"I'll be right back. Try not to fall over."

Nodding hurt too much, so Rhys just grunted and began scrubbing off the mud. The longer he was on his feet, the steadier he felt, until he got brave enough to bend over and pick up a clean scrap of his T-shirt to use as a washcloth.

She came back a moment later with another blanket like the one he'd lost when he attacked Jacob. Rhys turned off the water and wrapped it around himself.

"Interesting couple of marks there on your hips and thighs. Last time I saw a set of bruises that looked like that, they were on a guy who'd been beaten with a cane."

Rhys flushed but said nothing, clutching the blanket tighter.

"The old man had a cane beside him where he died."

He glowered and stomped out of the bathroom, trying to ignore her when she followed.

"I noticed that guy you tried to clobber the shit out of wasn't wearing rags like you were."

"Yeah, well, he didn't outgrow all of his clothes," Rhys muttered. "I was twelve when we got here."

"And how long ago was that?"

"Seven years." Why was she following him, much less asking all these questions?

"So, it was—what? Just you and your sister, and Jacob and his father?"

"No."

"That's right, there was a kid, too. Who else was here?"

He sighed in annoyance. He shouldn't be so unfriendly to her—after all, she did help save his life and stitch him up—but he really wished she'd stop probing for information about things that weren't any of her business.

"My mom died a couple years ago," he answered shortly. "We think it was cancer. She had some, uh, lumps. Gabe—Gabriel—ran away about a year before that, and his parents went to try to find him and never came back. Guess they must all have died, too." Rhys grimaced, trying not to think of why Gabe had run off. "The eleven-year-old boy you found out there today was Gabe's little brother, Jeff. When they went after Gabe, they left him behind here, where he'd be safe. There was another family, too, in the beginning. The Merkles. Holly got appendicitis, we think. Her dad committed suicide. Her mom was stung by a bee. Now we're all that's left. Anything else you wanna know?"

Xolani shook her head and took his arm without asking, helping him down the stairs. Her grip was really strong, but then, her shoulders were broad even though she wasn't tall, and she had a solid, muscular build. A scar ran down her cheek, a light line puckering and pulling at the skin and making her look tough. Even without it, she wouldn't have ever been called pretty. Darius was a lot bigger than her, but something told Rhys that if it came down to a fight between them, she could probably hold her own.

And she didn't try to apologize or sympathize as he cataloged their losses. He appreciated that.

"Look, I'm sorry. I don't mean to be a jerk, and you're being nice and all, but my head hurts, and can we just not talk about all that?"

"Okay," she said with perfect equanimity and fell silent.

Darius was outside—along with some of the others whose names Rhys hadn't gotten yet—standing beside a large pile of scrap wood. Father Maurice, Jeff, Cady, and Caleb were lying on top of it, and Rhys swallowed hard seeing them just draped limply like that with their throats torn out. On the far side of the pyre, Jacob was watching him with eyes that glittered with hatred, but Rhys couldn't be bothered to care. All he could do was stare at the dark gold of his sister's blood-matted hair hanging down.

When he drew near, he could smell kerosene fumes.

Darius grabbed a length of wood and lit it from the fire still burning the remains of the revenants. But before he could touch it to the other pile, Jacob lifted his head and intoned, his voice loud and dramatic, "Dear Lord, we commend to you these loved ones: my father, wife, and son . . ."

No mention of *sister* or *nephew*, of course.

"Oh, shut up." Rhys snatched the torch out of Darius's hand and set the pyre ablaze. The last damn thing he needed to hear was about God and heaven and salvation. After a moment of glaring, Jacob continued droning on, but Rhys didn't hear the trite platitudes over the roar and crackle of the flames.

He stood there staring into the embers long after everyone else, even Jacob, had drifted away. The wind blew smoke in his face, stinging his eyes. He watched it burn until the bodies were charred beyond recognition and the disgusting smell of seared flesh had stopped twisting his empty stomach, making him gulp against dry heaves.

"It's getting late, son." He turned when Darius spoke behind him. "We gotta close the gates, so you need to get inside. Not safe to be out in the open after dark. My people brought some clothes for you."

Rhys's throat tightened at the idea of leaving Cady and Caleb, even now, but he nodded, blinking rapidly and hanging his head as he turned to go inside. Darius fell in step beside him.

"Can you not call me 'son'?" Remembering how snippy he'd

been with Xolani, Rhys made an effort to be a little more polite. "Father Maurice used to call me that."

"Okay."

"There a reason you're following me?"

"Gotta make sure you don't haul off and attack anyone else." Rhys couldn't tell from the soldier's wry expression if he was serious or not. "Bags of clothes are in the chapel. Didn't know which room was yours, and my people had to get to work locking things down."

All but the front row of pews had been stripped from the chapel to make the fires, just like he'd suggested. Rhys wondered briefly what they'd used to break them down into scrap wood; he hadn't seen any saws or sledgehammers. Against the wall was a garbage bag full of clothes and a large backpack that looked military issue.

"Find a few changes that'll fit you," Darius said, gesturing toward them. "Leave the rest; you won't have room to carry it. Choose big. You could stand to put on some weight, and if you do, you might need something larger than what'll fit you now."

"Okay." Rhys nodded and tried not to feel self-conscious over Darius's presence as he tried on the clothes, since he had no idea what size he wore. He chose two pairs of jeans that were just a little too large. They had to be belted to keep from dropping off his hips. Most of the T-shirts hung loosely, but he took some anyway, as well as a pair of sweats. There were a bunch of socks and several pairs of hiking boots that looked almost new. He found the ones that fit him best, figuring he couldn't outgrow those.

He also took every pair of underwear, regardless of the size. Despite the grief of this abysmal day, he couldn't help but be pleased at the presence of those. It had been years since his last pair—so small the elastic had bit into his skin and left blisters—had fallen apart.

"So, who are you people?"

"Used to be Army, back when there was an army. Now we look for survivors and hunt revs."

When he was dressed, Rhys followed Darius to the industrial-grade kitchen where the monks—who had fled the monastery before Rhys had ever arrived—had once made the cakes and confections they'd sold to keep the monastery self-sustaining. That operation had been the reason Father Maurice had urged them to seek shelter there; they had staples laid away in large quantities. With careful rationing and supplements from the garden and orchard, those staples had lasted Rhys and the others almost seven years.

Darius's people were perched on the stainless steel tables and counters, eating a combination of vegetables and fruits from the garden in the courtyard and dried rations they had brought themselves. For once there was light in the monastery after sunset; they had brought lanterns with them and placed a few around the kitchen.

Jacob was there, as well, turning on the charm, yukking it up with several members of the squad as if he hadn't just lost his family hours before. The sound of his voice made the throbbing in Rhys's head worse. Jacob paused only long enough to give Rhys a scathing look before ignoring him completely. Rhys dismissed it as someone offered him a strip of smoked meat, the smell of which turned his stomach. He murmured a polite refusal and stuck to a handful of nuts from the trees in the orchard.

He turned his attention back to Darius after he'd swallowed, picking up the thread of their conversation. "What do you do once you find them? Survivors, I mean."

"Quarantine 'em, make sure they're not infected with Beta or Gamma before sending them on to join the rest."

"Beta?"

"What you'd call the Rot," Xolani explained. "Gamma's what makes the revenants."

"I've never heard them called that, though I knew they were different versions of the same virus."

"How much do you know about where they came from?"

"I was just a kid when we went into hiding. Father Maurice just said it was God's punishment for, you know, immoral . . . *stuff*." He blushed, unwilling to get into what particular sins Father Maurice had claimed the plague was punishment for.

Xolani and Darius scoffed in unison.

"My father—God rest his soul—was often confused about many things." Jacob looked almost sheepish. "Rhys has apparently been paying too much attention to him."

Rhys turned his head with an incredulous stare. Seven years at the monastery and Jacob had never once said anything that indicated he wasn't in perfect lockstep with every one of his father's opinions.

"Well, that's bullshit," Xolani said flatly. "Beta's a mutation of a virus known as Bane Alpha. Gamma's a second mutation that sprang from Beta. The Beta and Gamma strains coexist in an infected person, though only symptoms of one will manifest, which means exposure from revs can spread either one."

Rhys frowned. "So . . . there's a *third* virus? The, um, Bane Alpha?"

Darius and Xolani shared a tense glance Rhys couldn't interpret, and the rest of the conversation in the kitchen quieted.

After a moment, Xolani narrowed her eyes at Darius and set her jaw almost defiantly, turning away as though ignoring some silent argument he'd made. "Exactly," she answered Rhys. "Though technically it's the *first* virus. The wellspring, as it were. McClosky's Bane, named for the general in charge of the R&D brain trust at the Pentagon whose brilliant idea all this was."

Rhys blinked. He recalled reading about those sorts of things years ago, back in the bunker before they'd left Montana. The neighbor who'd owned the bunker had been something of a conspiracy nut, and his books had been a lot more interesting than the ones Rhys's mom had brought for his homeschooling.

"It was a weapon?" He tried to remember what the books had called it. "Bio—Biolog—"

Xolani nodded. "Biological warfare. Yes. It started with a bit of genetic engineering called Project Juggernaut. It was an attempt to engineer a virus that—when it delivered its genetic payload and began replicating in the RNA—would rewrite certain genes to make the infected subjects superhuman. They would have radically increased in strength, stamina, reaction speed, and so forth."

Rhys set the remaining half of his handful of nuts aside, uneaten. The pounding in his head was making him queasy. "Wait. They gave that to their enemies? Why would they do that?"

"No, not the enemy. Well, not entirely. Bane Alpha was meant for *our* troops. They wanted more effective soldiers, see? They were having a recruitment crisis that started way back in the early twenty-first century. More than twelve years in Afghanistan. Nearly as many in Iraq. Syria. Iran. Venezuela and Guatemala. Libya. Palestine. Iran again. Russia, and so on." She sighed tiredly, packing up the uneaten rations. The soldiers who were finished eating began to do likewise. "There wasn't a day in over a century that we weren't occupying at least one country, and often more. The economy was shit, the national debt was astronomical from more than a hundred years of insupportable military budgets, and people were tired of us fighting wars we couldn't win in places they couldn't give two shits about. Unless they reinstated the draft—which would have been political suicide for anyone in charge—the military had to make do with fewer troops than they actually needed."

Rhys nodded slowly. That part, he knew. His mother had covered history—particularly recent history—thoroughly. "Did they succeed? In creating the super soldiers?"

"After a fashion."

"I don't understand. How would that turn into the Rot?"

"Because the virus was designed with a second purpose—to weaken the enemy. Imagine you're one of these super soldiers, and you're wounded in battle. Maybe even killed. Any force strong enough to do that needs to be weakened, either to slow their offensive or cripple their defense. So when the infected troops were wounded, the Alpha strain in their blood would mutate into a Beta strain, which would infect enemies within contact range—and part of the mission was to make *sure* they got into contact range."

Rhys's eyes widened. "How is that possible?"

"Short version is that exposure to air and the clotting agents in an open wound would trigger the mutation. It was an utterly idiotic plan destined for disaster, but they thought they could keep it under control." Xolani shook her head, a long-suffering sigh expressing her opinion of that idea. "At any rate, enemies would then take it back home with them to infect their comrades. Beta was airborne as well as blood-borne and highly contagious, which meant they could spread it easily. It wasn't supposed to be permanent or fatal. Just a bad rash and a flu-like malaise for a while, nothing more. Enough for our guys to get in, wipe them out, and leave or set up shop and take over while they were weakened."

"Oh." Rhys hesitated, trying to make sense of it. The kitchen had gone virtually silent, the attention of the strange soldiers a little disconcerting. "But wouldn't that end up making our soldiers sick, too?"

Darius shook his head, giving Xolani an irritated look. "Alpha gave them immunity."

Rhys took that in, his mind still churning to process all this new information. "But the Rot *is* deadly. It's not just a rash and a flu."

"Yes." Xolani looked grim, zipping her pack shut with a hard jerk. "That's because in that hundred-plus years of nonstop warfare, standards at the top got pretty damn lax. Someone cut corners to rush things through the testing phase, so the live trial went to shit once it was deployed in the field. No one really knows what happened. There wasn't ever time or manpower to figure it out. Best theories are that it was influenced by another virus, something local to the region of Russia where Alpha was first administered to a battalion of test subjects—who ended up calling themselves Jugs, for Project Juggernaut. Or possibly it was affected by radiation from all the uranium that ended up floating loose around there. At any rate, it didn't do what it was meant to do. The rash became necrotic lesions, and what was intended to be an exhausting malaise was so severe and debilitating that the infected victims were left pretty much catatonic, trapped inside their bodies while their tissues decayed." Rhys wiped a hand over his mouth, the nausea redoubling. He'd known the Rot was bad, but hearing it described that way sounded a lot worse.

Xolani continued. "But before all this became apparent, some wounded, Alpha-infected troops brought it home when a bureaucratic snafu sent them back to the States to recuperate instead of into quarantine, so Beta started spreading back here, as well. That's when reports of the Gamma mutation first appeared. There were probably revs in Russia, too, but the military just managed to hush it up."

"Well, it's wonderful you folks came along when you did!" Jacob said brightly, right on schedule. Obviously Rhys had been the center of attention for longer than Jacob found tolerable. "Who knows what would have happened to me—us—otherwise?"

Rhys managed to avoid rolling his eyes. Barely. "What *is* going to happen to us? Are you going to quarantine me and Jacob like you do the other survivors you find?" That would be just great, stuck with Jacob alone, without even Cady there.

Darius sighed. "No. We're not taking you back to base and putting you with the other survivors."

Something in his voice made Rhys's head snap up. "Why not?"

"Because there's very little chance—statistically speaking, zero, really—that you're not infected." Xolani's eyes passed between Rhys and Jacob, gentle and full of pity. "I'm sorry. You took a faceful of blood there, kid, and even if you hadn't, your proximity to those revs was too close. Both of you."

"Oh." Rhys swallowed hard. The voices became fainter as a low humming grew steadily louder in his ears. His headache kicked up another notch with the increased force of his pulse in his temples. "I'm still going to die. Okay."

There was something wrong with his numbed acceptance of that fact, though he couldn't pinpoint exactly what. After all, he'd known he would die from the moment Father Maurice ordered him to use himself as bait to distract the revs so the rest of them could get away.

Then he looked up in alarm, and the humming in his ears became an unnerving drone. A cold sweat prickled his skin. He felt dizzy, and his head throbbed mercilessly. "You have to kill us. Both of us. Now. We're endangering you."

Everyone shuffled.

"*What?*" Jacob squawked in alarm and started protesting, but Rhys had no attention to spare him. His eyes were fixed on Darius and Xolani, who were having another silent conversation made up of glares. His knees felt weak, and he gripped the edge of a stainless steel table for support.

"Don't worry." Xolani never took her eyes off Darius, though she spoke to Rhys. "You won't infect us."

The droning turned into a deafening claxon, and dark spots began to spread across his field of vision. His whole body tingled like every part of him was falling asleep, except his head, which hurt so terribly he almost wished they *would* kill him.

"Oh. You're the Jugs." He gave a short, hysterical giggle. "Guess that explains how you broke up the pews, then."

The terra-cotta tile floor leaped up to smack him in the face before he could decide what he thought about that.

3

HOPE

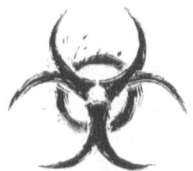

"If you won't do it, Darius, Titus will."

Rhys awoke on a pew in the chapel with the same old odors of decay filling his nostrils. From the way Darius towered over him, he didn't have to wonder how he'd come to be there. Xolani stood almost nose to nose—well, nose to shoulder—with Darius, though she broke off arguing as soon as Rhys opened his eyes. Titus was there, too. He was barely taller than Xolani, and he looked to be in his late forties or early fifties. He leaned against a wall, scraping under his fingernails and paring them down with a pocketknife.

Darius's jaw flexed. "*Why* are you so fucking set on this?"

Rhys blinked as Xolani gave Darius a glower. "Because he's just a kid."

"What's going on?" Rhys tried to push himself up on the pew, mortified at having passed out again.

Darius glared back at Xolani, his gaze dropping to Rhys for a second. "Nothing. How are you feeling?"

"Fine. Sorry about that. I don't know why—"

Xolani turned and shushed him, her mannerisms brusque as she reached down to check his pulse and then lifted his eyelids to examine his pupils. Her touch was gentle despite her callused fingertips, not to mention her irritation. "It's the concussion. And you've had a lot of shocks today, Rhys. I've seen bigger, tougher guys than you face-plant under less stress."

The solicitude felt good. It brought to mind his mother again, and for a moment, Rhys was humiliatingly certain he would start to cry. He blinked it away, shaking off her touch.

"You were talking about me?"

"Yes, we were." Xolani ignored Darius's frustrated growl.

"You're trying to decide who'll kill me."

"We're trying to decide whether or not to attempt to save you. Or more specifically, who's going to do it."

"Save me?" Rhys bolted upright, the motion setting his head throbbing again as he stared at them in astonishment. "There's . . . there's what? A vaccine? A cure? Tell me!"

"Not a vaccine, no." She sighed, tugging at her braid. "Look, this is all purely hypothetical. We've never had an opportunity to test it. But, like we said, people infected with the Alpha strain are immune to Beta and Gamma. Problem is, there's no stockpile of Bane Alpha left. That was lost or destroyed years ago. And there's no use exposing you to our blood because then it'll just mutate into Beta."

Darius stalked away, pacing the chapel, then spun to face off with Xolani again, ignoring Rhys. "There's also the question of whether or not we want to make any more Jugs. I mean, how many super-humans can we have running around before some psychopath ends up infected and tries to take over everything?"

Xolani gave him a long look that Rhys couldn't read. "A valid point, but you can't stick your finger in the dam on that one, Darius."

"Fine. But it's not a good life. We don't *get* to have homes and families, except the ones we make with each other."

"Oh, don't you *dare* talk to me about the lack of family. You're not the one who takes care of our people when they get knocked up."

That seemed to give him pause. "You're right. I'm sorry. Still, the fact is, we're too dangerous. But if we can destroy everyone who's infected before we die off ourselves, well, then Bane's gone. It's over. Eradicated."

Rhys tried not to be hurt. "You'd rather let me die than make that take any longer than it has to." It was the second time today someone had summarily decided to sacrifice his life for the greater good. He should be getting used to it by now. Maybe it would be selfish for him to expect Darius to do anything else. He blew out a resolved breath when Darius didn't respond. "I guess that makes sense. Not like it matters anyway, if there's no, um, Alpha strain left, right?"

"Oh, there's a way. Again, hypothetically." Xolani patted his knee. "But we have to start now if we're going to do it. Tonight."

Darius snorted. "What's this 'we' shit?"

"How?" Rhys demanded at the same time.

"The Alpha virus only mutates to Beta when it's blood-borne and exposed to air and an open wound. That was a deliberate choice on the part of the virologists who designed it. They didn't want friendlies accidentally exposed to Beta by, say, kissing or sex. In fact, the Jugs were to be quarantined except for combat situations. We weren't supposed to have contact with civilians at all because it's transmissible as Alpha in semen and vaginal fluids."

Rhys stared at her, blushing to hear a woman talking about semen. Then he went cold and dizzy. "What are you saying?"

"She wants me to fuck you," Darius snapped.

"Or me." Titus shrugged, tucking his pocketknife away, as though Xolani had volunteered him to make dinner, not . . . do what Darius had just blurted.

"This is our best hope if we want to save your life." Xolani's fists were tight at her sides, as if she wanted to punch something. Rhys suspected "something" was Darius. "But we didn't come out here with a squad equipped for recruiting. We've got two subjects to try to expose and only so many males who aren't either in strictly monogamous relationships or inflexibly heterosexual. Gina doesn't sleep with men. I could do it, or at least *try*, but female-to-male transmission of just about any viral infection found in sex fluids has a far lower rate of incidence than male-to-female or male-to-male. Same problem with Jamie. He'd be willing, but he's anatomically female."

"Not to be picky, but I'm in a committed relationship, too," Titus drawled, still relaxed and sounding slightly amused. "And I'm not queer."

Xolani smirked, and her aggressive posture eased. "Yes, but luckily you're an open-minded man who will do what it takes, and your woman is a wonderful, caring person who understands this sort of thing."

Rhys stared at them all as if they'd gone insane—which he was fairly certain was the case. "You people are sick. Jesus! You know, this is a really shi—crummy time to be playing a stupid joke!" He flinched, pure instinct telling him to expect a hard cuff or a rap across the knuckles for even beginning to utter a swear.

"It's no joke." Xolani strode up and down the aisle runner. "We need to get the Alpha strain spreading through your body before Beta starts to work. We caught a break, there. Alpha was engineered to replicate in the RNA faster than Beta, because Beta has a long incubation period to ensure maximum contagion before anyone caught on. What we need to do is expose you to Alpha, immediately and repeatedly. We have no idea just how much of the virus is present in sex fluids, so we need a lot of it. Daily exposure, multiple times a day. Multiple partners would be even better." She reached the end of the aisle and pivoted on her heel to face Rhys. "Five or six weeks at least, which is on the long side of the amount of time it takes to see if someone is infected. It's not perfect, and the longer we wait, the less likely it is to work. It could be that your exposure to Beta and Gamma already has you producing antibodies to Alpha, especially if we delay. You need at least one male sex partner, and you need him *tonight*."

"This is crazy." Rhys's fingers tingled, and his head buzzed. He wasn't certain he wouldn't pass out again. He should pray, he thought distantly. If Father Maurice were alive, he'd be shouting a sermon at the top of his voice right now, telling them to repent of their wickedness and condemning Rhys for allowing himself to be led into temptation, even if he hadn't *done* anything.

Of course, Father Maurice had been full of crap most of the time. Rhys still recalled the burning shame and resentment he'd felt each time Father Maurice had berated him about unnatural lust and perversion after he and Gabriel had been caught almost kissing. Gabe had felt right. Safe. Closest to him in age—except for Cady, of course—Gabe had been Rhys's best friend and constant companion in those first few years at the monastery. That near kiss had been the most thrilling moment of his young life. He'd never understood how it could be considered a sin.

Rhys stared at them all but mostly at Darius. Was he honestly supposed to have sex with him? Or one of the others? He didn't know Titus or those other men. He didn't really know Darius, either, but—

"It should be you, Darius." Xolani gave Rhys a sympathetic look. He struggled to know how to respond to it. His outrage and annoyance over what still felt like a horrible prank were at odds with his gratitude for her kindness. "Titus or someone else will do it if we have to. *I'll* do it if we have to, though I'll give him long odds for success if it comes down to that. But look at him. It's you the kid's imprinted on. If anyone can make this easier on him, it's you."

"I'm not a kid," Rhys snapped.

"Well, I'm not doing the honors with that other guy," Titus muttered.

Darius overrode them both, his voice cold. "And if I don't think we should be spreading the Alpha strain?"

"You want to sentence him to die unnecessarily?" Xolani stared him down. "Fact is, Darius, Bravo Company may be onto something."

"I can't believe you'd argue in favor of that."

"I'm trying to survive in a world that's gone to shit. We don't have time to be squeamish. We've lost people. We need to begin replacing them if we want to keep our fighting force effective. This kid's going to die anyway if we don't help him, so really, where's the risk?"

Darius looked grave. "At what cost, Xolani?"

She crossed her arms over her chest and set her jaw. "We do what we have to do."

Rhys would have been more annoyed at being left out of a

conversation that concerned him so intimately if it had made any damn sense. His eyes ping-ponged from one to the other as half their words went over his head.

Who the hell was Bravo Company?

The muscle in Darius's jaw jerked. "Fine. Someone find me a cup and a goddamn turkey baster, then."

"Dammit, Darius!" Xolani looked like she wanted to punch something again. "We have no idea how long the Alpha virus will survive in sex fluids once exposed to air. Beta's short-lived when airborne. Moreover, it's an unstable virus prone to radical mutations. Even if it doesn't die prior to transmission, there's no predicting what it *will* do under those sorts of uncontrolled circumstances."

Darius looked back and forth between Titus and Xolani.

"Get out, both of you. Let me talk to the kid alone."

Xolani looked like she wanted to argue, but Titus gave her a tight shake of his head, and she swallowed it down. Pulling her scarred face into what Rhys suspected was meant to be an encouraging smile, Xolani ruffled his hair in a quasi-maternal gesture, as if she hadn't just moments before suggested that she'd have sex with him if necessary.

Then they were gone, and he was left alone in the dark chapel with Darius's forbidding presence. He wasn't sure if he was grateful for the lantern someone had brought into the room; it made the shadows even creepier. The rev he'd bludgeoned to death earlier had been removed and burned with the others, but the bloodstains remained on the floor. In the dim light, the brownish-black smudges looked oily and ominous. They filled Rhys with a horrified fascination. Short of this bizarre scheme and Darius's good graces, that blood might end up killing him.

"You're a virgin, aren't you?" Darius sat on the altar with an utter lack of reverence, the same altar at which Father Maurice had made Rhys kneel during prayers for seven years. Rhys's mom and Gabriel's parents had tried to protest Father Maurice's insistence on religious observation, but no one had been willing to fight over it once he'd grown volatile.

They'd tolerated a lot for the safety of numbers.

Rhys had listened at that altar three times a day from the time he was twelve as Father Maurice went over well-told tales emphasizing the importance of obedience to God's will, of chastity and purity and self-denial. He'd listened to endless rants about how immorality and sexual deviance had resulted in the destruction of civilization as they knew it.

He'd listened as Father Maurice had all but blamed him personally for a plague that, if Xolani was telling the truth, had seen its first scattered cases not long after Rhys had mastered a two-wheeled bike.

Now his only hope of survival was to agree to be part of the wickedness Father Maurice had condemned.

With Darius.

He swallowed hard, trying and failing to see Darius's dark shape as something other than terrifying. "Of course I'm a virgin." At nineteen years old, with no eligible partners and no prospect of ever encountering any, he'd resigned himself to living and dying that way.

Darius drummed his fingers on the altar in a rhythmic patter. "Do you *want* to do what Xolani is proposing?"

"I don't want to die."

"That's not the same thing."

"Well, then, no, I *don't* want it. I think it sounds sick. But I don't want to die, either, so what am I supposed to do?"

The drumming stopped, and Darius rapped his knuckles against the wood in a hard, sharp strike. "Well, *I* don't want to fuck an unwilling kid, so I'd say this is a shitty situation for both of us."

Rhys folded his hands in his lap, as much to stare at them in embarrassment at having insulted Darius as to hide the fact that, despite himself, he was getting a boner. Wasn't that pathetic? Even as warped as the whole situation was, apparently all his body heard was *sex*.

"Sorry." He was glad for the shadows that kept his face from looking as red as it felt.

"Sick, huh? I suppose that means you don't even like men?"

Oh, God help him, could his head actually explode from too much blushing?

"Actually, I do." He squirmed on the moldering velvet padding of the pew, thinking of Gabriel. Daring, defiant, larger-than-life

Gabriel, who'd left him behind. "I mean, I know some people think it's a sin and all, but . . ."

Darius waved him off with an impatient flap of his hand. "Shut that down. I don't want to hear what your preacher had to say about it."

Rhys looked down at his hands again. His erection wasn't subsiding. "Sorry," he repeated.

"Is there . . .?" Darius sighed, running a hand down the ponytail that hung to his shoulder blades. The altar creaked as his weight shifted. "Shit. I wish this could wait until we get back to base. If there's somebody else here you'd rather have your first time with, I could talk to them. See if they'd be willing to do it. If I can at least give you a choice in *that* . . ."

The rest of them were even less familiar to him than Darius, who was a complete stranger himself. The rest of them hadn't saved him seconds before he was about to die. They hadn't been so concerned with his safety that they'd climbed fully clothed into the shower with him to try to get the blood off.

"No." He looked away, suddenly feeling vulnerable, humiliated by the fact that, twisted as it was, some part of him—a very singular part, at least—wanted this. It shouldn't be arousing. It should be the least arousing thing imaginable, because it *was* sick. What Xolani had proposed was a humiliating, degrading farce, but his cock didn't seem to care.

If and when he had sex, he wanted it to be for a better reason than being forced into it because he had no choice other than dying. Now he understood what had offended Darius earlier. After all, Darius was only considering doing this to save him, not because he *wanted* to. He didn't want *Rhys*. That stung, pricking his vanity for some absurd reason. It would have been nice to at least be desired. Maybe Darius didn't even like men as a rule. "I don't want anyone else."

"Then this is how it's gonna go down." Darius paused. That measuring gaze pinned Rhys, stripped him down to all his deepest secrets. "You need to understand: If you're not infected with Alpha, you're infected with Beta or Gamma. Either you become one of us or you die. We can't have you running around, no matter what strain you've got. The reasons you can't be let loose infected with Beta or Gamma are plain, but even if it's Alpha, you'll still be too dangerous to leave uncontained. One cut and you could infect any survivors you come across. You'd be strong enough to take captives and set yourself up with a harem and slave labor somewhere out of the way. So no matter what happens, boy, you're with us until you die, whether that's a few weeks from now or when you're an old, old man. You understand what I'm saying?"

Rhys shook his head. "I don't— No."

Darius glowered. "I'm saying if you back out, I'll kill you. I don't like it. It's a little too close to raping someone under threat of death for my comfort. Hell, I suppose that's exactly what it is. I don't consider that much of a choice to give someone. But if you don't agree to this tonight, or if you agree to this and back out, sooner or later I'll end up putting a bullet in your head. I'll have to. Now do you understand?"

Worried for a moment that he might faint again, Rhys waited for the dizziness to pass and nodded, his mouth dry and the sour taste of terror on his tongue.

"All right, then." Darius pushed himself up off the altar. "We're all in, both of us, or we're finished. So for the next five or six weeks, or however long it takes, your ass is mine. If I give the word, you drop everything and do what I say. I don't care if we're in the middle of the fucking mess hall. If I tell you bend over, you do it. We clear?"

Rhys didn't know which reaction was the strongest: offense or fear or, God help him, arousal. His heart hammered in his chest as he stared at Darius wide-eyed. He should protest, he thought, licking his dry lips. He should tell Darius to go to hell, and then he should go pray for the serenity to accept his eventual death.

Problem was, he wasn't sure he could actually walk just now, much less kneel.

"We're clear," he heard himself agreeing. His pride groaned in protest, and the thrill of terrified arousal redoubled.

"Then come here." Darius beckoned him toward the altar.

"What, here?" In his head, Father Maurice's voice screamed condemnation and accusations of debauchery and blasphemy.

"Don't question me, boy." Darius's eyes narrowed, somewhere

between challenge and annoyance. "Come to me, or I'll come get you. Think I can't do it?"

Of course he could. He was a Jug, right?

His face burning with shame, Rhys pushed himself from the pew and came.

Literally.

4

INITIATION

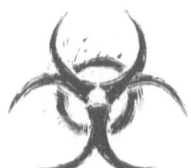

"**O**h God." Was there still time to opt for death? Better that than the wet stain spreading across the front of his new jeans.

Darius's mouth twitched. "Plenty more where that came from, boy," he murmured, not unkindly. "Now come here."

Rhys looked over his shoulder at the door the revenants had splintered earlier. "Someone might—"

"Who cares? You think they won't know that I fucked you?" Darius crossed his arms over his chest. "I could take you back to the kitchen and do you in front of everyone if you think they won't."

"No!" Rhys shook his head violently. His eyes burned again, this time with the agony of humiliation. He wanted to call the whole thing off, but he didn't want to die and—*dear Jesus, please*—even after that embarrassingly easy and unfulfilling orgasm, he still felt the pull of arousal tugging at his balls. "No, please." He lowered his voice lest anyone, particularly Jacob, overhear his unmanly whimper. His hands and knees shook as he approached the altar.

Darius reached down and opened the belt of his fatigues, then the fly, and pushed them and his boxers down his hips. Holy Lord, what was Rhys supposed to *do* with that thing? The sight of Darius's thick penis ratcheted up his terror, and suddenly this wasn't about his fear of God's wrath or Jacob's petty torments or the humiliation of having his first time under duress with someone who didn't really want him. There was no possible way he could ever do *anything* with . . . that.

Not that he knew exactly what he was supposed to do with it to begin with, beyond some vague ideas. Going into seclusion to escape the plague as a kid meant he'd missed out on a lot of schoolyard talk. His mother's homeschooling—even the birds and bees for gay boys part—hadn't quite covered this sort of situation.

"Look at me, boy." Rhys tore his eyes away from the heavy cock Darius was slowly stroking to full erection and met his severe gaze. "This doesn't have to be a bad thing. You like men; I'm a pretty damn good-looking man. You could do a lot worse. I won't be unkind unless you start giving me shit, and I won't hurt you any more than necessary to get the job done. When it's all said and done, *if* this works, you'll be one of us. You'll be strong and fast and less easily tired. You'll be able to kill revs like the ones who murdered your sister in job lots." Rhys tried to keep his focus on Darius's eyes, but he couldn't quite manage to break the half-appalled spell of that rhythmic stroking. "The people I lead, they're good people, for the most part. Decent. They'll welcome you as family. You'll never have some creepy old fucker preaching to you about right or wrong again, trying to make you deny your God-given urges. Now, you can be reluctant, if you want, or you can find the good in it. One way or the other, we're doing this."

None of that sounded bad, and Rhys's horrified soul seized upon it for hope. "What do I need to do?"

"You'll just suck me off tonight. Chances of passing the virus through giving head aren't great, but there's no way I'm doing a virgin who just blew his load up the ass. Problem is, time's not really on our side here, so we have to get creative. Strip."

Trembling, agonizingly aware of the *wrongness* of doing this in the chapel, Rhys peeled the T-shirt over his head. He felt Darius's eyes upon him, taking in his thin chest. Rhys had worked long hours trying to keep the monastery repaired and growing food in the small courtyard garden inside the gates, and there had never been enough to eat. Compared to Darius's muscular build—or at least what he assumed was muscle from the firm bulk he'd felt pressed against him when Darius had pinned him to the door earlier—he felt scrawny and ugly.

Darius smiled kindly, as though he understood the root of Rhys's self-consciousness. His hand had slowed on his cock as though half-forgotten, and he began stroking again when the lack of stimulation—or maybe it was just the sight of Rhys's skinny body—had the predictable effect. "You'll have more to eat with us, too. Now the pants."

Stripping off the cold, wet denim and sticky underwear was humiliating. Even more so was the fact that he was already half-erect again. Darius seemed pleased to see it.

"Well now, you're a sweet thing, aren't you?" Rhys didn't think Darius was asking him. "Cute little ass on you. Bend over the altar."

"I thought you weren't going to—"

"No questions." Darius's gentle expression quickly became severe. "You do what I tell you when I tell you to do it. I'm helping you here, remember?"

"Right. Sorry." Rhys felt heat spread upward from his chest as he flushed crimson, and his dick rose a little more. His limbs quaked as he made himself obey, kneeling and bracing his elbows on the altar and trying not to think of God's—or Father Maurice's—opinion on his position. The tang of antique pine and waxy varnish filled his nostrils, and the sticky surface of the altar dragged at his fingertips.

"That's it, boy." Darius trailed his hand down Rhys's spine. The contact was electric, tightening everything along its path all the way to Rhys's belly. "Just give in. Relax and enjoy it. Trust me."

Despite the instructions, he tensed at the feel of Darius's hands on his butt, squeezing and kneading. He made a dismayed sound, shrinking from the touch, but Darius didn't let go. He pushed Rhys's cheeks apart and teased the tight knot between them with a finger. Rhys groaned in confused longing, getting louder when his erection bumped the altar. He yelped when something warm and wet replaced that careful finger. It wasn't until he felt the steamy heat of Darius's breath along his crack that he realized what was happening.

Oh God. With his *tongue*?

Rhys's knuckles turned white as they tightened around the ornately carved edge of the altar. He wriggled, trying to escape the stroking—or possibly to greet it. Revulsion mingled with perverse pleasure.

This shouldn't feel good. It shouldn't feel— Oh, Jesus, save me.

Darius's sweeping, slurping tongue began to probe, trying to squirm into Rhys's opening.

Somewhere along the way, Rhys forgot to be disgusted. As Darius's firm hands spread his cheeks and his tongue tried to insinuate itself inside him, Rhys began to relax. He moaned softly, getting louder the more energetically Darius licked and prodded. Darius grunted and grumbled against Rhys's butt, making noises that didn't sound at all like he wasn't enjoying himself.

Then his finger replaced his tongue, pushing inside Rhys's wet, semi-relaxed hole. Rhys cried out, more from surprise than any actual distress. The finger didn't feel *bad*, just weird. And getting less weird all the time. It began to stroke in and out, and that *definitely* didn't feel bad.

How could he be hard again this soon?

"Just take it, boy." Darius's breath brushed Rhys's back. "Not gonna do any more than this tonight. Just get used to it. In a minute here, I want you to suck me off, just like I said you would. But don't spit and don't swallow. Now."

Darius drew his finger out of Rhys's twitching hole, and Rhys had to take a moment to shake off the pleasured daze before he could obey. In the time it took him to collect himself and begin to turn, Darius stepped up beside him and that intimidating cock touched his face. He opened his eyes and stared at it, mesmerized by the way the loose sheath of skin rolled under the strokes of Darius's fist.

"Open your mouth," Darius demanded. "Suck me."

Could he even get his mouth around all that?

Salt and sweat and musk touched his tongue an instant after it hit his nostrils. Silky skin over rigid flesh slid between his lips and invaded his mouth. However bizarre the whole situation was, he knew he'd never forget that sensation. Sensory gratification conflicted with his rational mind, which told him this shouldn't be happening. It was the wrong person, the wrong circumstance, the wrong cock, just plain wrong. But he'd dreamed about it, long ago, with Gabe, wondering how it would taste and feel. Now he knew.

Darius's groans sounded good. The salty droplet of fluid that touched Rhys's tongue tasted good. He even *smelled* good. Warm and rich. He filled Rhys's senses, quieting all the reasons Rhys shouldn't be doing this. His jaw began to ache before long, but he managed it with less difficulty than he'd anticipated when he'd seen the cock in question. Darius's hand pumped up and down the lower portion of his shaft, bumping against Rhys's lips as they stretched around his dick.

"That's it, boy. Good. Go ahead, and suck on it. Use that sweet little mouth."

Rhys flinched and tried to draw away, the words crude and vulgar in his ears, making him ashamed. Darius pulled him back, but he also fell silent for a moment, and Rhys wasn't sure if that was better or worse.

He tried to suck. He tried to lick and move. He even stopped thinking about Darius's words and just obeyed. Darius took his hands away, and Rhys began to use his own, stroking where his mouth couldn't go without making himself gag.

"Give me your hand, boy." Obeying, Rhys felt his hand drawn inexorably between Darius's thighs as they shifted apart, and Darius's fingers closed his own around the fragile, wrinkled lumps of Darius's balls. They were large and heavy, and felt similar to his own but different, the hair springier and less wiry. Wonder shot through the surreal sense of disbelief that this was honestly happening, that Darius was making Rhys *pleasure* him.

"Good. Go ahead, and squeeze. Not too hard. Make it feel good." Darius's moans grew louder, and his cock grew harder, the head swelling until Rhys's jaw began to cramp.

"Remember, don't swallow." Darius's hand took over for Rhys again, pumping hard and fast as Rhys sucked. Against his tongue, along the underside of Darius's cock, something moved, rushing up the length of it. A salty, bitter torrent of Darius's semen hit his palate a moment later.

Rhys struggled for a moment not to spit it out. It wasn't just that he had another man's cum in his mouth—he'd imagined doing that, once upon a time, with Gabriel—but the idea that it was *infected*. A virus lived in that thick mass sitting on his tongue, the same virus that killed people with the Rot or made them into mindless cannibals.

He tried not to gag, but then Darius bent down, muttering, "Put it in my mouth," before closing his lips over Rhys's.

It wasn't a kiss, and Rhys tried not to think of it as one, though Darius's hand cupped the back of his head, refusing to let him pull away. Rhys spat the mess into Darius's mouth and bent over the altar when Darius pushed him forward. Rough hands spread his cheeks again, and Darius's tongue thrust into him.

Rhys groaned, lost between dismay and arousal, as he realized what Darius was doing. As he forced his semen into Rhys's rear, his hand wrapped around Rhys's dick.

Oh God.

It was nothing like the reluctant arousal that had ended in an unsatisfactory rush in his new underwear just minutes earlier. Jesus, no. This was better. The strokes of Darius's hand made the tension in his balls reach deep into Rhys's gut, pulling and straining and *good*, so very, very good. He hadn't touched himself in years, not since Father Maurice had screamed at him about self-abuse and damnation when he saw stains on the sheets of Rhys's bed. Not when he and Jacob had frequently barged in on Rhys in the showers, expecting to find him engaged in something sinful. With the pressure of Darius's hand, though, the impending orgasm became not something to dread, but something to chase, to yearn and strive for.

With just a few strokes, Rhys's second climax spent itself against the altar. His strangled yell echoed off the stone walls of the chapel.

Trembling and panting, Rhys whimpered and rolled off his knees beside the altar to give them a break from the hard floor. He didn't dare sit, for fear that what Darius had spat into him would seep back out, so he curled up on his side instead, his eyes closing as he tried to make sense of the world again.

Darius's breath was only a little labored, and he seemed otherwise calm as he hitched up his fatigues and looked down at Rhys.

"Take your time, boy."

Rhys couldn't open his eyes to confront any of the images of the

Lord or the apostles around the chapel looking down at him in his blasphemy and shame. He wanted to weep, or he wanted Darius to just touch him, to pet him or hug him or *something* so that he didn't feel so horribly alone and confused in the aftermath.

But Darius kept his distance, because this wasn't like that. They were only here because they had to be. Which made something that should have been intimate and amazing into something completely perverse and demeaning.

"You all right?"

At length, Rhys gathered his dignity and pushed himself up from the floor. He reached for his clothing, grimacing at the state of his jeans and underwear. He didn't let himself look at the mess dripping down the side of the altar as he pulled his shirt on, feeling the bottom hem of it brush his bare thighs and spent cock. "Yeah."

Darius leaned casually on the altar again, apparently unaware of Rhys's struggles to make sense of his own clothing. "Keep that in as long as you can. Soon I'm gonna get you a butt plug that you'll wear at night. It'll keep the jizz inside your ass and help you get used to relaxing and letting something in there. We're gonna work on that in the morning. Maybe sooner if I wake up with a hard-on. A Jug's got stamina all the time, not just in combat. That's good news for keeping you alive, but you can expect to get a workout."

Rhys nodded, trying and failing to envision what exactly a butt plug was. His knees were weak, and he still felt wrung out by the force of his orgasm and wretchedly intrigued by the whole perverted scheme.

God help him, he wanted to do it again, and for reasons that had nothing to do with survival.

"Which room's yours?"

Rhys braced himself to pull on his sticky briefs. "Upstairs."

Darius snatched them from his hands with a grimace of distaste. "Don't be nasty, boy. You ain't got nothing I'm not gonna see again. Might as well get used to it. You can wash these and hang them up in the bathroom to dry overnight, and you've got a change of clothes if they're still damp when you wake up."

"But what about . . .?" He looked at the door, unsure where the rest of Darius's team was now.

"They're probably all hitting their bunks by now. If they're not, well, you don't have anything they ain't seen, either. No questions. Just go."

As they made it through most of the monastery without encountering anyone, Rhys relaxed, but just before he reached his room, Jacob stepped out of a bedroom that wasn't his. He opened his mouth to say something—no doubt scathing—but then he saw Darius come up behind Rhys.

His eyes traveled up and down Rhys's half-nude body and hardened, his expression twisting.

"There a problem?" Darius's hand landed on Rhys's shoulder. The gesture felt almost . . . protective.

"No." Jacob forced a smile. "I just wanted to thank you for giving me—giving us *both*, of course—a chance to live."

"Well, don't make sense to waste lives if we can save 'em." Darius shrugged as if he hadn't argued against the idea. "If you want to help us fight revs, you're welcome on the team."

Rhys stared at Jacob in disbelief. "You—you took the offer? *You?*"

Jacob, who had echoed all Father Maurice's condemnations of Rhys. Jacob, who had helped Father Maurice torment and punish Rhys for infractions real and trumped-up. Jacob, who had assured Rhys that he was going to hell for being a faggot and that Jacob would be happy to help him on his way there.

Why had he accepted? Who had attempted to infect him?

"Well, maybe you'll have better luck murdering me next time." Jacob managed a tragic look and let them pass. Rhys glanced over his shoulder, at least a little satisfied to see Jacob walking with an uncomfortable-looking gait.

Darius followed Rhys to his room, and by the time Rhys returned from washing his clothing in the bathroom, he'd moved a mattress from one of the narrow beds in another of the monks' empty chambers into Rhys's room. There was barely enough space for both of them.

Rhys gave the suddenly even more cramped quarters a dubious look, prompting Darius to explain. "You're staying where I can keep an eye on you and where you're available when I want you. The next few weeks, that's your first job. Be ready anytime, and don't give any lip."

Dear Lord, was his cock actually twitching to life *again*? Rhys ducked his head and dug into his backpack, hoping Darius wouldn't notice.

He hesitated, though, once he had the fresh pair of underwear in hand, looking at Darius for permission.

Darius shook his head. "You'll just be taking 'em off in the morning. Go to bed."

Blushing miserably, Rhys climbed into his bed, rolling to face the wall. The crack of his butt felt strangely slippery, and he tried not to think about it. He lay there listening to Darius settle in, wishing the man would say something encouraging.

Finally, the murmur came in the dark, awkward and sounding a bit forced. "You did good tonight, Rhys. You'll be okay."

As comfort went it was lacking, but at least it was something. At least it gave him an indication that Darius hadn't dismissed him entirely from his thoughts.

A reddish glow flickered against the wall, and Rhys realized it was the still-glowing embers from the fires they'd built to burn the bodies. That inevitably led to thoughts of his sister and nephew, which really weren't any better.

Grief and confusion, humiliation, torment, and fear of the future all joined forces to overwhelm him.

Hoping desperately that Darius was asleep, he finally let himself cry.

5

CLAIMSTAKING

Darius awoke to an unaccustomed sense of remorse. He'd lain awake listening to Rhys sniffle long into the night, and despite his irritation with Xolani for pushing this whole fucking situation, he couldn't help but feel for the kid. Considering what Rhys had been through, he'd actually been fairly levelheaded about it all.

At least when he wasn't attacking people.

Darius had tried to get an explanation out of Titus about that incident, but the other guy—the one who'd barged into the conversation and introduced himself as Jacob Houtman—had started on a tirade about Rhys. How he'd gone crazy, how he'd always been trouble, making life difficult for the survivors who had sought refuge at the monastery, how he'd tried to create problems for his sister and begrudged her the smallest bit of happiness when she'd married Houtman. He'd even insinuated that Rhys had been jealous and felt an *unnatural attraction* to his sister.

Darius was reasonably certain now that at least that last insinuation was bullshit.

He wasn't sure how much he could trust Houtman. He gave the smarmy impression of a bad used-car salesman, of someone who was a lousy liar but too full of himself to realize no one was buying it. Titus had taken an instant dislike to Houtman, and Titus had damn good judgment when you could pry two words out of him about anything. Darius wasn't sure what to make of a man Houtman's age marrying a girl who'd been only sixteen, but it wasn't as though the polite strictures of society that had kept those sorts of arrangements in the realm of the forbidden—or at least the deeply frowned upon —existed anymore.

If rumor out of the clean zone was to be believed, any fertile pairing was encouraged, with much greater age differentials disregarded. Besides, Darius couldn't exactly point fingers when he was fucking a nineteen-year-old kid at the ripe age of forty-three.

No matter if he trusted Houtman or not, the question of whether Rhys was stable, much less a troublemaker, was a significant one. In contrast to the bravery he'd exhibited trying to save his sister and her baby, there were moments when he was stubborn and sullen, snapping at Darius and Xolani, though mostly that came across as bravado. Still, Darius couldn't afford to bring someone into the unit who would disrupt operations. Delta Company had rid itself years ago—often messily—of anyone too egotistical, power hungry, or unstable to be trusted with the strength of the Alpha strain. If Rhys was prone to flying off the handle and attacking people, they'd be better off killing him than taking the chance of him creating chaos in the ranks.

Was there a good reason for Rhys's behavior? Yesterday he'd lost the last of his family and come close to death himself. He might have been provoked by Houtman, and even if not, he might simply have been reacting to the grief and trauma. His mood could be swinging like a weather vane in high wind, and he might settle down once he had a chance to process it all.

Or he could just be a troublemaker, like Houtman said. Then again, Xolani seemed to think he was worth saving, and Darius trusted her judgment in general, even when he disagreed with her on the specifics. There was a reason she was his second-in-command.

At any rate, the least Darius could do was not be such a bastard with the kid. He didn't know how to interact with civilians anymore. He'd grown too used to the restrictions of the search-and-rescue effort. They sent the uninfected people they found on to Colorado Springs for quarantine and reintegration and never saw them again.

There was no sense getting to know the survivors, even if Darius and his people could get close enough to try without jeopardizing them.

Jugs weren't welcome on the other side of the trenches and razor wire surrounding the clean zone any more than revenants were.

He knew that some companies of Jugs weren't sending all the people they recovered to join the civilian population. He also knew some had taken advantage of their strength against the vulnerable survivors. He didn't want to be like them, and he certainly didn't want to discover the point at which a person who was physically more powerful began to believe they were, in fact, superior, that they had the right to take what they wanted from those who were weaker. So Darius kept his distance, made his people keep theirs, and sent the civvies on their way.

But Rhys was different. He'd never be welcomed inside the perimeter, either. He wasn't a civvie, not anymore, and quarantine was useless. He would be one of Darius's people. Maybe. There really was no telling what the odds were that this scheme of Xolani's would fail. Sex with uninfected people was known to transmit the Alpha strain—Bailey was proof of that—but no one had tried it with someone who had already been exposed to Beta and Gamma. Anything could happen, and Darius might still have to put a bullet in Rhys's brain before all was said and done.

Which reminded Darius why he was annoyed with Xolani. How was he supposed to do what he needed to do if he let himself get a soft spot for the kid?

How was he supposed to do what he needed to do if he *didn't*?

He heard the moment when Rhys awoke, the catch in what had been deep, even breaths, the soft snort, the sudden tension as awareness came flooding back to him. He lay stiffly on his cot, his back to Darius, refusing to roll over. Did he hope to con Darius into thinking he was still asleep? Did he want Darius to go away?

It would help if he could coax the kid into being a little less reluctant. Rhys's body was willing enough, but then he'd been a nineteen-year-old virgin last night—of *course* his body was willing. But the fact that he'd only agreed to this because the alternative was dying wouldn't ever sit right with Darius.

You did what you gotta do, man.

Really? Then why'd you get so fucking horny the moment you went all Dom Hardass on the kid last night?

Because it had been months since he'd fucked anyone, that's why, and ages since he'd gotten his hands on someone as soft and sweet as Rhys. The people of Delta Company had either claimed each other or weren't compatible for whatever reason. In fifteen years of being an exclusive company, they'd tried pretty much every combination that could work. The ones who were inclined toward commitment—the ones who weren't played musical beds at will— had made it.

And Darius kept to himself except for the occasional tension-relieving fuck because the ones who might be attracted or attractive to him didn't work on other levels.

He stared at Rhys's thin back, wondering just how long it would take the boy to quit playing possum and roll over. The window was open, but the night breeze had barely cooled the spartan cubicle masquerading as a bedroom. Rhys had started with his blanket pulled up to his chin, covering his nudity, but in his sleep he'd pushed it down to his hips while his T-shirt had rucked up, so that the only thing hidden was that cute, skinny ass of his.

It would be easier for Darius to convince himself he was a better man if he weren't so fucking certain that ass would feel like heaven clamped around his dick.

There were disproportionately few female Jugs, so almost all the males had learned to be flexible in their preferences, which meant they all carried lube with them everywhere. He had it there in his pack. Hell, it was on the list of items the reclamation crews routinely scavenged. So he could have that ass right this minute. He could roll Rhys over, pull the blanket off him, and just plow right in. The boy was his for the taking, however much circumstances had coerced his compliance. Darius could drive his cock into that tight, sweet ass, seed him, and tell himself he was doing Rhys a favor.

He wanted to do it. He *wanted* it. That was the worst part. He knew heightened aggression was a signature of the Alpha strain, but sometimes he wondered if the virus hadn't also had its effect on the moral centers of the Alpha recipients. Not to the extent of the revs, of course; Jugs weren't mindless animals. But it was tempting to believe that animal-like strength, agility, and endurance had the side effect of bestial urges for gratification in all forms. His people certainly were a hedonistic lot, after all, every one of them prone to living hard, loud, and lusty. Sometimes it took a concerted effort to remind themselves of the things that kept them human.

So yeah, he wanted it, but he didn't want to traumatize the kid. Forget the six weeks or however long Rhys would be anyone's meat until they knew whether or not he would live. If they successfully infected him with the Alpha strain, he'd be one of Darius's people for the rest of his life. Rhys needed to start thinking of Delta Company in terms of being a safe place, a family. That was worth exercising a bit of patience, however strongly Darius's instincts demanded otherwise.

"I know you're awake, boy," he rumbled. "You can quit pretending."

Rhys rolled over reluctantly. From the way he clutched the covers at his hips, Darius was willing to bet he was trying to hide some morning wood.

Darius smirked and shifted onto his back, taking way too much pleasure in seeing Rhys's eyes widen.

Rhys licked his dry lips, looking away from the rise over Darius's hips. "What should I call you?"

"Something wrong with my name?"

"No, except it feels weird when you're always ordering me around and calling me *boy*."

"I order my people around and they call me by name." He flashed Rhys a grin. "Though if you wanna call me *sir* I won't stop you."

Rhys blushed and tried to cover it by burying his face in his hands.

"You got a toothbrush?"

Rhys nodded, lowering his hands to reveal a grimace. "Yeah, but it's in pretty bad shape. We haven't had toothpaste here for years, and we ran out of baking soda last winter. I've been trying to make do."

"Sometimes that's all you can manage. I'll see if anyone is carrying a spare. If not, we'll get you a new toothbrush on the road when we move out, and you can use the toothpaste from my kit until then." Darius rolled from his pallet to his feet and grabbed his rucksack, slinging it over his shoulder. "Come on."

It was worth the tiny kindness to see Rhys's delight at having access to real toothpaste. No one should look that ecstatic to be brushing his teeth. Darius's mouth twitched with amusement at the whole passel of innuendo that came to mind watching Rhys spit masses of creamy foam, humming happily all the while.

"When you're done, we'll hit the showers." Darius tucked away his own toothbrush after he was finished, pulling a carefully wrapped block of soap out of his pack.

In an instant, Rhys's exuberance dimmed. "We?"

Darius lifted an eyebrow, letting his eyes travel possessively up and down Rhys's body. The sooner Rhys got comfortable with that, the better.

"Any reason we shouldn't?"

Rhys dropped his gaze miserably, crossing to the shower. "No, I guess not." He turned it on and stepped under the cold spray.

After a moment, Darius made himself unclench his jaw and join him. "Turn around," he said when Rhys refused to look at him. He proffered the soap. "Wash me."

"What?" That got Rhys's attention, at least.

"You're in a pretty rotten position to be overly modest, boy. Sooner you get used to seeing me in my skin and me seeing you in yours, the easier this will be for both of us."

Rhys nodded and accepted the soap. His movements were fast and light as he worked the lather over Darius's skin, as if he was trying to touch as little of Darius as possible for as short a time as he could get away with. Darius closed his eyes, grasping for patience.

"Slow down." He opened his eyes again, catching Rhys's gaze. "Touch me. Learn me. Get used to me, 'cause I ain't going anywhere."

A visible shudder rippled through Rhys, though he stopped his brisk soaping. He flinched but opened his palms and laid them against Darius's chest. Darius responded with a small shiver of his own at the electric feel of another person's hands on him, truly *on him.* The hypersensitive nerves that enabled the swift reaction speed of the Jugs tingled.

Rhys's palms began to move in widening circles, eking scant lather out of the homemade lye soap on Darius's skin. The suds made crisp noises in the whorls of hair sprinkled between his nipples. Only the chilly water kept Darius from responding physically.

"That's it." Darius had to force himself to speak rather than simply grab Rhys. If he could just get the kid to *trust* him . . . "I'm just a guy, not a monster. I got no interest in hurting you."

Strictly speaking, that wasn't quite true, but he let it slide.

"I know." Rhys ducked his head, his voice small. "You're trying to help me. Even though you don't want to."

"Well, it's more I just don't like having my choices taken away."

Rhys swallowed. "Me either."

"Then we got that in common." Darius offered the boy a small smile, and Rhys's slippery hands moved down the ridges of Darius's ribs, forgetting to hesitate. "We can make the most of this, you and me. We gotta do it, so why not let ourselves enjoy it?"

"Because it's not right." Rhys looked away.

"Says who? Your preacher?"

He shrugged. "This just isn't the way it should be."

"What's your basis for comparison there, boy?" A bit of Darius's gentle solicitude melted away with the unplanned detour into moralizing. He knew his voice had hardened again when Rhys's hands shrank away. Dammit. He firmed up his grip on his temper. "You seen so much of the world you can say at a glance what's right and what's wrong?"

Rhys fell miserably silent. The passes of his hands as he worked on washing Darius became perfunctory once more. Darius clenched his jaw and tried again.

"I've seen evil, Rhys. Hell, done my share of it and then some. Sometimes I was following orders. Sometimes I didn't know any better. Sometimes I just didn't care. I'm not gonna pretend to be a good man. I'm way more interested in getting the job done than in being good."

"You don't think there should be something more between

people than . . . nothing?" Rhys's hands went still as he looked up, something stubborn hardening his eyes. "*That's* my problem. It's not even about what Father Maurice said, though it seems a lot of people think that way. It's just . . . demeaning when it doesn't mean anything."

Darius snorted. "What, you waiting for true love, boy?"

Rhys rolled his eyes disdainfully. "No. Just something a little less warped than doing it because I don't have any other choice."

"Damn, you're young." The boy's hands shrank away from his chest as if he'd only just become aware that he was still touching Darius. "Look, far as I'm concerned, only thing evil about sex is rape. Now, that puts us in a real gray area, but I'm trying to avoid it. You said you don't wanna die. I'm trying to help you live. I told you what would happen; you said you understood. I can't get bogged down in the rest. If fucking you for a few weeks to save your life is wrong, that's fine by me. I don't flinch, boy. If you've changed your mind, tough shit. I didn't compromise my beliefs on this to have you back out on me."

"I'm not going to change my mind," Rhys muttered. "Just don't expect me to be thrilled about it."

Perhaps he was expecting too much, too soon, to ask for any enthusiasm.

Shit, the kid's spent his life shut away from the world since before puberty.

He hadn't seen the shithole society had become: desperate, starving, ragtag people stabbing each other in the back for a chance at survival and fucking their brains out for just a few moments of comfort in the midst of all the terror. The boy could afford to be idealistic.

Hell, if he'd had time for it, Darius might have admired Rhys's innocence and the balls it took for him to stand by his ideals when expediency demanded a change of heart.

And at least one part of Rhys was enthusiastic. It was a start.

"I don't recall asking you to be thrilled." He backed Rhys against the shower wall, turning off the water. "Just compliant."

"Yes, *sir.*" If Rhys's voice twisted the last word with a touch of rebellious irony, Darius let it pass. He stared into the boy's eyes for a long moment, watching the breathless fear mount. Then something nudged his hip as that one interested part responded predictably.

His hand closed around Rhys's beautifully curved cock and drew up its length in a slow stroke from root to tip. Rhys's head bumped on the tile wall, his face crumpling, his expression trapped somewhere between despair and quasi-orgasmic pleasure. And Darius noticed something he'd missed the day before, when the gaunt kid with the brutally hacked-off hair and patchy beard had just been another civvie to be rescued or a victim to be put out of his misery with a merciful bullet to the head.

Rhys was lovely.

Darius stopped after only a few strokes, by which point Rhys was already trembling on the edge of coming. Now wasn't the time for that.

He wished he could wait for more comfortable surroundings and a more relaxed mood. Or rather, he didn't. He liked this setup just fine, but he knew another way would be better for Rhys. If he could take the time to seduce to boy, get him relaxed, it would be less frightening—and less uncomfortable—for him. He should just order Rhys to his knees and tell him to put that mouth of his to better use than sulking, the way he had last night, but something much less patient took over. This time he wanted that ass.

Darius turned Rhys to face the wall and grabbed the little bottle of lube he'd pulled out of his pack.

"What—?" Rhys's startled question was cut off when Darius's fingers slid between his ass cheeks. He gently worked a blunt fingertip into that tight, virgin hole until it gave up resisting. When it let him add another, he rewarded himself for his patience by introducing Rhys to his prostate, smiling when Rhys groaned and jolted, his fingers scrabbling futilely for purchase against the slick tile.

Darius gripped Rhys's shoulder with his free hand to keep him still, rumbling in his ear, "Relax, boy. I can't promise it won't hurt, but it'll hurt a helluva lot less if you don't fight it. One way or the other, you're taking my cock up your ass this time."

Darius didn't know if the half-sobbed cry Rhys gave was need or distress, but he wasn't sure he cared. He worked his fingers into Rhys until the tension eased as much as it seemed it would, then he tried to press the swollen head of his dick in as gradually as he could while Rhys's muscles struggled to push it out. It was all he could do not to just *drive* into the boy.

"I can't! God, it hurts. Please!" Rhys's fingers clawed at the mildew-stained tile. His entire body quivered, and good Lord, the way his ass clenched. Trapped between his own primal urges and the desire not to injure Rhys, Darius wrestled just one more moment of self-control from the clutches of his lust. He stopped moving, but he didn't draw back.

"Shh. Quiet, boy. Just relax." Rhys shook his head urgently, and Darius pressed his body against the boy's, trapping him against the wall when he tried to escape. One hand pinned Rhys's shoulder against the tile, while the other pulled his hip back. "If I pull out now, it's just gonna hurt all over again when I go back in. It'll get better. Just be still and wait for it to come. Push back on me if you can. It'll help. You'll get used to it."

"I can't. I can't. Please, stop." Rhys moaned, shuddering as Darius pushed in a bit further, trying to get the head through those struggling muscles without rushing it and causing the boy unnecessary pain.

"You can, baby. Just relax. Almost there. It's gonna feel good, I promise. Maybe not today, but soon." His hand smoothed Rhys's wet hair, then pulled Rhys's head back. His hips nudged forward again, and . . .

Fuck, yeah, there it was. The wide ridge of his cock passed through that ring of resisting muscle, and then it was like he was being pulled in deep as Rhys slumped against the wall with a moan of abject relief.

"See, not so bad, is it?" He pushed aside the urge to kiss or nuzzle behind Rhys's ear. Fuck that. This wasn't about romance, no matter how sweet and tight Rhys was. "It'll get better." Darius let an amused smile dance about his lips and color his tone as he continued to wrestle his own urges under control. "Just your bad luck to wind up with a dude hung like a bull elephant first time out. Tender thing like you should start with some training wheels, but we don't have time for that. So for now, I'm gonna be as gentle as I can, and you're just gonna take it. Someday, though, you're gonna beg me to shove my dick in your cute little ass."

"God, *please*." Rhys whimpered brokenly. Darius wasn't sure if Rhys was begging him to stop or continue.

And honestly, he no longer cared. He drew back and eased in again, rocking slow and shallow. Rhys cried out as Darius groaned against the back of his shoulder, picking up the pace after a moment.

"*Fuck*, you feel good," he muttered into the skin of the boy's wet neck.

If all his people there in the monastery didn't hear the wet slap of skin on skin, they definitely heard Rhys's yells echoing in the bathroom, amplified by the tile. Darius didn't *think* the cries were entirely distressed, and he *knew* the hard length of cock he found when he wedged his hand between Rhys's body and the wall sure as hell wasn't. He didn't dare jack the boy off. Not yet, not before he bent Rhys over, hauled his hips back, and set about *really* fucking him.

The contrast of his hands on Rhys's pale skin, thick and blunt on the sharp-boned hips and emaciated back, should have reined Darius's lust in. It should have reminded him that not only was he a veteran hardened by years of fighting for his survival while Rhys was just a soft kid trapped in bad circumstances but that he was far more powerful by virtue of the Alpha strain. He could quite literally *break* the boy if he wasn't careful.

None of that seemed to carry any significance, though. He *wanted* Rhys . . . not broken, not exactly, but taken right to that edge. He couldn't remember the last time he'd been so horny for someone, so eager to claim and possess.

Of course, Rhys wasn't a lover. Maybe that was the difference. Not a lover. Rhys was just . . . *his*.

His burden. His responsibility. His to have and to save.

Gripping Rhys's hips, Darius drove into him over and over, slamming against his flanks. Rhys's cries faded away to groans as Darius's body tightened. His balls drew up, and his hands trembled where they clutched Rhys's soft skin. He came with a sharp grunt that echoed off the tile.

The thought of his cum inside Rhys, claiming him like a flag planted on newly explored ground, awoke a primal, triumphant possessiveness that mingled with concern. He finally seized Rhys's cock and jerked him off. It didn't take much. Darius figured the boy would be on a hair trigger until he got used to regular orgasms. Rhys's spunk splattered the wall, mingling with the droplets of water.

Afterward, Darius pulled out carefully, and Rhys slid down the wall of the shower, gasping, his expression stunned. Darius turned on the water to finish bathing but turned it off again as it sprayed Rhys's face without the boy making any effort to dodge it.

Jesus, what had he done?

"You okay, boy?"

No answer. Darius squatted beside him, hesitating to reach out until he could control the instinct to pet and soothe Rhys. He couldn't afford to coddle the kid, but that nagging sense of remorse reared up again.

Shit. This was why they didn't do civvies. Jugs were too strong, too dangerous. He should have been more careful. He'd meant to be more careful, but once he'd gotten a taste of Rhys tight around him, *careful* hadn't been any part of his vocabulary. He didn't *think* he'd been that brutal, but Rhys was acting broken.

"Come on, talk to me, boy. You okay?"

Slowly, Rhys's eyes tracked toward him, wide and shocked. He stared for a moment, his brow furrowed as he tried to make sense of the question, then he nodded slowly.

Darius breathed a sigh of relief.

"I'm sorry. I shouldn't have—"

The crease between Rhys's eyebrows deepened, and his mouth pulled down.

"Why?"

"I didn't think how new you are. I—"

"Why are you sorry?" Rhys's voice rasped, and he cleared his throat. "It's what we have to do, right?"

"Right." It was Darius's turn to be confused as Rhys collected himself with visible effort.

Not broken, no. Not even close.

There was an aloof dignity about the way he pushed himself to his feet, a detachment that Darius wasn't sure he liked. It felt too much like that eerie lack of emotion he'd exhibited when staring at the remains of his family the previous day. Like he'd just shut down.

"Then you shouldn't apologize," he said, no inflection in his tone, and he left Darius behind on the floor of the shower. Unsettled and at a complete loss as to what to make of the reaction, Darius watched him go.

He wasn't sure he wouldn't have rather actually broken the boy.

6

INTRODUCTION

The Jugs gathered in the kitchen for breakfast, but Rhys couldn't bear to go in. Not knowing they must have heard him, must know how he—

He decided to skip breakfast. It didn't matter. He'd lost the ability to feel hungry a few years ago as his rations had become leaner and leaner, especially once he'd begun giving some of his small share to Cadence when she became pregnant.

He tried to avoid the Jugs as they went about their duties. It felt like they were all staring at him. They weren't, of course. Not really. They were all too busy ransacking the monastery for salvageable supplies. There weren't many, but with it getting into late summer, some of the plants in the garden were starting to yield.

No, the only one taking notice of him was Jacob, whose sneers damn near had physical weight.

"How's your new boyfriend, faggot?" he hissed as Rhys passed him in the hallway.

"How's yours? Or should I ask, who's yours? Did you even get his name?"

Some of Jacob's disdainful swagger faded, and Rhys smiled tightly at having scored a hit. It took Jacob a moment of bluster to get back into his well-rehearsed riff of insults and accusations. "I wouldn't have to do this if you had distracted the revs like you were supposed to, you sick freak. You did it on purpose. You wanted us all to die. How's it feel to have murdered your own sister?" Rhys fought not to show any hint of the pain that shot like a spear through his chest. "You let Cadence die because you wanted them to get me. Don't think you won't pay for that."

"Better watch out. Without Daddy here throwing you on top of little girls because he's too old to get it up himself, you just might find you like it." Rhys smirked. He'd learned long ago never to let Jacob see him wince or cry. "Maybe you already do. That would explain why you're always after me about it."

Sudden impact with the wall drove the breath from Rhys's lungs. *Ow.* His headache from the concussion awoke with a vengeance as he thudded against the stone. Jacob's features loomed so close Rhys could feel Jacob's breath slashing across his face with each word he spat. "You're going to hell, you perverted little shit, and before this is over, I'm gonna be the one to send you there. You did this to me, and don't think I won't take the Lord's vengeance on you. The moment I can arrange for you to have an accident, you're dead."

"You know, you've been threatening to kill me since I was thirteen." Rhys tried to push away from the wall, but Jacob slammed him back. *Ow* again. "One of these days, I'm gonna start to think you don't mean it."

"There a problem here, guys?" Rhys's head whipped to the side to see Xolani coming down the hall.

"No problem, ma'am." Jacob backed off, smoothing Rhys's new shirt and pasting on a charming smile. He was a good-looking man, Rhys thought bitterly. Pity he was such a prick. "Just making it clear to my brother-in-law that I won't tolerate him creating trouble for you folks the way he's always done for the rest of us here."

Xolani regarded him with a level stare. "Thank you, but if there's a problem, we can tend to it ourselves. Today, you help our people gather what we can carry of your provisions. There's no sense leaving them behind. We'll be here another day, maybe two, then head out at first light. Pack up your gear. I see you've got a few changes of clothing you'll want to bring."

Oh yes. Jacob had clothes. He'd brought quite a bit of it as they'd crossed Montana and Idaho on their way to Oregon.

"Of course." Jacob smiled again. "Can I also say just how kind it was of you to get my brother-in-law some new clothes? He outgrew all his, and mine wouldn't have fit him."

"He's smaller than you," Xolani observed, looking Jacob up and down.

Jacob beamed at her. "Exactly."

"So, he *could* have worn yours. They just would have been too big. I'm surprised no one thought of that when he was reduced to wearing rags."

Jacob's broad smile fell.

"Haul ass to the courtyard. Darius needs to explain some things to the men, and I got better things to do than breaking up school-yard fights. After that, get to work. We all help out where we can in this unit."

"Of course, ma'am." Jacob was considerably more subdued as he sidled past Xolani with a polite bob of his head, giving her an uncertain look, which Rhys unconsciously mirrored.

Had she just taken his side?

Once Jacob was gone, she clapped Rhys on the shoulder. "You can breathe now."

Rhys swallowed, blinking rapidly. No one had taken his side against Jacob and Father Maurice since Gabe had left and his mother had died and Cadence had lost the will to fight pretty much everything.

He didn't want to discuss that, though, so he sought for something else to say, and failed miserably.

"So, how are you holding up, kid?" Xolani asked. Her tone was neutral, but her gaze was searching. "Sorry. Rhys."

He fell into step beside her as she led him downstairs. "Well as can be expected, I guess." He shrugged, trying not to blush. She, of all people, knew exactly what he'd been up to since last night. He had no secrets, right? Certainly not after the way he'd moaned and yelled in the showers that morning.

"You know, Darius is a blunt guy, and he can be pretty tough, but he's not bad." She gave him an encouraging smile. "If he's agreed to look after you, you'll be okay."

"I know that."

"Then why am I detecting a bit of a sulk?"

He tried to push away the surge of bewildered shame that threatened to undermine the air of dignity he was striving for. "No, no. I'm not. I just don't like everyone *knowing*." He dropped his voice. "Darius seems bound and determined that they're all gonna see or hear. Why can't we keep it, you know, *private*?"

Xolani sighed and closed her eyes. "Oh shit. Did you think . . .? Jesus." She swallowed and laid a firm hand on his shoulder. "Look, Rhys, it won't be just—"

"Hey, come on!" One of the other Jugs, whose name Rhys didn't know yet, jogged past them. "Darius is about to begin."

"Fuck." Xolani shook her head, muttering. "I don't have time to explain this. Darius wants to introduce you to the squad. Let's go."

Well. Whatever she'd been about to tell him sounded ominous. Wondering what he'd gotten wrong, Rhys couldn't even be excited over the fact that in a couple days, he'd be leaving the place that had been as much a prison as a refuge these past seven years. He didn't know what the world was like now. Were there still packs of revenants hunting everywhere? When they had fled to the monastery, revenants had been so plentiful that Gabe's dad had hotwired an armored bank truck and simply mowed over any revs that got in their way between Bozeman and Portland. They would never have made it in weaker cars. Obviously, there were still enough revs that Darius's people needed to track them down. The thought of traveling in the open on foot, even surrounded by armed soldiers, filled Rhys with an instinctive terror that not even the allure of escaping the monastery could overcome.

Shuddering, Rhys followed Xolani out to the courtyard. Darius looked around. "I think most of you have met Cooper and Houtman by now?" The Jugs nodded. "They probably don't have all your names yet, so feel free to introduce yourselves when we're done here. As you know, these guys are dead men if we don't manage to infect them with Bane Alpha ASAP. Now, what that means for our recruitment policy in general is for me and Luis to decide when I talk to him back on base. Until further notice, assume these two are an isolated case. That means you still don't get to touch any other civvies we find, got it?"

"Are we taking after Bravo Company now?" The question came from the only other woman Rhys could see in the company.

"I guess you could say that, Gina." Darius's eyes landed on Rhys. Even just catching Darius's gaze made him blush. Great. "Xolani says the more people try to pass the virus to them early on, the better their chances of being infected are. So our recruits here are gonna be real friendly to anyone who's in a sharing mood."

Rhys's jaw dropped in perfect sync with the bottom falling out of his stomach. Horrified, he stared at Darius, willing him to mean something other than what he'd just said.

Darius glanced away. "Be sure you mind yourselves. Hopefully, these men are gonna have your six someday. Any of you decide this means you get to mistreat them, you'll be hearing from me."

"And I'll dispose of what's left." Xolani favored the courtyard at large with a glower. Rhys turned his disbelieving stare on her, and she met his eyes briefly, offering a nod she probably meant to be encouraging.

"Bottom line," Darius continued. "They'll be our brothers. Treat 'em like it."

Another man, a guy with a dark complexion and a perpetually smiling face that suggested he or his forebearers hailed from the South Pacific, chortled. "Oh, is *that* how it works in your family, Big D?"

"Only a lucky few know, Kaleo." Darius bantered with them easily, obviously unaware of Rhys's mortification. More people called out questions, and Rhys ducked back into the monastery the moment no one seemed to be looking at him. He darted from one dusty, abandoned chamber to another, seeking a hiding spot, someplace to wait until they were all busy with other things. Once they were distracted, he'd run away. If he was sick, he'd kill himself quietly and no one would miss him. Better that than face the degradation they had in store for him.

"What do you think you're doing, boy?" Rhys turned, his heart drumming painfully hard. Darius was standing in the doorway, dark eyes narrowed in irritation.

Shaking down to his very bones, Rhys mustered the last ounce of defiance he could find after all the blows of the past two days. "I won't do it. You and Xolani didn't say it would be like this. Not with *all* of them!" His face burned in the darkened chamber, humiliation at the very idea of what they proposed dragging at him, making him want to crawl into a hole and never emerge.

"You said you'd do what I told you to do. No questions."

"I didn't know you meant—"

Darius went still, and his expression shifted, his eyes growing cold. He was a huge, looming presence, blocking out the light. If he'd seemed to be God for a few moments yesterday, today he was Satan instead. Rhys thought he'd never been so terrified of anyone in his life, even if some part of his body still burned in the most wonderful way with the memory of what Darius had done to it.

"You backing out on me?"

Swallowing hard, Rhys watched Darius's hand drop to his hip where a sidearm hung in a snapped holster. Too late he remembered Darius's warnings of what would happen if he tried to refuse.

"I told you: I don't flinch, boy. Not ever."

Strange how his determination to face death if necessary fled when he thought of Darius blowing his brains out right here, right now, before he had a chance to prepare himself for it.

"I didn't *know!*" He screamed in a whisper, hoping the shadows of the unused bedroom kept Darius from seeing the way he fought to blink back desperate tears.

"Well, now you do. Get it straight in your head, then get to work. Now."

As he slunk down to the garden to begin harvesting whatever was ripe enough to be of value, he hung his head to avoid meeting anyone's eyes. If they were leering at him, thinking filthy thoughts about him, he didn't want to know.

⚠ ⚠ ⚠

BY THE TIME Rhys had finished working in the garden and returned to the monastery with his bucket of beans, there was a large fire burning in the courtyard with slabs of meat roasting on a spit above it. While he'd worked, he'd seen the blond Jug Darius had called Gina go out the gates and return with a deer. Except for the occasional squirrel or rabbit they'd managed to snare, meat had been an unheard-of luxury at the monastery. If not for beans and the filbert trees in the orchard, they all would have been severely protein deficient. The unaccustomed scent of fat sizzling on the flames sent Rhys fleeing into the monastery. It reminded him too much of the bodies burning yesterday.

He sat on a ratty chair in what had once been Father's Maurice's office. Here, Rhys had felt a cane across his knuckles or shoulders or backside more times than he could count, often with Jacob holding him down. And if he wasn't being held down for the cane, it was for the scissors as Father Maurice brutally hacked his hair almost down to the scalp.

He hated this room almost as much as the chapel, but the kitchen had too much traffic from the Jugs, and Rhys's bedroom now had unwanted memories of Darius. No one was likely to come looking for him here, so Rhys could huddle in on himself, sick, aching, and exhausted.

He wasn't sure how long he'd been hiding when the door opened. He looked up to see the guy Darius had called Kaleo grinning at him.

The churning in Rhys's gut began anew.

"Darius says we're supposed to make you feel welcome. Well, I got no problems playing the welcome wagon." Kaleo sauntered toward him.

Rhys nodded, hoping his expression looked less miserable than he felt. Trying to beg his way out of his obligation wasn't an option. He could see all too clearly the look in Darius's eyes as his hand had moved toward his sidearm. "Yeah. Um, where would you like me to go?"

Still smiling, Kaleo sat on the desk, his thighs parted, swinging his feet with all the bouncy energy of a little kid. "Anything wrong with here?"

Oh God. Just what he needed. Someone else doing something painful and humiliating to him in this room.

"Guess not." Well, if he was going to be miserable, it might as well be here as anywhere else. He tried to ignore the shaking in his legs as he rose to approach Kaleo. He pressed the back of his hand to his nose as he realized Kaleo's clothing had absorbed the odor of smoke and roasting meat. It took an effort not to gag. Instead, he concentrated on forcing his reluctant feet forward.

Kaleo frowned as Rhys drew nearer. "You okay, cutie?"

"Just tired." Rhys attempted a shaky grimace he hoped would pass for a smile.

"You know, I'm not a bad guy." Kaleo reached out to stroke Rhys's jaw just above the line of his patchy beard. "Just wanna help you out, have a good time."

Rhys's eyes darted away. "I-I know. I appreciate it, sir."

"*Sir?*" Kaleo hooted, sliding off the desk. "Jesus, call me anything but that!"

Rhys ducked his head, blushing. "Sorry. I just—"

"Call me Kaleo. Or, you know, do like everyone else. 'Asshole,' 'shithead,' and 'numb-nuts' are all valid alternatives."

A small laugh bubbled up from Rhys's chest, short-lived and unexpected. "Sounds like you're real popular."

Kaleo gave a tragic sigh. "Just misunderstood. No one gets my sense of humor. Philistines."

Another laugh and Rhys found some of his tension ebbing. Kaleo beamed, looking pleased with himself.

"You're especially cute when you smile." He trailed his finger down Rhys's neck. It should have felt good, but Rhys fought not to flinch from the touch. It would be easier, he thought, if Kaleo wasn't trying to be so nice. It made him feel like he had to respond encouragingly. Or at least it made him feel guilty for not *wanting* to respond encouragingly.

Kaleo slid off the desk, and his hands came to rest on Rhys's hips. Rhys's breath quickened at the look in his eyes. The teasing had bled away to lust, dark and intent upon its purpose. Kaleo leaned forward, nuzzling Rhys's ear, and his hands found the buckle of Rhys's belt.

Rhys swallowed again and stepped back, his hands replacing Kaleo's. He didn't want Kaleo to see the full extent of his reluctance, not when he was trying to be nice. Rhys turned his back and pushed down his jeans and underwear, then leaned over the desk in a position he'd been in far too often, hiding his face in the cradle of his arms.

At least Kaleo didn't say anything about the bruises on his thighs like Xolani had. His fingers were wet and chilly as they wedged between Rhys's cheeks, and Rhys bit his lips to keep from hissing at the sting. His hands balled into fists, and he squinted his eyes as Kaleo worked his fingers inside him, stretching and twisting as Darius had, only now he was sore and he wasn't sure he could endure it again. Not like this, not hating it.

But when Kaleo's other hand snaked around his hip, his cock was at half-mast. Rhys groaned at its betrayal and again at the lurch it gave when Kaleo's fingers brushed that spot Darius had touched inside him. He grunted, trying to shrink away, grateful when Kaleo withdrew both the hand wrapped around Rhys's dick and his fingers. The burning stretch of Kaleo's cock was both better and worse. Better because it did away with that unwanted arousal, and worse because it simply *hurt*.

"Mmm, you feel good, cutie." Kaleo's hips brushed Rhys's backside, his breath hot and moist, gasping against Rhys's ear. His arms around Rhys felt too much like an embrace, but Rhys couldn't spare the breath to object as he gripped the edge of the desk, white-knuckled and moaning. He fought to keep from crying out and begging Kaleo to stop.

It got a little easier after the first few thrusts. Not good. Still painful, but endurable. It had hurt with Darius, too, but not like this. With Darius, there had been pleasure despite the pain, but now Rhys was just too sore, and he wanted Kaleo to finish and go away. He grunted when Kaleo gripped his hips and began thrusting harder, slapping against his ass, groaning. The increased force made the ache worse. Rhys cried out as Kaleo's thrusts stuttered to a halt with a low shout.

He whimpered softly when Kaleo's weight slumped against his back. He wished the panting breaths on the back of his neck would stop. Finally, Kaleo pushed back and reached around Rhys's hip once more.

"Well. That's not very flattering."

Rhys flushed, hiding his face against the surface of the desk.

Great. Kaleo must have heard him with Darius this morning and assumed he'd enjoy this. "Sorry. I'm just . . . I'm tired. The attack yesterday and . . ."

With a sigh, Kaleo pulled out of him, and Rhys forgot to suppress the hiss.

"Aw, man. You should have said something if it hurt!" Kaleo sounded genuinely distressed.

"Sorry. I just— Sorry," Rhys muttered. "Thanks for, um . . . helping me out."

Kaleo scoffed. "Not sure I did you any favors here." Rhys felt him shifting, fastening his pants.

Rhys ducked his head and pushed away from the desk, pulling up his own pants, trying to ignore the slippery wetness between his ass cheeks. "It's what I've got to do to live, right? You're trying to help. I get that."

"I'm trying to keep my ego under control here." Kaleo gave him a wry look. "C'mon, cutie, have a seat. Talk to your Uncle Kaleo. Is it that bad?"

"It's nothing." Rhys shook his head, trying to muster another smile. He was out of practice with the whole *everything's okay* routine since his mother had died. "Like I said, I'm tired, and you know, a little sore, and I lost my sister yesterday and . . . I'm fine."

"Right." Kaleo sighed, gripping Rhys's shoulder. "Sorry about your sister."

"It's okay. Thanks again for, um . . ." Rhys waved his hand vaguely between them. "Helping. Do you think I could have a few minutes alone?"

Kaleo nodded. "Sure, kid. Come out to eat soon, though. You're too skinny." Rhys stared at the dingy carpet, its pattern faded to an indistinguishable gray muddle, as Kaleo loped toward the door. He stopped, backlit by the fading sunlight outside, and turned a bright grin to Rhys. "Don't think I don't plan to try again. When we get back to base, Schuyler's gonna *love* watching me with you."

He was gone before Rhys could stammer a suitable protest.

7

FIRES

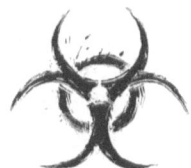

When Rhys overcame his humiliation and ventured outside again some time later, the Jugs were sitting around the fire eating strips of steaming venison. He saw Kaleo with his head bent, murmuring something to Xolani, who slid a troubled glance to Rhys. The smell of the meat almost sent Rhys back inside, but someone pressed a dripping cut of meat into his hand, and Rhys made himself take a bite.

The flavor flooded his tongue, awakening taste buds that had long since gone dormant on an inadequate diet of bland fare. Humming as he chewed, he gobbled the rich, dripping meat for a few bites before his stomach lurched. He bolted up from where he sat cross-legged on the lawn and ran toward the crumbling, ivy-covered garden shed, staggering to a halt around the corner as he retched.

Xolani joined him a moment later with a canteen of water.

"You have to take it slow. Small bites. Your body's been starved so long, it doesn't know what to do with food anymore. I'll make you a broth. That'll be better until your stomach's used to having richer food in it again."

"Sorry." Once the nausea passed, Rhys's stomach gave a hungry pang—the first he'd felt in years.

"It's okay." She rubbed his shoulder. "Kaleo says you're in some pain."

Rhys looked away. "It's nothing."

"I'm sorry, Rhys. I wish we could give you time to heal up and get used to it all, but we can't. Sad fact is, those abrasions are probably your friend right now. They increase your chances of exposure. I'll get you some ointment, and it'll get better in a few days, once you're used to things." She continued stroking his shoulder, and again, the gesture reminded him so much of his mother, he wanted to turn and lean on her, to hide his face against her arm until the burning in his eyes went away. "If you actually tear or start bleeding badly, you let me know. Otherwise, there's not much I can do but make sure the guys know to be gentle with you."

"Okay." Anything to make her stop talking about it.

"I also put something in your room. Darius sent Titus and Jamie out for some creative scavenging." She laughed softly. "He wants you to wear a butt plug, and I agree it will probably help you get used to stretching. There's some lube, too. Keep that with you in case the guys don't have theirs. Tonight, when you go to bed, try putting the plug in for a while to get used to it."

Rhys's face flooded with heat, and he refused to acknowledge that last bit. If he could get away with it, whatever that thing was would find its way into the coals of the fire tonight, but Xolani didn't need to know that.

After a moment she patted his shoulder again and led him back to the fire—either she was confident in his cooperation or didn't want to push him for an answer. "After dinner we'll start teaching you how to shoot. Try to nibble. Suck on the juices if you can't make yourself swallow until the broth is ready."

Nodding, Rhys accepted a scavenged barbecue fork with another strip of warm, rare venison on it. He gnawed gingerly but offered it to Kaleo before it was half gone.

"Sure you don't want any more?" Kaleo frowned. "You're skin and bones."

Rhys shook his head with a thin smile. "I'm full, thanks."

As he waited for the others to finish eating, Rhys realized he was staring at Darius across the courtyard and ripped his gaze away.

Whatever his twisted fascination with Darius was, he needed to stop. He'd already made too much of a fool of himself in the shower that morning, hollering the way he had. God only knew what they must think of him now. Like Kaleo, they probably thought this whole warped scenario was something he enjoyed.

Why was he the only one who seemed to care how sick all this was, how much it made a mockery of everything intimacy was meant to be?

And Jacob . . . Jacob was no doubt waiting to pounce triumphantly, crowing that Rhys was every bit the deviant Father Maurice had always accused him of being.

When they were done with supper and the first watch had secured the gate, one of the Jugs tapped Jacob on the shoulder, murmuring something, and Jacob followed him into the monastery. Titus and Xolani took Rhys out past the garden shed and taught him how to carry, load, and sight a handgun, shotgun, and assault rifle. They didn't fire, as there was no sense wasting ammunition until he had mastered the basics, but he began to learn how to aim.

It offered Rhys a distraction, at least. He knew he was just biding his time, waiting to see if someone would take him inside as well. Would it be Darius? The thought made his stomach tighten with something he tried to convince himself was reluctance, but he couldn't quite manage it. It hadn't done that with Kaleo.

After a while, when Rhys was too tired to attend to their instructions about the guns anymore, Xolani turned to throwing knives at a target drawn on the trunk of one of the trees. When the sun set, they all retreated into the monastery and secured the door. In addition to the gate being closed, all the exterior doors were barricaded and guards were posted.

Darius didn't acknowledge Rhys as he retreated to his room, hoping no one would waylay him. It was too much to ask, though. Just as he was about to reach his door, someone came jogging up behind him.

"Hey, kid! Um, Cooper." Rhys turned to see a Jug he hadn't met yet, who smiled broadly. "Hi. I'm Bailey."

It was like Kaleo all over again. Bailey was friendly, and his intentions seemed good. Rhys wanted to burst into tears at the idea of going through it again. Instead, he bowed his head and let Bailey follow him into his room. He couldn't help but whimper in pain this time—he was so *sore*. Apparently Xolani had warned Bailey about that, though. He did try to be gentle, and he wasn't offended when Rhys wasn't aroused. He murmured soothing reassurances that it would get better, that they'd all been there after their first time on the bottom. Then he did his thing and left Rhys lying on his cot in dry-eyed despair.

Feeling filthy and shamed, Rhys curled into a ball and tried not to spew up his meager supper. He glanced over at the dresser and saw the plug thing Xolani had talked about. Rhys gave it a disgusted look and jerked on his clothes, snatched it up, and stormed out of his room to look for someplace to throw it away or destroy it. With the monastery barricaded for the night, he couldn't get out to the fire like he'd planned, so he went for the kitchen, instead. Just as he was about to start hacking at it with the meat cleaver, footfalls came behind him.

"Don't do it, boy," Darius growled.

"I don't want it," Rhys grated, tightening his jaw.

"Good. Glad you got that off your chest. Now ask me if I give a shit."

For a moment, he considered telling Darius to just go ahead and kill him. What was the point of trying to live if he was going to be degraded and dehumanized this way, violated not only by people he didn't want and couldn't care less about, but by *inanimate objects*, not allowed even the tiniest bit of privacy and dignity?

But even now, he didn't want to die. Not like this. Not pointlessly. It had been one thing when he'd been willing to do it for Cady and Caleb. But not now that he finally, *finally* had a small chance to discover what life might be like outside the monastery and out from under Father Maurice's hellfire-and-brimstone tyranny.

Rhys's shoulders slumped in defeat, and he laid the cleaver down.

"Upstairs. Now."

He was already wet after Bailey, so once Rhys was bent over his bed, Darius's fingers slid right in. Rhys heard Darius behind him, stroking himself hard and fast. Darius pressed the head of his cock to Rhys's sore hole, inserting just the tip, and then his hand moved between them along the shaft, slapping against Rhys's backside with each stroke. He pushed in just a little more, just enough to wrench a pained cry from Rhys, and then went still, groaning and pulsing.

Afterward, he grabbed the plug.

"You're gonna wear this every night, boy, and I don't want any complaints."

The plug was wet when Darius pushed it against Rhys's entrance. He began to work it in and out with gentle thrusts that eased the gradually widening bulges into Rhys's hole.

"Oh God . . ." Rhys pushed back despite the ache, arousal surging up in a dizzying rush.

"That's it. Take it, baby. Feels good, doesn't it?" That voice. That was why Rhys couldn't remain unaffected by Darius the way he had with Kaleo and Bailey. He wished he could. "Next time you take my cock up your ass, it's gonna be so good. You'll beg me for it."

That was what he was afraid of. All day, he'd been hearing echoes of the crude promises of pleasure Darius had made to him in the shower that morning. But Rhys forgot to protest as he rocked back again and that final, widest knob eased past his aching ring. His ass spasmed around the narrow stem. He moaned into the bedding, shuddering, waiting to adapt. Then Darius's hand wrapped around his cock, and it was all over at just a touch. The sheets of his cot were wet and sloppy as Rhys collapsed onto his belly and waited for the twitching to pass.

"Good." Darius patted his rump an almost paternal gesture, sending outrage zinging through Rhys. Darius sounded far too satisfied with himself. "You sleep with that tonight. Take it out for a while in the morning, then try it again for longer in the afternoon and evening."

Rhys nodded, hating Darius and hating himself for responding. He drew up the covers, hiding his nudity, and Darius stretched out on his mattress on the floor and didn't say another word. Unfortunately, Rhys had no chance of drifting off to sleep anytime soon, despite his exhaustion. Not with that strange, stretched, full feeling inside his guts. Not knowing he had the semen of three different men trapped inside him. He lay there long into the night, resenting everything, with that plug driving him mad and a boner he couldn't quite will away.

△ △ △

THE BOY WAS DEFINITELY GOING to be trouble, and not just because of that quiet streak of rebellion. No, the trouble had started the moment Darius had seen Rhys lead Bailey into his bedroom and something had twisted uncomfortably inside his own gut.

He almost hadn't gone to Rhys's room at all that night, deciding it would be best to avoid the boy entirely. If Rhys hadn't sneaked downstairs, Darius might have succeeded in ignoring him.

So much for that idea.

They hadn't intended to stay more than one night at the monastery when they'd hunted down the revs, but Xolani had suggested they add a couple days to their stopover, arguing that their men would have an easier time exposing their recruits to the Alpha strain if they weren't on the march. Darius had agreed, but it hadn't been until he'd seen Bailey shutting the door to Rhys's room that the idea of Rhys having multiple partners had shifted from abstract to concrete in his mind.

His response hadn't been pleasant.

That uncomfortable feeling told Darius he needed to step way back. Possibly not touch the kid again at all. There was no way he could permit that hint of possessiveness to take root and sprout. Rhys needed to be fucked by as many men as were willing. Darius couldn't stand in the way of that, despite his unexpected urge toward territorialism where the boy was concerned. And he certainly couldn't develop anything resembling affection for a kid he was likely to have to put out of his misery in a few weeks' time.

The second day was worse. He saw at least five of his men tap Rhys and lead him away. The boy looked fucking miserable, and Darius gritted his teeth and forced himself not to pay any attention. Then Kaleo came down the stairs before supper, his expression a little wistful as he buckled his belt, which made Darius want to put a fist through his face.

Fuck this shit. Darius laid his strip of leftover venison aside and tapped Houtman on the shoulder. "Upstairs."

He didn't like the quality of Houtman's smile at that. It made the tense twisting in Darius's gut even worse than knowing his men were fucking Rhys. Houtman's expression was far too smug and calculating, and his voice was irritating as he led Darius to his room.

"Of course, I understand what the Bible says about all this, but you know that old story about the man facing the oncoming flood and refusing the rescuers the Lord sent him, right? I assume if this is the means God has provided me to survive, He must have some higher purpose for me. He means for me to endure, to bring His word back into the world now that the worst of the plague has passed and humanity is rebuilding itself." Houtman made a satisfied sound as he dropped his pants. "He has great things planned for me, for all of us. Like Moses leading the Children of Israel out of bondage . . ."

It took all of Darius's patience not to snap at the guy to shut up. Luckily, driving himself hard into Houtman's ass had the same effect.

What it didn't do, though, was relieve any of Darius's irritable tension. Instead, he just felt vaguely sickened and couldn't wait to get out of there. He didn't speak a word to Houtman as he walked away, pausing after he closed the door behind him to fasten himself up again.

When he glanced up, Rhys was standing in the hallway outside his room, staring at him. For the briefest instant, he thought he saw distress in the kid's eyes. But then that strangely empty expression wiped all animation from his face. Turning with a jerky, almost robotic precision of motion, he slipped back into his room and shut the door.

That was it, Darius decided, storming downstairs to send Gina to bed so he could take her watch shift. He couldn't allow Rhys to become dependent upon him any more than he could let himself be territorial about Rhys. It would only prevent them from doing the job they had to do.

He wasn't going anywhere near that fucking kid again.

8

TRANSIT

"Something wrong, Rhys?" Xolani leaned against his dresser, looking at him closely. "The guys say you're hardly speaking a word to anyone."

Rhys shrugged.

"Are you still in a lot of pain?"

Another shrug. He was, but it didn't matter. Answering didn't seem worth the bother. After two days of being everyone's sex toy, it was pretty damned clear that what he felt or wanted was irrelevant. All he could do was just get through it.

Xolani stood by patiently as Rhys sat on his cot, feeling disgusted. Three of the Jugs had approached him already that morning, all with the excuse that they wouldn't get a chance once they were on the road today.

"I can wait for as long as it takes you to talk."

Something snapped. "What, so now I can't even have any privacy in my own fucking *head*?" He glowered up at her. "Bad enough I've got to do all this with everyone knowing that I'm some *pervert* . . ." He huffed and fell silent. Dammit. Xolani didn't deserve him taking his frustration out on her.

Xolani's expression smoothed over, became neutral. "Pack your gear while we talk. We're late. We meant to break camp at dawn."

Maybe they wouldn't be late if the Jugs could have kept their dicks to themselves that morning.

He didn't bother to say that as he rose from his cot to begin stuffing his clothes into the rucksack they had scavenged for him.

"Let me ask you something, *kid.*" Rhys winced at her emphasis. "What makes you think a single one of us gives a shit?"

Rhys flushed, his chin touching his collarbone as his shoulders crept up self-consciously.

"Get over yourself." Derision gave Xolani's advice a biting edge. "So you're getting fucked. You're taking it up the ass like a big nelly fag. Think any one of our people here is gonna take out a front-page ad to trumpet the news to the world? Think they don't fuck every chance they get? Think there's not one of them—even the straight dudes—who wouldn't drop to their knees and blow an entire battalion if it meant a chance at survival? People are dying faster than they're being born, kid, and *we're all fucked.*"

Rhys stared at her in shock, his mouth working wordlessly. His eyes stung, betrayed by her harsh words after the comfort and kindness she'd seemed to offer him before. It felt awful that she wasn't even angry, just unflinchingly honest. Or worse, disappointed.

"I tell you what they will care about." Her voice softened, her eyes becoming gentle. "You feeling sorry for yourself. No one has time for that. They'll respect you doing what you have to do to live, because every one of them is doing the same. But they won't respect moping and self-pity."

"I don't mope." Rhys drew his chin up, his jaw tightening. Seven years of dealing with Jacob and Father Maurice and she thought he was going to mope over *this*? "I've put up with worse, and I didn't feel sorry for myself then, either. I just want some time alone so I can feel like a person again and not some . . . Whatever."

Xolani's eyes flicked toward the door and the hallway beyond where she'd saved him from Jacob the other morning, and her mouth tightened. "Yeah, I can see you may have had some hard times. I imagine you just keep things to yourself a lot. But now wouldn't be a good time to start pitying yourself. Like I said, any guy here would do the same thing you're doing in your situation."

He couldn't let himself cry in front of her, though confusion and the crushing weight of his shame made his hands shake as he zipped the bag shut. He had to clear his tight throat twice before speaking. "Yeah, but they wouldn't . . ."

"Wouldn't what?"

He forced the reluctant whisper from his throat. "Wouldn't *want* it."

"Oh." Now it was Xolani's turn to look bewildered, and possibly a little embarrassed. "Wait. You mean, this isn't because they're men?"

"*No!*" Rhys turned his back with a groan of frustration at having to explain. He punched his rucksack and flung himself down on his bed, grinding the heels of his hands into his eyes. "I don't want them, and they don't want me."

Xolani's eyebrows crept up. "Um, given the mechanics involved in the situation, I'm pretty certain that's not the case, or it wouldn't work."

"Huh?"

"Well, they're getting it up for you, aren't they? So where is this coming from?"

Rhys flushed miserably. "That's not what I mean. They're only doing it because they have to, or maybe they just feel sorry for me, and I don't have a *choice*. They're going to do what they want with me, and there's nothing I can do about it. Which makes it all wrong, and I shouldn't . . . enjoy it."

"You're upset because you *liked* it?" Xolani sounded befuddled.

"Not . . . not all the time."

No, definitely not all the time. With Bailey and Kaleo and the handful of others, Rhys just felt miserable. But those first couple times with Darius . . . Rhys shuddered with the memory of arousal and a fresh surge of accompanying shame. With Darius, it hadn't mattered *why* they were doing what they were doing. He'd been so turned on, and he'd come so hard. *God.*

But he couldn't tell her that. He didn't have the words. He couldn't explain how Darius had told him that someday it would feel good and how that promise kept replaying in Rhys's head, not with dread but with a terrible arousal. Couldn't explain how *good* it had been that first time with Darius, after the burning ache had passed.

He'd heard his own yells and knew everyone else must have been able to hear them, too, so they all knew how much he *loved* it.

And despite himself, despite everything he knew was right or decent, he was waiting for Darius to make good on his promise, but Darius had all but disappeared. And it was wrong that he could want something as *twisted* as the pleasure Darius had told him he'd feel someday, especially since Darius didn't give two shits about him, as evidenced by the fact that he hadn't come near Rhys since that second night.

He shouldn't have liked what Darius had done. He shouldn't *want* Darius, or want more of what Darius had done to him. He shouldn't have come so easily the moment Darius put his rough hands on him. He shouldn't have spent every minute afterward hoping it would happen again.

He shouldn't feel so hurt and abandoned that Darius had fucked Jacob and refused to even look at him anymore. Like he'd just been used and thrown aside.

Xolani was still staring at him, waiting for him to explain.

"Yeah, I guess. Kinda." He gave up. Xolani was nice when she didn't think he was being an idiot, but he couldn't make her understand—he'd probably just make more of a fool of himself trying.

"What feels good, feels good." She ran her silver-shot braid through her hand. "Hell, if you can actually get some enjoyment out of all this, do it. Virtue out of necessity and all that."

"I guess," Rhys repeated with a grimace. "Well. At least I don't have to do it anymore, now that we'll be on the road and there won't be any privacy."

Her head tipped back, and she groaned. "Oh, Rhys. Is that the idea you've got?"

"That's what . . . The guys this morning . . . They said once we were on the march . . ." Despair started to squeeze his lungs at the idea that his ordeal wasn't over yet.

"No." Xolani's gaze was kind but unyielding. "They won't be able to fuck you anytime they want, the way they have the past couple days, but when we make camp at night, you're still going to need to have partners. As for privacy, we're hoofing it south to Salem. We're all gonna be on the road together for weeks. There are plenty of abandoned buildings to sleep in, but on a first sweep, the protocol is that we all camp in a single space where we can't be cut off from each other if there's an attack. No separate rooms. Do you understand what I'm saying?"

Rhys's stomach dropped.

Xolani sighed and pushed herself away from the dresser. "No one cares. Keep your head down, do what you have to do, hold the bitching to a minimum, you'll be just fine."

Jacob cared. Jacob would never let him hear the end of it. Jacob would probably manage to get out of having to do it, somehow. And even if he didn't, Rhys had learned long ago that the same standards didn't apply to Jacob and him. Rhys would be held at fault for things Jacob could get away with easily, and Jacob would have no problems making Rhys miserable for doing something Jacob himself was doing as well.

If he had to do it publicly, in front of Jacob, he'd rather choose death.

Xolani patted his shoulder on her way to the door. "It's not that bad, you know. Actually it can be kind of fun. Kinky, to do it where you know everyone can see and hear." She met his surprised look with a smile. "What? You think Hurricane Titus has never set upon my shores in the middle of camp?"

ΛΛΛ

IF RHYS HAD HOPED for any sort of acknowledgment from Darius as the company left the monastery behind, taking with them anything they could carry by way of supplies and provisions, he was disappointed. The only thing Darius bothered to say to Rhys was to ask if he could use a gun with any proficiency. When Rhys admitted Xolani and Titus had been teaching him how to work one but he hadn't actually fired it yet, Darius ordered him to stay in the middle of the group, where the people with the weapons could protect him in the event of a fight.

He began to understand just why Darius was in charge as he stood back and watched him oversee the decampment. He gave orders with easy, sure authority, and people obeyed them without hesitation. At his command, the squad departed the monastery on foot, except for Titus and a man Xolani had introduced as Jamie, who went zipping away on strangely quiet motorcycles with an array of weapons strapped to their bodies, from pistols and knives stuck in their boots to assault rifles slung across their backs.

Even in their company, it took everything Rhys had not to freeze when the moment came to walk past the rusted-out gates for the first time in seven years. Leaving the monastery had been forbidden after they'd arrived. Father Maurice had said anyone who left wouldn't be permitted back, for fear they might have been exposed and infect the others. In fact, the gates had been chained and padlocked after Gabe left and his parents went to find him, and they had remained that way until this last year when rust and damage from the last earthquake had caused one of the gates to snap off its hinge. That was how the revs had been able to get in.

Terror and elation mingled as those gates fell behind and the whole world opened up in front of him. Outside the walls that had kept him both safe and captive since he was twelve, Rhys felt like maybe there was finally enough room to stretch, enough air to breathe. Like maybe there was a place for him in the world that wasn't dependent on Father Maurice's and Jacob's begrudging graces or kept by virtue of making himself as small a target as possible.

But there was danger out here, too. No vast packs of revenants came swarming at them the moment they started down the road, but it took Rhys a significant portion of that first day to relax and accept that fact.

After a while, Rhys realized the squad was in formation around him, keeping him protected on all sides. Even at their cautious, attentive pace, it was hard to keep up with them. Before long, he was panting and sweating, and they weren't even winded.

Jacob seemed determined to win the Jugs over, which was both worrying and a relief. Worrying because Rhys knew all too well how bad Jacob could get when he had others on his side and Rhys had no one on his, but a relief because with Jugs surrounding them on every side, Jacob had to refrain from his usual active taunts and petty torments. Whenever Rhys caught a glimpse of him, though, Jacob looked positively triumphant. He was probably congratulating himself that he'd managed to lure away Darius—who had seemed like he might become a possible ally to Rhys—and now in private, he could start telling Darius any tales he wanted about Rhys, turning the Jugs against him.

Refusing to think about what that might mean for him, Rhys watched as Jacob jogged to catch up to Gina when they were on the road again after stopping for a brief lunch. He gave her an ingratiating smile. "Excuse me, ma'am. Can I ask why you aren't taking us back to Fort Vancouver?"

"Don't have time to spare." She didn't even look at him, which Rhys imagined must've been a blow. Jacob was well aware of his own good looks, and he'd been trying to get Gina's attention for a couple of days. "You're infected anyway. No need to get you into quarantine."

"Of course, ma'am, but we wouldn't want to be in your way." Jacob's attempt at a charming smile seemed stilted, and Rhys knew all too well what his real concern was. Jacob was never one to risk his own safety. "Unarmed and untrained, won't we slow you down?"

Rhys bit his tongue against the impulse to call Jacob out on his cowardice. No sense looking like he was trying to make trouble, or give Jacob reason to threaten him again.

But from Gina's flat look, she wasn't buying it anyway. "You'll slow us down more if we have to divert to drop you off at base."

Jacob appeared on the verge of issuing another argument, and Gina's eyes narrowed. So instead, he smiled again and bowed his head, falling back. "Of course, ma'am."

Rhys studied the ground until his lips stopped twitching. He looked up when Titus fell into step beside him and chucked a thumb over his shoulder. "Kaleo, take the rear guard."

Kaleo nodded and fell back as Rhys looked at Titus expectantly. He had noticed Titus at lunch handing his motorcycle off to a red-haired guy named Toby and wondered why he'd done that.

"You got a problem with not going to Vancouver, too?"

"Nah." Rhys shook his head, refusing to say anything about his distress this morning once he had found out what going to Salem with the Jugs would mean. "Xolani told me to keep my head down.

Seems if you're making exceptions and changing plans on my account, it's harder to do that."

Titus grunted his approval. "Good man." He fell silent, walking alongside Rhys, and when Rhys glanced at him, his jaw flexed as if he were chewing on his thoughts.

"You know, I'm not the comforting sort, but Xolani thinks it's not a bad idea for you to have someone to talk to who isn't trying to get into your pants. I figure I agree."

"Thanks." Rhys's shoulders twitched awkwardly, and he looked at his feet, kicking up dust that had drifted across the crumbling asphalt. "Not sure I really want to talk about anything with anyone though. No offense."

"None taken. But here's what you need to get, Cooper. Xolani really wants to make this work. We're invested in you now. We all want you to be part of the team, even Darius, or he wouldn't have agreed to it in the first place. So you're going to need to deal with this, whatever it takes. Got it?"

Rhys looked over his shoulder at Jacob, always on the alert for whether he was lingering somewhere nearby, waiting to pounce on Rhys. But Jacob was schmoozing a huge guy Rhys often saw in Toby's company. Joe, he thought the man's name was. One of the few who hadn't approached him for sex.

Rhys dragged his attention back to Titus. Keep his head down. Right. "Got it. I'll try." With a sigh, he sought another subject. "What's Bravo Company? Xolani mentioned them the other night."

Titus made a grumbling sound. "Another company of Jugs. Bravo's clearing their way up through California. Because of the high population centers they're dealing with, their job pretty much sucks. Same with Echo and Tango out on the East Coast. Lot of survivors in the big cities, and a lot of revs. Some areas are no better than war zones because the survivors are either fighting each other for the remaining supplies or worried that anyone who approaches might be infected. Bravo's taken some pretty heavy losses, and they've had to start recruiting to replenish their numbers."

"You mean, making more Jugs? The same way—"

"Yeah. Recruitment into Bravo Company is voluntary, and recruits know what they're signing on for in advance. But it's necessary to get them up to speed ASAP, so the policy is that once they agree, they're anyone's meat for eight weeks, with no right to refuse unless there's a serious problem. And since a Jug's too dangerous to leave uncontained, once you're recruited, only way out is feet first. So if someone joins up and changes their mind, well . . . You get what I'm saying."

"So it's not just me, because I might be infected with one of the other strains." Rhys stumbled and reminded himself again to be careful where he walked. The weeds growing up through the cracks in the pavement kept catching his unwary feet. "But if others are doing it, why is Darius against it?"

"Well, few years ago, down around Texas, we had a company go bad. Charlie Company. Their CO died, new guy took over, didn't see why we Jugs—being superior—couldn't just take what we wanted when we wanted it. After all, we're stronger, faster, and better trained, and keeping those chumps settled outside Cheyenne Mountain alive, aren't we? Exterminating the revs and all. The civvies owe us, right? So they started taking their pick of the survivors they found before sending the rest on. Creating harems and menial laborers for themselves. Slaves, in other words."

"Oh."

"Yeah." Titus grimaced. "The reason it's taken us so long to make our way this far north is because our company, along with Bravo and Sierra from up around Chicago, joined forces to take Charlie Company out. They were pretty well entrenched, and we might not have succeeded if their harem slaves hadn't realized they were Jugs now and risen up to attack from the rear. Bailey over there led the revolt; he'd been one of the slaves. That's how we learned Alpha strain could be transmitted by fucking. So, now Charlie Company's under new management. But a lot of us took the way they went bad to heart. Set them up as an example of what we need to not let ourselves become. Darius is one of those, so this whole recruitment thing pokes him in all the wrong places."

The pavement blurred beneath his feet as Rhys considered how easily Darius might have refused permission to try to save his life. He hadn't appreciated that night just how close he'd come to being written off.

"So, why'd he agree, then? Is it just because Xolani bullied him into it?"

Titus guffawed loudly. "Cooper, there ain't no one makes Big D do what he don't want to do."

"But then why—" Kaleo came jogging up from the rear, summoning Titus with a question.

"Sorry, gotta handle this." Titus clapped Rhys on the shoulder, nearly sending him toppling over, then dropped back toward the rear of the formation. "You figure it out, kid."

9

OBJECTIVES

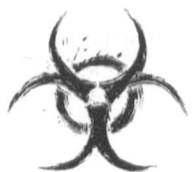

"Get your ass down, boy!"

Darius grabbed Rhys's shoulder and slammed him back against the brick wall that shielded them. He ignored Rhys's pained grunt, peering once more around the corner at the windows of an ivy-covered dormitory that had once been part of Linfield College.

"Fucking colonies," he heard Toby mutter behind him, where the rest of the squad had their backs pressed against the brick wall to stay out of the line of sight. Darius silently agreed with him. They were pinned now, the alley in which they hunkered a dead end. Whoever these people were, they had spent considerable time barricading off every approach to the dorm except one, which created a perfect shooting gallery. It hadn't appeared that way at first, though. It just seemed like the survivors here had tried to make it easier for themselves to spot revs coming. There'd been no warning that they'd be hostile until they'd opened fire. Now, if Darius and his people broke cover, they were targets on the open lawn.

They'd walked into a trap.

"What is it? Why are they shooting?" Rhys rubbed his shoulder, and Darius slid a glance further down the wall to where Houtman had hit the ground at the first shot. He wasn't sure which was worse: Houtman's cowardice or Rhys's brave but ill-advised attempt to find a better vantage point from which to aim his assault rifle against the surprise attackers.

Xolani cut off the question with a gesture, closing her eyes. Darius watched her lips move as she counted the number of different weapons pinning them down by sound. Darius did likewise.

"Six," she said. Darius nodded, his own count matching. "Maybe eight. No less than five. The way they're burning through ammo, unless they're exceptionally well provisioned, they can't keep up this rate of fire for long."

"Idiots." Darius could tell by his tone that Kaleo was rolling his eyes. "They'd be better off handing those munitions over to us."

"We'll try to get their attention again once they stop playing cowboy." Darius peered around the corner again, trying to avoid making a target of his head, to get a fix on which windows the shots were coming from. "Have some rations. We could be sitting here a while, might as well eat lunch. After that, we'll give them two chances to surrender. If they don't, there's nothing we can do for them."

"I don't understand. What's going on?" Rhys dug through his pack. Darius was pleased to see he was finally nibbling on some jerky and not just handfuls of nuts and hard bread.

"It's a colony," Toby answered, passing out some of the apples they'd found the day before. Darius bit into his, savoring its tartness as he listened to his people explain the situation to Rhys. That they were bothering to help the boy understand was a good sign about how they felt regarding his addition to the team. "That's what we call it when enough survivors band together with sufficient firepower to effectively defend themselves in a secure and well-provisioned position. Unfortunately, a lot of them are survivalist types. Anarchists. Doomsday preppers. Religious zealots. Paranoid fanatics. They've been entrenched so long they think they're the only ones left. Anyone else who comes along must be hostile or dangerous. They don't want rescue."

"Explains why we've found no revs in this town." Jamie examined a hole in his sleeve where the first bullet had come way too close. Fortunately, there was no blood. Darius would hate to have to sideline him. "They've been patrolling."

"Can't we just leave them?" Rhys asked.

Bailey shook his head. "Not while they're shooting at us. Unfortunately, we may just have to kill them to get them to stop."

Xolani grimaced, mirroring Darius's annoyance. "Fucking waste."

The gunfire tapered to an occasional smatter as they ate and eventually halted altogether. Gripping his weapon, Darius crept as close to the corner as he dared.

After drawing a deep breath, he began to shout. "Attention, survivors, this is Sergeant First Class Darius Murrell, commanding a squadron from Delta Company, 1st Juggernaut Battalion, formerly of the US Army. We are not infected. Repeat: *we are not infected*. Surrender and lay down your arms so we may approach to discuss your reintegration into the general population—"

Gunfire began again with renewed fury. Chips of brick erupted from the corner of the building that sheltered him, thanks to a bullet that came uncomfortably close to his head.

"*Shit!*" Darius wiped at a wet sting half an inch below his eye, nerves all over the rest of his face complaining about the scouring hail of brick residue. His fingers came away smeared with blood. "Idiots could've blinded me."

Xolani dug in her pack and crab-walked forward. She glued the edges of the cut together and slapped a bandage over it with little fanfare while Darius hissed from the sting. She met Darius's eyes, and he gave a grim nod, assenting without words to the requisite change in command.

Xolani raised her voice so they could hear her at the far end of the line. "Okay, people, you know the drill. This is my operation now. Darius will hang back with the recruits and maintain a distance of no less than twenty yards from any survivors we recover."

Darius glared at a divot a shotgun blast had torn in the sod, disgusted with the entire fucking debacle. Beached for a fucking little scrape. Sucking it up, he gestured Rhys and Houtman back with a jerk of his head. "Into the corner. Go."

Rhys looked surprised at this development and Houtman derisive. Darius could see the question sprouting on Rhys's lips and answered before it could form. "Standard procedure when one of us is wounded, no matter how minor. We don't want to take a chance that the wound will open or begin bleeding in proximity to a civilian and infect them with Beta."

A moment later the gunfire tapered off again, though this time Darius had no hope that it was due to a lack of ammunition. This colony was too well outfitted for that.

"Clear out from under the second-story windows," Xolani ordered, and everyone backed away from the wall, retreating further down the barricaded alley while trying to remain out of the line of sight of the hostiles. The first-story windows had all been sealed long ago or they would have already sought shelter inside the building. "Here's the plan, people. First priority: find a path of egress out of this alley for the rest of us that doesn't include crossing that lawn. Failing that, find a way to subdue those shooters. Lethal force only if we're out of other options. This is still a recovery mission if we can make it one. Go."

Kaleo stepped forward with a cheeky grin, drawing something out of his pack. "Allow me."

He hurled a can of peas, long past their expiration date, at a second-floor window, sending shards of glass raining down into the alley. Rhys cringed, ducking and covering his head like the rest of them, and it was only after the tinkling of falling slivers had stopped that Darius realized he'd moved in and covered the boy. He drew away before Rhys could realize what he'd done.

Xolani looked up at the window and nodded in satisfaction. "All right. Toby, you're up first. Clear away the glass. Try not to get cut. If you do, come back down once Gina and Jamie are up."

Toby handed his rifle off to Joe and slipped his rucksack off his shoulders, digging into an outer pocket, probably for a pair of tight leather gloves. Darius saw Rhys frown in confusion, and then his eyes widened as Toby, the smallest man in their squad after Jamie, sprinted two strides and launched himself the seemingly impossible distance. Toby caught the window ledge by a finger-grip and began sweeping glass away with his gloved hand, reaching through the broken pane to find the latch and push the window open. He swung his legs over the ledge and reappeared a moment later, peering down at them and holding out his hands.

"No cuts. All clear."

Joe tossed Toby's rifle to him, and then Gina and Jamie went up the same way Toby had, each receiving their guns in turn from someone on the ground.

"Those three are our best jumpers," Darius heard Kaleo murmur to Rhys. "That's why Xolani tagged them to go. Darius isn't nimble enough to make the jump or she would have sent him, since he's already wounded. Of the three, Toby's the least accurate marksman, which is why he got tagged to go first and chance getting cut. We couldn't risk Gina's hands when she's our best shot."

Houtman made a disgruntled sound. "If she's such a good shot, why doesn't she just take out the shooters from here?"

Xolani favored him with a narrow look, her lips thinning. "Because our primary mission is search and recovery of survivors."

"Even if they're trying to kill us?"

"They pose no immediate threat as long as we're pinned down in here. The gene pool isn't as big as it once was, Houtman. We need every survivor we can get helping to rebuild in Colorado Springs. If it comes down to them or us, we'll kill them, but not unless we've exhausted all other options."

"Seems if they're too stupid to listen to reason, the gene pool is better off without them." That won Houtman several guarded looks, which from his smile he apparently took as agreement. Darius restrained himself from snorting in disgust. Houtman had no clue just how quickly he was spending the limited currency of goodwill he'd been fronted by Darius's squad.

Xolani's eyes hardened. "If that was the extent of the mercy we exercised, Houtman, you'd be dead. Now shut it."

His expression grew tight and resentful at that, but Xolani ignored him, looking up at the window. A moment later they heard the creaking of old hinges as a window opened on the other side of the barricade, which had been welded together from rusted desks and lecture-hall chairs so that it blocked the walkway between ivy-covered buildings. The colonists must have been raiding the college classrooms for years, dragging out furniture to build their fortress.

Here in the alley where the sunlight was never direct, the rusted metal had acquired a silver-green overlay of lichen and moss. Unfortunately, the structure was far too rickety to scale, and all that jagged, rusty metal was a case of lockjaw waiting to happen. Otherwise, Darius and his people could have saved themselves a lot of trouble.

Toby reappeared above them. "The doors and first-floor windows are all welded, but we can climb down from the second-story window past the barricade. Toss me a rope."

Darius met Xolani's eyes, which flicked sideways at Rhys. Darius didn't need to be told that even a fifteen-foot climb might be a challenge for him, depleted as his condition was. Darius wasn't sure why Rhys was so malnourished and Houtman wasn't, but six days in the Jugs' company hadn't been enough for him to build up the sort of strength he needed. He ended each day's march at the point of collapse, endured the attentions of two or three men a night and every morning with silent but palpable misery, and tossed on his bedroll almost until second watch began their shift, waking with dark circles under his eyes.

But despite all that, he kept his head down and tried to pose as little inconvenience as he could, calling into doubt all Houtman's assertions that the boy was a troublemaker. Everyone was beginning to genuinely like the kid. Despite his weariness, he made every effort to pitch in without being asked, and his questions—when he couldn't sit on them any longer—were pertinent and thoughtful.

It would sting that quiet dignity of his to fail in front of them all.

Xolani's mouth pursed. "Houtman, you go up first. Darius, you'll go last, after Rhys. The rest of you, get up and get Houtman down the other side pronto. Then we'll decide on our approach for trying to talk to these assholes again."

Darius nodded his agreement, suppressing a smile. Houtman no doubt thought he was being given precedence over Rhys, rather than realizing that Xolani had just arranged it so that no one else would be present when Rhys tried to struggle up that rope. Darius hung back with the boy, who watched in trepidation as Houtman clumsily worked his way up to the window.

The rest of the squad went after him, only the bulkiest of them, like Joe, needing the rope at all. Xolani was alone at the window when it was Rhys's turn. He grabbed the rope and began trying to haul himself up, his thin arms shaking after just the first couple of pulls. Darius put a hand under his scrawny ass and hoisted him.

Xolani's soothing murmur floated down from the window. "It's okay. Just hold the rope, Rhys. I'll pull."

"I can do it," Darius heard him mutter mulishly. He was willing to bet that sunburned face was blazing with embarrassment.

"Let us help you, boy. You're still building up your strength. No one but us three will ever know."

Rhys groaned, and Xolani hauled the rope up as if it—and the boy clinging to it—weighed nothing. She helped Rhys over the windowsill before tossing the rope back down to Darius. A moment later, he joined them in a cobweb-filled classroom, where calculus formulae were still faintly visible on a dust-coated whiteboard.

Rhys glanced at Darius and Xolani self-consciously from under his brows. "Thanks."

Xolani gave him a tight smile of encouragement and turned to follow the footprints in the dust to the other broken window. Rhys trailed after Darius, forcing him to stop and turn.

"Keep ahead of me. Always stay where we can see what's coming at you." Rhys's mouth tightened, and Darius snorted at the suspicious look the boy threw him as he passed by to take the middle position. "Relax. If I wanted my hands all over that skinny butt of yours, boy, I'd only have to wait until we made camp tonight. Or help you up another rope."

Rhys's footsteps stuttered, but he continued on his way without response. It was too dark to see if the boy was blushing again, but Darius imagined he could feel the heat radiating off his face. He hadn't touched Rhys since that second night at the monastery, five days ago. Not since he'd begun to feel inappropriately possessive about his men fucking Rhys. He hadn't even taken the time in the evening to force Rhys to wear his butt plug. The last thing he needed was for the boy to become attached to or reliant on him. But he often felt Rhys's eyes on him as Kaleo or Bailey or one of the others led him away to a private corner or stepped over to his bedroll as they settled into camp for the night. As if he were waiting for Darius to do something.

It was an appeal that was getting harder to resist.

Kaleo caught Rhys by the waist as he slid carefully down the rope on the other side, and Rhys broke contact and shrank away as soon as his feet were on the ground. But his gaze sought out Darius's once he'd landed. Darius felt the eye contact tighten things south of his gut. There was no denying the fear in Rhys's eyes, but there was something else, too. Something that wasn't there when Rhys looked at Kaleo or the others, something only for Darius. Darius wasn't sure he could call it lust, but it sure as hell wasn't a lack of interest.

Damn, but he wanted that boy again.

"All right." Xolani gathered them into a huddle. "Do we have a way into that dorm they're in over there?"

Toby shook his head. "Not unless we expose ourselves long enough to figure out which of the doors they didn't weld shut. They have to have a way in and out. There's an ash heap over past the fifth building that suggests they've been hunting and burning the carcasses, and clearly they've exterminated most, if not all, of the revs in the area. Whoever these people are, they're good. They planned well. They blocked off every approach to that lawn there, where they planted their crops, so that anyone entering would be running a gauntlet. I'm betting the only entrance to their building is through there, too."

"Do we have rooftop access on this building so Gina can take out the shooters in the windows if we have to?"

Gina nodded. "First thing I checked. They didn't weld that door. They were guarding against ground attacks by revs. The roof wasn't a consideration, unless revs have learned to fly."

"Bite your tongue. What about a basement? Any underground corridors connecting this cluster of buildings?"

Jamie pursed his lips thoughtfully. "There was one door with basement access, but it was welded shut. We could break it down, but we'd make a lot of noise doing it. My money says if there's any approach that way, they have it barricaded as well. Maybe even booby-trapped. Otherwise, they'd be shooting at us from the building we just came through, too."

"Any estimate on how many civvies we've got in there?"

"Hard to say with all the movement but I'm picking up eighteen or more heat signatures." Titus glanced at Kaleo—who had the other scanner—for confirmation.

Kaleo nodded. "Maybe as many as twenty-five."

"All right." Xolani considered for a moment, then pushed briskly to her feet. "Gina, Jamie, up on the roof. Darius, they already know your voice so you're going to call out that second warning they've got coming to them. We'll take position at the mouth of their 'gauntlet' while we try to negotiate, but we won't enter again unless they throw down their arms, or Gina and Jamie have taken out the shooters. Houtman, Rhys, you stay back, but not so far that you're uncovered if something manages to come up behind us. Titus, hand your scanner off to Darius so he can monitor the rear, since he's going to be hanging back there anyway."

Darius nodded his approval of the plan, not that it was necessary. This was Xolani's show, and she'd kick his ass if he even considered having anything less than absolute confidence in her. Gina and Jamie went back up the rope into the building, and Darius brought up the rear as the rest of the squad crept around to the one open approach, well out of range of the colonists' weapons. He could see Xolani ticking off seconds silently as she waited for Gina and Jamie to get into position, and then she gestured him forward.

"Attention, survivors! This is Sergeant First Class Darius Murrell again. I will repeat: We are not infected with the Rot. Lay down your arms so we may approach to ascertain your status and discuss whether there are any of your party who wish to relocate to the clean zone in Colorado Springs. We have a medic with us if anyone needs treatment. We just want to make sure everyone is okay. Once we've done that, we'll be on our way if none of you want to go with us."

There was no answering hail of gunfire, not even aimed toward the alley where the colonists must assume they were still pinned.

"Looks like they're congregating in one area now," Kaleo reported, looking at his scanner, where the heat signatures were converging in the middle of the building.

Xolani nodded. "Hopefully they're having a conference to decide if they want to let us in or not."

Silent minutes dragged out as Darius fell back to wait with Rhys and Houtman. He watched Xolani as she watched the dormitory where the colonists were entrenched. When the first gunshot came, they all hit the ground, but the shot was muffled. Indistinct. Followed by others. Darius watched a horror that mirrored his own dawn on his people's faces.

"*Shit!*" Xolani sprang up from her crouch. "Find a way into that building, *now! Go! Go! Go!*"

As a single body, the rest of the squad dashed forward, heedless of their own safety. Darius grabbed Rhys to keep him from charging with them. The boy looked alarmed, and even Houtman seemed bewildered. Only instinct-deep habit kept Darius's attention on his scanner and searching their exposed rear for threats. He needed to be in that dormitory with his people, though he already knew what they'd find in there.

Heat signatures approached from the right, and then Gina and Jamie dropped down from the roof nearly on top of them. They both looked ill.

"Well. There aren't any shooters in the windows now." Jamie dragged a hand over his mouth, his eyes wide and his lips bloodless.

"What happened?" Rhys was so pale Darius wondered if the boy would faint. He could see in the appalled hazel eyes that Rhys had put it together already. He just didn't want to believe it.

"They killed themselves," Darius said starkly, and looked away.

10

COMFORT

The vermilion glow of a funeral pyre danced on the wall in red and gold flickers as night fell. From the corner of his eye, Darius watched Rhys stare at them. He'd been silent since the colonists had begun shooting themselves, and Darius wondered if the massacre was reminding the boy of his own losses just days before. His expression had gotten more and more pinched with each body they'd carried out of the dorm. Especially the small ones.

"Final count: Seventeen adults. Four adolescents. Five children young enough to have been born after the plague, including two infants." Toby's voice was nearly inflectionless as he reported to Xolani. Darius saw the scar on her cheek twitch, but she just nodded.

Hard-ass though she was, Xolani always took it a bit rougher than the rest of them each time they were reminded that they couldn't save everyone.

"Any clue what their ideology was?"

Toby shook his head. "No, but it looks like maybe not all the women and boys were with the colony willingly."

Xolani hissed a curse between bared teeth, and Darius felt the almost imperceptible ripple of anger that ran through them all. It wasn't the first time Delta Company had come across that sort of situation, but it was guaranteed to piss them off every time. They all sat with food in their laps, but no one seemed to have an appetite, tense and unhappy to a person. Xolani'd had to harangue Rhys to get even a few bites down his throat.

"The second dormitory was uninhabited?" Xolani asked. Darius picked up on her train of thought and nodded in agreement. No one wanted to sleep in this building, with the splatters of blood and brains so fresh in the common room.

Kaleo nodded. "Yeah. They'd sealed it off the way they did all the other surrounding buildings, to prevent anything approaching from that direction, but they weren't living in it. The roof's still sound for the time being, though the moss is eating away at it. They hadn't been clearing it off like the dorm they were using."

"Then that's where we'll camp tonight. This town's clear, and we can seal off the floor we stay on. No reason we can't have our own rooms, sleep in beds for a change."

They all nodded, but no one looked as jubilant as such good news normally would have made them. Only the smallest flicker of relief brightened Rhys's shadowed eyes, though the boy had to be grateful after days of sleeping rough. Mostly he just looked miserable as his eyes flicked from one person to another from beneath lowered lids.

The only thing more troubling than the reluctant resignation with which the boy waited to see who would claim his company that evening, was the fact that none of Darius's people were looking at Rhys. Darius couldn't blame them. After a day like today, they either wanted to be alone to process what had happened, or they wanted willing company for solace and reassurance. Darius had watched morning and night when his people approached Rhys. The kid was miserable, and there were rumbles that the men were getting increasingly less comfortable with his obvious unwillingness.

Darius couldn't make sense of how the boy could be so responsive with him—albeit grudgingly so—but not with the other men. If Rhys could just relax and enjoy himself, the whole business could be accomplished easily. His men were more than willing—they'd had only the company of other Jugs for nearly a decade, and the boy was definitely a sweet piece of ass. But Rhys seemed determined to hate it, and Darius couldn't understand why.

Gradually, the Jugs were learning to stop asking if he wanted them to get him off as well.

"I don't get it," Darius had heard Kaleo say the second time Rhys had pushed his hand away. "You know, it feels a lot better if you're into it. Why not try to enjoy it?"

"Because I don't have a choice." Rhys hadn't volunteered any more, pulling his pants up and fastening his belt tightly, as if girding himself. Kaleo had returned to his bedroll, still looking confused.

Somehow Darius didn't think it was just prudery. Rhys had made it pretty clear that one morning in the shower that he didn't mind the idea of sex; he just didn't like being forced into the situation by circumstances. Darius could respect that, even if the kid was carrying it to an irritating extreme. But he couldn't shake the feeling that there was something more keeping Rhys stubbornly unenthusiastic. The boy couldn't bring himself to meet their eyes after one of the men had fucked him. He looked *ashamed*, humiliated, but why would he if he didn't have trouble with the concept of sex?

Frowning, Darius glanced at Houtman. Rhys often slid furtive, fearful looks toward him once he'd pulled his clothes back on. Like he was worried about how Houtman was going to react or what he was going to say. Which didn't make a lot of sense, since Houtman was in the same boat as Rhys. It wasn't like he had grounds to criticize anyone. So why did Rhys always look like he was waiting for someone to point the finger of condemnation at him?

Hell, maybe it was just the ghost of the old preacher the revs had killed.

When they sealed off the third floor of the abandoned dormitory, Darius saw Rhys look around again, but his men were still avoiding eye contact with the boy. They weren't looking at Houtman either.

Shit. At this rate, no one was going to attempt to infect either of them tonight. Darius watched Rhys as the others began to filter away, reciting to himself one last time the list of all the reasons why he needed to keep some distance from the boy, trying to determine whether any of them were worth taking the chance that Rhys might miss an opportunity for exposure to the Alpha strain. Then Darius crumpled the list and tossed it into the wastepaper basket of his mind. He wanted to be reluctant, but he couldn't quite manage to regret the failure of his intentions to keep away from the kid. He took Rhys's arm and pulled him toward one of the empty rooms. Breaking the lock on the door, he gestured Rhys inside. The tattered remnants of posters for bands and athletic teams long gone clung to the walls, and dust coated the furniture and piles of laundry strewn about. The covers of the twin beds were in a heap on the floor, and the mattresses were propped against the walls. The bed frames had probably been claimed by the colonists for building the barricades or for firewood at some point.

"Lay the mattresses down and spread out the bedrolls, boy. Try not to stir up too much dust. I'll be back when I've seen to setting up watch shifts for the night."

When Darius returned, Rhys had laid the mattresses side by side and covered them with the bedrolls. The boy was pacing restlessly about the small room as if unwilling to settle on the makeshift pallet. His look at Darius was fretful, but there was heat in his eyes, Darius would swear it, and a noticeable bulge under the fly of his jeans.

"Rhys." Darius shut the door, and the boy flinched as if the dull *thud* had exploded like a gunshot. The smell of dust and decaying fabric filled the room, as though something foul lurked in the shadows beyond the glow cast by the single flickering candle Rhys had lit. Darius's hand rose without any deliberate intent to touch the boy, instinctively reaching out to try to soothe Rhys's jumpiness away. He made himself lower it again. "How have you been feeling?"

"Fine." Rhys wouldn't meet his eyes.

"Really." Darius crossed his arms over his chest, his lips twitching. "How's your ass? Heard you were sore as hell for a while."

Rhys groaned, closing his eyes for a moment. "Yeah, okay, but —" He shrugged, opening them again to stare past Darius. "It's better now."

Darius sighed, leaning a shoulder against the cinderblock wall. "When I ask you how you're doing, I'm looking for a status report, boy. There's a time and a place for toughing it out, and there'll be plenty of times you'll be expected to handle your own problems.

When I'm trying to assess the state of my people isn't one of them. I can't fix what I don't know is broken. You hear me?"

Rhys gave him a resentful look. "Yes, *sir*."

"Take a load off before your legs collapse." Darius gestured to the pallet. "I'm guessing you're not used to the sort of marches we've been doing the past few days."

Rhys shook his head, though he didn't move. It looked like his limbs were frozen, his muscles locking him in place, as if he couldn't make himself take those steps toward the mattresses.

Enough was fucking enough.

Darius's gaze slid over him, sizing Rhys up. He pushed himself away from the wall. "Just what is it you're afraid of, boy?" He prowled toward Rhys. "Think if you sit on that bed I'm gonna throw you down and pound you into the mattress?"

Rhys's eyes darted to meet his and then raced away like frightened rabbits. The bulge under his jeans hadn't gone away, though, and he looked miserable and confused, as though his own impulses made no sense even to him. Darius was reasonably certain he hadn't imagined the expectant looks Rhys had been giving him for days, waiting for Darius to take him again, so why was the boy so anxious?

Darius's deliberate perusal dropped to the kid's groin. "Or maybe it's not that you're afraid of it, but that you're just *dying* for it? Is that it?"

"Please don't." Rhys closed his eyes, shutting Darius out, and turned away.

"There's no shame here." Darius ignored the pointed rejection, pressing against Rhys's back. His cock nestled against the crack of Rhys's soft ass as if it had been waiting for the opportunity to rest there again. Which wasn't far from the truth, however good Darius's intentions had been. Pushing against that scrawny, fragile body felt good in ways logic didn't account for, and he was damned if he was going to let Rhys pretend he didn't feel the same. "I don't care what your preacher or anyone else said. You can just let it happen. Enjoy it. Trust me. Let me make it good for you."

Rhys swayed, as though his body yearned for Darius to embrace him in spite of himself. But Darius merely reached around, making quick work of Rhys's belt and fly and drawing his cock out of his underwear.

Rhys bit off a strangled moan as Darius's wrapped a hand around him.

"Let it go, boy." Darius's whisper brushed Rhys's ear. "Just let it go."

"*I can't.*"

"Would you prefer I hurt you? Force you? Is that what you want?" Darius drew his hand up Rhys's cock, rolling the foreskin over the flaring ridge. His breath dampened the skin of Rhys's neck, and Darius caught himself wanting to suck and nibble, to taste the boy. "I could do it. You know I could. You want to blame it all on me? Go ahead."

"Please, I don't know . . ." Rhys's ass tensed as his hips nudged forward, pushing his cock into Darius's fist.

Darius's other hand crawled under Rhys's shirt and across his chest to tweak his nipple, and he felt Rhys's knees melt. The boy sagged until Darius tightened an arm around him, catching his weight. Darius scraped his teeth along Rhys's neck.

"Give it up, boy." Darius pumped his hand faster, pinched his nipple harder, until Rhys moaned, and not in a way that sounded pained. "Give it up to me. Don't make me take it."

Rhys whimpered. "Please. *Please.*"

Darius didn't have a clue what he was begging for, but Rhys didn't seem to, either. Darius growled softly and bit the back of Rhys's shoulder, using pain to pull the boy back from the edge of orgasm. It wouldn't do for him to come too soon. He bucked between Darius's hands and his body, crying out before Darius released him.

"Strip."

Rhys looked dazed and bereft once Darius let go of him, but he obeyed. A battle was being waged in his eyes, though, and Darius wished he could figure out just what the kid was fighting against. His hands shook as he stripped out of the clothes Darius's people had scavenged for him. While he worked, the look of stunned arousal began to fade, and shame started to creep back over his expression, though his dick was still stiff when he pushed down his jeans and shorts.

He wanted it, but he didn't seem to *want* to want it.

Dismissing his own musings, Darius stripped off his fatigues, still watching Rhys. It was alarming how skinny the boy was. Darius could break him easily, and it was an effort to remind himself to be gentle. Something about Rhys made him want to cut loose and fuck the kid with everything he had, but the boy was ambivalent enough without Darius adding roughness to the mix.

Nude, Rhys watched Darius, transfixed, his eyes locked on Darius's cock with a look somewhere between fear and hunger. If the boy kept looking at him that way, Darius wasn't going to be able to restrain himself.

"Down. On your hands and knees," Darius commanded.

Rhys tore his eyes away, wetting his lips with a swipe of his tongue, and complied with gratifying haste. He looked even smaller and frailer there on the mattresses, and that made self-restraint a little easier. The boy was just skittish. If Darius could just be gentle, patient, show him how good it could be, he'd catch on. Darius seized the kid's ass cheeks and pulled them apart. Rhys jolted at the first touch of Darius's tongue like he'd been zapped. His spine arched as he moved into the caress.

Darius moaned his approval, and his hands kneaded Rhys's butt. The boy's responses were so sweet and genuine, it wasn't an effort to try to seduce more out of him. "Could eat this tight ass all night." His voice was muffled against Rhys's flesh, and he swept his tongue more energetically over the tense pucker, urging it to relax. He soothed with broad, firm strokes and tickled with teasing flicks. Rhys groaned and rocked, probably in spite of himself if Darius knew anything about the boy yet.

Words tumbled from Rhys's mouth, seemingly of their own accord, as Darius worked his tongue into him, probing ever more firmly.

"Please . . . I don't . . . I can't . . . oh God . . . God, please . . ."

He was nearly insensible by the time Darius rumbled, "Reach back, boy. Give me your hand."

He startled and immediately tensed, as if the bubble of pleasure had burst at the reminder that Darius was still there and still had plans for him. It took him a moment to obey. He dropped his shoulders to the blankets and reached back. Darius opened the bottle of lube and drizzled it over the boy's fingers and crack.

"Get yourself ready." He kneaded Rhys's hip but didn't touch him otherwise. "Go slow. Don't rush it. Get to know how much you can take, how fast."

Rhys's dripping fingers shrank away, and Darius's smacked his butt with a sharp *crack*, drawing a yelp that sounded more surprised than pained. "Do it. Just like I did the other morning."

Rhys groaned and slipped a finger into his own ass, his reactions fascinating. His movements were slow and hesitant, and the reach awkward, but he added a second finger without instruction. His fingers couldn't go very deep, but still he stretched and twisted, trying to go as deep as he could. As if he couldn't *not* obey Darius.

Or maybe as if he was too aroused to stop himself, even if he wanted to.

Darius rubbed a palm over his own swollen fly, watching those thin fingers sliding in and out. The sight alone had him almost ready to come. "This is your job—to keep yourself ready. You'll learn to fight, and you'll help wherever you're needed; we all pull our weight in this unit. But until we know you're in the clear, this is your first responsibility. Some days I won't have time to do any more than just bend you over and do my business before I go about my work, so you'll be ready whenever I've got time for you."

When Rhys's preparations stuttered to a pause and the boy looked back at Darius with confusion and questions in his eyes, Darius realized what he'd just done. He'd all but committed to not avoiding and ignoring Rhys as he had these past few days.

Shit.

Well, he'd been losing that battle for days, anyway. Probably time to surrender gracefully.

"Keep going." Darius smacked him again, the pink outline of a handprint blossoming on his pale skin. Rhys cried out, burying his face against the bedding.

Rhys's fingers resumed their movements. Darius watched the boy move his fingers, moaning as the stretch became pleasurable, and wondered if *gratefully* wasn't a more appropriate word to describe his yielding the battle to keep away from Rhys.

"That's it, boy. Open your ass. Get it good and relaxed. You've had some time to get used to it now. You should be figuring out it won't hurt if you relax. Here." Darius's finger worked in beside Rhys's, drawing an alarmed whimper from him. Darius didn't stop. "That's it. Stretch that ass. Lift your head, boy. Let me have that pretty mouth."

Darius shifted, moving to kneel beside Rhys's head. He drew his fist up the length of his cock, a bead of pre-cum welling at the tip. Rhys lifted his head and stared at it, transfixed, and Darius took a moment to enjoy the sight of the boy's face, waiting for his mouth. The only thing that could make it a hotter picture would be if Rhys didn't have all that scraggly hair covering his jaw.

"Lick it."

Rhys licked it.

The boy forgot to be reluctant as their fingers worked together to open his ass. He gave a breathy cry when Darius sought out and brushed against the knot inside him. His mouth wrapped around the head of Darius's cock, again without instruction. It muffled his groan as Darius took over, pushing Rhys's hand away and sliding another large finger into him.

"Good. Yeah . . ." Darius heard the strain in his own voice, could feel his patience unraveling. Jesus, the boy's mouth felt amazing. His hand hovered next to Rhys's head, hesitated, and then settled on his ragged hair. Rhys groaned at the hint of pressure, arching his back and offering his ass up higher as Darius's fingers pushed in a little more. "Suck me, boy. Harder. *Fuck* . . . yeah . . ."

The sound Rhys made when Darius's hand gripped the boy's hair vibrated along his nerves like shrill notes on violin strings. It damn sure wasn't distress. Not even remotely. The efforts of Rhys's mouth on his cock became downright enthusiastic as Rhys traced the veins with his tongue and slid the loose skin up and down with his lips, moaning when he dipped his tongue into the slit and wrenched an echoing groan from Darius.

Did the kid like it rough? Was that what got him past his misgivings? Darius wasn't sure he dared to cut loose without getting a better idea of Rhys's responses. He didn't want to traumatize the boy just because he'd misread a few noises.

"Deeper." Darius pushed on Rhys's head as his hips shifted, thrusting into Rhys's mouth. Rhys tried to flinch away, but Darius's hand held him captive, insistent but not too forceful, testing his responses to the pressure. Rhys made a muffled sound of protest, but it didn't seem urgent so Darius ignored him, repeating the jerky thrusts. A few more moments and Rhys's noises dropped in pitch and tenor, becoming groans around Darius's cock. The sound was almost enough to make Darius pop right there. He tore himself away before he lost control entirely and crawled behind Rhys, drawing his fingers out and positioning the head of his cock against Rhys's hole.

"Oh God. Please . . ." Rhys groaned, his head falling to the pillow. A shudder rippled along the bony ridges of his spine. Darius pressed forward, feeling the tension, the resistance. He'd barely worked the tip of his cock in before Rhys clamped down, crying out. "Stop! God, please, stop! Please, I don't want—"

"You know I can't do that, boy." Darius fought against himself for a few more moments of self-control, hearing the growl in his own voice. He stopped moving, but his hands shook where they gripped Rhys's hips. He released his hold on the boy, stroking up and down his back, over his shoulders, and up and down his arms, trying to soothe him. His other hand crept around Rhys and grasped his cock, which had begun to deflate when the fear had taken hold. "Relax. Open up, and let me in. Let me make it good. Take it. I'll force it if I have to. You know I will. Don't make me do that to you. Just take it."

Rhys went limp beneath him with an abject sound as he surrendered, loosening the clench of his muscles on Darius's cock. Darius pushed in slowly. Rhys quivered but didn't protest again.

The next sound he made couldn't be mistaken for anything but pleasure, and that was when Darius's fraying patience disintegrated. He began rocking into the boy, faster and harder with each stroke. Rhys's voice rose, shouting incoherent words with each snap of Darius's hips against his ass. For five days, Darius had watched from across camp as Rhys endured the pawing of other men in stoic near silence, but now he was melting down, damn near howling. The response pushed Darius right over the edge, and he gripped the boy hard, jerking and pulsing in the clenching heat of his ass.

He whimpered when Darius withdrew, but a grope around Rhys's hip made clear at least one cause for his distress.

"Stay there." Darius searched through their bags, and when he returned, Rhys's arousal had begun to recede, his body tense again as he hovered there on his hands and knees. Darius lubed the plug and slid it inside Rhys's wet, open ass before Rhys had a chance to protest. Then with a low, feral growl, Darius shoved him over onto his back. Before Rhys could do more than groan, Darius grasped his dick and began to jack it firmly, watching the boy's reactions. He wanted to see Rhys come completely apart.

Rhys screamed, a reedy cry of pleasure. His entire body seized, clenching, rising, thrusting. His fists twisted in the blankets as his thighs fell open, splaying him helplessly.

"Please! Oh, God, *please!*" With a savage sense of triumph, Darius added a twist and a curl around the head of Rhys's dick. He didn't give the boy the option of resistance, determined to shred all that aloof distance he stubbornly maintained. Surrender wouldn't be a choice he made; it would be the only possible response. With firm strokes, Darius sent Rhys tumbling into it, powerless before the onslaught.

When it was over, he gently released Rhys's still-twitching cock, licking a splash of cum from his hand. The boy even tasted sweet. If Rhys had been able to do anything but stare up at the darkened ceiling, shell-shocked, he might have noticed Darius's slightly smug smile.

Now maybe Rhys would understand there was nothing bad here, nothing he had to fight against.

"See, boy? Ain't nothing to be ashamed of." Patting Rhys's hip again, Darius sank onto the pallet beside him. Panting, Rhys fumbled for something to wipe himself off with, finally using a dusty old shirt from one of the piles of laundry, and crawled under the blanket.

Rhys lay there almost expectantly, and Darius had to quash the impulse to wrap his arms around the kid. Dammit, there was no way he was letting a civvie he'd probably have to kill get under his skin. He didn't let himself dwell on how nice it might feel to touch him, not for sex or because they had a job to do but for comfort and contact.

At least he tried not to dwell on it. The effort was made more difficult by that vulnerable, needy look in Rhys's eyes. Shit, how long had it been since the kid had had something as simple as a hug? His mom had been dead for years, and if Xolani's intimations were to be believed, life probably had been pretty grim for Rhys at the monastery.

After a long, laden silence, in which Darius felt Rhys's eyes upon him, he spoke. "I can just about hear you thinking, boy. Spit it out so I can sleep before it's my shift at watch."

Rhys rolled to his side. His jawline was taking on that mulish set that boded no good. He gave Darius an earnest, frustrated stare. "Look. I know there isn't anything to be ashamed of. God, I know Father Maurice and Jacob were full of crap with all that stuff." He bit his lip as if second-guessing his decision to speak, but then he plunged onward. "But everything I've ever known says this isn't right." He drew away in a tight ball, as far from Darius's body as he could. Almost as if he was expecting some sort of retribution for his temerity. "Don't try to take that away from me. It's all I've got."

A tense silence settled between them, and finally, Darius sighed. "Have it your way, kid."

Darius rolled and gave Rhys his back. Despite his exhaustion, he lay there a long while, aware of Rhys lying wakeful next to him. The kid was still chewing on that when Darius finally fell asleep.

11

DAYBREAK

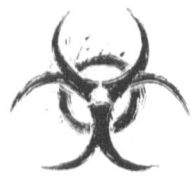

"You okay, sweetie?"

"Sure, Mom." Rhys pelted the trunk of a tree with another acorn.

"You did the right thing, walking away back there." She put herself between Rhys and the oak, forcing him to drop the handful of acorns he'd gathered. Her face was drawn with pain and seemed to be aging by the day. She flinched when she tried to cross her arms over her chest.

He rubbed his hand over the fine, uneven fuzz on his sixteen-year-old face. "You don't think he's right, do you?"

"You know I don't. I never have." She scowled, and Rhys knew it was because she lacked the energy to defend him from Jacob the way she had before she'd started to get sick. "Since Maurice declared himself Grand High Fucking Poobah around here, Jacob's decided that makes him the right hand of God."

Rhys shrugged. "It's no problem. I'll just keep ignoring him. Jacob's just a dick. It's not worth making yourself sicker."

"It is if I can stop him from hurting you."

"I told you, I can ignore him."

"I know it's easy to say that, Rhys, but having a message drilled into your head every day for years . . . even if you try not to listen, even if you know it's wrong, sooner or later it takes root and makes you question and doubt yourself. I don't want you buying into it."

Rhys rolled his eyes. "Please. I'm smarter than that. With any luck, someday soon the old fart will yell himself into an aneurysm and keel over and no one will be there to back Jacob up when he tries to make trouble. Then everything will be fine around here. Maybe Gabe will even come back."

She tried to smile, but it came off sad. They were humoring each other, offering false hope, of course. "It's not just you I worry about." She glanced toward the garden where Cadence worked beside Mrs. Merkle. Cady never left Rhys or the side of another woman these days, not since she'd begun menstruating last winter. "If he corners Cady one more time to lecture her on the proper duty of women to bear children, I'll stab him in his sleep."

"You rest. I'll keep an eye on her, Mom. He won't get to her with the rest of us looking out for her."

"I hope you're right, sweetie." Her voice sounded raspy, pained. The courtyard orchard became the dark walls of her bedroom. She lay on her narrow bed, gasping for each breath. Her eyes were yellow and sunken in as they rolled madly in the delirious panic of pain. The bones of her emaciated face and arms bulged through her paper-thin skin, and her flesh was mottled with the dark, oozing patches of the Rot, like bruised fruit gone bad.

"You killed her, freak," Jacob taunted over his shoulder. "You and your sick ways. Just like you tried to kill me."

"Repent, son," Father Maurice intoned severely beside him as his mother reached a skeletal hand toward him. The man towered over Rhys where he knelt by her bedside. Chunks fell from the ceiling as an earthquake shook the monastery.

"Rhys, don't leave me." Her breath rattled in her lungs, her voice cracking on the plea. He reached for her, but hard arms wrapped around him from behind, dragging him away.

"This is your fault, you perverted shit!" Jacob's face was rotting, too, and he glared hatefully at Rhys.

Somewhere out of sight, Cadence called to him. "Rhys, help me!"

He struggled to free himself of the arms encircling him, crushing the breath from his lungs. "Let me go!"

"They're gone, boy," a rich voice murmured in his ear.

AMELIA C. GORMLEY

"Fornicators! Sodomites! Perverts! Your fault! Repent!" Father Maurice thundered. The earth shook again.

"Rhys!" Cadence screamed, now standing beside the bed where their mother lay limp and motionless, the life gone from her sunken eyes. Jacob's rotten arms held Cady, pulling her away from him, just as the unseen arms held Rhys. Blood poured from her torn-out throat and splattered the front of her shirt. "Please! Rhys! Come back!"

"Give it up to me, boy," the voice near his ear entreated, dark and seductive. "Let it go. Let it go." The imprisoning arms dragged him further away as Cadence cried out. "Let it go."

"CADY!"

Λ Λ Λ

HE AWOKE WITH A BREATHLESS SHOUT. A sizzling pain at the base of his throat followed. His eyes flew open to see Darius looming over him. He struggled in a blind panic, his throat constricted, cutting off his air. Then he realized Darius had him pinned to the mattress with one hand on his larynx and a knife poised to slit his throat.

Awareness flooded Darius's eyes, and he tossed the blade aside and removed his hand, allowing Rhys a breath just as his vision was going black.

"Shit!" Darius grabbed the edge of a blanket and swabbed at Rhys's throat. It came away flecked with blood, and Rhys felt dizzy for a moment as he realized just how close he'd come to death for the second time in less than a week.

The wound burned, and Darius's weight pressed down against Rhys's morning erection. The thick ridge of Darius's cock lay alongside it, jabbing Rhys's belly. Rhys stared at Darius's mouth, mesmerized by his full lips, parted and panting. Rhys's lifted his head without any deliberate intent as he curled a hand around the back of Darius's neck. Then he pressed their lips together.

A shocked heartbeat passed as a shudder rippled through Darius. Then another. His powerful hands seized either side of Rhys's head, and his mouth angled, grinding down hard.

Rhys groaned as Darius's tongue plunged past his lips, insinuating itself against his own. It thrust and explored while Rhys's hands

108

grappled with Darius's muscled arms, trying to find purchase to pull him closer.

Rhys strained and writhed, seeking a way under Darius's confining weight to press harder against him. His nerves sang an electric chorus of awareness and *wanting*. God, he wanted. He wanted the sucking tugs and nipping pulls of Darius's lips and teeth, wanted the weight pressing him down, wanted the cock sliding against his own with each push of Darius's hips. His thighs opened, and his ankles hooked around Darius's legs. His hands moved down Darius's back, grabbing his flexing ass.

Darius tore his mouth from Rhys's, glaring down at him, looking angry and confused. Then Darius dipped his head to Rhys's neck. His tongue stroked across the cut still stinging at the base of Rhys's throat.

Rhys's body surged with arousal despite the shudder of shock and revulsion. He clutched Darius to him, urging him on.

Within moments, Rhys found himself facedown, his ass in the air, pushing and bearing down while Darius worked the plug out. He was tender from the night before—God, yes—but not nearly as bad as he had been that first day. He wriggled impatiently as Darius slicked his cock, then pushed in.

Rhys yelled into the mattress, his fingers clawing at the blankets. Caught at the dangerous edge where intensity could tip over into agony, his feet slid uselessly on the bedding, unable to escape.

"Oh, no you don't, boy." Darius grabbed him and jerked him back into the thrust. Rhys yelled again when Darius's hips smacked his ass, and Darius's heavy balls swung, knocking against his own. As he paused, Darius bit the back of Rhys's shoulder, adding just a little more pain before licking the spot he'd bitten. Rhys went boneless beneath him, moaning into the pillow.

The rocking push of Darius's hips that was shoving his cock deeper into Rhys faltered for a moment.

"You like that, boy? Is that what it takes? You like it when I force you?"

Rhys shuddered, unable to reply. The admission stuck in his throat, choking him. For the first time, everything felt *right*. No shame. No fear of what anyone else might say or think of him. No worry about how Jacob would use this to make his life hell or echoes of Father Maurice's indictments and condemnations.

But he couldn't confess that. He had to be better than this.

He groaned, shaking his head in useless denial.

"The fuck you don't." Darius withdrew and rammed back in, driving a shout from Rhys's throat. Darius grabbed his wrist, twisting his arm behind his back hard enough to put stress on the joint. Darius's other arm hooked around the front of Rhys's throat, threatening a choke hold if only it tightened a bit more.

Darius's weight bore down on Rhys, trapping him and threatening to break him. Inhumanly powerful muscles drove Darius's hips forward, slamming him into Rhys.

Between breathless cries and half-sobbing gasps, Rhys clawed at the arm across his throat with his free hand until it tightened in warning. He moaned each time Darius's cock stroked past the swollen knot inside his ass. The blanket beneath him grew wet. Denied any opportunity to struggle without risking injury, he could only give in.

It was even better when he did. Each thudding impact of Darius's hips rocked him, jolting his balls and cock, and wringing another shout from his raw throat. And it was good, so good. *God*, the stretch of Darius's cock reaming him open and the pressure of it running past his prostate over and over . . . Each pass took him to the edge of orgasm and held him there, rising and falling in surges. Trapped, helpless, defenseless.

Darius's teeth pressed into the fleshy part of his shoulder again. Between the pain and the pounding of Darius's cock and the brushes of his own dick against the sheets, the heat and pressure behind his balls searing along the base of his spine, became a full-scale nuclear event. It overloaded his senses and melted down his synapses with blinding, white-hot shockwaves exploding through his body. Rhys rode the waves, shuddering, seizing, groaning into the pillow as he clamped down hard on Darius. A moment later, Darius slammed into him for the final time, pulsing balls-deep in Rhys's clenching ass.

Darius released his wrist and moved the arm from across Rhys's throat, and the boy collapsed, moaning. His ass twitched and spasmed as Darius pulled out of him and replaced the plug almost in a single motion. Rhys lay motionless, stunned and trying to gather the ragged tatters of his composure.

Darius rolled off to the side, his dark skin shining with sweat, panting. Rhys began to curl toward him and then stopped himself, all the questions flooding back. Darius's hand rose as it had the night before, hovering for a moment before it stopped mid-reach, falling onto the hard ridges of his stomach. Rhys restrained the urge to close the distance between them.

"You okay, boy?"

Why had he kissed Darius?

"Fine." He turned his face away before he yielded to the stupid impulse to try to snuggle. He wasn't sure where it had come from; that first time in the shower, all he'd wanted after Darius had fucked him was to get away. And he'd certainly never felt any yearning for closeness with the other Jugs. Why did he now feel like he would burst into tears if he couldn't have a stupid *hug*?

This wasn't about that. *They* weren't about that. Darius fucked him because it was necessary. They weren't lovers, and Darius sure as hell had no interest in offering him comfort or affection. And Rhys couldn't let himself be weak enough to ask for it even if Darius did. He had to be strong, had to prove he was worth the effort they were investing in him, that he wouldn't be a burden or a drain on precious resources.

"Did I hurt you?" He felt Darius's finger touch the side of his neck, not far from the place the knife had nicked him.

"I'm fine," he repeated, grateful that Darius couldn't see the way he squeezed his eyes closed against the wave of longing that small touch aroused.

He wanted to press himself against Darius and breathe in his scent until he felt like he could face the world again. But nothing had changed since that first night in the chapel. It was bad enough Darius was doing all this to save Rhys when he really didn't want to, and was even trying to be nice about it. He didn't need Rhys turning into a big baby on him.

He was alone. Everyone was gone now, even Father Maurice. Everyone except Jacob, and that was *worse* than being alone. He needed to get used to that. Pull his weight. Don't complain. Don't do anything to make Darius and his people think he'd be more trouble than he was worth, or that Jacob was right about him.

Numbers meant safety. Survival. Especially if the numbers were trained soldiers with weapons. Rejection would get him killed, just like running off must have killed Gabe and his parents.

"I'm okay." He sat up and reached for his clothes. "I'll go get our rations for breakfast."

He left before Darius could ask him any more questions.

12

ROUTINE

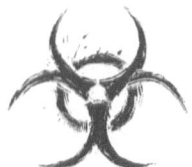

He was sore again that day, but Rhys couldn't bring himself to mind. They left behind that empty town and the site of the tragedy that had taken so many lives for so little reason. As they marched on, his body still sang with remembered pleasure. His heart raced as he recalled those breathless moments when his life had been in Darius's hands, and he couldn't recall why he was supposed to not feel excited by it. Or he could, but he couldn't seem to make those reasons actually matter.

As the suburbs yielded to farmlands along a crumbling two-lane highway, he finally found the courage to ask the question that had been plaguing him since they'd heard those muffled gunshots.

"Why did they do it?"

Walking beside him, looking as hard-edged and cool as ever, Xolani frowned. "You mean this particular group? Most likely, they didn't want to be held accountable for whatever they might have done to the people who were with them unwillingly. They destroyed everything, even the babies, rather than face the consequences. Fucking cowards."

"You say that like this isn't the first time."

"It's not. Sometimes single survivors who have been isolated too long panic and kill themselves. Once with a small group. Never a colony this size." She puffed her cheeks, blowing out a breath and tugging on her braid. She looked off into the distance and some large bird—what was that? A falcon? Hawk? Turkey buzzard?— skated across the sky, searching for prey in the weed-choked fields below.

"So many years cut off from everyone else, not even sure if there *is* anyone else, it does something to people. The last thing they knew, they ran away from the world because the world was dangerous. Being anywhere near other people meant they risked getting sick or being attacked. I think eventually that's all they remember, that the world is dangerous. That people are dangerous. They think coming out of hiding or allowing anyone near is certain death. Maybe they just can't handle the idea of things changing once they finally feel safe. Or maybe they just go crazy. We'll never know."

Rhys swallowed hard, nodding. "I think that's what Father Maurice started doing."

"Yeah?"

"He wasn't always in charge. When we left Montana, it was more equal. He was pushy and bigoted, but we could argue against him. By the time we'd been at the monastery a few years, though . . ." Rhys bent and picked up a chip of broken asphalt, slinging it to the side into an overgrown field that had clearly once been farmland. Parts of it were now covered in massive blackberry brambles, especially at the edges, where they sometimes spilled over onto the road, snagging at Rhys's clothes. They had tried to walk one residential street that had been so overgrown and covered by the uncontrollable vines that they'd needed to find another way around or risk the thorns scraping the Jugs and exposing their dangerous blood.

Rhys turned back to Xolani. "He was the only one with a gun. The rest had either broken or run out of ammo. He said anyone who wanted to 'forfeit the sanctuary' was welcome to leave the monastery, but if they stayed, he intended to see that we lived *righteously*, as God meant us to do, and that meant he'd be making the rules, seeing to it we kept God's law. None of us could stop him, especially not with Jacob watching his back. Not unless we were willing to try to get that gun. Though—" Rhys grinned broadly "—my mom did threaten to stab him in his sleep."

Xolani laughed. "Your mom sounds like a lady after my own

heart." Then she sobered. "But it's a hard step to take, making the choice to kill someone."

"I said *threaten.*"

Her dark eyes went flinty. "Don't ever make a threat you're not willing to carry through. The other guy just might be."

Rhys shivered and looked away. "Anyway, he started getting weirder and weirder. Laying on the religious stuff a lot thicker. Acting like we were the only people left in the world. Talking about Cady being the new Eve. It was creepy."

"Being cut off from the world can do that to people. It removes what grounds them, what keeps them somewhat connected to reality. It's easy in those circumstances to get paranoid. Or power hungry."

Silence fell, punctuated by the scuff of their feet on the crumbling blacktop, the rhythm occasionally broken as they sidestepped a clump of weeds sprouting up through a crack. It was shaping up to be a hot late-summer day and in the distance, mirages shimmered where the road met the horizon. In a moment when no one spoke, Rhys could hear the distant shriek of the bird that had wheeled overhead.

When had he gotten used to the eerie quiet of a world with no one in it?

"Do you find many survivors?"

"A few dozen a year." Xolani pulled a large knife out of a sheath on her hip and fished a whetstone out of her pocket, honing the blade as they walked. The scratching helped fill the vast and empty silence. "More if we're sweeping larger cities. We detach two squadrons to escort them back to Colorado Springs in batches, one in the spring after the mountains thaw, and one in the fall before they get snowed in again."

"I heard Darius mention the clean zone in Colorado Springs. Why there?"

"Cheyenne Mountain. Back before the batteries ran out on the satellite radios and everyone had used up all the fuel cells, a lot of survivors were in contact that way. The doomsday-prepper types all knew the locations of various underground government installations and broadcast the info. They were looking for safe places to wait for the plague to pass, like NORAD." Rhys blinked at her in confusion. "Oh, uh, that's the North American Aerospace Defense Command. It used to be a critical installation a century or more ago, but other, more modern facilities had taken over. Still, it was a big hole in the ground, essentially a huge bunker, and people flocked to it."

"That's how so many survived?"

Xolani flipped the knife in her hand once and returned it to its sheath without even looking at it. Somewhere behind them, a low voice began to sing a song Rhys thought he should have recognized but couldn't remember.

"It wasn't as easy as you make it sound, but in the end? Yeah. Now they've got a large perimeter established around the city, trenches lined with razor wire, with rusty scrap metal cut into points or sharpened wood stakes where they ran out of wire." Xolani shook her head with a soft snort. "There're two levels of that. Like that colony we just found, there's one route in and out of the clean zone, and the entrance is heavily guarded. When new people arrive, they're greeted by armed guards in hazmat suits who process them and assign them housing in the outer perimeter. They pass three months of quarantine there—that's on top of already being quarantined up to six months after we find them—then they're allowed inside the inner perimeter."

"Then what?" Rhys watched the dust rise beneath his feet. Weird. He'd never thought about how traffic had kept dirt from building up on the roads.

"Most of them work farming crews. They've razed a lot of the unused property and turned it into farmland. Everyone has a garden in their yard, and they're expected to grow their own food as best they can. They've got chickens in the city and herds of cattle outside the perimeter. Hunting parties are permitted in and out since the region has been swept clear of revs. Everyone works to keep what's left of society going. And we bring them more survivors when we can. If we can."

Xolani's mouth tightened in a grimace, and Rhys gave her a worried look. "It wasn't your fault they killed themselves."

She blinked at him, then scoffed and cuffed him on the back of the head. "Shit, kid, I know that."

"I just thought maybe since it was your operation, you might . . ." Rhys flushed and looked away, muttering. "Never mind."

She shook her head. "Nah. That operation would've gone tits-up on Darius or anyone else in charge, and frankly, I'm not the kind of person to dwell on shit like that. No, it was just talking about the clean zone. We're not allowed past the outer perimeter."

"The Jugs?"

She nodded, looking out over the waving yellow grasses of the fields. "Yeah. Like you saw yesterday, all it takes is a cut and we become dangerous to anyone we come in contact with. When we deliver the civilians we find, we're not allowed within fifty yards of the checkpoint."

"So you save them, but you can't ever have a home with them?"

She sighed. "We're home with each other, Rhys. We're not a part of that anymore, and neither will you be. Someday . . . someday when we're done patrolling for revs and civvies, we'll probably set up a permanent base somewhere, sort of like what we have at Fort Vancouver. We'll make our own settlement somewhere out of the way where we're not a threat to anyone. But that's a long way off in the future."

Rhys hung his head, watching the cracked asphalt pass beneath his feet again. It seemed terribly tragic to him that the Jugs should be exiled when they were protecting the people who had exiled them.

They reached a small community hospital in the early afternoon. The sun was high and the heat oppressive, especially when they had to stand around while Kaleo and Toby hacked through the ivy climbing the building to find the doors. Everyone's clothes clung to them, dark with sweat, and the dusty interior of the hospital was a gruesome relief. Faded scraps of banners declaring the hospital under quarantine still clung to the barricades and outer doors. Rhys's mother had explained to him that when the plague had begun to get bad, the National Guard had cordoned off the hospitals treating plague victims, condemning not only the sick people, but the doctors, nurses, orderlies and even the people working in the gift shop and cafeteria. Anyone who tried to escape was shot.

The air inside was stale and rank. The bodies of the last patients were mostly skeletal, lining the halls and filling the rooms to over-crowding. Even if anyone had been allowed in or out of the block-ade, there had never been enough manpower to inter them properly.

Or perhaps, by that time, those victims hadn't had any family left to claim the remains.

Rhys allowed himself a moment of smug satisfaction that Jacob lost his lunch at the sight of the corpses covered in dust, hair, scraps of leathery skin and stringy sinew. Rhys managed to contain his gorge, just barely, which was good because otherwise Xolani might lecture him about being underweight again.

They made no effort to burn the bodies. It would have taken too long to collect wood for a pyre large enough. They would have to remain where they were, a haunting remnant of a world that no longer existed.

What supplies they couldn't carry, they left behind. Darius marked the coordinates of the hospital in a logbook he kept for the reclamation crews. By the time they had finished scavenging, the sun was low enough that Darius declared they would camp near the hospital. Rhys would have preferred to be far away from that grisly place, but he said nothing. Titus and Jamie did another circuit of the area with the infrared scanners to make certain there were no revenants who might attack in the night. No one wanted to sleep in that giant mausoleum, and the nearby medical office buildings had been converted into overflow space for the hospital and were just as bad. So for the first time, the Jugs set up camp outdoors, in a field outside the hospital campus. They pushed rusted-out cars from the parking lot into a large circle to form a barricade around the camp-site, moving them with ridiculous ease.

It was far too hot to require a fire, but Gina had shot another deer while the rest were inside. Jugs required a lot of food, Xolani explained, to fuel their enhanced performance. Thus when they made camp, it was around a large fire that threw far more light than the lanterns they usually employed when they slept indoors. Rhys settled onto his bedroll with the sickening certainty that tonight he would not even be afforded the semi-privacy of darkness.

He lay awake, waiting, knowing at least one of the Jugs would approach him, sooner or later. After first watch had taken positions and everyone else had settled in, he saw Bailey look his way and swallowed something that hovered between relief and disappointment. At least with Bailey, he could be quiet. He could keep from humiliating himself with the sort of vocal responses Darius dragged from him. But the part of him that craved the near-agonizing intensity of what had passed between them that morning couldn't help but wish Darius was approaching instead.

Drawing into himself, Rhys dropped his gaze to the ground and pushed down his pants and underwear. He rolled to his knees and grunted softly as Bailey did what he wanted to do. When it was over, Bailey sighed in annoyance, and the partial erection Rhys hadn't been able to avoid quickly flagged.

"You're a nice kid, man, but I gotta say, this ain't workin'." Bailey fastened his belt with irritated jerks as Rhys righted his own clothing. "We finally get some fresh meat around here, and it turns out one of 'em is a smarmy asshole and the other might as well be a plastic doll." He patted Rhys's shoulder awkwardly. "I get that it sucks, kid, and I wanna help you out, but I don't know how much longer it's gonna be worth it, feelin' like I'm forcing someone who doesn't want it. That hits me all wrong, after what I went through with Charlie Company."

"I'm sorry." Rhys's face burned. He curled into a miserable ball on his bedroll and tried to ignore the unwelcome wetness down the cleft of his ass.

He didn't know how much time passed while the flickering of the campfire threw dapples of light around the circle of bodies settling in. His troubled mind had just about quieted enough to sleep when he felt someone drop to one knee behind him. His heart leapt into his throat as Darius grabbed his shoulder and rolled him onto his back with a brusque pull.

"Please don't," Rhys whispered desperately even as his cock filled, and his skin *ached* for the feeling he remembered from that morning.

Darius didn't answer. He merely dragged Rhys's pants roughly down his legs and tossed them aside, then made quick work of his own fly. He hauled Rhys toward him with his arms wrapped around Rhys's thighs and pushed into him—already wet and loose after

Bailey's attentions—with an abrupt thrust. Rhys cried out, his shoulders coming up off the ground with the combined pleasure-pain of that intrusion, but Darius gave him only a moment to adjust before he began plowing into Rhys at a brutal, rough pace, jerking Rhys into each thrust with that grip on his thighs.

There was no hope of staying quiet. No hope of not responding. His shouts filled the night air, underpinned by Darius's low groans and the slap of Darius's hips against his ass. He didn't even know if anyone awoke or heard them. All he knew was that lightning sizzled through his body each time Darius rammed into him, and it was better than he thought he could possibly bear.

With a final deep thrust and a groan, Darius shuddered and pulsed inside him. Rhys stared up at him, dazed, panting, yearning. His balls hurt, they were drawn up so tight, so ready to let go. Darius leaned down over him, grabbing a handful of his ragged hair.

"You ain't no plastic doll, boy," he growled, inches away from Rhys's lips. "You just need to be handled right."

His other hand wrapped around Rhys's cock and began jacking, and his teeth nipped firmly at Rhys's bottom lip before traveling down Rhys's throat and closed over the spot where the knife had nicked him that morning. Rhys came with a howl, surging through Darius's fist.

Darius's dark eyes seemed to burn with their own fire in the flickering light as he held Rhys's gaze captive. He reached for something, and when his softening cock slid out of Rhys, the cold, graduated ridges of the plug replaced it, sliding in easily.

"Get dressed, and get some sleep." Darius fastened his pants and walked back to his own bedroll farther away from the fire.

Burning with shame, Rhys pulled his clothes back on and curled up on his bedroll again, feeling so alone it ached.

13

POSSESSION

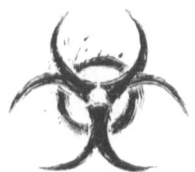

"Convenient when the wildlife pitches in," Darius heard Toby quip as he fired two shots into the head of a fallen rev, blasting the back of its skull off in a small fountain of bone chips and blood. A pack of five revs had been facing off against an angry moose defending her calf when the squad found them. One had already been trampled and the others had been easy to take out, distracted by the cow's pummeling hooves.

"*Shit!*"

Kaleo, who'd nearly been trampled by the moose when she'd decided her rescuers were another threat, rolled in the grass with the rev that had already been on the ground when they'd arrived. Distracted by the other revenants and the moose, and assuming it was down for the count, no one had delivered the coup de grâce. The rest of the squad formed a semicircle around Kaleo, their weapons aimed, waiting for an opening that would keep them from hitting Kaleo. He finally got the clearance to slug the thing and throw it off, but before anyone could fire, Kaleo jumped on it again and began pounding it with fists as powerful and punishing as the moose's hooves.

"Back off, Kaleo. We've got the shot." Toby's voice was steady as he sighted his gun, but Kaleo drove another fist into the rev's face. Darius heard bone crunch.

"Stand down, Kaleo!" Darius barked. Kaleo froze with his bloody fist cocked back, something feral sparking in his normally twinkling eyes. Darius held his gaze until humanity leached back in. Panting, Kaleo pushed himself up off the revenant. Its groaning stopped when Toby took the shot.

Kaleo's shoulders rose and fell with each harsh breath, his muscles quivering with unspent fury. After a moment, he turned his gaze to Rhys and Houtman, who were coming up from their crouches now that all the hostiles had been neutralized.

It was Rhys Kaleo stared at the longest, still breathing heavily, an erection swelling the front of his fatigues. Rhys swallowed audibly and stared back, paling beneath his sunburn and frozen in place like a terrified animal. Darius felt his own muscles bunch, anger churning in his gut, seeking a reason to intervene before Kaleo could grab Rhys and loose that uncaged aggression on him. But in the end, it was Houtman whose arm Kaleo grabbed, dragging him off toward a nearby barn.

Looking shaken, Rhys stood there in the tall, golden grasses long after they were gone, while the rest of the squad went to work disposing of the corpses. As if compelled by Darius's stare, Rhys turned his head and met Darius's gaze, a visible shudder running through the boy's thin form. Fear shadowed Rhys's wide eyes, but there was also something hungry and yearning there. Darius's hands curled into fists as he fought his own urge to haul Rhys off. After an endless moment, Rhys shook himself and walked away to begin gathering firewood, but not before Darius had seen the fly of his jeans bulging.

Darius growled to himself as he went back to work. Understanding that boy was going to make him crazy.

FAR TOO MUCH OF Darius's attention was spent contemplating Rhys the rest of the day, all the way up to making camp that night.

How was the kid who responded to all the others with such reluctance the same kid who was turned on by Kaleo nearly going bestial on his ass back in that field? Or by Darius damn near killing him? Was it just the lack of privacy driving the kid's self-consciousness when he refused to respond?

Darius couldn't offer Rhys the sort of solitude they'd had in the dorms two nights ago, but he could do better than the previous evening's campout near the hospital. They chose the clubhouse of a long-overgrown golf course north of Salem. The only piece of furniture that didn't get recruited to barricade the windows and doors was the pool table. They left that where it was, less because of its weight and bulk and more for the entertainment it would provide for the evening. Someone had actually put a cover over the pool table before the clubhouse had closed for the final time, and the felt was intact and dust-free, unlike every other bar they'd ever bunked in. Such a rare and unexpected find gave preparing camp an almost festive feel.

Even better, there was a bar that partitioned off one end of the room. Darius laid his and Rhys's bedrolls behind it, hoping being out of sight of the others, at least, would ease the boy's embarrassment.

As usual, Rhys kept his head down and went about silently lending assistance wherever he could. Some days it seemed like Xolani was the only person he spoke to, probably because she was one of the few people he was reasonably certain wouldn't bend him over, ream his ass open, and breed him. He was reserved even with Toby and Joe, who to Darius's knowledge hadn't touched Rhys yet.

Of course, given the way Rhys seemed to like a rough and dangerous edge to his sex, maybe it was time for that to change. Toby and Joe might be right up his alley.

The problem was that the more Rhys drew into himself—and he was withdrawn, even for all his responsiveness when Darius fucked him—the less Darius trusted what might be going on behind those skittish hazel eyes. Even when he was compliant, there was a deep-rooted streak of rebellion in Rhys that was never extinguished. He didn't surrender; he just chose his battles, awaiting his moment.

In a way, that was good. Reassuring. However weak he might be physically, Rhys was no one's victim. On the other hand, that stubbornness kept creeping up at times when it was unproductive, not to mention bad for the boy's chances of survival, which left Darius in the position of needing to protect the boy from himself.

At the rate things were going, he would lose both his recruits. Until that afternoon with Kaleo, no one had touched Houtman since those colonists had killed themselves days ago, and Rhys was so unenthusiastic the men were starting to feel uncomfortable fucking him. Darius didn't know what to do about Houtman. If he was making himself disliked by the squadron, there was nothing Darius could do about it. He certainly wasn't going to order his men to fuck the guy. On the other hand, they were perfectly willing to fuck Rhys. Just about everyone liked the kid. If he could just muster a little enjoyment so they didn't feel awful doing it, there would be no problem.

If Darius could just tell his people to use more force with Rhys, not to give him a choice, to *demand* a reaction from him, it might just work. But of course, they weren't supposed to mistreat the recruits, so everyone was being nice. Rhys didn't respond to *nice*, though.

None of this was helped by the fact that Darius had wanted to break Bailey's jaw again when he'd fucked Rhys last night. That same part of Darius had been willing to pummel Kaleo if he'd gone after Rhys there in that field earlier this afternoon. Darius had seen heat in Rhys's eyes. He wanted that heat to burn for him and only him, and a part of him didn't seem to be the least fucking bit interested in all the reasons why that could never happen.

"You got a problem?" Xolani gave him an inquisitive look as she passed by.

"Nope." Darius leaned casually against a wall, trimming his fingernails with a pocketknife to keep from hurting Rhys next time he had his fingers up the boy's ass.

"Just glowering for shits and giggles. Got it." She snorted and continued on her way. After a moment, Darius tucked away his knife and fell into step beside her, making a circuit of the clubhouse to double-check the security.

"How long do our recruits have to have multiple partners?"

Xolani's eyebrow quirked up a fraction of an inch. "I'm playing a complete fucking guessing game with this whole thing, Darius. We don't even know it will work."

"Well, what do we know?"

She tugged at her braid and stopped walking, leaning against a doorjamb and ticking off points on her fingers. "One: we know Alpha is sexually transmissible. Two: we know Alpha infection produces antibodies against Beta and Gamma. Three: we know there is a small grace period after Beta and Gamma exposure before it begins replicating in the RNA, due to the time delay designed into the virus, and that Alpha works a little faster. Four: we know certain other inoculations to various diseases in the past have worked prophylactically soon after bacterial or viral exposure. Think rabies, tetanus, a few others here and there. Based on that knowledge, I've formulated a scientifically questionable hypothesis that timely, prophylactic Alpha infection will combat Beta or Gamma exposure. I could be totally wrong."

"All right, then, tell me what your *hypothesis* says about this whole multiple partners issue." Darius braced a hand against the wall opposite her, forcing his restless fingers not to pick at the peeling wallpaper.

"Well, first of all, we don't know what the viral load is in sex fluids. It might vary from person to person, and it might be low to begin with across the board. So the more exposure our recruits get, the better their chances are. Second, some viruses undergo micromutations from one infected person to another, producing different strains that could be more virulent than others. It happened with HIV. Infected people were supposed to use protection even when having sex with other infected people because they might get infected with a different strain of the virus. Bailey or Joe or Kaleo might be more infectious than, say, you or Toby. So right now our recruits' best chance of infection is to be exposed to as many possible microstrains—for lack of a better word—of Alpha as we can manage."

"If we wanted to do that, we should have taken them back to Fort Vancouver."

Xolani crossed her arms over her chest, nodding thoughtfully. "Yeah, we probably should have, but it would have set our initial sweep south of Portland behind by at least a week or two based on nothing more than a maybe."

"So back to my original question."

She gave him a carefully shuttered look. "Frankly speaking, the odds are if they're not infected with Alpha and producing antibodies by now, after over a week of exposure, this probably isn't going to work. Beta or Gamma will be replicating in their RNA soon, if it isn't already, producing antibodies to Alpha, and a few weeks from now, we're going to have to kill them."

"You're saying we could stop now."

"*Possibly*. But not definitely. That's the problem. Because I don't *know* what's happening in their RNA, I have to go for the most conservative approach, which is maximum varied exposure until we're absolutely *certain* we know what they're infected with."

"So it could take up to seven more weeks?" Darius's fingers curled into a fist.

"On the outside. Most cases manifest between three to six weeks." Xolani tugged at her braid again. "Let's call it three more weeks at the minimum until we can pare back on at least the multiple partners aspect. Another couple weeks beyond that until there's no point trying to infect them at all."

Darius nodded tightly. "I'm just wondering if one of our recruits is gonna make it that long."

Another small twitch of an eyebrow on Xolani's normally impassive face. "He might not look it, but he's a tough kid. Are you worried about him making it, or you?"

Darius's jaw tightened. No hard-ass of Xolani's caliber should be so damned perceptive. "Fuck you."

She caught up with him before he'd taken more than a couple of strides away from her. "Quite a show you two put on the past couple nights. One might even call it a demonstration. Guys are wondering if they can top it. Getting that reaction from Rhys is going to become a competitive sport."

"That boy don't wanna react." He refused to let himself bristle at the idea that Rhys might respond to anyone but him.

"And yet . . ." Xolani spread her hands in an expansive shrug. "Quite a show you put on."

Darius grunted, testing a door to make sure it was sealed. "You got a point?"

"Use it."

"The fuck are you talking about?"

"Use it. Whatever you're doing. Whatever it takes to make him less miserable, expose him to as many microstrains as possible, and keep you from bashing skulls in."

"Don't ask for much, do you?"

She gave him a flat look. "I want that kid to live. You do what you have to do to see that it happens or I'll kick your ass."

Darius glared after her for a moment before he strode across the room, grabbed Rhys's arm, and dragged him to the corner behind the bar where Darius had dropped his rucksack. He'd chosen the spot thinking to indulge Rhys's need for privacy but what Xolani had said made sense. Under the circumstances, privacy was a fantasy, and the kid was just going to have to get used to it.

Now he had a better idea.

Snickers and soft chuffs of laughter followed them through the semidarkened room. The lanterns were all clustered around the pool table and balls clicked against one another.

"Drop 'em, boy." He pushed on Rhys's shoulder. "On your hands and knees."

Darius's cock began to rise, hot blood swelling eager, heavy flesh. He pictured the way Rhys had been that morning two days ago in the dorm room. Desperate. Out of his head with need. So damned willing. Darius's body tightened, demanding gratification, demanding to spend its heat inside Rhys's tight, skinny ass.

The boy looked away and took down his drawers.

The problem here was that Rhys wasn't going to respond to the relatively gentle Bravo Company model they'd been trying to emulate. The harder Darius was on him, the better he responded. Xolani was right; he had to use that.

"Spread your ass for me."

Rhys whimpered softly and dropped his head and shoulders, then arched his back, pushing his ass up. Darius growled and grabbed both his cheeks, parting them roughly. "Now put your hands back here and spread it."

Rhys made a distressed sound, but he laid his cheek against the blanket and reached back, holding the halves of his ass open.

"That's right." Darius squeezed his soft flesh roughly.

"Remember what I said that first night? This ass is mine, boy. Seems you been forgetting that."

"Please," Rhys panted. "I don't want them to hear—"

Darius dropped down above him and ground his clothed dick against Rhys's bare ass, hissing in his ear. "You think I *care* what you want? Told you the rules right from the start, didn't I?"

"Yes."

Darius's hand rounded his hip, and Rhys gasped. His cock was hard, pulsing, the slit dripping pre-cum. "Oh, you want it, all right." Darius's voice dropped to a caressing murmur as he stroked Rhys's lean cock. "You just don't wanna want it."

Pushing himself up, Darius dug in his pack and lubed the plug. Rhys startled at the first touch of the cool plastic, looking back at Darius in surprise, but his eyes slammed shut as Darius began to work it in.

"Oh God." He shuddered and arched his back, pushing his ass toward Darius like an offering. Darius eased the plug in slowly, almost to the widest part of the last bulge, when Rhys's noises began to sound genuinely pained. He drew it out and worked it back in, repeating the process, fucking Rhys with it.

"You're mine, boy. That's the rules." He tried not to think how close the pretense was to the very thing he most despised, how easily one could be mistaken for the other. "It's what we agreed on that first night, isn't it? I can spread you open, stuff you with my cock, and shoot my load in there anytime I want, can't I, boy?"

Rhys whimpered. His hips bucked, and his hands gripped his ass so tightly he was bound to leave bruises on all that pale skin. The widest part of the plug slid easily in and out, and Darius had to restrain the urge to drive his own cock in where the plug went so readily.

"God, please!"

Darius gripped what ragged sandy hair he could seize. "Don't you beg God, boy. He ain't got nothin' to do with this. You beg *me*."

Rhys groaned, humping back to meet the plug, his hand moving toward his cock.

"I own your ass. And I mean to share what's mine. So you get up and get out there with my men." He lodged the plug in Rhys's ass with a firm push and rose. Rhys knelt there a moment longer, blinking as awareness set in again. He turned his head to stare at Darius in incredulous inquiry.

"I said get up." The color fled from Rhys's face, and his eyes widened as he rolled off his knees. But more importantly, his cock twitched and jerked against his belly, dripping from the furiously swollen head. Darius crossed his arms over his chest, leveling a severe look at Rhys. "Move."

Flushed, Rhys rose from the floor and reached his pants. The tense knot in Darius's chest loosened a little at the lack of rebellion. He pulled the jeans out of Rhys's hands and dug in the boy's pack for a pair of sweats. "These. Easier to get into and out of."

Despite his arousal, Rhys's expression was grave as he pulled them on, and for a moment his eyes darted around as though he might try to make a break for it. Darius snatched a handful of the kid's hair, pulling his head back. His other hand rubbed up and down the wood pushing at the front of Rhys's sweats.

"You still mine, boy?" His teeth scraped Rhys's neck, below the patchy growth of hair.

Rhys groaned. Melted. Clung to him. "Yes." And something melted in Darius in response. Relieved. Almost content.

"Good. Go eat your supper."

14

RECREATION

Rhys froze when he rose up from behind the bar and saw everyone's head, except Jacob's, snap around, making it all too obvious they'd heard him and Darius. The clicking of pool balls had stopped, and he hadn't even noticed.

His face blazed, misery edging out arousal. It gracelessly spilled him out of the peaceful mindset he'd managed to find when Darius had done . . . whatever it was he'd done that had driven Rhys out of his head for a while. Rhys wished he could get it back. All he had to do was listen to Darius, obey Darius, be Darius's *boy*, and everything would be fine. No blame. No guilt. No shame.

But that assurance was a fragile thing, and the reminder of his lack of privacy and dignity almost undid it.

"Didn't tell you to stop walking, boy." Rhys made himself take another step forward at Darius's growl. The plug nearly buckled his knees with each ill-considered movement. When he eased himself down to sit, it was almost worse than standing, the pressure of the plug sending bolts of sensation searing along his cock. Xolani dropped down beside him, pushing a bottle of Scotch into his hands.

"I've never—" He cut himself off, grimacing at the absurdity of observing the legal drinking age from a system of law that had disintegrated almost a decade ago.

Xolani eyed him up and down. "Hrm. Underweight as you are, I bet you're a damn cheap date. All right. One sip, then give it back. You need to relax."

Rhys grimaced, taking up the bottle. The fumes from the liquor within were strong enough to singe his nasal hair, and actually drinking it made him shudder and wheeze, coughing as his throat burned.

Titus reached over and pounded his back, laughing. "Welcome to the team, recruit!"

Rhys blinked his watering eyes, strangely warmed by the epithet. It seemed to imply he had a place within their ranks. Perhaps not as a full member just yet, but getting there.

Definitely better than *kid*.

"I'll give him something to choke on," Kaleo quipped from the other side of the loose circle where they were sitting, passing the bottle around. Rhys felt Jacob's eyes trying to incinerate him on the spot.

Blushing, Rhys turned his attention away, trying not to hear the retort someone made about how Kaleo was doing the recruitment thing wrong if Rhys was choking. Across the bar, Darius was in conversation with Toby and Joe near the pool table while Bailey and Jamie played.

"Is this a party? What's going on?"

Kaleo shrugged. "When we make camp in a bar, if we can secure the location well enough, we usually get to drink a little and have some fun."

Titus grinned as Xolani used his lap as a pillow, his hand drawing small circles on her abdomen. He kept his voice low. "Wait 'til you see what happens when a patrol gets back to base. Makes this look like a tea party."

Xolani rolled her head on Titus's thigh to look at Rhys. "That's the thing about this life. There's fuck-all to be hopeful about, so we take what good we can out of it. We fight to stay alive and we fuck to *feel* alive because there's nothing else left."

"How can you live that way?" Rhys gave her a troubled look, but Xolani just shrugged.

Glancing back toward Darius, Rhys realized for the first time that Toby and Joe were *together*. Though Toby was shorter than Joe by nearly a foot, there was something almost protective about the way he had his arm around Joe, the way Joe leaned against him with that dazed look on his face. Rhys wondered if Joe was drunk. He watched as Toby nodded to Darius, left Joe's side with a stroke of his hand down Joe's arm, and crossed the bar, headed straight for Rhys.

"Wanna play some Delta Company pool, recruit?" he asked. Rhys blinked in surprise at the invitation. He'd only had a chance to talk with Toby a few times since that day with the colony. He seemed nice enough. He had a bouncy sort of intensity, and his features were delicate, pretty in an almost feminine way. His gestures and mannerisms were sweeping and flamboyant.

Rhys looked over to Xolani. "Go on. It's okay," she urged. Across the bar, his eyes found Darius. His attention was fixed on Rhys, and he gave a tight nod.

"Sure, Toby." Rhys forced a smile, forgetting the plug until he rose. He bit back a groan as standing reminded him.

"Great!" Toby grinned and slapped Rhys on the back, his hand dropping to brush Rhys's ass. "We could use someone to be the side pocket."

Rhys jerked back, and Toby's smile faltered. "Sorry, did I—?" he began, with an uncertain look at Rhys.

A hard hand landed on Rhys's shoulder, squeezing, and Darius's scent surrounded him.

"Good to see you making friends, *boy*." Rhys imagined he heard a slight growl to the last word. "Don't mind if I watch your game, do you, Toby?"

Toby's ready grin flashed. "Sure you don't want to play, Big D?"

Darius chuckled, though Rhys felt tension in the hand that still lingered on his shoulder. "You'd lose, son. I don't play by your rules. But you enjoy yourself with our recruit."

Toby snorted. "Oh, I think you play a close enough variant, but spectators are always welcome."

Darius stepped away, leaning against the wall nearest the pool table, with his arms folded across his chest and his eyes on Rhys. His stare was a physical weight, holding Rhys rooted in place. Rhys didn't know what sort of consequences there might be if he refused.

It was tempting to push back, to see what would happen, but he didn't dare.

Toby stepped nearer. "Don't worry." His eyes traveled down Rhys's front, to the undeniable bulge under Rhys's sweats. "Joe and I just like a little variety now and then. You can trust us. We'll take care of you, and we'll show you a good time."

Darius's presence nearby kept the questions on Rhys's tongue from escaping. Toby and Joe had never approached him before. He'd begun to assume that, like Titus, they wouldn't do so. What had Darius said that made them come to him now?

"Okay." Rhys met Darius's gaze over Toby's shoulder as Toby pressed even closer, settling his hands on Rhys's waist and drawing him forward. Rhys turned his head to dodge the kiss Toby would have landed, but Toby didn't seem to mind. His lips went to Rhys's neck instead, sucking and nuzzling below his beard.

He smelled like sweat and the alcohol being passed around, just like the rest of them. Despite Rhys's nerves, the brush of Toby's lips on the sensitive skin of his throat felt good. He had no idea why it should when it had been so easy to remain unmoved by everyone but Darius until now. Toby moved up to Rhys's ear, catching the lobe between his teeth before murmuring, "It drives Joe wild to watch me make the boys melt."

It's working. Rhys bit his lip from saying it aloud, and his eyes drifted shut. He moaned in spite of himself. Somehow it was harder to remember the lack of privacy when Darius was there with him, compelling him to go along with this. His nerves awakened in ways that were different from what Darius did to him. Toby's slow, sensual approach was like liquid heat flowing through his veins, instead of the violent electricity that charged him with Darius's displays of raw power or the cold apathy that came from the perfunctory awkwardness of the others.

He could still feel Darius watching him as Toby's hands crept up to his chest, thumbing his nipples through his T-shirt. Toby's erection brushed his own, and Rhys gritted his teeth, pulling his hips back.

He didn't *want* that arousal.

Toby didn't seem to mind that, either. He merely resumed his attention to Rhys's ears and throat. Then he drew away and spoke over his shoulder. "Joe, come on over here."

Another pair of hands landed on Rhys's shoulders, massive paws that felt like leaden weights. He opened his eyes to see the towering giant of a man pressing against Toby from behind. There was no way around it: Joe was huge. He was also quiet. In over a week, Rhys didn't think he'd heard more than two sentences from the enormous man.

Joe's hands rubbed almost soothingly along Rhys's upper arms. He still looked a little dazed. Toby pushed back against Joe, and his hands gripped Rhys's ass and pulled his hips forward. Rhys allowed it this time, tightening his jaw against a groan.

Joe smiled almost sweetly. Toby was all flamboyant sass and slow, deliberate sizzle, but there was something guileless about Joe.

"Darius tells us we might have something in common," Toby said conversationally. His hands roamed from Rhys's ribs to thighs.

Rhys blinked, frowning in confusion. "W-we do?"

"Mmhm." Toby grinned. "Darius says you like someone else in control, being a little rough, giving orders."

Rhys tried to jerk back, flushing with humiliation. Darius had told him that? "What? No—"

Toby's eyebrow lifted. "Really? That's a shame. Joe's *very* good at taking orders. Aren't you, Joe?"

Joe's eyes brightened, and he nodded eagerly. Around them, everyone but the guards was drinking. No one was paying any attention, not even Jacob, who was pinned beneath Bailey in the far corner.

"Lift up your shirt, Joe. Show Rhys just how well you take orders."

Joe stepped away and peeled up his tight, Army-green T-shirt revealing his barrel of a chest. Though his arms were covered with thick hair, his chest was devoid of even the slightest smattering. Instead, shiny, white lines of knotted scars traced across his skin, and after a moment of staring without comprehension, Rhys realized they were words.

Slut.

Whore.

Pig.

Slave.

Thick metal rings were looped through his nipples, and other, smaller, round scars occasionally dotted his skin. A fresh one was red enough for Rhys to understand, after a moment, that they were burns.

Joe watched Rhys take this all in, his eyes calm.

Rhys's alarmed gaze flew to Toby, whose smile had taken on a sharper, more dangerous edge. He no longer seemed so innocuous. "Now you see why Darius won't play with me. You're okay. I only hurt the ones who beg for it, like Joe here. If that's not your thing, fine. I just wanna toy with you for a while."

Rhys's mouth felt dry, and his heart was racing too fast with a horrible, terrified fascination and arousal. His eyes flew to Darius, who was still leaning against the wall, apparently unconcerned.

Darius wouldn't let them harm him. Would he?

"What—" He swallowed hard and tried again. He had to do this. He had to. Darius had made it clear he wouldn't brook any refusal.

I own your ass. And I mean to share what's mine.

"What do you want me to do?" Rhys asked tremulously.

"I want *you* to do what you're supposed to, sweet thing: follow orders." Toby smiled, all charming menace, and gestured Joe forward. "Bend him over the table, and get him ready for me."

"Yes, Toby." Joe caught Rhys by the back of the neck and pushed him down over the pool table, his strength undeniable even in his relative gentleness. As he started working down the waistband of Rhys's sweats, he murmured, "You should feel honored, recruit. Only place I get Toby's cum is on my face."

"Maybe someday our recruit'll get that, too." Toby waved his hand loftily, leaning on the pool table near Rhys's shoulder, watching Joe work. There was a surprised pause when Joe encountered the plug, then he began wriggling it out. "But if I came on his face this time, he wouldn't get to see just what a whore you are, Joe. You're such a pig, sloppy seconds don't even faze you. You'll just wallow in someone else's spooge, won't you?"

A shudder passed through the hand on Rhys's ass, and Joe's voice became quieter, so much softer than anyone his size should be able to speak. "Yes, Toby."

"Speak up, cumslut. I didn't hear that."

"Yes, Toby!" Nearby conversation stopped, and heads began to turn.

Rhys groaned, wretched with humiliation. Toby admired the lube-slick plug that Joe set on the pool table. "So courteous of Big D to make sure you're ready for action." He pushed himself away from the edge of the table and brushed Joe aside. "Saves us both a lot of time."

Rhys felt a few jerky movements behind him, and the tail of Toby's belt tapped against his buttock as he unbuckled. It seemed to take forever while Rhys bent over the table, his twitching hole exposed to the whole bar. Only Darius's intent presence across from him kept him from wanting to die.

"Spread that sweet ass for me, Joe." Joe reached over from where he stood to Rhys's side, his massive hands closing on Rhys's cheeks, and pushed them apart. "Look at that." Toby plunged a finger inside, then withdrew it. "Practically gaping. This kid may be a sloppier slut than you, Joe."

Rhys tried to stand straight, an outraged protest on his lips, but someone—Joe or Toby, he couldn't tell—shoved him back down. Toby drove into him without delay, setting a quick, hard pace almost before Rhys's first loud groan faded. Toby angled himself to run firmly past Rhys's prostate on every stroke.

"Wonder just how much it'll take to make you come." Toby's dark chuckle spoke of wicked amusement. "We're gonna find out. Maybe after my pig stuffs you full of his fat dick. I bet we can make you scream."

Rhys clenched his hands, fighting to hold back and not respond. Insensible, caught up in the struggle between pleasure and self-control, he buried his face against the felt of the pool table. The utter abandon of those hard, savage times Darius had fucked him hadn't prepared him for Toby's skilled onslaught. He didn't dare cry out a refusal, even if he could've found the breath for it. Darius had commanded him to do this.

The fear and uncertainty helped keep him from the brink, at

least until Toby was finished. He barely paused to catch his breath before he patted Rhys's ass and pulled out. Rhys shivered at the obscene feel of the air on his wet, exposed asshole. It was even worse when Toby plunged two fingers into him and drew them back out quickly.

"Time for some slops, piggy," Toby crooned, and then there was a vulgar, lapping sound. Rhys whimpered, fascinated and revolted, and Toby added, "If he didn't need that load I just dumped in him so badly, I'd make you suck it out of his ass, you filthy cumdump."

Joe groaned, and the lapping got more enthusiastic. "Yes. Please, Toby. Let me eat your cum out of him." His voice was breathless, transported.

A sharp, hollow *thwack* made Rhys jump, as though Toby had cuffed Joe sharply upside the head. "I said no, pig. Now get to work, or I won't even let you play in my mess."

They were insane, Rhys thought. All of them. Especially Darius and Xolani if they thought he was okay with these two lunatics. It was too much. He pushed himself up off the pool table as he heard Joe frantically unbuckling behind him.

Darius's severe gaze stopped him. His brow drew down in a frown, and he gave a subtle shake of his head.

Toby's hand landed on his shoulder in an amicable clap, and he leaned in close to Rhys's ear. "It's just a game. This is how Joe and I get our kicks. He's got a humiliation kink a mile wide, so I'm just taking the opportunity to work him up. You're safe. Relax and enjoy it, recruit."

Toby's other hand slipped down to grasp Rhys's cock, which was still hard despite his nervous revulsion. The stroking felt good, and Rhys made a noise somewhere between a distressed whimper and a pleasured moan as Toby pushed him back down.

And then Joe shoved enthusiastically into his wet ass, and there was no more chance for protest, for thought, for fear. There was only the incredible stretch, the pounding impact, the slick, sloppy noises, the bruising grip of Joe's mighty hands on his hips. Rhys groaned, slumping onto the pool table as he fought to cope with the attack on his senses.

Joe didn't have Toby's skill, but he had size and power. Rhys clung to the ledge of *too much* with Toby's obscene taunts in his ear.

"You're so fucking hard. Look at you. Look how horny it makes you, being fucked by a pig in front of all these people. Does it hurt? Is that chubby of his hurting you?"

Rhys shook his head, rolling his face on the felt even as a whimper hinted at just how close the gesture verged on a lie. Between sobbing gasps, he groaned, biting back the urge to beg for mercy.

"Maybe you like it that way." Toby's sounded almost conversational, twisting his fingers in Rhys's hair and pulling hard. "Maybe you're just a little baby pain slut, too green to know it yet. Darius should try spanking you. Use a belt and leave welts all over that pretty white ass of yours. How about a nice switch, turn your back black and blue? Maybe he'll even draw blood."

As a spasm of fear shot through Rhys, coupled with an image of the other morning when Darius had leaned in and licked the cut on his neck, tasting his blood. With a desperate cry, he came—for the first time with someone other than Darius—spurting onto the dusty floor. An insensible moment later, he realized Joe had followed him, going still and pulsing deep in his ass. Rhys lay over the table panting, too depleted even to be self-conscious about the display he must be making in the moment before Toby handed the plug back to Joe. Joe pulled out and slipped it easily inside his dripping hole, before easing Rhys's sweats back up. His hands were oddly polite and gentle.

Toby rubbed Rhys's back, the gesture at odds with his wicked menace from just a moment before, and hummed softly. "You're okay. Take your time. Getting boned by Joe can be an experience."

When Rhys dared rise and show his crimson face again, Joe had sidled up to Toby and was snuggled against him, ducking down to lean against Toby's shoulder as Toby wrapped an arm around him. "You did good, baby. We'll get Cooper back to Darius and go lie down, okay?"

A pang of envy awoke underneath the fear and mortification at what he'd just done, what he'd *allowed* them to do to him. Seeing the sudden shift to tender solicitude made something ache in Rhys's chest. Their intimacy emphasized how alone he was. It made him want what they had.

For a crazy moment, the yearning made it seem as though every-thing Father Maurice had ever told him was right. He *was* a pervert, and now everyone knew it. If he were any sort of decent human being he would have opted to let the virus kill him.

He was sick, and he was alone, without anyone to offer him even the twisted sort of comfort Joe seemed to take in Toby's petting and murmured words. Jacob had surely heard the whole thing, and he'd make Rhys's life hell. No one would understand.

Then Darius stood beside him, stern and hard as always, with none of the reassurance Rhys craved. Toby smiled good-naturedly. "Take care of him, Big D. I got into his head a bit."

Darius would never soothe him the way Toby was soothing Joe. Darius would never hold him or pet him like that. Rhys didn't know just what Darius had in mind after this, but it wouldn't be good.

Or rather, it would. Which made it even worse.

Rhys followed Darius's gaze to the puddle of milky fluid on the floor at the base of the table and cringed. Darius looked pleased, but for Rhys, those streaks were a sign of defeat.

"Come on, boy." Darius's warm tone didn't offer much reassur-ance. Rather it seemed to gloat. Wretched and ashamed, Rhys followed him to their space behind the bar.

15

PRIMACY

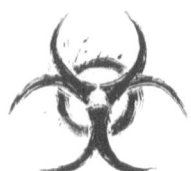

Darius was ready to punch something—possibly himself—at the sight of Rhys's hangdog expression. He'd thought Toby would strike the notes Rhys needed, boss him around a bit, add that kinky edge the kid seemed to react to, but Toby and Joe played too hard. Yeah, Rhys had responded, but seeing what they did had scared him. Or maybe he felt like nutting there against the pool table was some sort of defeat. Whatever it was, now the boy looked as if he'd committed some horrible crime.

But then, of course, there was the fact that Toby had taunted Rhys into coming with conjecture about Darius hurting him. That was . . . interesting.

Way too fucking interesting.

What had the kid so fucking miserable? Clearly he'd enjoyed himself, at least on some level. Why did he keep trying to resist that?

It would be easier if he didn't have to strong-arm Rhys into all this, if he could just respect Rhys's ambivalence and leave him alone. But taking no for an answer might mean Rhys's death, and that wasn't acceptable. Not now. It might have been possible once, if Darius had refused from the beginning. He could have written Rhys off then. But now he was in it. No turning back.

It would also be easier still if he didn't *like* the way Rhys responded when he leaned on him so hard. Darius *liked* the nervousness, the almost fear, the distress as Rhys struggled to take his cock. Every bestial urge Darius had never known he had roared to life when Rhys looked at him with trepidation shadowing his eyes. Darius might be too practical to make any claim on being a *good* man, but he'd never wanted to scare or hurt anyone. He'd always kept a lid on his rougher impulses, aware of his own strength and power. He'd cut loose rarely and then only the smallest bit, even with other Jugs.

Until Rhys.

Perhaps he was becoming a monster. Like the people of Charlie Company. Perhaps he just wasn't a decent enough person to resist the lure of Rhys's vulnerability and the advantage his own strength gave him over the boy.

He didn't want to be that man, but something about Rhys brought it out in him. He'd tried keeping his distance, and it hadn't helped. He couldn't give Rhys up, not now. He knew that without a doubt. Watching Toby and Joe going to town on Rhys, he'd had to clench his fists and grit his teeth not to tear them off and drag the boy away to re-stake his claim. He couldn't hand off Rhys to someone else who might handle him better now.

But that left the question of just what he *was* supposed to do with Rhys. Darius knew what he wanted to do, but it probably wasn't the same thing as what he should do. Regardless, he'd reclaim what belonged to him and deal with the rest later.

Once behind the bar, Darius grabbed Rhys and shoved him back against it. He belatedly remembered the plug when Rhys groaned, but he still pushed up against Rhys, claiming the boy's mouth, devouring his moans.

Perhaps he might have been able to stop himself if Rhys had protested, but instead, Rhys welcomed the kiss with a desperate sound, clutching at him and opening to it. Darius drew back only long enough to remove his own his shirt before diving for another kiss, too hungry for those needy noises Rhys made to figure out how he was going to get their clothes off.

It was Rhys who pushed him away. Rhys who stripped in an awkward, wriggling effort before he sank to his knees and reached for Darius's belt. Astonished by the boy's eagerness, it took Darius a

AMELIA C. GORMLEY

moment to lend his assistance. When Rhys would have rolled to his hands and knees, Darius pushed him onto his back on the blankets and shoved his knees up to his chest to get at his ass.

If there was anything sweeter than listening to those pain-pleasure moans as he worked into Rhys's loose, wet hole, it was seeing the need on his face, the strain, the struggle. Too spent from his ordeal over the pool table, Rhys never got more than half-hard as Darius hammered into him, but when he wasn't pleading for mercy, he begged for more.

"Please . . . I can't . . . *oh God, yes.*"

He shouldn't be doing this, Darius thought afterward, as sanity seeped back in and his cock softened. He lay panting and dripping sweat, his weight crushing Rhys against the floor. Remorse gnawed at the edges of Darius's afterglow, but Rhys clung to him, trembling and whimpering softly.

Forget the age difference and the fact that he'd been sexually active longer than Rhys had been alive. There were just too many things in Darius's favor, things that gave him too much power over Rhys, things that skewed all of this in ways that would be far, far too easy to take advantage of.

Rhys wasn't mistaken in what he'd said that night in the dorms. It *was* wrong. Very wrong. Darius could tell himself he was saving Rhys's life all he wanted, but the fact was, he liked that power differential too much for it to ever be right.

He should distance himself again. Trying to leverage Rhys's need for a little dominance to make things more pleasant for everyone had been a stupid idea, no matter what Xolani had said. It wouldn't be good for Rhys to be dependent on him in that way. The balance of power between him and Rhys was fucked up enough already without throwing that into the mix. Now that Rhys had realized letting other men screw him and enjoying it wasn't the end of the world, he'd be able to deal with it better next time, without Darius compelling him.

But Darius couldn't make himself quit.

Reluctantly, he rolled off Rhys, unable to decipher whether the sound Rhys made in response was relief or protest. He grabbed another plug, thicker and smoother the one they'd been using, out of his pack. Rhys's eyes were fixed on Darius, wary and somehow expectant. He wished he knew what Toby—far more experienced with all this than Darius himself—had been trying to say when he'd given Darius that loaded look and told him to take care of Rhys.

"Roll over, boy." Darius cleaned up the semen that had leaked from Rhys's ass before lubing the new plug and easing it in. Rhys's moans didn't sound at all distressed, and Darius wondered what he'd find if he rolled Rhys onto his back again. Would he be hard?

How would he taste if Darius sucked him off?

"I want you to keep wearing this, even if you're doing better at taking a cock without it hurting." Darius seated the plug, and the muscles in Rhys's skinny buttocks twitched and flexed as his body worked to try to expel it. Rhys tried to stifle a soft moan, and when Darius turned him over, his lean cock curved up over his stomach.

The mindless, brutal possessiveness Darius had tamped down howled awake once more as he remembered that Rhys had roused to someone else, responded to someone else. And then his best intentions and resolutions to back off didn't matter. He shoved Rhys's thighs open and engulfed Rhys's cock in his mouth, taking him down deep, all the way to the root in a single lunge. No one else would have this. The first time Rhys came in another man's hand, it had been Darius. The first time he came with another man fucking him, it had been Darius.

The first mouth he felt, the first mouth he came in, that would be Darius's, too.

So many firsts, and he'd claim them all. Sooner or later, he'd have to let Rhys go. Sooner or later, Rhys wouldn't need him. But for now, Rhys was his, and Darius would leave his stamp on every experience the boy would ever have.

He caught Rhys's wrists and pinned them down when Rhys would have grabbed for his head. He wasn't sure whether Rhys intended to push him away or try to control him, but neither one was acceptable.

This was his. *His.*

It took Rhys longer than it might have if he hadn't come earlier. The harder Darius worked—taking Rhys down his throat, pumping up and down Rhys's cock, sucking, tonguing, devouring those tight, high balls, rolling them in his mouth—the more desperate Rhys's panting groans and helpless struggles against Darius's grip on his arms became. He erupted with a shout, pulsing salty and bitter onto Darius's tongue.

Darius drank it down.

His.

Once Darius settled in his bedroll, Rhys lay staring up at the ceiling, tense and expectant, and Darius didn't think it boded very well that the boy was thinking again. Why couldn't he be one of those guys who just drifted blissfully to sleep after sex?

"What is it?" Darius felt weariness tugging at him.

Rhys turned his head, his eyes filled with unexpected vulnerability. He hovered on the brink of saying something, need and yearning plain on his face. Then he seemed to shut it down and shook his head. "Nothing."

He rolled away, giving Darius his back.

∧∧∧

DARIUS AWOKE with a gasp hours later.

The wisps of the nightmare dissipated, blown apart by consciousness almost immediately. But his pulse hammered in his head and his trigger finger spasmed in its curled position.

He could still see Rhys with the barrel of Darius's gun at the bridge of his nose, his hazel eyes pleading for mercy as the rotten-fruit patches of the Beta strain spread corruption across his pale skin. Beyond Rhys, Houtman had stood, smirking.

"Are you okay?" Rhys's voice was a groggy mumble beside him. He sounded like his nose was stuffed up, giving Darius cause to suspect he'd cried himself to sleep again.

"Yeah." He was too damn tired to play the hard-ass. He sat up and glanced around. In the light of the few lanterns that had been left burning, he could see that third watch was in place, but it wasn't light enough outside to be morning yet. He lay back down. "Problem with living in hell, boy. Plenty of nightmares to go around."

"You don't think there's any hope, either." His voice was a whisper in the predawn stillness.

Darius snorted softly. "Don't let Xolani and the rest of them fool you. They try to be cynical to protect themselves, but as long as there's people still breathing, there's hope. Why the hell you think we try so hard?"

"I guess you're right." Rhys rolled to face him, his eyes bloodshot and puffy. "When do you think we'll all stop being scared?"

Darius closed his eyes, looking ahead to the years left of his own life. The endless patrol and exile, moving from place to place, securing safety for people who wanted nothing to do with him. One of a dying breed of freaks who never should have come into existence.

"Not in this lifetime."

Rhys didn't answer, but after a moment Darius felt a hand, trembling and tentative, settle softly on his shoulder, offering comfort.

Without thinking, without questioning whether it was a wise idea for either of them to become attached to the other, he curled his arm around Rhys and drew him against his body.

Rhys tensed for a moment, and then he shifted. Settled. He laid his head on Darius's chest and let his arm slip across his waist. He was so thin. Soft. Fragile. So unlike anyone Darius had touched in the last fifteen years. That softness softened something within Darius in turn. Made him feel like something other than a Jug for a while.

Made him feel human.

"Go to sleep, boy," Darius muttered, weariness beginning to draw him under once more.

After a moment, Rhys's eyes closed, and he obeyed.

16

DISCOVERY

"**Y**ou haven't done much traveling, have you?" Toby asked Rhys as they trudged along an empty street, working their way through the outlying towns toward what had once been the state capital. As his third week among the Jugs began, they were starting to ask him questions like this, trying to get to know him.

By now he'd learned to keep to the middle of the formation, especially in urban areas, where revenants seemed to be more common. Somewhere in the distance, Jamie and Titus were cruising each block on the motorcycles with the solar-charged batteries, looking for heat signatures or other signs that someone or something living was nearby.

"No." He shook his head. "I was twelve when we moved from Montana to the monastery. We were in a bunker for a while before that, but our supplies ran out. Until you guys found us, I'd never been anywhere else."

"What sort of education did you get?" Darius glanced back over his shoulder again. "Most schools closed when the plague was declared pandemic. You remember how to read and write?"

Rhys nodded. "Yeah. My mom was a teacher. She homeschooled us and made sure to bring plenty of books and paper when we went into the bunker. Even stuff that wasn't appropriate for kids. She said we wouldn't have a chance to absorb the inappropriate stuff from the rest of the world the way we normally would, so she'd have to make sure we saw some of it however we could because she didn't want us to be . . . unprepared for reality, I guess?"

Kaleo smirked. "So were you? *Prepared?*"

To everyone's amusement, Rhys blushed and shook his head in rapid denial. After a moment, he began to smile as well.

Darius's dark eyes were intent upon him. "But you didn't have those inappropriate books at the monastery when you were old enough to need 'em."

"No." Rhys grew quiet. For a while, Gabe had been the one he'd gone to when puberty had left him a mass of confusion and conflicting impulses. But soon it had been Gabe who had been the inspiration for most of his confusion, making it harder to talk freely with him. "I didn't."

The others fell silent as though they were considering the implications of what Rhys had revealed, of just how sheltered and ignorant he'd been when they'd found him.

"Shit," Kaleo murmured finally.

Rhys offered him a wan smile. "I'm . . . trying to catch up."

Another beat of silence passed, and then they all burst into laughter.

Kaleo clapped Rhys on the shoulder. "You're gonna be okay, Cooper." He grinned, and Rhys grinned back.

It felt good to laugh, to be accepted. He met Darius's satisfied smile and began to understand just what he'd meant when he'd spoken of the good things that could come of embracing his situation. As he began to be receptive to the Jugs, they started to receive him as well.

His enthusiasm for the new camaraderie waned, though, whenever he felt Jacob's eyes upon him. The previous day, he'd been gathering supplies in a pharmacy when he'd overheard Jacob approach Darius about the fact that none of the Jugs were trying to infect him anymore. He'd complained about Rhys receiving preferential treatment, and he'd all but propositioned Darius to infect him if he wouldn't order any of the other Jugs to do it.

"My men make their own choices," Darius had said. "And so do I."

Jacob had sniffed. "And what do you choose to do about me?"

"You'll know when I decide." Darius had walked away then, shutting down any further argument. Jacob's glares at Rhys had been particularly murderous for the rest of the day.

From the first day they'd met, Jacob had hated him for reasons Rhys couldn't begin to understand, but it seemed the longer they were with the Jugs, the more virulent that hatred became. It wore an edge of madness, his eyes burning the way Father Maurice's had in those last years. The farther south they traveled, the more convinced Rhys became that Jacob might actually harm him, if he could find the opportunity.

He could only pray he'd become a Jug and have the ability to defend himself before that day arrived.

⋀⋀⋀

IT WAS ASTONISHING the way the vegetation had taken over, Rhys observed during the endless hours on the road. Grass and weeds took root in thick layers of moss on the roofs of houses. Endless patches of ivy climbed trees and the slumping, splintering skeletons of telephone poles, and it carved lines in the rotting wood siding of houses. In some places, it had even managed to work its way inside the buildings, as though nature were trying to reclaim the space within, as well.

Leaves and debris had long since clogged all the gutters and drains, allowing the rains to cut runnels through the asphalt, hastening the crumbling of the roads. Wind and ice storms had brought down trees and large branches and even entire hillsides in landslides they had to pick their way across.

Block by block, the Jugs systematically canvassed one neighborhood after another, looking for signs of human habitation. The motorcycle patrol periodically circled back to report in. A few packs of wild dogs had to be convinced with gunshots that no one in the squad would be easy prey.

Mostly, though, if they weren't making camp, they just walked. Questions passed back and forth were about the only way to break up the tedium.

"Why the capitol?" Rhys asked once they had reached Salem proper. He was chewing on a piece of jerky and sharing a water bottle with Toby while they chatted. "We're heading straight there. Why?"

"Because survivors head for places that can be barricaded or might have plenty of nonperishable food supplies," Toby explained, tearing into his own rations. "Basements. Fallout shelters. Cafeterias. It was no accident we found that colony on a college campus: dormitories are popular. So are prisons. Thinning out the revs is just a happy consequence of first sweep. The primary objective is recovering civvies. It won't do us a damn bit of good to kill the revs if they've already killed the survivors we failed to extract. So we hit the most likely shelters first, then we divide the area into sectors and begin clearing it one sector at a time."

Rhys nodded and looked down at the crumbling map. "All right. So, um, after the capitol, we'll head . . . here?"

He tapped the Willamette University campus with his index finger, and Toby grinned.

"Exactly."

Patrolling urban areas was far more exhausting than the country had been. Rhys's arms ached with the strain of carrying a gun at the ready across his chest, because despite the advantage the scanners afforded them in seeing ahead around blind corners, they still proceeded as if danger might leap out from behind the next wall. Stops for meals were brief and conversation terse before they continued on, everyone sober and alert despite the silence and apparent calm.

He nearly dropped the damn rifle when Joe's scanner chimed.

"Signature?" Darius murmured, and Joe nodded once.

"Two o'clock. Five heat sources. Definitely human."

"Get ready, people. Someone's just signed our dance card."

Sweat had begun to trickle down Rhys's forehead long before they reached the street where Joe had detected the heat signatures. Though he should have been used to it by now, he still jumped when Darius shouted.

"Attention! This is Sergeant First Class Darius Murrell, formerly of the United States Army. We're here on search and rescue, looking for plague survivors on behalf of the civilian interim government. None of us are infected with the Rot. You will be safe in our presence. Repeat: we are *not infected*. If you are human, put down any weapons you're carrying and acknowledge. We are fully armed. If you do not acknowledge within five seconds of visual contact, or if you make *any* hostile move, we *will* open fire!"

He hadn't finished speaking when a low, savage growl echoed down the silent street.

The revs moved inhumanly fast. How did he always forget how fast they moved? Rhys hit the ground beside Jacob at Darius's barked order, only to be deafened a moment later by the rapid explosions of assault rifles firing. He cringed for a moment, then got his weapon out from underneath him and scanned the perimeter formed by the Jugs to see if anything had gotten past them.

Nothing had. In a moment, the gunfire ceased, and five bloody bodies lay dying.

Like the revs that had attacked him in the monastery, they were nude, or clothed only in the rags they hadn't managed to shred or discard in the months or years since they'd been infected. They looked small and pathetic, broken in the street as the Jugs approached and systematically shot them in the head, one after the other. By now, Rhys knew to stay down until Darius gave the all clear.

A sudden chill went through him, the hairs on the back of his neck prickling, and Rhys's eyes tracked toward Jacob, who crouched to his left.

While Rhys held his rifle aimed forward, Jacob's was across his body.

Aimed at Rhys.

Jacob's eyes gleamed with malice, and his finger stroked the trigger. After a moment, he pulled it away so that it wasn't trained on Rhys but not before he'd made his message clear.

They didn't have to be alone for Jacob to arrange an "accident." He could have shot Rhys at any time during the engagement, and no one would have known until the gunfire had died down. And he could have claimed it was just a mishap.

"You look like you're gonna puke, dude." Kaleo clapped Rhys on the shoulder as Darius gave them permission to get up. "Surprised you haven't in all this time. Yo, Toby! He's made it over two weeks. You owe me ten, man."

Toby jogged back to them from helping to deliver the coups de grâce and drew a tattered bill out of his pocket, snorting. "Enjoy your toilet paper, dude."

"Enough chatter." Darius's eyes scanned Rhys intently. He said nothing, but Rhys felt the concern in that perusal. "Keep searching for heat sources, and hope the gunfire and smoke doesn't draw more. Gather wood to burn the bodies. It'll be approaching dusk by the time we're done, so we'll start looking for somewhere to camp."

Nodding, Rhys shouldered his rifle and began gathering scraps of wood from all the rotting fences lining the properties along the road. No other revenants appeared as they set fire to the bodies, and they left the blaze behind once they were certain it was contained.

The danger from the revs was gone for the moment, but every time he sneaked a look at Jacob, Jacob smirked and began whistling a tuneless ditty.

⚠ ⚠ ⚠

Willamette University had a haunted feel about it, and after the squad's last experience on a college campus, everyone was understandably tense. What had likely once been a broad lawn overlooked the capitol. Rhys could imagine it once upon a time as a picturesque place to study, as he'd seen characters do in videos before the plague. Now, it was a nearly impassable tangle of weeds, brambles, and saplings. A stone sculpture that had formed the centerpiece of a fountain had toppled, probably during an earthquake, and the fountain itself was nothing more than a dry pit filled with dirt and matted, half-rotten leaves. A quintet of massive sequoias towered on one of the lawns defiantly, as though they alone were untouched by all that had befallen the world and its population since their planting.

"We've got survivors here," Rhys heard Toby murmur as they approached the first building. "Or there were not long ago. Look."

He pointed to the basement windows nearly buried in the tall grasses. One of them had been wiped free of grime in a hasty circle.

Darius gave a tight nod. "If we find anything human, Joe and Xolani, you get Rhys and Houtman out. Until they're confirmed positive for Alpha, we have to assume whatever they do have is airborne." He turned his grim gaze to Rhys and offered the slightest hint of an encouraging smile. "Remember that: *Beta's airborne.* Just to be safe, you keep a distance of at least twenty yards until we get the survivors on the boats and headed back to base."

"Okay." Rhys nodded with a tense, jerky motion.

The basement with the peephole was empty, and the disappointment settled like a weight on the company. The murmured chatter dropped away to grim silence as they braced themselves to leave empty-handed.

"Dining hall next." Darius looked up and down the empty passages. "If they're not here, that's where they'll be."

A discovery on the quad made Kaleo break into a wide grin. "Whoever it is, they've left us a bread-crumb trail."

Scraps of industrial-grade terry cloth too pristine to have been in the open for long formed a path across the weed-eaten field.

"They've been holing up in the laundry." Toby began smiling.

Darius nodded, studying the scraps. "Probably nesting there to keep warm in winter."

Rhys frowned. "Why leave a trail?"

"He probably heard the gunfire." Darius pushed himself up and continued leading the way, wading into the tall grasses. "Like we saw last time, survivors can be skittish. If they're alone they might be suffering isolation psychosis. They've been holed up so long, they don't like being in exposed positions. So most likely, he came to see what was going on, but he didn't feel safe out in the open, close to the action, and went back to his hidey-hole. He really didn't want to be missed, though, and he doesn't know we have the infrared scanners, so he left a trail, hoping it would be us who found it, not the revs." He looked around, as if hoping to see the survivor emerge from somewhere. "Go slowly, people. We don't want to panic him or miss a pack of revs because we got too excited."

They slowed their pace across the quad, Bailey and Kaleo paying even closer attention to their scanners.

Rhys sidled up to Xolani, pitching his voice low. "Why do they think it's only one person?"

"If it were a group—assuming they weren't intent on remaining isolated like the last colony we found—someone would probably be brave enough to break cover and approach us."

"So, Darius thinks Jacob and I need two people watching to keep us away from one survivor? We know not to go near anyone by now."

She smirked. "No. I'm just beached for the next few days where contact with civvies is concerned."

"You're wound— Oh." Rhys's face began to burn. "Oh."

Xolani chuckled and took the lead, which thankfully meant he wouldn't have to see the wicked amusement in her eyes.

"Definitely only one heat source." Kaleo nodded toward the building they were approaching. "Dining hall. Right on the money."

They shuffled Rhys and Jacob toward the back of the formation as they filed into the derelict building. Darius began calling out warnings long before they found anywhere that a survivor might be hiding.

They found the survivor in the industrial laundry room in the basement beneath the kitchen.

"I'm not armed!" a male voice called, his voice rough from disuse, from behind a barricade of laundry machines as Darius barked another warning.

"Out." Darius jerked his head toward the door, looking at Rhys and Jacob. "Wait at the end of the hall."

Rhys didn't need the pressure of Joe's hand nudging at his shoulder. He turned and walked out the door with Joe and Jacob, Xolani bringing up the rear, as he tried to contain his curiosity about the first other civilian he'd met since he and Jacob had been rescued.

After a few minutes, the rest of the Jugs emerged from the laundry room with the survivor in their midst. Rhys wasn't able to garner much of an impression of him in the dark corridor, save that he was painfully thin and his face was nearly swallowed by a wild mane of dark hair and beard. Rhys couldn't get close enough to smell the stranger, but he suspected the guy hadn't bathed in a while. Kaleo took position with them, and they waited until the rest of the Jugs and the survivor had turned toward the exit at the opposite end of the corridor before following twenty yards behind.

The daylight didn't offer any more clues about the sort of person they'd found. His thin back was to Rhys, and all Rhys could see was that his clothes were in fairly decent condition. He must have been scavenging in the dormitories for things to wear.

Rhys listened as the breeze carried wisps of conversation back to him. In spite of understanding the reasons he had to keep his distance, he felt exiled.

Infected.

"Too much rev activity . . . any length of time." Fragments of Toby's words were lost when the wind gusted. "Especially with Cooper . . . We gotta . . . back to the boats . . . quarantine."

"Agreed." Darius raised his voice over the wind. "Okay, people. We're on recovery protocol now. We're heading back to Portland to get the boats. Xolani, Joe, stick with Rhys and Houtman, make sure they stay out of contagion range. We'll take the most direct route, no detours for patrolling. Move out."

Rhys had mostly been watching Darius, but he couldn't miss the sudden, rigid tension that straightened the survivor's spine when Darius had said "Rhys and Houtman." He had only a split second to pray that God wouldn't be that cruel when the black-haired man turned. His indigo eyes widened beneath strong, unmistakable brows.

Rhys took a step forward without even intending to, stopped only by Joe's huge hand.

Suddenly, everything hurt.

"Gabe?"

17

SACRIFICE

"Please!" Darius scowled as he watched Rhys try to shove past Xolani and Joe, each gently holding him back.

"Sorry, Cooper," he heard Joe murmur, his voice carrying downwind. "Can't let you do it."

From the corner of his eye, Darius saw the civvie they'd rescued looking back and forth at them in confusion. "That's Rhys! Why won't you let him go?"

"We're waiting to make sure he's not infected with the plague, son." Darius never took his gaze off Rhys.

Rhys gave Darius a pleading look across the yards separating them. "Please! I just want to talk to him. Can't I talk to him?"

Xolani gave him a sympathetic look. "You might infect him. You can't go near him until we know you're safe. Stand down."

"But—"

Joe's jaw flexed, and the hand he'd held up as a barricade dropped. He reached down and jerked Rhys's sidearm from its holster, thrusting it butt-first at Rhys.

"You want us to let you go, Cooper? Fine. But only if you tell me you're ready to put this to his head if you have to. Because if he gets infected, someone's gotta do it. You gonna be the one?"

Rhys's struggles stopped abruptly, and he gave Joe a horrified stare. "What?"

"Well? Don't you want to go?" Joe thrust the gun toward Rhys again. Darius and the rest of his people stirred uncomfortably, because they knew—even if Rhys didn't—where gentle Joe's sudden anger had come from.

Rhys looked pale and ill as he shook his head quickly, the tension leaving his body. "No."

After a moment, Joe backed down as well, offering Rhys the gun much more gently. "Good."

Something in Darius ached at the way Rhys shut down, his usually expressive face growing stiff and blank. Off to the side, Darius saw Houtman's eyes seeming to gleam with malicious pleasure, and Darius wasn't at all happy with the way he was looking at their newfound civvie.

"Sorry." Rhys put the pistol back in its holster and glanced at them all before dropping his gaze to the ground. "I'm sorry."

"Don't sweat it." Xolani ruffled his hair. "There's not one of us wouldn't want to do the same."

Darius cleared his throat, breaking the tense silence that fell when Rhys didn't respond. "That's enough, people. We got a lot of ground to cover. Let's move out."

Rhys followed them, his head still bowed.

Darius couldn't blame Rhys for his reaction. Xolani had nailed it. There wasn't a single person in Delta Company who wouldn't struggle with the same impulse if they were suddenly confronted with someone they thought they'd lost. But his people had had years to get used to their losses. Rhys didn't understand yet that he could never go back to who and what he'd been before.

Would he choose to go back, if he could?

It shouldn't matter what Rhys would do in a perfect world. None of Darius's people were particularly happy with what life had dealt them. They'd just learned to live with it. Rhys seemed to have been doing the same this last week.

That was what Darius had been trying to get him to do all along, wasn't it? Make the best of a bad situation? This had never been about what they would choose. Rhys would never be with him out of choice, except as an alternative to death.

All that mattered was what they had to do to survive.

The squad was quiet as they made their way through the silent city toward the interstate heading north. They gave Rhys his space, not attempting to draw him into conversation as they usually did, letting him hold his sullen silence. Every single one of them had confronted their own moments of futile yearning for the past.

Darius saw Toby's concerned eyes slide toward Joe, but Toby shook it off when he caught Darius looking. "Don't worry about it," he said with a shrug. "Joe's okay. You better handle your boy, though. Joe says he holds on to things too tight."

Darius flicked Toby a look, thinking about those nights of furtive tears. Rhys never cried when he thought anyone might see or hear, even when the last of his family had died. Darius recalled the detached dignity with which Rhys had walked away after the first time Darius had fucked him, and about the days of dutiful apathy that had followed. He'd been doing so much better that Darius had almost forgotten how miserable Rhys had been before.

He could almost hate this new civvie for putting that look back on Rhys's face.

"I need to find a way for them to talk. Not fair to deny the boy that chance."

"We weren't planning to ship out the next batch of survivors for another month. Our civvie will still be at base by the time we're sure Cooper's not infected."

"If you were him, would you be willing to wait that long?"

Toby shrugged again, scuffing a toe on the cracked asphalt of the old interstate. "Can't be helped. We've all made our sacrifices. He's a good kid, but that doesn't mean he's not going to have to do it, too. Give him something else to think about in the meantime." He flashed Darius a grin. "He turned a bit green when he saw Joe's burns, but I bet a belt or a good willow switch would get him back in line."

"You're assuming way too much, Toby." Darius forced a chuckle, refusing to let himself dwell on the image of Rhys with angry, red welts covering his back. That wasn't something he could ever do to someone who didn't want to be with him in the first place. "He might like being pushed around a bit, but it ain't like that."

"Maybe you're not assuming enough." Toby scoffed and shook

his head, dropping back into formation. "If I know anything, it's pain sluts, and our sweet little ingenue back there's got it written all over him, even if he doesn't know it. Keep him out of his head until his head gets right again. He'll be okay."

∧ ∧ ∧

THE REAL TROUBLE began after dinner that night, as they prepared to bed down in two adjoining conference rooms of a waterfront hotel.

"We've got a problem," Xolani murmured near his shoulder.

"I know." Darius gritted his teeth. In the past twenty minutes, he'd watched Rhys flatly refuse Kaleo, Bailey, and now, even Toby. He'd shrugged off their attempts to draw him aside, getting testier and more insulting each time.

As Darius watched, Rhys gave Toby a baleful look. "Leave me alone. Go play your sick games somewhere else. I'm not doing it."

Xolani glanced at the sliding partition separating the conference room, on the other side of which Gina, Jamie, and Titus were bunking with Gabriel. "He doesn't want to let them screw him where his friend can hear."

"Can you blame him?" Darius scowled. "What's the story there?"

"I don't really know. Rhys doesn't talk much about what happened at the monastery."

"Why not?"

She puffed out her cheeks in a sigh. "Because on day one I told him to keep his head down and not complain. I think he interpreted that to mean no one wanted to hear how bad things were for him in the past. Or maybe he's just conditioned to think no one will believe him or do anything to help."

"Just how bad do you think things were?"

"Bad." She cast a stinkeye at Houtman.

"Well, he talks to you all the time. He has to be saying something."

"A bit about his mom and sister. Enough about that guy"—she gestured toward the other room—"to make me suspect a bit of puppy love back in the day. But mostly he just asks questions. Wants to know what we're doing and why we do it. It's his first time out in the world. He's trying to get a handle on it."

"Does Houtman give him shit?"

"Not that Rhys will cop to, but yeah." Xolani pressed her lips together, the corners of her mouth whitening. "I've caught Houtman menacing Rhys several times now. And we've seen what happens when bullies and megalomaniacs become Jugs."

Darius gave her a sharp look. "You think it's that bad?"

Xolani rolled her eyes. "For a smart guy, you miss a lot of shit happening right under your nose."

"I'm busy running this unit. That's why you're my eyes and ears. So, report."

"Fine. See how skinny Rhys is? Houtman doesn't have that problem, now does he? Nor did any of the casualties whose bodies we found that day. At least not to such a severe degree."

"Been wondering about that." Darius laced his fingers behind his head, stretching. "Could he be sick? Have some sort of wasting illness?"

"He's been starved. Maybe you missed the padlock on the pantry back at the monastery. Guess who had the key?"

Darius's eyebrows lifted. "Houtman?"

"I heard him bragging to Toby about all the responsibility he had, running the monastery with his dad, making sure no one got more than their due. He was in charge of supervising their food stores." Xolani's scar twitched. "How much you want to bet withholding meals was a favored punishment of the late, unlamented Father Maurice? Rhys will be lucky if he doesn't have organ damage from muscle loss."

"Shit." Darius folded his arms across his chest. "But that's still just conjecture. We don't know what happened."

"Maybe not. But if I had that night at the monastery to do over again, I wouldn't offer to infect Houtman with Alpha. I don't trust him with that sort of power."

Darius looked at her a long moment and sighed. "Noted."

"Guess that leaves the question of what we're going to do about Rhys tonight. You know, we did a pretty good scan before we set up camp. There's nothing around this hotel. If we wanted to take separate rooms . . ."

"No." Darius stared her down. He tried to think like their leader, to consider the greater implications for future recruiting efforts, the slippery slope of changing the rules at the whims of their recruits. "We don't break safety protocol. Not to baby a shy recruit. When we camp in an area that hasn't been thoroughly swept, we bunk together in a secured location where we can't be cut off from one another."

"I know the protocol," she snapped. "But that doesn't leave us very many options for getting Rhys to bend over for someone tonight."

"I made it pretty fucking clear what would be expected of him that first time." Darius glared at her. He didn't even know why he was irritated, except that the thought of what would happen if Rhys chose death over allowing himself to be infected was way more upsetting than it should be. "Unless you're willing to tell me there's no point in continuing trying to infect him, then none of us have a damn bit of choice, short of killing him or letting him die."

"*I don't know.*" She met his glower with one of her own. "It might be pointless by now, but I'm not willing to gamble his life on a maybe."

"Then we do what we have to do." Darius felt a bitter satisfaction at throwing her words from that night in the chapel back at her. He rose and stalked away before she could manage a retort.

Rhys stood against the far wall with his arms folded across his chest, staring at the partition as though he could see past it to his friend. Darius grabbed his thin arm in a bruising grip, wrenching a soft cry from him. Heads came up, gazes falling upon them. He knew Xolani was watching, possibly itching to interfere, and his irritation became anger. Anger at her for talking him into this scheme in the beginning, anger at himself for agreeing to it, anger at Rhys for being a recalcitrant little shit with such a misplaced sense of modesty.

"You got ten seconds to get your ass to your blanket, boy, or I throw you over my shoulder and carry you there."

Those dark-fringed hazel eyes widened, darting around the room to the other Jugs.

"You think they're gonna help you? Five."

Scowling with far more defiance than he usually mustered, Rhys jerked his arm out of Darius's grasp and stalked over to his bedroll. Darius followed, grabbing the back of his shirt and yanking it up.

"Strip, or I cut it off you."

Rhys's eyes flashed furiously. His body quivered, and Darius could see the snarl of rebellion twisting his lips. Darius seized his bony arms, snatching Rhys against him.

"I told you from the start how this would go, boy." He fought to check the frustration that wanted to tighten his hands on Rhys's arms until he cried out in pain, until he wore bruises for a week. He made himself pull it back, trying to remember how easily he could injure Rhys. "We're all in, remember? Both of us. No backing out. That was our agreement. You only got one other choice here, and I ain't letting you choose that. Not now. Not after all this. So you strip and lay your skinny ass down."

If Rhys's glare could burn, it would have incinerated Darius on the spot. The boy wasn't afraid; he was livid. His hands shook as he pushed his jeans down with rough, jerky movements, and frustrated tears gleamed in his eyes.

Sweet Jesus help him, even the boy's anger was a turn-on. That was the worst part. Darius would do this, and he would like it.

"Shirt, too." He didn't even know why he needed Rhys totally nude, except that he had to break down any bit of resistance Rhys mustered, to strip him bare in every possible way. He had never wanted to break Rhys, and yet now nothing less than the boy's total capitulation would do. Darius could tell himself he was trying to prevent this happening again, but it was more than that.

Now he understood, Darius thought in some deep, sickened part of himself, what they meant about it being an act of power.

This was the path they had put themselves upon, he and Rhys, that night in the chapel. He couldn't flinch. Not if it meant letting Rhys die. Too late to back out now.

Too damn late.

One of those angry tears spilled from the corner of Rhys's eye, but he obeyed. He didn't resist physically until Darius refused to let him roll to his hands and knees. Then he began to fight, and Jesus have mercy, that was good, too. The boy was hard, and that wood knocked against Darius each time Rhys tried to thrash and writhe. He pushed at Darius's shoulders as Darius loomed over him, trying to clamp his legs shut when Darius shoved them apart to work lube into his ass. Finally, Darius pinned both of his wrists to the floor above his head with one hand, stretching out that thin torso as he guided himself to Rhys's struggling, bucking ass and thrust.

His mouth covered Rhys's, not to kiss but to swallow his scream. He wondered if it sounded as loud to the rest of them as it did right there above the boy.

Despite it all, being inside Rhys was as close to being in paradise as Darius thought he'd ever get. Rhys didn't give up the fight right away. He kept resisting, even pinned as he was, and he was so hot and tight and amazing, seizing Darius's cock with each effort to writhe away. And then the contact of Darius's mouth upon Rhys's *did* become a kiss, his lips crushing, grinding against that soft, pink mouth, his tongue invading. He took possession of Rhys's unwilling mouth as surely as he had the rest of Rhys, until the struggles stopped, tapering away to sobbing gasps.

Only then did Darius begin to move, driving into Rhys, releasing his bony wrists to grab his thighs and shove them up to his chest. He half expected Rhys to begin fighting again. But when those hands gripped Darius's biceps and moved up to his shoulders, it was to pull him closer.

"Say you want it, boy." Darius panted, plunging into the incredible heat of his ass.

Rhys shook his head violently, his lips clamped shut. Now, even now, as he reached down Darius's back to grab the flexing muscles of his ass, he still tried to resist letting anyone hear that he enjoyed this. That he wanted it.

That wouldn't do. He'd make Rhys yield everything to him.

Another brutal, bruising kiss. A hand in Rhys's hair, yanking his head back. Teeth at Rhys's neck, so hard and gripping he might have broken the skin with a little more pressure.

"Say you want it, boy!" Another rough, driving thrust punctuated by the slap of Darius's hips against Rhys's ass.

Rhys cried out before he could stop the sound, his face

contorted with the struggle. His lean cock was a furious shade of red, shining with trails of pre-cum and jabbing against Darius's belly. Rhys bit his lips again, trying to stifle any more sounds. When Darius forced his tongue between them, he tasted blood.

"Say it."

A near scream on the next thrust, and the one after. A torrent of sound like the first furious surge of water from a breaking dam.

"Say it!" Hard. He was fucking Rhys so hard they'd both be sore in the morning. But he couldn't yield. He couldn't. He wouldn't let Rhys die because someone, somewhere, had taught him shame.

"*Please!*" Rhys wailed. The fingers of one of Rhys's hands tightened into claws on Darius's ass, and the other moved between them, gripping his own cock. Rhys cried out as though the contact hurt, and it very well might have, as stiff and swollen as he was.

"Oh no, you don't." Darius jerked the hand away. "You say it or you don't come."

"Please. Pleasepleasepleaseplease . . ." A breathless, desperate litany as Darius drilled him over and over. "Oh God, please! Please! Darius!"

"Say it. Say it!" Darius's breaths were explosive pants against Rhys's collarbone. Sweat dripped down his shoulders, and his muscles began to vibrate with the effort of holding back.

He wouldn't stop. He wouldn't. Not until Rhys had given him everything.

Rhys howled again. Yearning. Full of agonized pleasure. And when the cry had faded, a whisper followed.

"Please. I want it. I want it. I want it. God, please . . . Please . . ."

Darius groaned and devoured Rhys's yells, biting at those bruised and bloodied lips, roaring his own release into that captive mouth as blinding white light strobed behind his eyelids. He pumped and pumped into Rhys until he was certain he'd spent everything he had. Not just cum, but every ounce of fluid within him—blood and tears and sweat and bile—leaving Darius wrung out and bone-dry. But before he collapsed, he jacked Rhys off, fast and hard, until the boy spurted over both of them.

He wanted to be tender as his weight crushed Rhys, but he

couldn't. Not after what he'd done. He'd lost the right to ever be tender again.

Sickened with himself, he pushed his body off Rhys and pulled up his fatigues with jerky movements. He looked down at the pale belly streaked with jizz, at the dingy carpet, at anything but those wide eyes, where he was certain a hundred accusations must be written.

"We all make sacrifices to live in this shithole of a world, boy." Even through his remorse, Darius's body hummed with satisfaction. If not for the circumstances, he would have called that the best fuck of his life. "Told you from the start I didn't have time to be a good man. Now I've gone and done the one thing I swore to myself I'd never do. At least you'll live. Sure as hell hope that's worth something."

He walked away to the other half of the room, beyond the partition, before Rhys could answer.

18

SURVIVAL

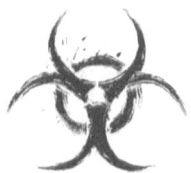

"You okay?" Gabe asked as Rhys propped his rake in the rotting shed. "Yeah." He shook his head in disgust. "I just don't get why he hates us so much. We've never done anything to him."

"He doesn't need a reason. He's just an asshole." Gabe shrugged. "You're younger and smaller, which makes you an easy target. And I'm competition."

"Huh?"

"Come on. Cady's growing up. Few more years down the line, he's going to get tired of dating Rosy Palm, and I'm the only other eligible guy in the way of the obvious target. Unless he wants to make a play for Mrs. Merkle."

"Ew. Gross." Rhys shuddered. "Why would he even think you'd be interested?"

Gabe gave Rhys a look that said he was being stupid. "Because I'm eighteen, and someday I'm going to get tired of dating Rosy Palm, too, and there aren't any other options around here."

"But what about—" Rhys broke off, profoundly grateful for the dark shed that hid the heat in his face. Did Gabe really not consider him an option?

After three years, how could Gabe still not understand the infatuation Rhys had developed almost the moment they'd met on the journey from Montana? Did he not realize that Rhys lay in his small room each *night replaying every little kindness, every time Gabe leaped to his defense against Jacob's bullying? Did he not know that when Rhys's hand stole under the blanket to ease the tight ache in his nuts, he imagined Gabe? Brave, courteous, playful, older, wiser, knowledgeable Gabe?*

"What?" Gabe watched him patiently.

"What about me?" Rhys whispered, trembling at his own daring.

Gabe stared for a confused moment as Rhys's heart pounded, his palms sweating. He didn't know which of them moved, but they were only a breath apart when Father Maurice came thundering out of the monastery.

ΛΛΛ

"So, WHO'S YOUR TYPE, RHYS?" Xolani asked, pulling Rhys from his reverie as they loaded their packs into the inflatable boats Darius's people had stored in one of the empty luxury condos on the riverfront in downtown Portland. The boat carrying Gabe and half the Jugs in the squad had already left the dock, and the motorcycles had been stashed in one of the waterfront buildings for the next patrol to grab when they came down this side of the river.

"Sorry?" He was aching again. The two-day walk from Salem to Portland had been exhausting, and each night it had ended the same way it had the day they found Gabe. Each night he fought not to give in to Darius, not to debase himself where Gabe would hear and know. Each night, Darius inevitably overpowered him. He was covered in bruises from the struggle, and God help him, despite his misery, every sight of them, every flash of memory about how they'd been acquired, sent a surge of arousal pulsing through him.

He was a pervert. Just like Jacob and Father Maurice had always said.

"What you see here is only a small part of Delta Company." She idly flipped one of her knives in her hand, waiting to pass him the next pack. "Some of the other squads have been scouting east toward the Cascades, some are going west toward the coast, but at any given time at the fort, we have around seventy troops stationed, working in teams to scavenge supplies, repair infrastructure, even tend the crops we plant when we settle in one place for long enough to need them. Only about twenty percent of the company is female, which means most of the rest either like men or have learned to be fluid enough about such things to consider it. Whether or not they're spoken for is another matter. Darius told me to figure out who to introduce you to. See if there's someone you'll like better than him."

Rhys stumbled, quickly turning away to keep her from seeing the shock that had punched him in the gut. Darius was just going to get rid of him, hand him off to someone else?

"You'll be the belle of the ball, cutie." Kaleo wandered by in time to overhear and earned himself a glower. "Not often we get fresh meat."

The look Jacob shot Rhys from behind Xolani's back could have incinerated him. Somehow, Jacob hated him even more now that he was fighting it than he had when Rhys had been reluctantly willing.

Xolani scoffed. "You're full of shit, Kaleo. I know Schuyler. You might be able to do who you want out in the field, but back on base?" She smirked. "She'll have your balls if you even think about doing someone else without her permission."

"Who says I won't have permission?" Kaleo wandered off with a grin and a cheeky wink, leaving Rhys's face burning with humiliation.

Xolani's look was almost pitying, and that was even worse.

"Don't worry about it." She sighed. "Kaleo gets inappropriate with everyone who hasn't kicked his ass at least once, no matter how much he actually likes them. Sooner or later, someone breaks his nose and he behaves himself for a while. We'll toughen you up, you'll beat him down, and he'll be your friend for life."

Rhys grimaced, unconvinced, as he accepted the next bag Xolani tossed to him. "So, what, am I supposed to *date*?"

She snickered. "Well, I doubt anyone expects you to buy them dinner."

"I think—" Rhys swallowed, looking away across the river where it ran between high concrete banks. The docks of the marina had long since begun to rot into the river. The boards of the short stretch remaining creaked alarmingly any time they put weight on them, which was why Rhys and Jacob, the lightest of the party, had been nominated to load the inflatables. Rhys stepped cautiously around Jacob and onto the dock to tuck the rucksack in the boat.

"What?" Xolani watched him carefully when Rhys hesitated to continue.

"I don't want to do that. Meet anyone, I mean. Not for . . . that."

"Pay attention to where you're stepping," Xolani snapped at Jacob. The rotting boards gave a particularly loud creak as he pushed past Rhys with a bag of his own, exercising much less caution. Rhys saw Darius turn his head to watch them from beyond Xolani, his dark eyes squinted against the morning sun and his mouth pulled down as he listened to Titus and Jamie report. "I already told you why this is important, Rhys."

"Why isn't Darius enough?"

"I've already explained that, too. Exposure from multiple partners could make all the difference."

"Isn't that my risk to take?" Rhys demanded, tucking the last bag into the inflatable and straightening to face her as Jacob preceded him toward land. He dropped his voice to a near whisper, choking on the humiliating surge of desperation at the idea of doing what he'd done with Darius and these other Jugs with more strangers. He couldn't bear the things Jacob would say to him every time he caught Rhys at an unguarded moment. He couldn't bear the thought that word would somehow reach Gabe of the deviant he'd become. "Please. It has to be enough. I can't do it."

Xolani's eyes softened with sympathy, but before she could speak, a loud *crack* split the eerie silence of the downtown waterfront, and the dock beneath him disappeared. Rhys tried to lunge forward to safety, colliding with Jacob, who was already leaping for the ramp leading up the concrete retaining wall. Jacob's foot caught Rhys square in the chest as he kicked back to push off against something solid, and with a startled yell, Rhys flew backward and plunged into the Willamette. Even in high summer, the mountain-fed waters were cold. He seized in shock and sucked in a lungful of liquid before he began flailing.

The splintery wooden piling that had supported the dock caught

Rhys's jeans, stalling his climb for the crystalline surface overhead. His lungs burned, and his efforts to tear himself free became frantic.

In the midst of his panicked struggles, a thread of peace tried to pierce his fear.

Maybe this was for the best. Maybe this was the way to save himself from the choice between horrific death and becoming something he couldn't stand to be.

Better than facing Jacob's hostility and the degradation Xolani and Darius were determined to press him into. Better than shaming himself in front of Gabe. All he had to do was stop struggling and he could join his mom and Cady and baby Caleb. No Rot. No perversion. No warped fight to survive and endure.

Hands plunged through the water and found him, pulling at his forearms. Already aching from three consecutive nights of trying to fight off Darius, Rhys felt as though his arms were being wrenched from their sockets. When he didn't budge, another body sliced through the water past him. The thick piling broke with a *snap* that was audible even in the water, and whoever had dove in ripped his jeans away from the snag. Another mighty heave jerked at his arms, and he broke the surface, gasping a desperate breath before spewing water from his lungs.

More hands hauled him up the concrete wall. They pounded on his back as he coughed and retched. When he managed to open his running eyes, Titus and Jamie were helping Xolani and Darius from the water. They each shook themselves as if unaffected by the impromptu swim and dropped down next to him.

"You damned lunatic!" Jacob was ranting, his clothing wet from the waist down. He looked pale and furious. "You grabbed me! You tried to drag me down with you! You did it on purpose! You're just not going to be happy until you manage to kill me, are you? Do you see what I've had to deal with all these years?" He glanced from one Jug to the next, beseeching.

"I didn't—" Another fit of coughing seized Rhys, and he vomited more water. He shook his head, but he knew it was useless to defend himself when Jacob tried to pin the blame for something on him.

Darius's hands—hands capable of snapping a wooden piling like a twig—began feeling carefully up and down Rhys's body, assessing for injury. "You okay, boy?"

Xolani's blunter inquiry overrode his. "Talk to me, Rhys. You all right?"

"Yeah, yeah." Rhys shivered, though the heat was making a steamy wrap out of his wet clothing. He turned his face toward Darius's thigh without thought, trying to block out light and activity and questions until he could gather himself again.

He thought about that moment of terrifying, seductive peace beckoning him to yield the fight and trembled even harder at how close he'd come to honestly giving up.

"Please don't make me do it." The whispered plea left him involuntarily, heedless of the presence of others.

After a moment, he felt Darius's hand on his hair, stroking the uneven hanks back. "Don't worry about that now. It's okay. I've got you."

When Rhys finally looked around again, the others had all left them there on the riverbank. They had all gone still, staring at Jacob, who stopped glowering at Rhys long enough to become aware of their regard.

The tension felt like a suffocating weight pressing Rhys into the ground. He pulled away from Darius's soothing hand, embarrassed by his frailty next to Darius's strength.

"What is it? What's happening?"

"Houtman sent you flying when he kicked you." Xolani's voice was flat, her mouth tight. "A good ten feet or more."

"I don't understand." Rhys coughed again. Jacob's eyes began to gleam, and his mouth curled into a diabolical smile.

Darius's hand tightened on Rhys's shoulder.

"He's a Jug."

19

BASE

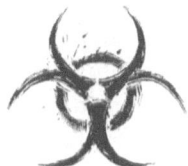

Darius watched Rhys swaying on the landing near Fort Vancouver. Little wonder. With all the kid had been through, Rhys probably hadn't slept more than a handful of hours combined in the past three nights. Not to mention the fifty-mile march and the nightly struggle that Darius couldn't let him win. Only the fact that he'd turned green once the boats had been in motion, and the looks of terror he kept giving Houtman since they'd realized he was a Jug, had kept Rhys from falling asleep during the trip downriver.

His feet practically dragged on the ground, but he still tried to pitch in, attempting three times to heave a supply-laden rucksack out of the boat until Kaleo took it from him.

"Take a break, cutie. You look ready to fall over. We got this."

Rhys flushed, but he made a point of getting out of the way. The same couldn't be said of Houtman who, for all his new status, wasn't doing much more than Rhys to help but who kept making pointed remarks about Rhys expecting everyone to wait on him. No one was paying Houtman much attention since his outburst on the waterfront. They could excuse knocking Rhys into the water when the dock began to fall apart as being a reflex response, but his accusations afterward had disgusted everyone. Darius felt a surge of pride in his people that they didn't mind Rhys not helping when he was obviously on the verge of collapse.

"I need to check in with Luis, give him our report," Darius told Xolani as they unloaded their gear from the boats. "Can you get the boy settled in?"

She lifted an eyebrow. "And just where's his billet gonna be?"

"My quarters." Darius gave a resigned shrug. "Doesn't make sense to put him anywhere else."

Her eyebrow crept higher. "You're not still thinking of foisting him off on someone else if you can find a taker?"

He glanced over at Rhys again, in time to see his chin touch his chest and then jerk up again as he nodded off. "I don't know." Darius pulled his rucksack out of the boat. "After all I've had to do to get him to this point, not sure it's right not to stick by him until it's done. Assuming he can stand having me there. If there's still a way to salvage this fucking mess after what I've done to him, maybe we can find it."

Xolani tugged hard on her braid, giving him an impatient look. "Bullshit angst isn't like you, Darius. You don't wear it well. Yeah, in a prettier time what you've been doing would be going over the line, but times sure as fuck aren't pretty right now."

"You think he sees it that way?"

"I think he's going to live," she answered frankly. "I think for his age, as isolated and abused as he's been, he's one damned self-possessed kid. But I also think he's just one more trauma away from cracking if we don't give him a chance to find his footing. He needs something stable, and handing him off to a stranger isn't going to do him any favors. He's tough, but everyone has a breaking point. I think a few days of at least being able to have some privacy for what he has to do and getting to know more of our people can only be a good thing. Besides"—her gaze flicked toward Houtman—"I'm not sure Rhys would be safe in the barracks."

"Right." Darius grimaced, handing her his pack. "Put him in my quarters. Tell him to get some sleep if he can. Put Houtman in the barracks. I think a few weeks of bunking with people who won't put up with his shit might just adjust his attitude. Let Rhys know I'll check on him later."

⋀⋀⋀

DARIUS WAS WELL aware that he'd made everything worse.

Yesterday, it had seemed essential to ask Xolani to scout for candidates among the other men at the fort who could take over shepherding Rhys through the process until he was a Jug. It would be better for the kid. Rhys couldn't possibly trust Darius any longer, and it wasn't like he'd had a lot of interest in Darius to begin with, however strongly he responded when Darius pushed him. Maybe someone who was more his type would be able to help him along more effectively. Darius had thought he would pawn Rhys off on someone new, someone nicer, someone who understood the kid, and go about his business.

Now he didn't know what to do. Rhys's despair at the idea of being available to everyone had been obvious, and his fear of Houtman was palpable. Darius wasn't sure he could safely let Rhys out of his sight. Either Rhys would kill himself or Houtman would do it for him. Which left it up to Darius.

Had he done the unforgivable? Or would Rhys understand that Darius just wanted him to live? And when had it begun to matter so much?

That morning in the dormitory, after the failed operation with the colony, of course. That was when it had started to matter what Rhys thought and felt. Darius had nearly killed the boy on sheer reflex when Rhys's nightmare-driven scream had jerked Darius out of his sleep only an hour or so after he'd gotten off watch. If he had been just an instant slower to come to his senses, Rhys would have bled to death there on those musty mattresses.

Rhys should have been petrified once he'd realized how dangerous the man fucking him was.

Instead, he'd kissed Darius with so much goddamn *need*.

Darius wasn't sure why he'd turned rough in response. Maybe he'd just wanted to avoid the urge to make love to Rhys, or maybe he'd wanted to *show* Rhys just how dangerous he could be, to convince him that Darius wasn't anything close to what he wanted. Either way, he hadn't been prepared for Rhys's eager response. And he couldn't have been prepared for just how addictive that response would be.

Darius might have been able to work things out if Rhys's

intractable reluctance to consider having sex with anyone else was the only obstacle. But Darius's possessive streak was back and worse than ever. The closer they'd drawn to base, goaded by the presence of Rhys's adolescent crush, the more willing Darius had become to pulp the face of anyone who even considered sticking his dick in the boy. Rhys had kept his distance from his onetime friend, but Darius had seen him looking at Gabriel with yearning naked on his face.

And Gabriel himself had been worse.

"What have you been doing to Rhys?" he'd demanded furiously after that first night, after Darius had made Rhys scream. Gabriel's hands had been fisted at his sides, his body tense and ready to launch himself at Darius. He'd had no idea that Darius could pulverize him with a single blow. And that he wanted to. And that challenging Darius wasn't helping the situation. So before either of them did anything stupid, Darius had told Gabriel everything.

He wondered if Rhys would thank him for trying to make his friend understand. Or would he hate Darius for exposing what he considered his shame?

It wasn't acceptable. Rhys *needed* to be exposed to other partners for at least another week for his best chance at survival. Darius couldn't spare him that, no matter how reluctant both of them were.

So now what the fuck was he supposed to do?

Darius shook his head at himself and headed across the grounds to the barracks where Luis had set up his office. He didn't have time to figure all that shit out right this moment. Now he had to check in with Delta Company's *other* CO.

Luis Martinez was Darius's best friend, for all that Luis had been an officer. They'd fucked occasionally, when neither of them had anything better to do, but they weren't really compatible. So when the Jugs had been exiled from Colorado Springs and split into companies, he and Luis had divided the responsibility of leading Delta Company. Luis was the natural strategist and administrator while Darius oversaw operations. The partnership had worked well.

Luis greeted Darius with a smile when Darius entered his office. Sitting on the desk were two glasses of what could only be Titus's moonshine, so strong Darius could damn near see the distortion of fumes rising from it.

"So, what's this I hear about you taking on recruits?" Luis asked when Darius finished reporting on the patrol's efforts to clear south and west of Portland. Darius knocked back his shot. The alcohol burned pleasantly in his stomach, and he relaxed for the first time since Titus's motorcycle scouting had tracked the infrared signatures of a suspected pack of revenants to the monastery outside Newberg. "I thought we'd agreed—"

"I didn't have a choice." Darius offered him a wry smile. "Xolani's big-sister switch got hit or something. She would have gutted me if I'd let Cooper die. As for the other one—" Darius's smiled became a grimace. "There was a chance he'd been infected, too. I couldn't make the offer to one without making it to them both."

"Well, that's a problem for us." Luis swirled the liquor in his glass. He was still on his first shot. Darius realized he'd probably given away a lot of his present conflict with how quickly he'd downed his first drink in comparison. "How the hell are we supposed to keep telling our people hands off the civvies now?"

"These weren't exactly normal circumstances. We didn't decide to fuck these guys just to do something new and different, you know?"

"Yeah, but we had a deal, man. After we took out Charlie Company . . ."

"I know," Darius snapped. "Xolani's starting to think we need to implement Bravo Company's way of doing things. I'm not really comfortable with that, but we may have to open the door to other exceptions in tightly controlled circumstances. But right now, it's these recruits I gotta deal with." He subsided and held his glass out for a refill. "I think I screwed up."

Luis topped them both off. "How?"

"Offering someone no one seems to like a spot on the team, for one. Houtman has been rubbing everyone the wrong way. And Rhys . . . Jesus, I have no idea what the fuck I'm doing there. Kid's got no business anywhere near this life, but the other option was him dying so what the fuck was I supposed to do?" Darius took a burning gulp of the hooch. "He's been through a lot, and he's stayed tough, but he's pushing back on doing what he needs to do to survive. I'm not even sure anymore if it's that he's been screwed up by religion or if he's just too modest or what. If I can't find a way to get him to play ball, this may have all been for nothing."

Luis gave him a level look. "Are either of them going to contribute enough to the unit to make it worth the disruption?"

Darius fought the urge to glower and made himself look at the situation as objectively as he could, analyzing it with the cold calculus of survival. "Houtman? I doubt it, but that's a done deal. Rhys? Yeah. I think he will." Darius gave a firm nod. "He's untrained, but he's a survivor. Scrawny, but stubborn as all fuck. He works hard, takes orders well, doesn't talk back much, and except for having too much pride or morals or whatever to bend over for a bunch of strangers, he's willing to do what it takes without complaint."

"If he takes orders well, make it an order." Luis gave an offhand shrug. "If one of your people was wounded, would you waffle while he refused to have it treated? Our job isn't to hold their hands and make sure they're happy about everything. It's to make sure they get the mission done and that if we can't keep them alive, at least they die for a good reason, accomplishing something. *Pride or morals or whatever* aren't good enough reasons. His job is to help the unit to the best of his abilities, and if he's gonna die, it needs to be serving the unit or protecting the civvies. So right now his job is to do what it takes to keep himself from dying because his life ain't his to throw away. Not anymore, not in our unit."

Darius snorted softly, thinking of the way Rhys kept *melting* the more force he used. How he'd responded that night in the clubhouse bar after Darius had given him to Toby and Joe. How . . . almost content . . . he'd been for a few days afterward. Until they'd found Gabriel.

"He doesn't understand the life yet. What our duty is. That's not the kind of order he'd respond to right now."

Luis shrugged again, sipping his drink. "Then make it the kind he will."

Darius scowled. *That* was exactly where all this had gone to shit in the first place.

⚠ ⚠ ⚠

RHYS WAS sound asleep when Darius returned to his quarters. The boy's hair was still damp and his lips blue from the shower. In the fading daylight coming through the window, Darius could see the bruises he'd left on Rhys's wrists and arms over the last few nights.

Darius was never more grateful that he'd chosen to take advantage of being co-commander and claimed one of the private units rather than staying in the barracks. Here, Rhys could indulge that stubborn modesty of his, at least when he was with Darius. Maybe he'd even find the privacy sufficient to give it up without a struggle. He looked peaceful and agonizingly young curled up in Darius's bed. In another world, the old world, he'd be getting ready to go off to college or something, rather than waiting to find out if he was going to die. In that world, if he fucked strangers, he would do it willingly, chasing after adventure and new experiences with all the enthusiasm of his youth.

Darius wanted to join him in bed, to be tender and seduce him sweetly. God help him, he wanted to make love to the boy, and he could never do that. He'd lost the right. It was idiotic—a man his age getting hung up on a kid so young. Rhys would never be his lover, even if Darius *hadn't* forced himself on him the past few nights. In a matter of weeks, possibly days, Rhys would be a Jug or he'd be dead. Either way, he wouldn't need Darius any longer.

Annoyed with his own sentimentality, Darius decided to let Rhys have a few more minutes of bunk time while he showered and changed out of his fatigues, which smelled musty after getting soaked in the river. The shower was a glorious treat, one he hadn't experienced since they'd left the monastery. After so many years of living rough, the cold water had ceased to be a shock. At least this time it took the edge off his lust while he considered how he would fix the damage the last few days had done to his cease-fire with Rhys.

When he emerged, toweling water from his loose hair, Rhys's eyes were open, and he was staring at the bathroom door warily.

"Didn't mean to wake you." Darius scrubbed the towel across his chest before wrapping it around his hips. He wished he could get a handle on what was happening behind those somber eyes. Rhys had seemed so open and transparent that first night in the monastery, but now his gaze was shadowed and cautious. Darius could almost hate himself for destroying that innocence.

"Are you going to send me to someone else?"

Darius approached the bed carefully and sat down on the edge. His wet hair clung to the skin between his shoulder blades, itching slightly.

"After what I've done to you these past few days, you might find it easier that way." A muscle in his jaw twitched, but Darius made himself meet Rhys's eyes frankly. "I won't hold it against you if you can't stand me, but I won't apologize, Rhys. Not even for that. I told you from the start, I don't flinch. I can't, not if I wanna get by and keep my people alive in this world. Sometimes that means doing some ugly things, things that make me a fucking shitty person but that get the job done. My only other choice was risking you dying, and I couldn't do that. I wasn't gonna make one of my men force you, so that left me. We all do what we have to do."

"You were ready to kill me that first day at the monastery. Or let me die. You don't *care* if I live. You never have!"

"Is that what you think, boy?"

Those hazel eyes were hot and dry. Except for the first time Darius had forced him, Rhys still shed his tears in the dark of night when he thought no one could see or hear.

So much strength in such a thin, frail shell.

Darius didn't know even a fraction of what Houtman and his father had done to Rhys. But he knew the boy had faced the prospect of certain death so that his sister and her baby could get away and live. And every blow that he'd been dealt since, every act he'd considered demeaning, he still managed to lift his chin and cling to his dignity when it was over. Every fight he'd put up had been not to save his own life, but to save something more essential. The indefinable *something* within him that maybe, just maybe, was what made it so important that he live.

Maybe he'd rather die than break. Maybe Darius was wrong to deprive him of that option. In the process of saving Rhys's life, was Darius destroying the very thing that was so worth preserving?

But he'd do the same if he had to do it again. No looking back.

"If I didn't care if you lived, we wouldn't be here. It was always an issue of weighing the cost."

"But you *were* willing to let me die before, so why not now?"

"I could say because I've come too far, invested too much in seeing you live, compromised my principles too deeply to give up now. All that would be true."

"But?"

Darius frowned at the wall beyond Rhys's head. "But it wouldn't be the whole truth."

"Then what would?"

"That you give us hope." It had taken him some time to figure that one out, to realize the source of the fascination that had compelled Xolani to argue so hard in favor of Rhys's survival that day and that had compelled Darius to give in. "You gave us hope the moment you told us to kill you to protect ourselves. Knowing people like you exist, people who won't lie or kill or whore themselves out for another day of pointless breathing, people who actually *believe* in something—even if it's just yourself and what you know is right—it makes it worth it, boy. Everything we've lost. Everything we've destroyed. Everything we've fought for. Me. Xolani. Titus. All of us. We can look at someone like you and think that maybe this world ain't such a shithole after all. Maybe there's something in it to give meaning to spending the rest of our lives doing what we do now."

"It isn't fair to put that on me."

"No." Darius looked down at the bedspread, sighing. Rhys had never asked to be their talisman. "It isn't. But it's already done."

Rhys rolled to his back, staring up at the ceiling. It was getting toward evening, and the room was filling with shadows. "So, are you going to send me to someone else?"

"Is that what you want?"

Rhys scoffed. "Since when does what I want matter?"

"It matters in this. Given my choice, I'd rather keep you here. Can't send you to the barracks with Houtman there." Rhys's eyes flashed back to him with alarm. "I don't need to know what he's done to you to know you're scared of him, boy. I won't put you within his reach. But if you're scared of *me*, I can put you out of my reach, too. Titus and Xolani would let you bunk with them. Xolani would find men for you. There's about a week to go until she thinks having more than one partner won't make a difference. After that, she'll find you someone steady. Someone a lot nicer than me. Toby and Joe would probably take you. Maybe Luis." Darius's knuckles whitened around his knee, and he drew a deep breath. "What I can't do is give you the choice of quitting. I can't even give you a promise that I won't force you again if you try. But you can choose who it will be, as long as for the next week there's more than one and at least one for a few weeks after that. I can give you that much."

"And what'll happen if I stay with you?"

"If you stay with me, your ass is still mine." He met Rhys's gaze evenly. "You won't have a choice because I won't let you handicap yourself with that damn modesty of yours or whatever it is that makes you fight this. I'll fuck you wherever and whenever and however I want. I'll pass you around to others, and you won't have a say in it. And when the next week is up and you don't have to have anyone else, I'll keep you all to myself until you don't need me anymore."

And I'll enjoy every minute of it way more than I have any business doing.

Darius decided not to add that.

Was it fear or something else that made Rhys's breath come quick and shallow after that speech? That made his pulse throb visibly at his throat? Darius wanted to slip his hand under the blankets and check, but he kept his hand on his knee and made himself wait.

Rhys closed his eyes and swallowed once, hard.

"I'll stay with you."

20

ABSOLUTION

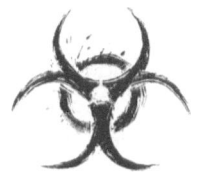

T he look Darius gave him was filled with so much heat, Rhys was certain Darius would rip the covers back and fuck him then and there. God, he ached for it. Even sore and bruised as he was, he wanted Darius again. Now. Here. In privacy, where he didn't have to be ashamed of who might hear him. He didn't know why Darius would want him, skinny weakling that he was, but if it would get him through these final few weeks, he wouldn't question it.

Darius did pull the covers back, but he didn't touch Rhys. He merely stared at him, his eyes passing up and down Rhys's body.

"Roll onto your stomach, boy," Darius said almost kindly.

Rhys obeyed, laying his face in the cradle of his arms. His cock had begun to fill, growing stiff and eager when Darius had described what life would be like if Rhys stayed with him. He felt no need to fight just now, not here in private, and wasn't that strange? He thought he might be fine with anything Darius chose to do to him as long as it was done where no one else would see or hear, especially Jacob. How could just that one detail make everything better?

Darius's hands settled on him, their touch odd. Not rough. Not arousing. They passed over Rhys's skin, manipulating his limbs, lifting and moving him until Rhys realized what Darius was doing.

Inspecting him. It had been three weeks or more since his exposure to the blood of the revenants at the monastery. The first patches of the Rot could appear any day now.

"Anything?" He could barely force the whisper through the narrow pinhole his airway had become.

"No. You're clean, boy."

Rhys blew out a long breath, his body melting into the bed as he relaxed. "Thank God. If, um, if I do get it, how much time will I have?"

"Hard to say." Darius's hand rested between Rhys's shoulder blades, its weight comforting. "Sometimes the catatonia begins before the Rot appears. You'll start . . . slipping away. Losing sense of time, unable to focus, finding it harder to speak and keep track of your thoughts, and it'll get worse over the course of a few days until you just zone out and don't come back. If the Rot shows first, the catatonia will set in soon after. You might have a day or two to decide how and when you want to go."

Rhys swallowed, rolling his head on the pillow to face Darius. "Okay."

"If it's Gamma, you'll become volatile. Temperamental. Aggressive. Violent. You'll get stronger, as if you were a Jug. In that case it'll be up to us to recognize it and put you down before you hurt someone. You won't . . . You won't have a chance to come to terms with it."

"Okay," Rhys whispered again. Darius's hand passed over him once more, this time caressing. Rhys closed his eyes and let that touch push away the fear until all he remembered was the anticipation he'd felt when Darius had first set hands upon him after coming out of the shower.

"Don't worry, boy. There's no reason to think that's gonna happen. So you just enjoy the ride until you're in the clear." Darius's touch disappeared, and when it returned, his slick fingers slipped into Rhys's crack. One thick digit worked into him, and Rhys moaned softly, lifting his hips to open for it.

"I'll be taking you to meet the rest of the company here on base tonight." Rhys *felt* himself clamp down around that finger as the words sank in. His head came up, tension instantly ratcheting through his body.

He heard the sharp *crack* almost before he felt the burn of Darius's open hand landing on his ass. Rhys yelped, twisting, trying to roll over to protect his vulnerable backside and dislodging Darius's finger in the process, but Darius grabbed him by the hip and pushed him down.

"Relax, boy. I got something special in mind for you, something you might even like. But you'll have to trust me. That might be hard after the last few days, but it'll be better for us both if you can manage it."

Another finger, prying his tight muscles loose, wedging into him. Rhys groaned, letting his head fall back onto his arms. A shudder rippled through him as the stretch started to burn, so much later than it once had. He almost missed the ache, missed the ordeal. Like fighting back, the pain made it better, somehow. *Okay.*

"I don't understand," he mumbled into his arms.

"What's that?"

He turned his head. "Why you think I'd be afraid of you. You haven't done anything you didn't tell me you'd do from the beginning."

The fingers within him stilled.

"Because I did something to you most people couldn't ever forgive. *Shouldn't* ever forgive." Darius's voice sounded a bit raspier, strained.

Slowly, Darius's fingers resumed their stroking. Carefully. Far more careful than Darius usually was with him. Rhys shook his head. "No. You made me do something I had to do but *couldn't.* It's like—"

"Like what?" Darius's question was a hoarse whisper.

"Like shoving someone out the window of a burning building into a river far below. Pushing someone out a high window is a lousy thing to do, and it might hurt, but if it saves their life . . ."

"Jesus." He barely heard the whisper behind him. Darius's hand, the one that had slapped his ass moments ago, caressed his back softly. "Is that how you really see it?"

"How do you see it?"

"That I raped you." Rhys startled at the bald statement, tightening around Darius's fingers, which had gone still again. He'd never considered that. "You chose to risk death rather than let anyone fuck you, and I took that choice away from you by force."

"I don't want to die. I never *wanted* to die." Rhys shivered as his eyes burned. "I was going to, to save Cady and Caleb. And earlier today when I was in the river it seemed like it might be easier if I did, but I never wanted it. I just . . . I *couldn't*. Don't you see? When I thought about letting Gabe hear what I was doing, what I've . . . what I've become, everything locked up. I couldn't move, couldn't make myself . . . So you threw me out the window to save me. That's how I see it."

He heard Darius swallow, and then his fingers were gone and something cold and hard—the plug, of course—was spreading him open instead.

"Maybe someday I won't think you're giving me more credit than I deserve." Darius snorted behind him. "I don't know if I'll ever understand the way your mind works, boy."

"Yeah, well, if I ever figure it out, I'll let you know." Rhys chuckled weakly, groaning at the first stretch, then sobered. "I didn't fight because I'd chosen to die. I fought because it felt good to fight."

"Why?" The in-and-out advance of the plug slowed, allowing him to think a bit more clearly.

"Because I never have. I've always given in. Father Maurice. Jacob. You . . ."

Darius was silent, silent enough that unease started to make Rhys's heart race. Rhys gasped and groaned as, with a final push, the plug slid the rest of the way inside him and lodged, seated by its narrow stem. But then Darius's hands went away, no longer caressing or working him open or doing anything at all.

"You're not fighting now."

Something in Rhys's stomach felt hollow and fluttery as he rolled up on his side, gasping when the plug shifted. "No."

"Why? Because now no one can hear?"

"Maybe. Partly." Rhys shrugged, struggling to meet Darius's eyes, which were dark and intent upon him. He looked deadly sober. "But mostly because of what you said about . . . about hope. About why you want me to live." He swallowed hard and made himself return the gaze, though his own pulse threatened to choke him. "I matter to you. You're not just doing it because you have to. And that makes it not feel wrong anymore."

That fierce stare pinned him in place, drilling into him as though Darius would strip Rhys down to the bone with just his eyes. Then Darius was on him, stretched above him, crushing their mouths together in a brutal, twisting grind of lips and tongues. Darius's towel was bunched between them, and they were both hard. So hard. Moving against each other, rubbing to get more.

More. Rhys wanted more. He wanted Darius to fuck him, not to try to infect him but just because Darius actually wanted *him*. That was more than Rhys could ask for, though. Maybe someday, once Rhys was a Jug, someone would want him just because. But not now. For now it was enough that he mattered.

When Darius pulled away, his breath was harsh and ragged, his dark eyes burning with something that both terrified and thrilled Rhys. He was hungry for Darius as he hadn't been since that morning in the dormitory. Rhys reached for him with groan full of yearning, but Darius dodged his hands.

"You'll make me forget what I was doing, boy." He chuckled, sounding somewhat pained. "Behave."

Suddenly self-conscious again, Rhys subsided, looking away as he tried to figure what to make of Darius's withdrawal. But Darius caught his chin and turned his head, compelling his gaze.

"Later. Don't think I'm stopping because I don't wanna keep going. But right now we got something else we need to do."

SOMETHING ELSE TURNED out to be a party. Or at least it felt like one.

The Jugs had converted one of the wards in the early twentieth-century hospital at Fort Vancouver into a lounge of sorts. Titus had set up his still there, Darius told him, and old hospital beds were clustered around the room like strange chaises, along with a number of mismatched chairs, sofas, and tables they had hauled in from houses in the area.

"We got a mess hall, but this is a little more cozy," Darius explained when Rhys asked, trying to distract himself from the pressure of the plug inside him. "There's the big ward on the main floor where everyone gathers to socialize, but then there are small rooms upstairs, too, for people who want more privacy than they can find in the barracks."

"Bet you didn't think of that, did you, Rhys?" Xolani patted the foot of the bed where she and Titus lounged, inviting him to sit. She offered him a glass of something clear that smelled like paint thinner as Rhys perched gingerly, trying to find a comfortable position. "Embarrassing as you may find it, the fact of life in this unit is, if it weren't for public or semipublic sex, a lot of us wouldn't get laid at all. Of course, Titus and I got lucky this time around and won the lottery for one of the private apartments."

Rhys flushed and took a drink of the liquor, wheezing and coughing as it seared its way down his esophagus.

"I guess I didn't think of that." He handed the glass off when he could breathe again. He didn't know what he'd assumed about the Jugs' communal living arrangements, but he'd thought surely they must get more privacy than he'd been afforded while they were out on patrol. He'd regarded the public sex as a perversion and an assault on his dignity, never considering that none of them found it degrading in the slightest because they all did it.

Just a fact of life.

Would he have felt better about it if he had known?

Darius squeezed his shoulder encouragingly and wandered off, shaking hands and making conversation, clearly catching up with people he hadn't seen in some time. Rhys scanned the crowd for faces he knew. There was Kaleo, reclining on another bed, nuzzling a redheaded woman who Rhys could only assume was Schuyler. Gina was there, draped over another woman. Toby and Joe, too, across the ward. Joe was shirtless, his scars visible for all to see. He knelt at Toby's feet and . . . was that a leash around his neck?

Then Joe turned to say something to Toby, and Rhys's stomach clenched in horrified fascination. Joe's back was a mass of bruises and welts, crisscrossing and striping him from his shoulders to the waistband of his fatigues.

Rhys knew those welts. He'd seen them in the mirror on his own backside after Father Maurice had done his worst.

Xolani nudged him with her foot, drawing Rhys's attention to the fact that he was gawking. "Remember, everyone celebrates coming home in their own way."

Rhys swallowed and nodded, tearing his eyes away from the sight.

People began to approach and introduce themselves, starting with Captain Luis Martinez, who welcomed him to Delta Company. He was followed by a stream of others. Cato. Jackson. Sanchez. Giovanni. Soon Rhys lost track of the names. Some of them tried to flirt with him, but he found himself tongue-tied, unable to respond aside from ducking his head and stammering. Lord help him, it was like that first time with Kaleo all over again. He *wished* he could be interested in them, but he couldn't. All he felt was a vague dread that they might expect a reaction from him or demand he accompany them somewhere for sex.

"Relax, Rhys." Someone passed Xolani a pipe. She took a deep drag off it, closing her eyes, holding her breath, and finally exhaling slowly. It was only after the sweetly cloying scent of the smoke hit him that Rhys realized it wasn't tobacco. She smiled and leaned back against Titus, looking softer than Rhys had ever seen her. "No one here's gonna bite you. Unless you ask, of course."

Relaxing would be a lot easier if he had the slightest idea what Darius had planned. But he couldn't bring himself to say that. "Where's Jacob?"

"Guess someone forgot to tell him where the party was."

"Damn shame, that," Titus rumbled, and Xolani chuckled, inhaling again before passing the pipe to Titus.

A whoop from the other side of the room made Rhys's head snap around to see Gina falling back on a sofa, pushed by the woman she was with. She laughed and arched her spine as the other woman reached for her belt. Rhys looked quickly away, his face growing hot, only to have his gaze land on Kaleo, whose hands were working Schuyler's shirt up over her breasts.

Rhys turned his attention to a spot on the floor in front of him and refused to look up, gratefully accepting the glass of hooch Xolani pressed back into his hand.

"You get used to it, recruit." Titus wrapped his arm around Xolani. Before the heat in Rhys's face could begin to cool, though, Darius was back, his hand on Rhys's shoulder, urging him up.

"Say good-night, and come with me, boy."

"'Night." Rhys ducked his head. If everyone was staring, knowing he was being led off for Darius to fuck him, he didn't want to know.

Instead of leading him back to his quarters, though, Darius took Rhys upstairs to one of the private rooms. In the thin moonlight that filtered through the dusty window, Darius lit a single candle. The hospital bed had been removed at some point, but there was a mattress on the floor, reminding Rhys of the dormitory.

"Take off your clothes, and get down on your knees." At Darius's instruction, Rhys nodded, beginning to undress.

Why now? Why here? Why hadn't Darius done this earlier, in his apartment? Why bring Rhys here for this, if not to shame him?

"I want you to be real quiet. No yelling this time." Darius knelt behind him, working the plug out and setting it aside. "If you yell, I'll have to gag you. Got it?"

"Yes, sir." Rhys hid his burning face in his arms.

"Sit up, boy." Rhys obeyed, glancing around, but Darius shook his head. "No. Close your eyes."

Frowning in confusion, Rhys did as he was instructed. A wide strip of fabric pressed against his eyelids, shutting out the meager light.

"Now, you listen to me." Darius kept his voice a low, steady murmur. "I want you to remember this: in this room, every cock that fucks you is my cock. Every load someone shoots up your ass is my cum. You don't need to see who it is because it don't matter. It's all me. Got it?"

Rhys whimpered. He couldn't help it. In an instant, the throbbing in his cock and aching pressure in his balls ratcheted up to full-on urgency. Everything was utter blackness as Darius tied the blindfold. He cupped a hand around the back of Rhys's neck and drew him into a long, hard kiss.

"Stay quiet and don't ask any questions," Darius breathed into his ear, and then Darius was gone. Rhys knelt alone on the mattress in the darkness, and silence followed the *click* of the door when it closed. Around him, he could hear the sounds of sex from other rooms, muffled grunts and groans. He tried to make out more sounds, to get an idea of where Darius was, but it was useless.

It was a warm night, and the hospital room was poorly ventilated. Rhys's skin grew damp and prickly as he knelt there for what felt like forever. Waiting. Waiting. His limbs began to grow heavy. Just as he planted his palm on the mattress, intending to shift from his knees and lie down, he heard the door open. Clothing rustled, a belt clinking.

He went still as a hand brushed his shoulder.

"Who—"

"Shh." Just that whisper, no more, and a bare body pressed against his back.

Don't ask any questions, Darius had said.

Rhys fell silent.

Whoever he was, he was a large guy. That much was obvious from the size of the arms that encircled Rhys. Joe, then? No. Not Joe. He couldn't feel the metal of the nipple rings Joe wore. Kaleo, perhaps? Or maybe Bailey? One of the others? Someone whose name he didn't even know yet?

Gentle despite their size, the man's hands slid across Rhys's front in a featherlight stroke that covered his scrawny chest. Thick fingertips brushed his nipples, and Rhys shifted, pressing back unintentionally. The leftover lube made his ass cheeks slippery as he moved. Moist breath ghosted across the back of his neck, followed by a brush of lips.

Body parts. Without a name, without a voice, without a face, it was all reduced to body parts and sensation. The person behind him rocked, and Rhys felt the firm pressure of a cock against his back, warm except for the spots where it left streaks of cooling moisture. Hands explored his chest and arms as if the owner had all the time in the world, rousing Rhys's nerve endings one slow caress at a time.

Skin damp with sweat slid against his. Lips tugged at his earlobe. A tongue trailed up the shell of his ear before teeth retraced its course, then nibbled their way back down. Phantom fingertips captured his nipples, squeezing then pinching until Rhys seized his bottom lip between his teeth to suppress a whimper. Anonymous nails scraped down his abdomen and along his thighs. A fist wrapped around his cock, pumping slowly, making no effort to bring Rhys to climax.

Nude and blind as Rhys was in the darkness, the stranger could have simply taken him. Used him. Done his business and left. Instead, he seduced Rhys, made love to him with a sensual gentleness. Freed from the awkwardness of facing the man under circumstances that reduced sex to a dutiful transaction, everything changed.

It wasn't Darius. Rhys would have known. Darius's touch, his scent, the feel of his body were indelibly imprinted on Rhys's senses.

It wasn't Darius. But whoever it was, he valued Rhys.

His throat vibrated with a silent moan, and the stranger urged him forward onto all fours. For the first time with someone who wasn't Darius, the dick that slid easily into his ass wasn't an unwelcome intrusion he endured in cringing humiliation. The semen it pumped inside him didn't make him feel filthy and polluted. Tender hands embraced him, warm arms engulfed him, hot skin stuck to his as the unknown man's breath slowed against the back of his neck and his shaking ceased.

"Good to have you here, little brother." The words were barely a whisper, not loud enough for Rhys to discern whose voice it was by tenor or accent. But the words were punctuated by the softest of kisses as Rhys turned his head, seeking the source of those words, and then the body behind his was gone.

Another replaced it in time. And another after that. And one more after that.

Each one kissed him and whispered a benediction, a welcome, before they left.

Rhys wasn't sure how long he lay there while they came to him, four in all, before Darius returned. After the first one, he stopped trying to figure out their identities. It didn't matter. They were avatars, emissaries of Darius's will. And they were his brothers, making him feel welcomed, cherished, wanted.

Darius, he knew. His fingertips, the cadence of his breath, the touch of his hot skin, were all familiar. As rousing as the caresses of the others had been, they didn't claim his flesh the way Darius did, even when he was gentle.

And he *was* gentle. Far gentler than he'd ever been. He unwrapped Rhys's eyes and inserted the plug again, then helped Rhys dress. Rhys's skin was oversensitive after so many caresses, the brush of his clothing an unbearable friction. But he was content as he followed Darius out the door and past the ward where the party still went on. Not self-conscious in the slightest.

He would never know which men had had him. It had been all of them and none. As if the time he'd spent in that room had been removed from reality. It had never happened. The men who had touched him were apparitions in the darkness, nothing more.

Then he was back in Darius's quarters, naked on the bed, and still Darius was gentle. Nevertheless, each touch felt territorial, branding him, marking his ownership on Rhys's skin. He overwrote every other caress Rhys had received, growling softly behind Rhys's ear, "Mine. My boy."

"*Yes.*" Rhys was lost in it. As Darius's thrusts came faster, harder, smacking violently against his ass, Rhys let his cries ring out without any effort to quell them. In the midst of his climax, he missed the moment of throbbing and twitching when Darius came. As Rhys sank, panting, onto the bed, Darius licked his own hand clean of Rhys's cum, then lodged the plug firmly inside Rhys's dripping hole again.

The bedroom was dark, but the moon shone through the windows, bleeding silvery light over the hardwood floor.

"Go to sleep, boy." Darius brushed a kiss across Rhys's mouth and drew the covers up over him. Rhys nodded and stretched, going still as Darius pressed close to his back and embraced him.

He fell asleep with a smile.

21

RESPITE

Rhys struggled to put Gabe's presence at the fort out of his mind. The urge to see him, to find out how he'd survived and why he'd run off, whether he'd missed Rhys and how he felt now, was an ache that never went away. Xolani promised that as soon as they were certain Rhys wasn't infected with one of the airborne strains, she would arrange for them to meet, but the fact that Jacob was already infected with the Alpha strain and Rhys wasn't gnawed at his nerves.

What if he wasn't going to become a Jug?

He learned dozens of names and faces those first few days at Fort Vancouver, and a good number of those he came to know in a far more physical sense. Each night, Darius took him back to that room in the hospital and blindfolded him. More anonymous men came to him, silent and unreal.

Darius had duties throughout the day while they were at base, but sometimes he would come to Rhys as he worked in the warehouses or fields.

"Come with me, boy." He'd lead Rhys back to his apartment and, there, he'd strip and blindfold Rhys. The door would open and some unknown man would come in. He'd have Rhys the same as the others did in the evening, though it was full daylight, and that was different somehow. It added a delicious thrill to know the anonymous man could see him, naked and vulnerable, available at Darius's command.

After the first couple of times, it became apparent that Darius was also there.

"He don't mind it a little harder, you know," he'd remark conversationally from the other side of the room. "Go ahead and breed him good. He likes it."

How was it possible to feel so dirty but not degraded? How could that blindfold and not knowing the men's names and faces make such a difference? Shouldn't that make it worse? Why didn't he feel like a filthy deviant anymore?

One time, Darius gave him to three men at once. It had taken the whole afternoon and a good part of the evening because they each took several turns. These men weren't silent, though they didn't identify themselves, and Rhys didn't think he recognized their voices. They egged each other on and talked about Rhys as if he wasn't even there. By the time it was over, Rhys was aching in every part of his body, because Darius had kept prodding them not to be careful with him. Cum was dripping out of his ass when the men had left, and then Darius did what he always did. Every day, he was the first man to have Rhys, and the last. When the others were done, he reclaimed Rhys, bringing him to a shattering climax, then stuffed the plug back in, stopping up that stream of semen spilling out of him. Then Darius held Rhys as he collapsed into an exhausted slumber.

The times when Darius wasn't there were much harder, though for the most part, the men who approached him were courteous and respectful. If it never came as easily to him as it did blindfolded, with instruction to consider every touch he received as coming directly from Darius, still he knew he could at least endure it until the week was over. Only one time did he feel truly shamed. Captain Martinez was kind and apologetic, but he made it clear he'd invited Rhys to his quarters only out of a sense of duty.

After it was over, Rhys returned to shower in Darius's quarters and scrubbed himself in the cold water until his skin stung. Then he dressed and went out in search of some sort of occupation to keep his mind off things.

Which was when Jacob found him, naturally.

"You know, you won't be Darius's pet much longer, faggot." Jacob backed Rhys against one of the warehouses where Rhys had been stacking crates of rations to be delivered to the quarantine zone. "The guys in the barracks are getting tired of seeing you get special treatment. They think you're stuck-up, especially after they heard how you tried to kill me so I wouldn't tell them just what a little degenerate shit you are. As soon as Darius gets tired of you, he'll send you to the barracks so they can all have their turns on you."

"What, feeling jealous that you haven't had *your* turn?" Rhys mustered all the bravado he could, looking for an escape. God help him if Jacob *did* try to fuck him. "I know you've always been on my ass, but sorry, Jacob. You're just not my type."

"Watch your mouth, freak. Now that I'm a Jug, I'm going to move up in the ranks fast. They know you tried to murder me, and that God wants me to triumph. This is my chance for real power. They respect me, but you're just the camp whore, and they know that, too. After all, what sort of man bends over for a whole company?"

"The sort that doesn't have his head up his ass." Rhys grasped for the emotional distance he'd always put between himself and Jacob's words back at the monastery. It was harder now. "And you're lying. Darius and Xolani wouldn't let them—"

"That nigger and his Arab bitch don't have the authority you think they have. These people are looking for someone decent to lead them back to God. The Juggernauts could reclaim this nation, become God's Own army. They could wipe out all the perverts and fornicators like you, bring what's left of civilization back to the Lord. All they need is a leader with faith to make it happen. I'm going to be that man, just wait."

Rhys rolled his eyes. "Without us *perverts and fornicators*, you wouldn't even—"

"There you are, Cooper." Rhys had never been so thankful to hear Titus's gravelly voice as he approached from the mess hall. Jacob stepped back, and Rhys made a grateful escape. "Been looking for you. Thought maybe you might want some more weapons practice."

Titus clapped a hand on Rhys's shoulder, and he felt stronger. Reinforced.

"Hi, Titus." Jacob pasted on an insincere smile. "If you two are heading for the target range, I'd love to join you. I feel like we haven't really had a chance to get to know each other. Now that we're brothers—"

"Pfft, not a chance. Go be unwanted somewhere else, shit stain." Titus propelled Rhys away by a hand between his shoulder blades.

"I don't get it." Rhys turned to Titus when Jacob was out of earshot. "How is he making himself so popular? If you and Xolani can see through him, why can't everyone else?"

"Popular?" Titus snorted. "Who told you that?"

"He did. He said the guys in the barracks really like him, that now that he's a Jug he's going to—" Rhys's shoulders slumped. "Never mind. It's not important."

"You think our people are stupid, Cooper?"

Rhys shook his head quickly as Titus's hand continued to guide him. "No, of course not. It's just that everyone always used to believe him. Why should it be any different now?"

"Everyone being his old man?" Titus scoffed. "You know, I'd just got the monastery in visual range on my infrared when the revs reached your family. I saw it happen, but I couldn't get to them in time. I saw that chump leave his wife and baby behind and run." Titus gave a low growl. "That's how I knew to chase him down, though I was really hoping the rev that went after him would catch him first. Sort of man who'll leave his family behind to be slaughtered while he bolts isn't the sort of man we want on the team. Our people can recognize that he's a coward who likes to talk big, even if they don't know the details. We're stuck with him for now, seeing as how he's a Jug, but we've gotten rid of troublemakers before, and we won't have any problem doing it again."

Rhys looked at Titus so sharply he missed an uneven crack on the paved path and nearly landed on his face. "You should know he's taking aim at Darius and Xolani. Trying to undermine them. He called her an 'Arab bitch.'"

"Did he now?" Titus's eyes, wrinkled with a perpetual sun-squint, glinted with amusement. "And just when I'd almost managed to convince myself stupidity isn't a terminal illness. Well, she's a *Persian* bitch, in the interest of accuracy. She ended up in the med corps during Iran because she could speak Farsi."

"Huh. I didn't know that. So Xolani is a Persian name?"

"Nope." Titus laughed again. "Darius started calling her that when she joined Delta Company. Means 'peace' in Zulu."

"Peace?" Rhys felt his eyebrows creep up.

"Well, he didn't have a word for 'will rip off your face and eat it with ketchup.'" Rhys laughed so hard he had to lean against a tree for support until he caught his breath. Titus stood by, grinning at him in the afternoon heat and seeming very pleased with himself for making Rhys laugh, but after a moment he sobered. "Look, I don't mind saying your pal's life expectancy just got a lot shorter, Cooper. He steps a toe out of line, I'll be there to put a bullet between his eyes, if Xolani doesn't beat me to it."

"I thought you weren't allowed to mistreat the recruits?"

"Well, he's not a recruit anymore, is he? Besides, who said anything about mistreatment? I'd kill him so fast it wouldn't even hurt. Much."

Rhys pushed himself away from the tree, and they continued down the path. "You know what I mean."

"Yeah, I do. And normally I wouldn't think it, but in this case, I'll make an exception. I've been part of Delta Company for twenty years, Xolani for eighteen. We're a family. We have our squabbles and trouble, but after this long, most of the assholes have weeded themselves out. You think there's a single person who'll question my judgment over the best way to deal with that asswipe?"

"No, I guess not." Rhys peered at Titus closely, trying to decide if he was serious about killing Jacob.

"You know what, Cooper?" Titus tilted his head, studying Rhys for a moment. "I think you need hand-to-hand training more than weapons training just now. We're gonna go back to your quarters, and you're gonna take out that plug I know you're wearing. Then we'll spar in the yard."

Rhys blushed and changed course toward the West Barracks area, where the duplex units like the one Darius occupied were located. "Yes, sir."

Titus burst out laughing, a deep, rumbling noise that sounded like boulders rolling down a hill, and Rhys blushed. He ducked inside Darius's apartment to remove his plug, and afterward, he and Titus walked down the cluster of divided houses to the unit Titus and Xolani had claimed. It felt strange, walking without the plug for the first time in days. Rhys hadn't even realized how accustomed to it he had become. But then he didn't have much time to think about it as they stood in the yard, and Titus showed him how to throw a punch.

"I brought you here because you need to start standing up for yourself." Titus held up his hands as targets as Rhys tried to aim for them with his fists. "I get why you don't. I bet Houtman hid behind his daddy back there at the monastery, got you in a lot of trouble. But things have changed now. Here's the thing, though. You can't just attack him the way you did that day at the water pump."

"Why not?" Rhys grinned when his fist hit Titus's palm with a satisfying *smack*. He tried one punch after another, at first missing more than he hit.

"Because you did that in a blind rage, which is a stupid way to fight. It'll just make things worse. You do that, people might start listening to his claims that you're trouble, that you're unhinged. So you gotta be smart about when, where, and how you draw the line." Another hit, square in Titus's palm. "Good! Do that again. You gotta make sure you got provocation, make sure you got witnesses—and he's smart enough to give you most of his shit when there's no one around, so that could be a problem. But when you finally do cut loose, you make that son of a bitch wish he'd never crawled out of his mama's cooch."

"How can I do that? He's a Jug now!" Rhys swung harder, missing more as he lost focus.

"Concentrate, recruit!" Titus shoved Rhys back, forcing him to charge forward to get more blows in. "Fight smart! He's a bully, and you're his favorite victim. Long as the two of you are anywhere near each other, he's going to try to make your life miserable unless you find a way to put the fear of God into him."

"How am I . . . supposed to do that?" Sweat trickled down Rhys's temple as he threw punch after punch, landing enough that

Titus began to make it a little more difficult by dodging. "Even if I get infected . . . he'll still be . . . bigger than me."

"Sure, he's taller and he's got a bigger frame than you, but you think anyone's teaching him to brawl just now? Put your body into it." Titus gave him a tight grin, pushing Rhys away again with what must have been relatively gentle force for someone with a Jug's strength. Rhys waded back in with a savage grimace, trying to actually move Titus's hands as he swung at them harder, throwing more of his weight into each punch. "Even a civvie can get the advantage if they take a Jug by surprise. It's just a lot harder to do."

"Didn't . . . you just tell me . . . that was a stupid way . . . to fight?" Sweat started to blind him, and his arms were beginning to tremble with effort.

"Stupid to do it without planning for it," Titus corrected. "Spread your feet. Ground yourself. Keep your balance. You pick your time. Pick your place. Pick your limit of just how much shit you're going to take from him. Then, when you finally take him down, you make fucking sure he *does not* get back up. Bullies like that, they're cowards. It's why they poke at your weakest spot, where you have no defenses. If he knows you can hurt him, he'll leave you the fuck alone. If he needs to die, you leave that to us. In the meantime, you make him fucking terrified to look at you sideways."

Rhys swallowed hard, dropping his trembling arms, unable to hold them up any longer. He stood there sweating, trying to catch his breath. Something inside him quailed at what Titus had suggested. His knuckles bore too many thick scars from Father Maurice's cane. It was never Jacob's fault for provoking him, always his own for reaching the breaking point. But here was Titus, giving him explicit permission to set Jacob down and assuring Rhys there would be no repercussions if he did so.

As his breathing slowed, Rhys realized he was calmer and more clearheaded than he had been since learning of Jacob's altered status the day he fell into the river. He finally felt capable of rational thought, less mired down in the helplessness that had set in when Jacob became a Jug. Titus waited, watching him impassively, as resolve took root in Rhys's chest.

Rhys began to grin. Titus grinned back.

ΛΛΛ

AFTER THE FIGHTING LESSON, Titus told Rhys to go see Xolani, who was waiting for him inside their apartment.

Rhys approached the open screen door to see her sitting on an armchair with a drink and knocked.

"Hey, you just missed dinner." She looked up and smiled, gesturing him inside. "I think I can scare up some more rations, though, if you haven't eaten yet."

"No, thanks." He felt a bit nauseated after his exertion, especially on top of working in the warehouses all afternoon. Now that he'd been with Delta Company a few weeks, he understood just why so many of them stayed behind at the fort rather than going out on patrols. Those people were tasked with reclamation and inventory. Any nonperishable food, clothing, and medical supplies they found that were still in usable condition were brought back to the warehouses at the fort. Most of Luis's job was to oversee the distribution of these supplies among the soldiers or the civilians they had recovered, particularly making sure they had adequate supplies for the journey back to Colorado Springs.

Like Gina, several of the soldiers were skilled hunters, and unused meat was preserved and added to the rations. In addition, the company had reclaimed and refurbished farm equipment. What had once been the parade grounds and an airfield at Fort Vancouver now yielded crops as summer approached its end, and each duplex and barracks had a kitchen garden. Rhys had spent a few days working in the fields as well as the warehouses. It was far more familiar labor after so many years of tending the garden at the monastery.

Xolani gave Rhys a sharp look when he declined to eat but didn't press him. "It's only been a few weeks, but I think you're starting to fill out a little."

He sat on the sofa at her invitation. "How much longer until we know whether I've been infected by the Alpha strain? I mean, with Jacob already—"

"It could be another two to three weeks, maybe longer." She took a drink and set her glass aside, leaning over the coffee table to pack a pipe. "You won't necessarily manifest on the same timetable as Jacob. The original Project Juggernaut cases took anywhere from three to eight weeks before physiological changes, such as increased strength and stamina, confirmed infection. Since we don't have the facilities to test by other means, that's the best indicator we have."

"Why does it take so long?"

"Virus was designed that way. If the physiological changes that come with the Alpha strain happened too fast, it would be too much for a body to handle and kill the carrier." A shadow passed over Xolani's face, and Rhys wondered just how long it had taken them to figure that out. "And if the onset of Beta symptoms had started soon after exposure, it would have been easy for hostiles to figure out the source of the virus and quarantine anyone who had been exposed to us. So it acted slowly, to guarantee the infected victims spread it around so it could do its job and incapacitate them. Unfortunately, that also made it impossible to combat when it got into the general population, because people were spreading it long before they were symptomatic."

"Oh." Rhys tried not to sigh in disappointment.

"Still struggling with it?" Xolani put the pipe to her mouth and lit it, taking a long drag. The oddly sweet, sharp scent of marijuana smoke wafted across the coffee table toward him.

"I guess."

She lifted an eyebrow and passed him the pipe. "Have some."

"You didn't offer me that the other night at the party." Rhys accepted it and took a cautious drag, holding his breath as he'd seen her do.

"The other night I thought it'd be better for you to be in control of all your faculties." She reclaimed the pipe for another puff, then returned it to Rhys before leaning forward to fill the bowl of another. "But since there's no one here waiting in line to bone you, no harm in it, is there?"

"I guess." They fell silent for some time, smoking until the pipes were finished. Rhys leaned back against the cushions of the sofa, feeling pleasantly relaxed, with a slight buzzing in his ears.

"So what's eating at you?" Xolani reclined in her own chair with a sigh. "Darius really isn't that bad, is he? I mean, he's a bit too alpha male for my tastes, but most of the people he's been with in the company have good things to say about him."

"What? No. Darius is great." Rhys's tension level was hovering somewhere around spaghetti al dente. Which sounded really good. He hadn't had spaghetti since he was a child, before they'd left Bozeman. "I just don't want people doing things they don't want to do to help me."

"Who the hell is doing that?"

"Everyone." His stomach rumbled, and Xolani tossed him an apple. The scavenging crew must have found an orchard somewhere. "Darius. Luis. None of them want to be doing this."

"Someone told you that?"

Rhys shrugged, chomping into the apple as Xolani grabbed a few strips of jerky and some fresh milk for him. That had surprised Rhys —to discover the Jugs had wrangled up some dairy cows. With no refrigeration or pasteurization, though, the milk was always warm, fresh each day, and rich with milk fat. None of that watery skim stuff he remembered from when he was a kid. They even made butter from the cream by shaking it forever in sealed jars—and had Rhys's arms ever hurt after spending an afternoon doing that. Xolani smeared some of the butter onto a thick slice of coarse bread for him. "You had to talk Darius into it. And Luis said he just wanted to get it over and done with."

Xolani blinked and blew out a breath. "Damn, Luis. That's cold."

"Why?" Rhys chewed the apple noisily, deciding its tart sweetness was the best thing he'd tasted in years.

"Well, no one wants to be treated like someone is doing him a *favor* when he screws him, no matter what the circumstances. It's degrading. Bravo Company tries to make it about welcoming people to the team."

"It's nice when they do that, but . . . never mind." Rhys grimaced, too relaxed for any genuine bitterness, and set the apple core aside. The jerky was even better, the salt of it stinging his tongue, the savory flavor of the dried venison urging him to gobble it hungrily.

"That's it." Xolani watched him eat with a wry smile. "I'm

prescribing a bong for you before every meal until you're back up to weight."

As he ate, he thought of the shower he'd taken after Luis and how filthy he'd felt. So much filthier than the things that actually *were* filthy. He hadn't felt that way after those faceless men had fucked him and welcomed him as their brother while he was blind-folded. "You know, you'd think after what Toby and Joe did, I wouldn't care."

Xolani frowned, looking confused. "What did Toby and Joe do to you?"

"Not to me, really. Just the way they are with each other."

She refilled a pipe and passed it to him. "Keep smoking. I like it when I don't have to drag explanations out of you. You got a problem with the way Toby and Joe act with each other?"

He inhaled deeply and held it, closing his eyes. "Toby *hurts* him."

"Ah. And you're put off by that because Father Maurice used to beat you, is that it?"

Rhys blinked, staring at her. "No, that's not it. I know what they do is different. I mean, Joe seems okay with it, but that's . . . Well, it's a little sick, isn't it?"

"Oh, is it?" He heard a tight, irritated note in her voice, but his brain seemed to have grown a layer of fuzz that was filtering out the reason for it.

"I didn't like Toby thinking we had anything in common. I'm not like that."

"Nobody says you have to be." She leaned forward and took the pipe from him, and Rhys pivoted to stretch out on the sofa. "But being a self-righteous prig and calling the people who are trying to be nice 'sick' isn't going to do you any favors, Rhys. So I'd really recommend you rethink your attitude."

He sighed. "Sorry."

"You don't seem to get how badly Delta Company wants to make this work for you. To make it so it's not traumatic. They're good guys, and you being ambivalent makes them feel like rapists." Her frown deepened, pulling on her scarred cheek. "I thought it was getting better. The guys haven't been complaining about feeling they're forcing you anymore."

Rhys felt too mellow even to flush. "Well, no, that's because Darius—well, he found a way to make it better."

"Yeah, I heard something about that, too. Wanna know where he found that way?"

"Where?"

"Toby and Joe."

"What?"

"That day we got back to base, Darius was just about at the end of his rope figuring out how to handle you. So he went to them for advice. Guy like Darius doesn't ask for help much, so you think about it for a while, what that means, what it took to make him do that." Xolani's tight smile looked more like a grimace. "Toby's not the only one who thought you might have something in common with him and Joe, apparently."

Rhys sighed again. "It's just . . . I spent years imagining how, if I ever had the chance, I'd prove Father Maurice and Jacob wrong. Show them that just because I liked men didn't mean I was . . . abnormal. Deviant. Immoral. Whatever. I was just a guy who wants the same thing everyone else wants. To care about someone, be happy with someone. Now look at me. At what I'm doing."

"Rhys . . ." Xolani hesitated a moment, and he cracked open an eye to see her run her hand over her braid. "Do you honestly think they would have cared?"

"Guess not." He let his head loll drowsily against the arm of the sofa. "Maybe I just wanted to know it myself, that they were wrong. But they weren't. They were right about me. I just wanted to know I was a decent guy."

Xolani's lips buzzed as she blew out a tight, annoyed breath, leaning forward in her chair. "Yeah, well, news flash, Rhys. Who you fuck and how you do it has *jack shit* to do with whether or not you're a decent guy. It never did, but before the plague, assholes like your Father Maurice didn't get the memo on that. But, hey! Now it's a new world, and you can fuck the whole damn company. You can get off on slapping people around and calling them cum-guzzling gutter sluts, or you can get off on *being* slapped around. Doesn't matter. Doesn't matter if you're doing it to survive or just because that's what gets your rocks off. As long as they're all of age and capable of consenting, you still get to call yourself decent, and most people are too busy trying to survive to give a damn. So there. If you're waiting for permission, you have it. I give you my blessing. Go forth and fuck whomever you want, however you want, and you'll still be an okay guy. I promise."

"Anyone ever tell you that you rant too much, Xolani?" Rhys mumbled sleepily, rolling onto his side.

She laughed. No, *giggled*. Xolani was giggling. *What?*

"All the damn time. It could be the Gospel According to Xolani is better reserved for a kid who isn't stoned off his ass, but there you have it."

"Mm, I hear what you're saying." He felt sleep tugging at him, but he didn't want to be rude. "I just don't think I'm like them. Can't be. Jacob'll make my life hell."

"Well, since their advice clearly worked, maybe you've got more in common with them than you think. Sick or not." Xolani shrugged. "And you don't have to worry about Jacob anymore. But out of curiosity, what is it that's got you so bothered?"

"Because I got off when Darius gave me to Toby." Rhys thought he should rise from the sofa and return to Darius's quarters before he fell asleep, but his limbs seemed to have melded with the cushions. "When he talked about Darius hurting me. I shouldn't have liked that. But Toby was so nice to Joe after what they did. Darius isn't like that with me, 'cept when he has nightmares. But then, he's only doing this because he wants me to live. Just like Luis . . ."

If Xolani replied, he didn't hear it. Sometime later, at the edge of his awareness, he heard Darius's low voice and Xolani's sharper one, replying in that frank way of hers. Rhys thought about telling her she was ranting again, but he was too damn tired to speak. And then strong arms lifted him, carrying him out of Xolani's quarters and to the ones he'd begun to think of as his.

△△△

HE CAME ABRUPTLY awake sometime in the night to the unmistakable feeling that something was missing. Then he felt Darius's cock rocking against his ass and realized he'd forgotten to replace the plug. Darius didn't appear to care. His slick fingers sank into Rhys, and then his cock replaced them, hard and thick. It no longer hurt, save for the initial burn; Rhys had finally learned how to make it easier on himself, how to push back and bear down. He did so now, arching his spine. He bent forward, curling almost into a ball on his side, drawing his knees to his chest. He opened to Darius, offered himself, too heavy with sleep to consider protesting even if he'd wanted to.

Without the plug, he'd tightened, and it was more intense, more like it had been those first few times. It was *good*, so unbelievably good. Relaxed with the peace of slumber, he rode the sizzling line between intensity and pain. Stretched and stuffed full, so close to the edge of endurance, Rhys groaned with each jolting impact of Darius's hips against his ass. He wriggled and begged and pushed back greedily into each stroke, angling to help Darius drive against the swelling knot of his prostate. He rode that line until Darius shouted into his hair and shuddered against his back. He seized Rhys's cock and brought Rhys to his own orgasm with little effort.

Lassitude began to overtake Rhys almost immediately, while his cum still dried on his belly. He mumbled a protest as Darius retrieved the plug to insert it again, and Darius paused.

"You don't want it?"

Too sleepy for discretion, Rhys answered, "Like it better . . . when it's harder to take . . ."

Darius went still behind him and something brushed Rhys's shoulder before Darius put the plug aside. Not Darius's lips. Couldn't be. Darius kissed him sometimes during sex, but nothing like that. No little sweet, fond gestures.

"You'll use it in the morning, then, boy. I'm the only one gets to fuck you when you're tight."

Rhys gave up the struggle and let sleep drag him under. "'kay."

22

RISK

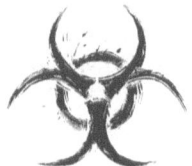

When Darius awoke, Rhys was snoring softly, his perpetually sunburned face even rosier with the flush his cheeks always took on when he got too warm in his sleep. Darius smiled, thinking once again that without the scraggly facial hair, it would be easier to see just how gorgeous Rhys was.

It was time to do something about that.

One reason he and Luis had decided to establish their base of operations at Fort Vancouver instead of a more modern facility was that all the buildings—most of which dated back to the mid- to late nineteenth century—came equipped with fireplaces. That, coupled with the windmill pumps that provided them with running water, allowed Delta Company to live fairly comfortably there on the base.

While Rhys slept, Darius built a fire and set a large pot of water to simmer, then retrieved from his bags a soft-sided leather case he'd carried with him since his first deployment. He didn't use it often, especially when out on patrol, but he made certain to maintain it carefully.

By the time Rhys stumbled from the bedroom—no doubt disturbed by the scraping as Darius stropped the straight razor—the water was steaming on the hearth and Darius had pulled one of the heavy wooden armchairs from the dining room table into the block of sunlight pouring through an east-facing window.

Rhys frowned at the razor. "What's that?"

"Have a seat, boy." Darius pointed to the chair.

Moving cautiously, Rhys obeyed, still watching Darius.

"You ever shaved?"

"No." Rhys shook his head. "By the time I grew anything worth shaving, Father Maurice and Jacob had used all the razors we had. I tried with a kitchen knife I sharpened once, but I wasn't stupid enough to try again."

Darius winced. "Lucky you didn't slit your throat."

"For all the blood I lost, I might as well have." Rhys gave him a crooked smile.

"Well, it just so happens my daddy used to run an old-fashioned barbershop down in Macon. This—" Darius held up the mother-of-pearl-handled straight razor "—used to be his."

Rhys eyed it skeptically. "Do you know how to use it?"

"I worked for him all through high school before I went into the service, so you bet your ass I do. You're gonna have your first real shave in style."

Rhys blinked at him. "Why?"

Darius grinned. "Because it's time to show the world that pretty face of yours, boy. You just keep still. I'll take care of the rest."

Looking wary and perplexed, Rhys tipped his head back when instructed and held still as Darius snipped his beard short with a pair of stainless steel barbers' shears. He closed his eyes and visibly relaxed while Darius worked, stifling the occasional groggy yawn.

"Want me to try to trim your hair, too?" Darius eyeballed the tufts, which looked like they'd been hacked at by a blind man with a hedge trimmer. His hair had grown quite a bit in almost four weeks, perhaps enough to salvage something with a little care.

Rhys shook his head adamantly. "I want it longer." His mouth tightened with that mulish expression he sometimes got.

Darius held up his hands to show he meant no harm. "Okay, then. Wanna tell me why you're acting like I just threatened to shave you bald?"

"It's nothing. Never mind." He swallowed, coloring.

"Hm." Darius went back to trimming Rhys's beard as short as possible. "You used to cut your hair yourself?"

"No."

"Didn't think so."

Rhys sighed. "Father Maurice used to have Jacob hold me down every few months so he could hack it all off. He said it was to protect against lice."

Darius lifted an eyebrow. "Same Father Maurice who died with hair longer than a prophet?"

"Yeah, that's the one." Rhys's mouth twisted. "Guess lice wasn't an issue for him and Jacob."

"Hm. Probably not a bad idea to grow it out a bit longer. That'll make it easier to trim neatly when you decide you want to."

Rhys met his eyes and ventured a cautious smile. "Thanks."

"Welcome. Careful now. This'll be warm." Darius wrapped a damp towel, still steaming from the pot of water, around Rhys's face. Rhys yelped and scrambled to uncover one eye as Darius began working the shaving soap into a lather. Out on patrol and on busy mornings, Darius used shaving lotion, but for Rhys's first shave, it felt appropriate to pull out all the stops.

"You've had all this since before the plague?"

"Most of it." Darius shrugged, adding a few more drops of water to the lather, watching for it to peak. "Have to replace the shaving soap once in a while, but it's not something most folks bothered with when they looted the drugstores, so it's always lying around."

"You know, it's hard to imagine you having a family, or a childhood."

"Well, I wasn't hatched full-grown from Project Juggernaut, boy." He gave Rhys a severe look. "That was a whole other project."

Rhys's eyes widened credulously, and Darius's lips began to twitch.

After a moment, Rhys laughed, a lighthearted almost giggle muffled by the cooling towel. Darius chuckled and removed the towel, using the badger brush to massage lather through the patches of shortened beard left on Rhys's jaw.

"Nah, there's not much to tell," he murmured as he worked. "Grew up poor in a big family. Joined the service right out of high school. Wound up in the wrong battalion—or the right one, guess you could say—and became a Jug."

"Did you lose your family in the plague?"

"Probably." He tilted Rhys's chin back to lather underneath. "By the time us Jugs were brought out of quarantine to fight the civilians rising up against the military government at NORAD, I couldn't find them. They might be in Colorado Springs now, at least a few of them. I don't know."

"I'm sorry."

"You talk to anyone in the company, they'll tell you the same story." Darius gave him a frank look. "It's probably for the best. You know, Joe found his husband. Wound up having to put a bullet in his head. Hold still now."

Rhys quivered under Darius's hands as he picked up the straight razor and dragged it slowly down Rhys's cheek. He listened to the quick, even snaps as the razor sliced each individual hair flush with the skin. Rhys closed his eyes, remaining carefully immobile, and Darius continued to speak to fill the silence.

"Everyone's lost their people, boy, including you. Just took you a while longer. We all got that in common."

Darius drew the razor away to wipe it, and Rhys's eyes opened as he seized the opportunity to speak. "So that's why Joe— I mean, that day when we found Gabe—"

"Yeah. Now quiet." With a thumb on Rhys's temple, feeling the beat of his pulse there, Darius turned Rhys's head and brought the razor down in another pass. "I imagine seeing you react that way stirred up a ghost or two for him. Toby tends to it, though."

"You mean that's why they—"

Darius snorted. "I don't know the details, but if you're asking if he and Toby do what they do because he's damaged, I'll say the answer is no. He's no more damaged than any of us. No, he does *that* because he likes it."

Rhys pulled a dubious face and closed his eyes again.

Quit fucking with his head, Xolani had told him bluntly last night. To say Darius had gotten an earful while Rhys had snored quietly on the sofa was an understatement. *You can't just go half in with a kid who doesn't know how to play the game so that you have all the authority and none of the responsibility.*

And if I have to put a bullet through his brain?

She had sobered at that. *I think it's a little late to try to maintain our distance on that one, don't you?*

Darius wiped the lather off the razor and tilted Rhys's head back, working down his jaw.

Rhys's breath picked up, and the pulse in his temple fluttered faster the closer Darius came to his neck. When the razor scraped down the vulnerable artery, his throat vibrated with a soft moan.

Blinking, Darius glanced down at Rhys's lap. The stiff rise of his dick was lifting his sweats.

"God Almighty, you really are a kinky little bastard, aren't you?" He shook his head, smiling.

"What—"

"Hold still." He drew the razor down alongside Rhys's Adam's apple. Experience guided his hands, made them sure and confident. He wished he could say the same for his words. "You gonna try to tell me it's not turning you on, sitting here with your life in my hands? You're helpless, boy. I could do anything I want to you right now, and you love that."

"Please. Don't." Rhys began to tremble, and he wouldn't meet Darius's eyes.

"Don't what? Don't say that? Why not? It's the truth, ain't it? Why shouldn't I say it? 'Cause someone told you it was bad, you were dirty, you were to blame for all the world's problems? So now the only way you can let yourself want what you want is if someone takes the choice from you? Because this world's so fucked up the only time anything feels right or makes sense is when it hurts? Because you're living every day knowing soon you might die, and when I got a knife to your throat you get a taste of that and it doesn't look so scary?"

Rhys made a soft, choked sound, his eyes squeezed shut and his thick lashes spiky. Unable to move with the razor along the underside of his jaw, he gripped the arms of his chair. "Why are you doing this?"

"Because it just so happens, I like seeing you afraid. Like seeing you hurt, too." Carefully, then, another stroke over the ridges and bumps of Rhys's Adam's apple, wiping the razor before turning

Rhys's head to expose the other side of his throat. "I even like seeing you bleed."

Rhys tensed, his breath catching as he tried visibly to control his shaking.

"You're the first person I ever admitted that to." Darius's calm was more the product of decades of remaining levelheaded under fire rather than due to any real serenity. There was every chance he might send the boy running for the hills if he played this wrong. If that happened, Darius wasn't sure he'd be able to salvage the situation. They'd lose Rhys, and it would be Darius's own damn fault for finally pushing too far. "Not sure if it's just you who brings it out in me, or if it's been there all along, but it's there all right. But we got a problem. The fact that you need me to save your life gives me leverage you don't got. I could do just about anything I wanted to you and you'd have to take it, and I like that fact too damn much. Way more than I should."

The razor stopped, pausing over the pulsing artery as it fluttered beneath the press of the blade. Darius hesitated a moment, then pulled away both the razor and the hand that had held Rhys's head immobile.

Rhys blinked at Darius in confusion. His pupils were large and his breath still rapid.

Darius regarded him soberly. "I ain't gonna say this while holding a knife to your throat. I'm not threatening you. I may wanna hurt you, but only in the ways it seems you wanna be hurt. That's something else, though, something way past what we signed on for. We get into that, it's not about saving your life anymore. I think I can do what you need, make things really great for both of us for a while, but not unless you tell me now you want it."

Rhys stared at him for a long moment, a thousand thoughts flickering across his frightened eyes. Then he swallowed hard and closed them.

He tipped his head back, offering Darius his throat.

Fuck. Just like that, Darius was rock hard. The boy was so fucking vulnerable, and *trusting*, despite everything Darius had done to him. He was fucking sexy, all soft and open like that. There was so much damn power in just that one simple gesture, and none of it had a thing to do with Darius's strength as a Jug.

Darius hesitated a moment more, wondering if he should press for an explicit and unambiguous *yes*. But the foam was beginning to dry on that last strip of stubble, and he didn't like wasting resources.

He laid the razor against that throbbing pulse and carefully drew it down.

If he'd believed in fate, he would have attributed the nick to it. It seemed too perfect, on the heels of what he'd confessed to Rhys. Most likely, it happened because Rhys had shuddered or moved in some imperceptible way, or the edge of the razor had dulled just enough after shaving off all that growth that it caught on a ripple of skin.

Rhys flinched, making a pained sound, and Darius pulled the razor back and watched the crimson bead of blood well up until its own weight pulled it down the pale line of Rhys's neck.

Rhys's breath hitched audibly. He stared up at Darius, and Darius stared back, a quiver of hunger tensing his muscles. The razor dropped into the bowl with a clatter, and his hand caught Rhys by the back of his neck, jerking him up and out of the chair into a hard kiss.

He set free the savage thing that snarled inside him every time he thought of Rhys. He shoved Rhys onto the table and reached for the bowl of butter. Without instruction, Rhys shimmied out of his sweats, his lean cock hard and eager. But when he began to roll to his stomach, Darius slammed him down onto his back, stunning him. He didn't want to look at the boy's back when he fucked him. Not when so much happened on his face.

Without the beard, Rhys's features were naked: vulnerable, open, beautiful. Pale and pink and so damn young. The savage thing inside Darius didn't care about Rhys's youth. It didn't care about his frailty compared to a Jug's strength. All it cared about was the desperate need written in Rhys's large hazel eyes. Need to be claimed, possessed, freed.

He hadn't worn the plug all night, and he'd be tight, just like he'd wanted it. And Darius would be able to see the struggle on his face as Rhys took his cock.

At his push, Rhys's knees came up, tilting his ass to a better angle. Darius smeared the butter on his dick and began to work it into Rhys's snug, gripping hole.

Rhys's head rolled back, exposing his throat. His mouth opened on a silent cry. His expression twisted, became strained. An entire saga of pleasure and pain composed itself in that grimace.

"Oh God . . . Ow. Oh yes. God, please. Oh, please . . ."

His ass seized Darius's cock, so hot, so incredibly tight, so eager and resisting all at once. Darius paused only a moment before he drove back into that heat, filled it with his aggression, his ferocity, his need to take Rhys's soft yielding to the very edge.

He still held too many cards; that hadn't changed and it never would, not until Rhys was a Jug himself. It would be far too easy for Darius to take advantage and become the monster he'd always feared he'd turn into as a Jug.

In the world that had once been, he would never have dreamed of doing this.

That world no longer exists, Xolani's blunt words had reminded him.

Darius didn't think she knew just how deeply Rhys's fascination with his own pain and destruction ran, or how willing the bestial instinct within Darius was to give Rhys what he craved.

"Take it!" Darius growled, setting a punishing pace.

"I can't . . . I can't . . . oh, God, please . . ."

"You will, or so help me, boy, I'll whip the skin off you."

Rhys gave a reedy cry, and his hands closed on Darius's upper arms.

Pulled him *closer*.

Fuck, he was sexy. Darius knew he should stop and explain to Rhys how the game was played, or had been in nicer times. He should give him a safeword and discuss boundaries and all that stuff people had done back when the world was sane and they had the luxury of making games out of anguish. But those pretty, clean rules had no place in Rhys and Darius's reality.

Rhys was right. It *was* warped. And Darius just couldn't care about that anymore. Not when Rhys went slack and still there on the table, soft cries and moans rising from his throat between gasping breaths. The only tension in his body that of the cock slapping against his belly with each thrust. The expression on his face was a study in agony and bliss. When he let go, the gripping pressure of his ass around Darius's cock eased. His body surrendered and received the hammering thrusts without struggle as Darius reamed him open.

Darius *wanted* that struggle. He seized Rhys's hair, jerked his head back so that his neck strained and his spine arched, the motion tightening him again.

"This what you want, boy?" Rhys's eyes popped open, full of uncomprehending fear and wonder.

Rhys's mouth worked, struggling to form even the simplest words, sobbing breaths exploding from his lungs. "I can't— Please!"

"Say it!"

"Yes!" It came out as a strangled yell wrenched from nearly empty lungs. "Please! Oh, *please . . . please . . . please . . .*"

With a satisfied growl, Darius drove harder, faster, pounding into Rhys's receptive body, urged on by his desperate cries. He dipped his head and dragged his tongue along the rusty streak down Rhys's neck, tasting iron and soap. He set his teeth in Rhys's shoulder, and Rhys screamed again, his ass clamping down on Darius's dick. With a groan, Darius exploded, the world flashing nuclear white behind his eyelids, sending shock waves down his dick to pulse and jerk in that clenching heat.

When the blood stopped pounding in Darius's ears and the fury subsided, Rhys was whimpering, limp on the surface of the table. A small puddle had collected under the head of his cock where it lay on his stomach, still rigid. Darius wrapped his hand around it, jerking it with fast, efficient strokes. He swore he could have come again when Rhys tightened around his cock, while ribbons of his own cream lashed across his belly.

Afterward, Darius slumped over his hands, braced on the table as Rhys lay there, staring up as if stunned. His thundering pulse and shuddering receded, and in their wake came a wave of unaccustomed tenderness.

So vulnerable. So fragile. He could break Rhys easily, and that savage thing inside him yearned to carry Rhys to the very brink of destruction. Rhys was his now, truly his, a fact that could still ruin them both.

But if Rhys was his to ruin, Rhys was also his to protect.

"I've got you." Darius bent down to kiss him. Not with the desperate passion and possessiveness with which their mouths had clashed every other time, but gently, reassuring and seeking reassurance.

Rhys gave it, embracing Darius with his arms and legs, pressing close to him. His mouth opened to the soft exploration of Darius's tongue, and he breathed a soft moan as Darius's cock slipped out of his ass.

It startled Darius how quickly his dick began to fill and ache again while they lingered in that clinch. Even for a Jug, that seemed excessive. Rhys had to be sore, and yet he kissed Darius as if welcoming him and held him as if he never meant to let go.

Not even when Darius gripped him under the ass and straightened. He clung to Darius like a limpet, without the slightest hint of mistrust for Darius's unnatural strength, and let Darius carry him back to the bedroom and do it all again.

23

RESOLUTION

R hys felt naked without the beard and self-conscious when all the men who had done their duty to help infect him with the Alpha strain looked appalled at the sight of him.

"They're afraid they robbed the cradle." Toby shrugged, easily hefting rucksacks into a pair of inflatable boats. They were equipping the next squadron to go out on patrol. "Can't say I blame them. The beard added a few years. No one knew it was hiding such a baby face."

Rhys groaned as he handed Toby another pack. "I'm nineteen. They can get over it."

"Yeah, well, you look a lot younger now. Luckily, I'm perv enough not to mind."

"Me, too." Kaleo came strolling down the sloping bank toward the river. "We still owe Schuyler a show."

Before Kaleo could collect, however, Rhys received a reprieve of sorts. Three days later, Xolani pronounced he no longer had to have sex with multiple partners if he chose not to. If he hadn't been infected by now, after four weeks of daily exposure to strains from multiple sources, it almost certainly wouldn't make any difference. Now they simply needed to wait for the Alpha strain to manifest.

The *or not*, hung in the air, heavy but unspoken.

She recommended he continue having daily sex with a Jug until infection was confirmed, just in case, a fact for which Rhys was grateful. He wasn't sure what he'd do once Darius didn't have to help him. Though to all appearances he was no closer to acquiring the immunity of the Alpha strain, neither did he show any signs of illness from Beta or Gamma. He could be content with that if it put off the day Darius no longer had to be with him.

Jacob was keeping his distance from Rhys since that day Titus had intervened. It helped that Rhys was rarely alone, and there were too many witnesses for Jacob to continue his covert harassment. But there were grumbles from the barracks, carried back to Darius and Xolani by Titus.

"Houtman's keeping his nose clean enough to not give us an excuse to take action, but pretty much everyone is sick of his shit," Titus reported when he and Xolani had Rhys and Darius over to plan their squadron's next patrol. "He's proselytizing. Talking about how God gave us the gift of the Alpha strain so we could redeem humanity. Fucker thinks he's Christ or something."

"His dad was insane," Rhys said grimly.

Xolani frowned. "You think he's absorbed his father's crazy?"

Rhys bit his lip and shook his head. "I don't think Jacob's crazy; I think he's just an egotistical dick. He liked being in charge at the monastery. He liked people being scared of him and his dad. He liked making people obey. If he believed all his talk about religion, he'd never have become a Jug. And he's talked about turning the Jugs into an army for God."

They all went still.

"He said that?" Xolani asked, looking grave. "He *actually* said that?"

Rhys nodded. "But Jacob's always talked big, you know. He's always been full of himself. He referred to his dad as our God-appointed leader at the monastery, stuff like that."

Darius leaned forward in his chair, his expression intent. "You know him best, boy. Could it be more than just talk?"

Rhys nearly replied with an automatic and emphatic affirmative, but the looks on their faces stopped him, and he remembered Titus mentioning that they'd kill Jacob if he got too far out of line. The fact that someone's death—even Jacob's, God help him—might result from his answer made Rhys swallow his reflexive *yes* and think about it.

Would Jacob take action? Rhys saw the look in Jacob's eyes that day in Salem when he'd "accidentally" pointed his gun at Rhys. But he hadn't shot. He could have, but he didn't. He was just threatening, and Rhys was used to that. Jacob had been making threats against Rhys's life since Rhys was twelve.

"I don't—" It went against the grain to say anything charitable about Jacob. "I don't *think* so. I mean, he's said a lot of stuff over the years and never really carried through on any of it. I mean, he hardly ever even touched me when we were at the monastery. He just tattled to his dad and had his dad do it."

Xolani's posture eased. "So you think he's just self-aggrandizing."

Rhys lifted one shoulder in a halfhearted shrug. "Probably."

Darius drummed his fingers on the arm of his chair. "Titus, get with a few of the most trusted people in the barracks and see if they'll monitor things for us and report back. If Houtman tries to actually recruit or make a real plan of action, the sooner we know, the faster we can take him down. I'll talk to Luis tomorrow, but I'm pretty sure he's not going to sign off on eliminating a guy we just recruited for showing off. Not without something more solid."

Titus snorted. "Let him try to recruit. He won't get far with that in Delta Company, that's for damn sure."

"Don't be so certain." Darius gave them both a long look. "Most of our people aren't listening because we took care of the ones who thought to set themselves up as dictators years ago, but there might be a few who've changed their minds since then. Could be they're tired of exile, thinking it's time to get their due."

"That sounds an awful lot like insubordination to me." Xolani fingered one of her knives. "Or the next thing to it."

"And if we were still actually in the Army, that'd be a problem we could do something about." Darius stretched his legs out in front of him, taking a sip of the liquor Titus had poured for them all. "It was different when we purged the ranks early on. We'd been serving with those people for years. We knew them, knew what they were capable of, knew which ones were seriously thinking about how they could use being Jugs in all the wrong ways versus the ones who were just bellyachin' about the situation. We take action against Houtman this soon, it's gonna raise a lot of questions about any recruitment policy we put in place, and even our judgment and fitness to command. If we do have people who are moving in the direction of being disaffected, it could give them grounds to challenge us. I'll answer to that if we have something real to go on, but we need to be sure."

"We'll keep an eye on him." Titus draped an arm across the back of Xolani's chair. "That's about all we can do right now."

Rhys bowed his head, an inarticulate dread scratching at the back of his mind.

His fears were pushed aside, however, when they left Titus and Xolani's, and Darius got him alone. The next morning, on Darius's command, he resumed wearing the plug throughout the day, even though no one else would be attempting to infect him now. His wearing it wasn't functional, and they both knew it.

He wore it because Darius wanted him to wear it. It pleased Darius to have Rhys walk around all day filled with Darius's semen. And it pleased Rhys for Darius to flex that sort of control. He spent the morning in the warehouse, helping inventory supplies for the winter at Fort Vancouver and cataloging provisions needed by the detachment escorting the civilians back to Colorado Springs. He worked cheerfully, with the omnipresent buzz of low-grade arousal singing along his nerves each time a movement reminded him of the plug's presence. He even went back to Darius's apartment at lunch hoping to find Darius there and in an indulgent mood, but in that he was disappointed. After a few bites of leftover smoked venison and scavenged fruit, he returned to the warehouse well before anyone else, hoping to make an impression on Delta Company as a whole by being useful and pulling his weight.

It was immediately apparent that someone had been in the warehouse. Several rucksacks full of supplies now sat by the door, ready to go. This wasn't unusual, since patrols were arriving and departing all the time. Rhys spared a moment to hope that whatever had been packed wouldn't mess too badly with the inventory counts he'd already completed.

"Still not dead, cocksucker?" Rhys whipped around from counting crates of medical supplies, panic lancing through him at the sound of the familiar sneer. He was completely alone here with Jacob. "It's been, what, four weeks now? Hear you're not a Jug yet, even though you're still bending over for the whole company. Guess it's just a matter of time until you die, huh?"

"Maybe, maybe not." Rhys made himself meet Jacob's glare without flinching. If Jacob decided to attack him, he'd be dead before anyone could reach him, but he'd be damned if he'd let Jacob see him afraid. Despite what he'd told Darius and the others, now that he was looking in Jacob's eyes, it seemed like maybe he was capable of anything. There was something off about Jacob today. His diction wasn't as crisp as it usually was, his words slightly less pompous than the arrogant speeches he usually made. "But seeing how you're a Jug now, it might be a good time to remind you that members of Delta Company aren't allowed to abuse recruits."

"I know the rules." Jacob loomed over him. "Not that you're much of a recruit. More like useless worm bait. But the company's enjoying having its own whore. I'm just here to put you to work. You're going to help me haul some packs. Let's go."

Unable to think of a reason not to help Jacob other than his fear and dislike of the prick, Rhys shouldered one of the rucksacks and accompanied Jacob from the warehouse, his mouth pressed into a tense line.

"Where are we taking them?" Rhys's shoulders began to ache from the weight of the pack as he tried to keep pace with Jacob's effortless stride. They passed out of the West Barracks area and began skirting the East Barracks, which was not the usual route either to the docks for the patrols that would leave by boat or to the gates for the ones leaving on foot.

"Officer's Row. The quarantine zone. We're outfitting the civilians for the journey back to Colorado Springs in a few weeks."

Rhys stopped in his tracks, setting down his burden with a vehement shake of his head. "No, I can't. I can't go near the survivors."

"I'm trying to help you, freak." Jacob gave him a taunting look. "Or don't you want to go see your boyfriend?"

"You don't help anyone." Rhys began to shake with adrenaline, standing near the old war memorial as Jacob set down his own rucksack and advanced toward him. Rhys had become so content with his situation, he almost hadn't thought of Gabe since the morning Darius had shaved him, but now another wave of panic surged. Whatever Jacob had planned involving Rhys and Gabe, it couldn't be good. "And you especially don't help me. Leave Gabe alone. That's over. He's got nothing to do with anything anymore."

Jacob's face twisted into an ugly scowl. "You pick up that fucking bag and follow me, or we'll see just how little your boyfriend has to do with anything when I throw my blood on him."

It was almost eerie, the calm that came over Rhys, a stillness that seemed to let him feel the contraction of each muscle in his arm as he clenched his fist at his side. He would die in the next moment. He knew that before he moved. Titus had been wrong. There was nothing strategic or thought-out in the instant when Rhys finally attacked Jacob. His only objective was to stop Jacob, or slow him down, even if it meant his own death.

And his only advantage was surprise.

He swung like Titus had taught him, trying to drive his fist *through* Jacob's face rather than landing the punch on it. His shout was as much an attempt to call out for help as a grunt of effort and pain as he threw every feeble bit of strength he had, from his feet upward, into the blow. Caught unprepared, Jacob rocked back, and Rhys pressed his advantage, turning his momentum into an immediate follow-up, fast and hard, and then another. Blood blossomed from Jacob's nose on the third blow. Rhys was dimly aware that his hand was a mass of agony, but he wouldn't let himself stop.

Then Jacob caught him by the throat, and it was over. He lifted Rhys off the ground before Rhys could land the fourth punch. It took only seconds for black spots to begin to dance in front of his eyes as the grip cut off his air and endangered the blood flow to his brain. In another instant, Jacob would crush his windpipe, and it would be finished.

He had a split second to regret that it wouldn't be Darius who killed him when the time came, and then he was on the ground, trying futilely to suck in desperate breaths through a useless throat. There were hands on him and commotion around him.

"That little bastard tried to kill me!" he heard Jacob yell. "I tried to stop him when I found out he was heading for the quarantine zone. He thinks he can infect his friend with the Alpha strain!"

He couldn't speak, could barely see, but Rhys shook his head in wild denial, sobbing for air. He could feel the suspicious looks he knew the Jugs must have been turning toward him. No one had ever believed him over Jacob's lies, and anyone in Darius's squad who saw his reaction to discovering Gabe down in Salem would be all too willing to accept Jacob's version.

"I didn't!" Rhys's voice was a barely audible gasp. He searched desperately for a supportive face. Most of the Jugs weren't the ones he'd come to know out in the field with Darius's squad. He knew they had no particular fondness for Jacob, but Rhys was an unknown. They regarded him uncertainly. A massive form resolved itself into Joe, and he stared down at Rhys with a grave expression. Rhys could hear other voices approaching and knew Darius and Xolani were on their way.

"I wouldn't," Rhys pleaded in a cracking whisper. After what Darius had told him about Joe, even more than Darius or Titus or Xolani, it seemed critical that he make Joe understand. "Joe, I wouldn't. I swear it."

His voice broke too badly for further speech, and so Rhys was left to listen in silence when Darius demanded a recounting and Joe overrode Jacob's blustering to explain what he'd found. Rhys wished he understood the sober, impassive look Darius turned on him when Joe shared Jacob's accusations. Rhys shook his head again in desperate denial, rubbing his throat and begging with his eyes.

But Darius was one of their leaders, of course. He couldn't afford to be partial. His mouth tightened as he looked back and forth between Jacob and Rhys.

"Xolani, stop Houtman's nosebleed and escort him to the barracks, then get Titus and meet me in Luis's office. Joe, take Rhys home, make sure he's all right. They're both confined to quarters for the time being. I'll be there to question both of them after I talk to the people who saw it."

Rhys accepted Joe's help up and followed him miserably back to Darius's quarters.

"I wouldn't, Joe." His voice cracked painfully as he stood at the threshold, making further explanation impossible.

Joe gave him a searching look, hesitating in the doorway. "I believe you," he murmured at last, ducking his head, and left.

Λ Λ Λ

"So who's telling the truth?" Luis folded his hands across his stomach as he leaned back in his office chair, after they'd spoken to all the witnesses and questioned both Houtman and Rhys. The questioning hadn't proven terribly enlightening. Houtman had been full of indignant bluster, and Rhys had barely been able to rasp out full sentences until Xolani had declared they could finish questioning him later. The boy's eyes had been huge with fear, and Darius couldn't quite manage to believe it was because he was afraid of being caught out at something. "Houtman says Cooper was heading for the quarantine; Cooper swears he wasn't. Who do we believe?"

Xolani scoffed. "Is this even a subject for debate?"

"I think after the obvious and blatant preferential treatment one of the recruits received from your entire squadron, we need to tread carefully." Luis flicked a glance toward Darius, whose jaw flexed as Xolani shot back a protest.

"If Rhys was treated better by all of us, it's because he acted better," she said bluntly. "Houtman has only himself to blame if he was marginalized. He's self-important, self-aggrandizing, and narcissistic. He's a coward and a bully. He thought he was big shit back at the monastery, and he thought he could become big shit here. Now that he hasn't, he wants to salt the earth instead. I should have found a reason to slit his throat two weeks ago."

"That's one way of looking at it," Luis temporized. Darius suppressed a growl and forced himself to listen fairly. "The other way of looking at it is that on the surface, Cooper is cute, sweet, and small. He seems harmless, which makes it much easier for him to pull the wool over everyone's eyes. Word is this isn't the first time he's attacked Houtman without provocation. And who is this civilian he was supposedly going after?"

"Xolani and I both witnessed that first 'attack,'" Titus grumbled.

"Kid had plenty of provocation. Houtman's so sleazy he leaves a trail of slime everywhere he drags his sorry ass. You go ahead and call it preferential treatment if you want, but fuck yeah, I'll believe Cooper over that guy any day."

"What about this civilian?" Luis gave Darius a level look, and Darius rubbed his forehead.

"Anyone on my squad can tell you Rhys was upset, finding someone important from his past and not being able to go near him. I was gonna try to find a way for them to talk, or write each other or some damn thing, if we didn't get confirmation that Rhys was infected with Alpha strain soon."

"You think he got impatient?"

Darius closed his eyes, feeling Xolani's expectant gaze upon him. "I wouldn't be doing my job leading this unit if I didn't say it was possible, but . . . no, I don't think he did. I think by now I got a pretty good idea how the boy works. He's offered to sacrifice himself for the well-being of others at least twice before. He may wanna find a way to talk to his friend, yeah, but he won't risk lives to do it."

Luis gave him a searching look born of twenty years of friendship. "And are you sure that's the analysis of my co-commander rather than a guy who's infatuated with the kid?"

"Can't it be both?" Darius kept his tone mild, managing not to wince while he cussed Luis out in his mind. Leave it to his oldest friend to bluntly point out the attachment to Rhys that Darius had been trying to avoid acknowledging. "Houtman's claim doesn't work. Plain fact is, Rhys doesn't have the ego to think he can pass on the Alpha strain when he's not showing any signs of infection himself."

"But you can be damn sure Houtman does," Xolani added with a bitterly satisfied smile at Darius's conclusion. "That sort of arrogance, believing he can just take what he wants and it will all work out in his favor, is just like him. The fact that he doesn't even recognize that not everyone thinks like him makes him a pretty fucking bad liar."

Darius nodded. "Ask anyone who has been on my squad with either of them, they'll tell you the same. Besides . . ." He fell silent for a moment, bowing his head as he searched for words. "The boy trusted us. He was a terrified kid looking death in the eye as bravely as he could until we hatched this crazy plan and asked him to trust that it would work, even though it forced him to go against everything he thought was right. He trusted us. You ask me, I think we ought to repay that."

Xolani's stubborn expression softened, and she offered Darius an approving smile.

Luis looked between the three of them for a long moment, then sighed, nodding slowly. "All right. I've never questioned your judgment before, and certainly not when you're all unanimous like this. Far as I'm concerned, Cooper wasn't doing what Houtman accused him of. So we need to figure out just what Houtman was trying to pull and decide what we're going to do about it. Was he just covering his tracks for attacking Cooper?"

"I think he had a plan." Xolani gave a decisive nod. "There were packs of supplies there. Maybe Rhys can tell us more now that he's had a chance to rest after the attack. I should go check on him soon."

"Do that." Luis caught Darius's eye, and Darius gave a tight nod. For all Luis preferred to administer with a light hand, Darius had been his friend for too long to entertain any delusions that Luis couldn't be a deadly cold motherfucker when something threatened his unit. "I want to know what his plan was. Now, what about Cooper? He's still not infected. Are we sure he's going to be?"

Xolani sighed. "It's been four weeks. The original Project Juggernaut cases could manifest between three and eight weeks. Nobody was quite sure what caused the disparity, since the ones with the healthiest immune systems seemed to be the *first* ones to manifest. Maybe that's the problem here."

Darius leaned forward in his chair. "Explain."

"Rhys's malnourished state. His lack of muscle tissue. The possibility of organ damage. It could be his body just doesn't have the resources to support the changes of being infected with the Alpha strain. Every test subject for Project Juggernaut was in prime physical condition, and Houtman was . . . well, he was at least a lot better off than Rhys. Something needs to fuel the changes, after all. It's why we have much higher metabolisms than civvies. Rhys just might be too depleted, which means he might not manifest until he's built himself back up a bit."

Xolani rubbed at her scar, and something bleak shadowed her dark eyes.

Luis narrowed his eyes thoughtfully. "I hear an 'or' in there."

"Or—and I completely fault myself for not thinking of this sooner—it could be that if Alpha infection *tries* to manifest, it could prove too big a burden for his already weakened body."

Darius had to keep himself from wincing. "You're saying we may have killed him." Even speaking the words felt like a punch to the gut.

Shit.

"He was already dead anyway, Darius," Xolani said softly. "We gave him a chance. And it might still work. This is pure speculation. We just have to start thinking in terms of the alternatives. For now, though, he's not showing any of the early symptoms of the Beta or Gamma strains, either. That gives us a lot of cause to hope."

"Except for maybe going crazy and attacking a Jug?" Luis dead-panned, then held up his hands in apology when Xolani favored him with a glower.

"If it were Beta, he'd be more likely to be slowing down, slipping into a catatonic state, rather than flying into a rage. If it were Gamma, he would have been far more out of control and powerful enough that we would have had a job of it subduing him. No. He's clean."

Luis murmured, "For now, you mean."

Darius flinched.

"Yes. For now." Xolani didn't seem any happier than Darius at that concession.

"I should go check on him." Darius stood, trying not to look as desperate as he felt to see Rhys again and make sure he was all right after all this talk of the boy's possible death. "I need to talk to him about—"

A sharp rap on Luis's open door interrupted him, and Toby stuck his head in, his eyes wide and his mouth tight at the corners. "We have a problem out on Officer's Row."

⋀ ⋀ ⋀

Rhys was curled up asleep when Darius and Xolani came in, tense and silent. He awoke with a start as Xolani sat on the edge of the bed.

"How are you feeling?" Darius could see by the way she examined the gruesome, finger-shaped bruises darkening on his throat that her hands were gentle in comparison to her usual brusque mannerisms.

"Fine." Rhys's voice was a painful rasp, and his eyes shifted from her to Darius. He looked so damned pale. "I didn't do anything."

"Hush." Xolani ruffled his hair, her thumb stroking his forehead. "We all know that. I'm gonna send someone to the warehouse and put the scavenge teams on alert, see if they can come up with some honey or lozenges for your throat. Maybe even some chamomile or jasmine tea. Slippery elm and licorice root would be even better, but that's probably too much to hope for. I want you to try not to talk for a day or two, if you can manage it."

"What about Jacob?" Rhys's voice cracked as he tried to force out the whisper.

"Hey, what did I just say?" She slid an arm around the boy and helped him sit up, propping pillows behind him. "If we tell you about Houtman, will you keep your damn mouth shut?"

Rhys nodded eagerly. He looked very alone, even with Xolani perched on the bed beside him. Darius felt foolish standing back in the doorway, as if he didn't feel like he was welcome in his own bedroom, but he was oddly reluctant to draw closer. Like he might be intruding on Rhys when Rhys wasn't well enough to deal with him. Or maybe like Rhys might shatter if Darius jostled him.

Infatuated. Fuck Luis for putting that word out there. It didn't even matter if it was accurate. It had been easier to ignore when it hadn't been spoken aloud.

Setting his jaw, Darius made himself stop acting like some bashful suitor and approached the bed from the other side, sitting down next to Rhys.

"Houtman's gone," he said bluntly.

"Not dead." Xolani clapped a hand over Rhys's mouth as it opened, giving him a stern look. "He's run off."

How? Rhys's eyes asked, widening as they passed rapidly back and forth between Darius and Xolani.

"Joe went to confront him after dropping you off." Darius gripped his knees to keep from patting Rhys to reassure himself that the boy was all right. "Joe tends to be real protective of anyone he's taken a liking to, so he was probably gonna pound the truth out of Houtman. Houtman must have seen him coming, because he got the drop on Joe and knocked him out. From what we can piece together of Joe's story after he came to and the reports of the civvies in the quarantine zone, Houtman grabbed several packs and went to Officer's Row. He threw blood on two of the women and one man and told them if they wanted to live, they needed to follow him. Then he loaded them up with supplies and set out. It's our fault for not setting guards. We've never had a survivor try to break quarantine; they're usually more'n happy to wait their turn to go down to Colorado Springs. And the idea that a Jug would kidnap any of them . . ."

Xolani rubbed the scar down her cheek, looking as troubled as Darius. "We'll go after them, of course. With three civilians, he'll be traveling slow. But it's already dark. He's going to have at least a twelve-hour head start, and he took one of the inflatables. We're not sure if he went east or west on the Columbia or south on the Willamette. Stupid. Fucking stupid. No one was paying any more attention to the boats and the water approaches to base than to the quarantine, because until now, it's been unthinkable that anyone would try something like this. The only thing we ever post guards for is to watch for revs. Now he could be anywhere in three states in a matter of days."

She wasn't fast enough to stop Rhys from speaking again. "Gabe?"

Darius nodded. "Yeah, that's the man he took."

"He wants me to go after him," Rhys croaked.

"If you don't shut up, we're done talking about this." Xolani glared at him. "No, I don't think his choice of hostages is a coincidence."

Rhys gave her a dirty look, flung himself off the bed, and stomped into the living room. Darius heard the roll top of the antique desk squeak in its track, and then he returned, thrusting a yellowed piece of paper at Xolani, which she scanned and passed to Darius.

He tried to make me go with him. I'm the one he wants. I have to go.

Darius caught himself before he began to growl. "Don't get any ideas, boy. You're in no shape to go anywhere, and we leave at first light." Just how many times was the boy going to volunteer for death before he understood that Darius was determined to keep him alive?

Rhys grabbed the paper back and used the pencil he'd brought to scribble another note.

It's just my throat. My legs work fine. I'm going.

"Oh, you think so?" Xolani hooted. "You're not a Jug, Rhys. Our major advantage is that we can travel at speed, and he'll be slowed down by his hostages."

Rhys strode back out to the living room and returned with a whole stack of papers.

Can you make the river flow faster? You don't even know which way he went. A lot of good Jug speed is going to do you.

Darius rubbed a hand over his mouth to disguise the twitching of his lips. He wasn't about to seriously consider letting the boy come, but damn if seeing him talk back wasn't an entertaining show.

Rhys scowled at them each in turn, his jaw set at a mutinous angle. Then he sobered and wrote another note, his eyes shining as he passed it to Xolani. *What will he do to Gabe if he gets pissed because I don't come?*

Xolani gave him an indulgent look. "Rhys, when we catch up to him, he's not going to see us coming, at least not in time to do a head count and kill his hostages if he realizes you're not there."

Darius affirmed her claim with a nod. "Besides, even if that wasn't the case, there's no reason to risk you, as well."

Rhys's eyes narrowed, and he scribbled another note and flung it at them.

They're civvies. I'm not. They come first. If something goes wrong and you don't surprise him, you need me there.

Fuck. Suddenly the argument wasn't so amusing anymore. Interesting how difficult it was to maintain that uninfected survivors were given the highest priority when it wasn't simply an abstract question.

Darius gritted his teeth. "That ain't gonna happen."

Rhys tapped the end of the pencil on the sheath of paper rapidly for a moment, then wrote another note and thrust it at Darius with a defiant look.

What about infecting me?

Xolani pulled the slip of paper out of Darius's hand and read it, cursing when she finished. "It's probably not necessary at this point, but . . . shit." The scar down her cheek tightened, and she sighed. "Look, we'll find you someone, Rhys. Someone nice. Someone you'll be comfortable with."

Rhys held Darius's eyes, and Darius knew he and Xolani were on the losing end of this debate. The boy would sooner court death than fuck someone else when Darius wasn't there to compel him to do it, and he and Xolani weren't going to risk that happening. Rhys didn't want Xolani's *someone nice*. And there was no way Darius could force the issue if he left Rhys behind. He certainly couldn't command anyone on base to fuck the boy against his will.

As they stared each other down, Rhys touched the spot under his jaw where Darius had nicked him, and the stubborn look in his eyes turned just a little pleading. They'd made an arrangement, the two of them, Rhys reminded him with that gesture. Reached an agreement. Rhys wanted Darius just as much as he *didn't* want anyone else— possibly more—and Darius had assented to that.

Rhys dropped his eyes and wrote something else. It seemed to Darius that the pencil shook while he scribbled. He handed the note to Xolani, and Darius swore he saw her olive complexion go a little gray as she read it. She crumpled it in her hand and threw it on the floor without passing it on.

"That's not going to be an issue, Rhys." She tossed an irritated look at Darius. "You want to jump in here?"

Darius scoffed, shaking his head in disgust. There was no answer he could make without conceding defeat. Somehow the runty little undernourished twerp had managed to argue them both down even without a voice.

A final note, passed gently to Xolani. Rhys's face was grave, and Xolani read it, then closed her eyes as if in pain, blindly handing it over to Darius.

It may be the last thing I do anyway. Let me help you stop him.

Fuck again. Darius cleared his throat, which suddenly ached. "Don't be so sure about that, boy. We got time yet."

Rhys looked away. He didn't seem very convinced. Darius couldn't let himself dwell on the possibility that Rhys might die, despite everything they'd done. And especially that it might happen while they were gone, unable to say good-bye. Rhys's connection to them might be new and tenuous, but they were the closest ties he had in this world now.

Xolani sighed and met Darius's eyes, looking troubled. They shared a moment of unspoken communication of their own, making joint decisions with a few glances as they'd done for years. The odds were far too good that Rhys was in greater danger from himself if they left him behind than he was from Houtman if he went with them.

Darius growled and nodded once, sharply. "All right, boy. You're coming along. We leave at first light."

Rhys sagged back against the pillows, letting his papers and pencil slide off the edge of the bed. He didn't smile or gloat, and Darius realized this wasn't a game to him. He wasn't just some stubborn kid who had to have it his way and didn't want to be left behind. He'd meant those protests, each one deathly serious.

Now he just looked drained, and it seemed the bruises on his throat had darkened in the short time it had taken for them to have their debate.

Xolani muttered a curse at the display of exhaustion, which Darius had to force himself not to echo. How was the boy going to keep up with them?

She rubbed her hands on her fatigues and rose. "Well. At least we'll be in a boat for the first leg of the journey, so you can continue to rest. You're probably still in shock after the attack. You'll be better in the morning." Giving Darius a loaded look, she added, "Make sure he gets some sleep tonight."

"That's not going to be a problem." He flicked a stern glance at

Rhys, who had the sense to look abashed. Xolani excused herself, and Rhys went to the bathroom, leaving Darius to stare at the notes scattered around the bed. He picked up the one Xolani had crumpled up and pried it open.

What if I get sick while you're gone?

Darius crushed it in his hand.

Fuck.

24

FUTILITY

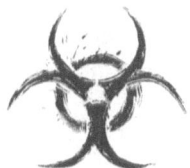

R hys folded his arms across his chest, glowering at the broken Bonneville Dam as water surged through it.

Jacob and his hostages weren't here, and there was no sign of the inflatable he'd stolen.

"He still could've have stashed the boat before heading out on foot." Titus rubbed his grizzled chin. He had to speak loudly to be heard over the roaring of water through the spillways.

Xolani turned a slow circle, looking in each direction. "We've been looking all afternoon. If he stashed it, he didn't do it anyplace within easy walking distance, and if he'd taken time to stow it farther away, he'd still be in the area and we'd be caught up to him by now. It's more likely he ported it by land upriver to continue past the dam."

"Assuming he even went east." Darius's rumble was filled with the disgust they all shared.

"*Why* would he go west?" Xolani turned to Darius with a challenging look. "Sooner or later he'd hit the ocean, and then he'd be pinned. It's not likely he went south on the Willamette, either. Very little south of Portland has been patrolled, but we have squads sweeping around there, which means he faces a greater chance of discovery by our guys. Heading east, he has better odds of finding other people and supplies."

"I ain't saying you're wrong, Xolani, I'm just saying there's a chance we're not finding him because we're going the wrong way."

Rhys remained silent, glaring at the river as if it were somehow to blame for his frustration. The first day of their hunt for Jacob was a waste. The longer they went without finding him, the greater the likelihood that some or all of his hostages would die.

Including Gabe. If Jacob didn't kill him outright, he'd still been exposed to Beta from Jacob's blood. Rhys kept replaying that first night at the monastery in his mind, hearing over and over Xolani's insistence that they needed to act immediately if they hoped to counter Rhys's exposure to the Beta and Gamma strains.

He had no doubt the squadron would offer to save Gabe and the other hostages the way they had Rhys, by infecting them with the Alpha strain, but how long was too long, before it wouldn't do any good to try?

Darius sighed, the muscles in his jaw flexing as he looked at the sky. It wasn't dark yet, but the shadows seeping out from the base of the trees were beginning to lengthen into inky tendrils, stretching across the landscape.

"Not much more we can do today. We'll make camp here, port the boats upriver in the morning. We'll give it until we reach the fork where the Colombia and the Snake River merge. If there's no sign of 'em by then, we turn back, try west."

Everyone nodded and turned their attention to eating before setting up camp. They had tents now; in the manner of the Pacific Northwest, summer had given way to fall seemingly overnight. The days were still warm, but the nights were considerably cooler. Without the safety of a being barricaded inside a building, however, tents meant extra men and women on the watch shifts to raise the alarm and give everyone else more time to react if a pack of revenants should attack.

Rhys wouldn't be taking a watch shift, naturally. He simply wouldn't be as capable at it as they were. So to make himself useful, he set up the tent he'd share with Darius. Beside him, Kaleo worked on his own tent. He'd been strangely quiet all day, his usual nonstop stream of good-natured joking absent. It had made the already grim attitude in the boats even tenser.

"What do you think, Kaleo?" Rhys tossed over his shoulder. "Are we heading in the right direction?"

Kaleo shrugged, his tent springing up into shape with a muffled *whuff*. "What the hell do I know? I go where I'm told and shoot what they aim me at."

Rhys looked up from spreading his and Darius's bedrolls to blink at Kaleo. He continued working with jerky movements, practically hurling his own gear into his tent, the corners of his mouth tight and white.

"I even fuck who they tell me to fuck, and hasn't that worked out well for everyone involved?" Kaleo sneered at his tent, as if it had somehow offended him, and stalked away, leaving Rhys frowning after him.

With an unhappy shrug, Rhys crawled out of the tent, heading for a stand of trees just beyond the campsite. This area had already been thoroughly scanned with the infrared detectors, and the Jugs assigned first watch weren't stationed far away. He couldn't go too far from camp, but he wanted privacy for a while.

Safely sheltered by the trees, he looked around to make sure no one was watching, then pulled a knife out of the sheath clipped to his belt.

∧∧∧

DESPITE HIS RESERVATIONS over Rhys's comparative frailty, Darius had to admit he was grateful that the boy had insisted on coming along. Unobtrusively, he'd brought over dinner rations as Darius organized watches and oversaw the camp setup. Then he'd erected their tent himself so Darius could sit with Xolani and Titus and strategize their manhunt. In all his years as a Jug, and the numerous relationships with other Jugs he'd test-driven during that time, Darius had never had someone so seamlessly integrate himself into Darius's way of working so that he could more efficiently go about what he needed to do.

Ignoring his constantly increasing appeal in bed—which was a damn near impossible task—Rhys made a damn fine assistant.

It wasn't that the Jugs Darius had been with were inept, of

course. They wouldn't have been in Project Juggernaut to begin with if they weren't highly competent. But they all had their own roles within Delta Company, their own duties. Never before had Darius had someone whose only purpose—at least for the moment—was to help however he could, filling in whatever random gaps he found. Perhaps that would change once Rhys became infected with Bane Alpha, and as Delta Company as a whole—and Darius's squadron in particular—figured out just where Rhys fit into their operations. For now, Rhys was one of theirs even if he wasn't one of *them*, which left his role within Delta Company something of a question mark.

When the watches were settled, Darius frowned to realize Rhys wasn't anywhere to be seen within the ring of tents erected around the campfire.

"Toby, you seen the boy?" Darius strode through camp to where Toby stood at his post on the perimeter with one of the infrared scanners.

"Don't you mean *your* boy?" Toby grinned, and Darius grinned back, though he didn't answer. Toby gestured to the scanner and showed its screen to Darius, where a single speck of warmth moved in the cooling evening. "Two o'clock, maybe fifty yards into the trees over there."

"Thanks." Darius clapped a hand on Toby's shoulder, driving an exaggerated *oof* out of him, and took off at a jog for the trees.

What did Rhys think he was doing, wandering so far from camp?

Rationally, Darius knew it was a ridiculous concern. Toby would see anything approaching Rhys's location in plenty of time to raise the alarm, and Rhys had almost certainly been deliberate in his choice to position himself well within range of the scanners. Still, Darius hadn't had time to get over his conviction that Rhys's as-yet-uninfected status meant he was helpless. He might not be a Jug, but he was intelligent and resourceful.

He was maybe ten yards out from Rhys's location and about to call for him when he heard the first wooden *thunk*.

Darius stopped jogging and began to creep forward, concern giving way to curiosity. As he drew closer, he heard a sequence of sounds. *Grunt. Thunk. Twang.*

Another few yards and Darius realized what he was hearing. He heard that sequence all the time when Xolani practiced throwing knives.

Grunt. Thunk. Twang.

This one was followed by a scorching curse, a word Darius didn't even know Rhys knew. He smiled. In just a few short weeks, the scrawny, half-starved, terrified, and traumatized kid they'd found had managed to wriggle his way out from under the old preacher's repressive boot. Rhys might not yet be a Jug, but he'd begun to blossom nonetheless.

When the clearing Rhys had chosen came into sight, Darius stopped his silent approach and stood in the shadow of a tree, watching.

Rhys wriggled a knife loose from a tree trunk, rocking it up and down to work the blade out, and backed up ten feet or so. He caught his tongue between his teeth, scowling in concentration, the knife held aloft by the blade near his ear.

Grunt. He used his whole body to give the knife force on its release, and it spun end over end through the air.

Thunk. It embedded itself in the tree, mere inches from where Rhys had pulled it out.

Twang. The hilt vibrated as the knife's momentum bled away.

Rhys stared at his results for a moment, then nodded in satisfaction, returning to the tree to rock the knife loose again. This time, it went back into the sheath at his hip, then Rhys knelt down on the ground, where he stretched out and began a set of push-ups. Fascinated, Darius forgot about making his presence known. He watched as Rhys's arms started to quiver after only a few presses and then collapsed beneath him, leaving him panting on the mossy earth. But the boy wasn't through. Once he'd caught his breath, he scanned the ground around the clearing, finally setting his sights on a decent-sized rock. It wasn't huge, but it was large enough that Rhys had to use both hands to lift it. Straightening his back, he began to do curls with the rock, bringing it to his chest and then slowly lowering it back to waist level.

Darius blinked in astonishment. Rhys wore that mulish look

Darius had become far too familiar with, and despite his obvious weariness, the boy kept working.

After only a few reps, Rhys began to pant and gasp. His tongue poked out between his teeth, and his thin arms started to tremble visibly with the strain as his muscles approached failure. He was still so painfully thin. The only definition to his chest, back, and abdomen were the ridges of his bones underlying the skin beneath his sweat-dampened T-shirt.

And still he was trying.

On the last attempt, he failed to lift the rock to his chest. The quiver in his arms had become a powerful tremor, and Rhys let the rock fall to the ground with a *thud*. He slumped against a tree, panting and shaking, with beads of sweat rolling down his temples.

"You don't have to do that, boy." Darius stepped out from the trees.

Rhys startled to see him, then relaxed. "Yeah, I do." His voice was still raspy, and Darius grimaced again at the blackened bruises around his throat.

It troubled Darius that he could no longer see the open inno-cence in Rhys that had captivated him from the start. All he could see was bitter determination. He should be thankful for that. The post-plague world devoured innocents whole and spat out their bones. But he'd miss Rhys's softness if it went away. Maybe it was just living two decades among hardened soldiers that made that vulnerable sweetness so appealing.

Darius gave him a sober look. "No one expects you to be like us, Rhys."

Scorn twisted the boy's lips. "Well, that'll be a real comfort next time I stand by uselessly while Jacob tries to tear my head off my shoulders."

Darius's mouth twitched. He might miss Rhys's innocence, but he was developing a healthy appreciation for the kid's quiet sass.

"Useless, huh?" Darius leaned a shoulder against a tree trunk, folding his arms over his chest. "Guess it wasn't you who broke Houtman's nose trying to stop him from endangering the civvies?" He arched an eyebrow, giving Rhys a sardonic perusal. "Must've been someone less useless."

To Darius's delight, Rhys began to blush, embarrassed by his own heroism. Darius had a hard time finding the situation as amusing. Houtman had already come too damn close to killing Rhys, but by the state of Houtman's nose and Rhys's bruised knuckles, it wasn't hard to deduce that the boy had gotten a few licks in before Houtman got the upper hand.

Civvies who got into punching contests with Jugs usually wound up dead.

After a moment, Rhys's blush faded, and he lifted earnest hazel eyes to Darius. "The only reason I got away with that was because he wasn't expecting it. He won't let me pull a sneak attack on him again. I won't stand a chance if he gets close in. I *need* to be able to shoot, to use a knife, to—" Rhys's voice cracked, and he cleared his throat, wincing as he did so. His bruised larynx apparently didn't approve of speechmaking. He opened his mouth again, but his voice broke on the first syllable, and Rhys's face tightened, his eyes burning with frustration.

"Hush, boy." Darius pushed himself away from the tree and stepped close, but he hesitated at opening his arms to Rhys even now. He held Rhys when they had sex or when they awoke from their respective nightmares. They didn't hug. But Rhys's bravado seemed to melt away with the loss of his voice, and all that was left were those soft, vulnerable eyes sending out a signal only Darius could receive, pleading wordlessly for reassurance.

Darius's hand closed on his shoulder, squeezing. And then his awkward indecision was overruled as Rhys stepped forward and pressed against him.

Fuck, he was an idiot for letting the boy get under his skin. But that didn't stop him from enfolding Rhys in his arms.

"You'll get there." Darius pressed his lips against sandy blond hair as Rhys slid his arms around Darius's waist. Rhys felt frail, still so damn scrawny. How did the boy expect to build up muscles when he hardly had any body mass to begin with?

Darius spared a moment to damn Houtman and his father to the hottest of hells. Did they know just how close they'd come to starving the boy to death?

"You need to give yourself more time. You could set yourself back, trying to take on too much. You're making progress. Your ribs ain't showing quite as bad as they used to, but Xolani says there's a chance that now you've got better nutrition, you might sprout up a bit more, if you got another growth spurt in you." Darius smiled, chuffing a soft laugh into Rhys's hair. "You might still end up taller'n me, boy."

Rhys laughed silently, his shoulders jerking. It wasn't an exaggeration, though. He had all the earmarks of a tall kid who hadn't reached his final height yet. His bony hands and feet seemed too long and big for the rest of his body. He was only an inch or two shorter than Darius, and a good growth spurt with proper nutrition could put him over the top.

"I'm nearly twenty." Rhys kept his voice to a breathy whisper, obviously trying not to engage his vocal cords. "Actually, if it's getting to be fall, I might be twenty already. You really think that's gonna happen?"

Darius shrugged. "Hell if I know. Xolani says it might, and I've never had reason to doubt her medical knowledge. Now stop talking. The sooner that throat of yours heals up, the better."

"Wh—" Rhys stopped at Darius's stern look, tilting his head in inquiry.

Darius stared into Rhys's eyes for a moment, then lifting his hand, brushed his thumb over wide, full, beautifully curved lips. He hadn't realized until he'd shaved him just how gorgeous Rhys's mouth was. He had lips just made to be wrapped around a dick.

He nudged, and Rhys resisted only a moment before letting Darius insinuate his thumb in the wet heat of his mouth. He let it rest on Rhys's tongue for a moment before beginning to move it in and out suggestively.

Darius let a bit of growl creep into his tone. "When the day comes that I don't have to fuck you every time to try to infect you, it might be good for you to know a bit more about sucking cock."

Somewhere deep inside he reminded himself that, assuming Rhys survived, he wouldn't *need* Darius anymore, much less want him. But that was a worry for another time. For now it was enough that Rhys was his.

Those wide eyes turned liquid in the twilight of the clearing, dark in the shade beneath the leaves. In sunlight, they had flecks of gold in all that earthy hazel, but now they were muted, like the bark of a moss-covered tree, gray and brown and green laid over one another. There was hunger in them, too, a hunger he'd never have guessed Rhys was capable of just a few weeks ago.

He'd done his job of seducing Rhys a little too well, and now he was the one who'd been seduced.

Rhys pursed his lips and began to suck on Darius's thumb until Darius's dick stiffened in sympathy with the lucky digit.

"*Not* until Xolani says your throat is healed." Regretfully, Darius drew his thumb out. He cupped Rhys's jaw, trailing saliva across his cheek. "You go too deep, you could hurt yourself."

A hint of mutiny sparked in Rhys's eyes for a moment, then quickly guttered. He nodded, not looking particularly happy about it. Darius stared at his lips again until he finally made himself break the spell. He wished he could think about the day when he could fuck Rhys not just for necessity's sake but because they both wanted it. But for now, they had a job to do, and they were out in the open in unswept territory so they'd better get it done and get back to camp.

He pushed Rhys against a tree and turned him around, bending him forward until Rhys grabbed the trunk for support.

"Same rules as last night, boy." He made short work of Rhys's belt. "Take care of your throat. No yelling."

25

HUNT

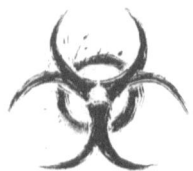

"Well, at least we know we're still heading in the right direction." Xolani surveyed the punctured inflatable on the banks of the Columbia just before the McNary Dam.

"We'd be turning around now if your friend hadn't managed to leave us a bread-crumb trail again." Titus gave Rhys an approving clout on the shoulder, but Rhys's return smile was perfunctory at best. He'd been thrilled when he'd caught the little clues someone—Rhys suspected Gabe because it was the same sort of thing he'd done the day they'd found him down in Salem—had been leaving, pointing them in the right direction. But now his fear, which had been numbed by shock and disbelief when he'd first learned what Jacob had done, was escalating the longer the hunt went on. Was Jacob infecting Gabe with Alpha after exposing him to the Beta strain? Or would he withhold that, just to watch Gabe die?

Would Gabe even allow it, assuming Jacob didn't just force him?

Darius picked up a folding knife. It appeared to have been used to slice the side of the boat in a deliberate act of sabotage, possibly an attempt by one of the hostages to slow Jacob down so they could be rescued. "Whose work is this?"

"I don't recognize the knife." It was small consolation, but Rhys was pleased his voice didn't crack, even if the bruises on his throat were still a hideous, mottled yellow-purple. "If it's Gabe's, he got it after he left the monastery."

Xolani shrugged. "Could be one of the women's."

"Whoever it was, they're on foot now. Next question is, which direction?"

Toby looked up from consulting a map. "Little bit east of here is where the river splits. North is the Colombia into Washington and Canada, east and eventually south is the Snake River into Idaho."

Titus frowned. "Is he crazy enough to head north into unswept territory with winter coming on?"

"Could be, if he really thinks he's untouchable," Xolani mused. "If he doesn't, he'll head south, knowing we've already done a sweep of Idaho and Utah. He might even be trying to get to the far southwest before winter hits so that temperatures aren't as big an issue. Arizona or New Mexico, maybe?"

"I know him. He wants me to find him. He's going to go wherever that's most likely." Rhys looked between them all, his expression glum. He wasn't sure just what Jacob planned to do when he did catch up with him. Kill him? Kill Gabe and make him watch? All he knew was that Jacob wouldn't find his newfound power nearly as satisfying if he couldn't use it to prove his superiority over Rhys.

Darius pushed himself up from inspecting the boat and brushed his hands on his fatigues. "Then he'll head south, where there's few —if any—revs, milder weather, and more supplies and shelter. Jamie, think you can find us a trail?"

He shrugged. "If the wind hasn't swept away the dirt on the roads, sure. Assuming he's kept to the roads in the first place."

"He will." Rhys grimaced, looking at the smudges of blood on the shredded side of the boat. Jacob had taken his fury out on someone for the sabotage. "He doesn't like to work any harder than he has to."

Darius pondered that a moment, then nodded again. "All right, then, people. We take the lazy man's trail, stick to the best roads. Scanners front and rear, and stay on your toes. We're not in patrolled territory just yet."

BY NIGHTFALL they came upon a small town that showed traces of human traffic recently, including an extinguished campfire no more than a day or two old. A large signature at the edge of the infrared scanner's detection range gave them hope that maybe they were closer to Jacob's trail than they'd thought, but it turned out to be a trio of revenants, no doubt drawn by the smoke. Unlike animals, revenants were intelligent enough to realize that fire meant people, which meant prey.

The revs were easily dispatched, but when the squad's attention was on building a pyre to burn the bodies, a second pack attacked. Rhys had fallen behind, struggling to carry an armful of scrap wood the other Jugs could have hefted easily. Kaleo was ahead of him and scanning forward when the growl came from behind.

Close. Too close.

For a moment, Rhys froze, struck motionless with the instinctive paralysis of an animal hoping to evade the notice of a predator. It was an instant, only an instant, then his muscles unlocked as he thought of how fast the revenants moved. His armful of half-rotten boards clattered to the asphalt, and he reached for the assault rifle hanging on his back, bellowing an alarm.

It was almost upon him by the time he turned around and got the rifle up. The rapid series of explosions staggered the charging revenant but failed to stop it. Rhys moved the stream of bullets in toward center mass, praying to hit the spinal cord before the rev caught up to him. Its legs dropped out from under it just as the rev reached Rhys, and it clutched at him, dragging him to the ground.

The rifle flew from his hands as he fell. The rev's teeth tore into the fleshy part of his waist where his shirt had ridden up as Rhys twisted to try to pull his pistol from its holster at his hip. He screamed as those mangling teeth cut into flesh. He freed the pistol, but he couldn't get the angle for a head shot amid the maddened flailing.

The world around him erupted in gunfire as the rest of the squad arrived, but he knew they were shooting at the other revs, taking down the ones that were still mobile and closing in for the kill. They couldn't shoot this one without hitting him, and by the time they got to it, it would tear Rhys apart.

Another snarl ripped through the air under the rattle of rifle fire, and a dark form dragged the revenant off Rhys. Powerful hands nearly tore the rev's head from its shoulders with a grotesque explosion of shattering vertebrae. The gunfire died down, and Rhys pushed himself up, gasping as he stared into Darius's flashing, furious eyes.

He looked almost as wild as the revenant himself, crouching over its body, hard, rapid breaths bursting from his lungs. It was like that moment in the field with Kaleo all over again. For an instant, it seemed there was nothing human in Darius's eyes. They burned as he stared at Rhys, and Rhys knew if he looked down, Darius would be hard. He stalked toward Rhys, and in that panicked moment, Rhys wondered if Darius would drag him off like Kaleo had Jacob. But Darius stopped short at the sight of Rhys's blood, and reason slowly bled back into his eyes. Darius blinked, his gaze growing concerned. He crouched beside Rhys and pushed him down, pulling up the bloody shirt that had fallen over the wound as Xolani hustled over.

Rhys lay immobile, staring up at the crystalline sky, all the bluer in the years since the plague, without the crisscrossing web of contrails he remembered from his childhood. Why was he even thinking about that? He giggled a little hysterically. He felt dizzy and nauseated as he became aware of the hot, throbbing pain of the bite wound. He didn't know who handed Xolani a flask of alcohol, but he sure as hell regained his focus when she swabbed it around the ragged bites, probing with a disinfected finger to make sure the rev hadn't left any portions of its rotting teeth behind. When it was over, Rhys shook with pain and shock, but he sat up so she could wrap bandages around his waist.

"I'm sorry," he muttered miserably. "I fell behind."

"It's not your fault." Toby patted his shoulder as Xolani worked on tying off the bandages. Darius, whose pardon he most wanted to hear, remained mute. "We forgot you can't quite keep pace with us yet."

"I know." The reminder didn't make his failure any less wretched. "I'm sorry."

"Fuck, Rhys, don't be." Xolani flashed him an encouraging smile over her kit as she packed away her supplies. "Take it as a compliment. It means everyone thinks of you as one of us."

"Oh." Rhys couldn't stop the lopsided smile that stretched across his face. It balanced out the nerve-shredding urge to dissolve into hysterics each time the feverish, pulsing pain at his waist reminded him how close he'd come to death.

"There." Xolani inspected her bandaging job. "Tomorrow we need to find a medical clinic and pray to God they have the dry-storage tetanus vaccine. I've got a supply back on base, but I don't usually inoculate our people out in the field. Stupid," she muttered with a disgusted look. "I've made sure every damn Jug in the unit is up to date on their vaccines before I let them go out on patrol, but I didn't think to update yours while we were back there."

Darius sat back on his haunches, and his strangely detached gaze traveled to Rhys's face before he dusted himself off and shot to his feet.

"Joe, give your scanner to Toby and take a bow. You just got promoted to bodyguard. You stick by Rhys from now on. Kaleo, I don't give a fresh fuck what your problem is, next time you fail to scan the rear long enough for something to get that close, you'll find my boot so far up your ass you'll have tread marks on the back of your teeth. Add these bodies to the pile and finish gathering the wood, people. We've got to make camp."

Rhys stared at Darius while he strode away, gathering spilled lumber as he went. Darius didn't look back.

"Don't feel bad if you're shaky for a bit," Xolani advised as Joe appeared by Rhys's side to offer him a hand up. Rhys accepted, groaning. "Everyone gets the shakes when they come that close to biting it. It's not a weakness. In fact, it'll get worse when you're one of us because your adrenal responses will be a lot more powerful and the crash afterward will be even more severe. So it's okay."

"All right." Rhys stared after Darius, only half attending her words.

Toby clapped Rhys on the shoulder. "You'll be fine, Cooper. So will Big D. He's just not gonna be fit for company until it wears off."

"He's not angry?" Rhys clamped his lips, refusing to moan again as the bending and lifting of gathering wood pulled at his wound.

"More like scared shitless." Xolani scoffed and walked away.

Joe was a huge, silent presence beside Rhys as they worked together to gather wood. For the first time since that night in the clubhouse near Salem, Rhys didn't find his quiet bulk creepy or frightening.

"Can I ask you something?"

"My husband."

"Pardon?"

"It wasn't Toby who wrote on me. It was my husband. Toby's left plenty of his own marks, but no one else will ever write on me."

"Oh." Rhys opened and closed his mouth several times. "I'm sorry."

"Why?"

"Um. Because he's dead? I mean, Darius told me . . . Sorry."

"Why?"

"For offending you?"

"Was that a question?" Joe took Rhys's armful of wood when it began to grow too heavy.

"I guess. I just— When I first met you, I wasn't—" Rhys shook his head and began to gather more, too bewildered to make sense of himself, much less express anything that would make sense to someone else. "I didn't understand."

"Now you do?"

"I think I'm starting to."

Joe nodded, and Rhys fell into step beside him as they carried the lumber they'd gathered back toward the pile of revenant bodies. Rhys almost dropped his when Joe spoke.

"Sheltered kid like you, coming that close to death. Surprised you didn't fall apart back there after it was all over."

Rhys's mouth tightened. "I can't. I've got to pull my weight, not be a burden. Right?"

"Don't let anyone see your weakness."

"Well, yeah. At least, I'm trying not to. Kinda hard when you're about five times weaker than everyone around you." Rhys ducked his head again.

"That wasn't advice." Joe dropped his boards on the growing pile where they'd burn the bodies. Rhys wanted to ask what he meant, but there wasn't time as Darius lit the fire.

That night in an old Grange Hall, Darius kept first watch, sitting near the barricaded door in grim silence. He hadn't spoken a word to Rhys since the incident that afternoon. Despite Xolani's reassurances, Rhys couldn't help but feel that Darius was angry with him. He hadn't been able to keep up. He'd gotten himself in trouble. He'd been too weak, too slow . . .

He lay on his bedroll in the cobweb-filled hall, thinking. As everyone settled into watchful stillness or slumber, he heard soft gasps and moans. Toby and Joe were making love. A couple weeks ago, it would have made him blush and squirm, both aroused and miserably ashamed of his arousal.

Now it only made him ache with a longing he couldn't put into words.

We fight to stay alive, and we fuck to feel *alive.*

That was what Xolani had said. He understood now.

He didn't realize he'd dozed off until there was a shuffle of motion around him as the watch shift changed. Rhys lay in expectant silence while Darius stretched out on his bedroll nearby. When Darius made no move to touch him, the pang in Rhys's chest grew keener.

Was Darius so annoyed with him for falling behind, for being weaker and slowing them down, that he'd bypass the opportunity to expose Rhys to the Alpha strain? Or was it simply, as Xolani had implied, relief and concern that kept Darius from reaching for him?

He could still see the eyes of the revenant that had nearly killed him, one bright and feral, the other an empty socket still oozing pus. He could see the eyes of the others, too, the ones back at the monastery Darius had saved him from. In those mad eyes, devoid of compassion or intelligence, Rhys saw the limited number of his days.

It had been almost five weeks since his exposure to the revenants at the monastery. The Rot could appear at any time. Each day might be his last.

He didn't want to waste time being ashamed or afraid.

Seizing his courage, he rolled toward Darius. He reached out in the darkness until his hand found the warm bulge of Darius's biceps. He ignored the pull on the feverish wound at his waist as he dragged himself those scant inches across the floor. His fingertips crawled up Darius's chest to his jaw and arrived at his mouth, helping Rhys locate his target.

He replaced his fingers with his lips, and Darius shuddered. His hands rose to rest on Rhys's arms, but they didn't seize him.

"One time's not gonna make a difference, boy." His lips brushed Rhys's as he spoke, not returning the kiss. "Not at this point."

Rhys froze for a moment, his resolve faltering in the face of doubt. Was Darius offering him an out because he thought Rhys had only approached him out of necessity? Or did Darius not want him? Should he back away rather than impose?

He began to withdraw and stopped.

What would he feel when Darius held the gun to his head? Would he be frightened or relieved?

What would Darius feel as he pulled the trigger?

He didn't have time for doubts. Not now.

"I know." Rhys reached for Darius's belt.

After a moment, Darius's mouth opened, slanting against Rhys's, taking control, and he pulled Rhys closer.

26

DELAY

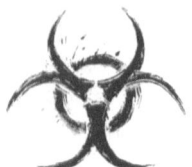

Two days later, Darius had overcome his irritability from the scare with Rhys and the revenant, though it had taken a few sharp words from Xolani. He didn't need her jabbing him in the ribs about just how terrified he'd been in the moment he saw Rhys fighting off that rev, and he certainly didn't need her scolding him for taking the backlash of that fear out on the rest of them.

Rhys hung toward the back of the formation with his head bowed. He'd been almost listless when Darius had fucked him at first light, though he'd tried to be gentle when Rhys complained about the pain of his wound. He'd become quiet and withdrawn since they broke camp. Darius allowed him his solitude, though he wasn't sure what exactly had touched off Rhys's sulk. More than any of them, Rhys had reason to be more furious the longer this manhunt dragged out. Perhaps that was it. At least Joe was a large, quiet presence beside Rhys, so Darius knew the boy was in good hands.

They ate lunch on the march, munching silently on dried rations between towns. Darius didn't really have a chance to check on Rhys; he, Xolani, Titus, and Jamie were discussing the status of the search and planning their route. As far as Darius could tell, Rhys kept his head bowed and didn't say a word to anyone the whole break. The mood of the entire squad seemed sullen, and they largely kept silent until Joe's deep-bass bellow shattered the stillness.

"Xolani!"

Darius whirled to see Joe catch Rhys as he staggered, laying him down on the road. Xolani rushed to his side, Darius only a step behind her.

"Oh, fuckitall." She pressed a hand to Rhys's forehead. His face was flushed damn near scarlet.

Rhys's wide, terrified eyes sought Darius, pleading with him.

"Is it the Rot?" His breath came in shallow pants, his gaze not quite focused. "Darius? Xolani?"

For a moment it felt like all the air around him had been sucked away, leaving Darius suffocating, his chest near to exploding. Xolani jerked Rhys's shirt up, lifting the bandage that covered his injury. Pink streaks radiated out from the crescent-shaped wounds.

"It's not the Rot, Rhys." She cupped his blazing cheek. "Listen to me. *Listen to me.* It's not the Rot. You've got an infection, that's all." Her laugh sounded a little choked. "Human mouths aren't known to be all that clean to begin with. Can you imagine how bad a rev's must be?"

She shrugged off her rucksack, digging into it for her medical kit.

"Do you know if you're allergic to any antibiotics?" His eyes rolled in her direction, half-lidded and confused. She patted his cheek sharply. "Rhys! Come on, kid. No napping on the march. Do you know if you're allergic to penicillin?"

His head rocked back and forth in a boneless shake. "I don't— I don't— I don't know."

"*Shit.*" Xolani bared her teeth in a snarl, looking up at Darius. "Okay, I've got some broad-spectrum antibiotics and a couple beesting kits in case he goes into anaphylaxis, but I don't have the equipment to intubate or trach him if his airway swells shut."

"Then do it," Darius snapped. "What's the holdup?"

"We need to get him someplace where we can monitor his condition, with IV antibiotics and epi if necessary. There's minimal streaking radiating out from the wound, so the infection isn't all that widespread yet, but we need to backtrack. There's that medical clinic where we got his tetanus vaccine back in the town where we camped last night. I don't know if we'll find anyplace suitable down the road."

Darius nodded once. "Say the word when you're ready to move him and we'll go."

Xolani opened a bottle of carefully sterilized water and loaded it into a syringe, injecting it into an ampule that contained a small quantity of fine powder and rocking it with a twist of her hand to mix. "Thank God for dry-storage drugs." Darius had heard her mutter that refrain before. The lack of climate control in the summers and winters had decreased the shelf life of many of the drugs they scavenged, but the situation was infinitely better than it would have been a century before, when most drugs had a short shelf life and often required refrigeration.

She cleaned Rhys's sweaty, dusty arm with an alcohol wipe and injected the antibiotics, kneeling beside him to listen to his heart and breathing for nearly half an hour before she gave Darius a nod, loading her pack again. "So far, so good. Let's go."

"All right. Joe, you carry him. You, me, and Kaleo will trade off every half hour. Move out, people."

"No." Xolani tossed her pack to Titus and scooped Rhys up in her arms, hefting him easily. "I need to monitor him. We'll trade off when I need to be relieved, but for now I'll carry him."

Her eyes met Darius's, and he gave a nod of agreement and turned to lead them away. Gina's mouth was drawn tight in irritation as they began double-timing it back the way they came. "What about Houtman?"

"We're not leaving a man behind."

"Understood. Within reason. But the question is, how much delay are we going to tolerate to take care of a civvie who can't keep up? Are we going to compromise our objective?"

"Would you say the same if it was Lucy?" Jamie asked shortly.

"Lucy's a Jug. She's one of us."

Darius had her by her shirtfront before he even realized he'd moved, winding his fist in the fabric. "Shut that down right the fuck now. Get this straight, all of you: the only *them* and *us* is *revs* or *not revs*. The second we start thinking we're worth more than anyone else, we become Houtman. We become Charlie Company." He released Gina with a slight shove and glared at them each in turn. "Don't say it again."

The sun had almost set by the time they burst into the medical clinic Xolani had scavenged the day before. They wouldn't have made it before midnight if they hadn't been Jugs. Carrying Rhys was no burden, even if he hadn't been so underweight, and they were able to move faster when they didn't need to slow their pace for him.

Xolani laid out syringes of antibiotics and epinephrine injectors, then began tearing through cupboards and cabinets for an intubation kit as Darius deposited Rhys gently on the examination table and Toby set up lanterns around the room. "Kaleo, Gina, take one of the scanners and go down to the pharmacy," she instructed. "Find me more bandages and Betadine. Search the town for any other emergency clinics where they might have bags of saline and IV epi. Benadryl, too."

Darius gestured the rest of them toward the door. "Joe, you stand watch here while Xolani works. The rest of you are with me. We're camping here tonight, so let's secure the location. Toby, Titus, take the other scanner. Scout the area, make sure nothing's on our doorstep. Go."

By the time all the possible entrances were secured, except the one Gina and Kaleo would use to return, Xolani had cut open Rhys's shirt and inserted an airway guard to keep his tongue down and his throat from swelling shut before she could intubate him if it became necessary. As Darius watched, she injected another dose of antibiotics.

"We're lucky so far." She tugged on her braid, her face drawn and sweat darkening the neck and back of her Army-green T-shirt. There was no ventilation in the clinic, and the day hadn't cooled yet.

Darius covered Rhys's blazing brow with his hand, surprised to realize the dark blond hair that had been so brutally hacked off when they'd first found Rhys had grown long enough to flop into his eyes and stick to his temples.

Xolani pushed his hand aside to check Rhys's temperature herself. "I'd be a lot happier if we had ice or cold packs to bring down his fever."

"How's he doing?"

"No reaction to the antibiotics yet. Heart rate and resps are holding steady. No wheezing or stridor. No signs of angioedema in the face or eyes. His skin is so flushed I can't tell if he's breaking out in hives yet in this light, but this is about the best we can hope for right now. If he doesn't react within the next few hours, we should be in the clear, at least as far as allergies are concerned."

"What about the infection?"

She flicked a worried glance at him. "Hope like hell it's not a resistant strain of bacteria requiring designer antibiotics that I don't have access to."

"Anyone ever told you you're a great comfort?"

Xolani snorted, then sobered. "Good job shutting Gina down earlier."

Darius shook his head. "Yeah, well, she had a point. We may have condemned those hostages to death to save him."

"Houtman condemned those hostages to death when he threw his blood on them." Xolani put her stethoscope in her ears again and listened to Rhys's chest. "No matter when we get to them, it's been long enough that unless he started fucking all of them on day one, multiple times a day, they're gonna die. With three hostages, even as a Jug, I'm not sure one man would be able to provide prophylactic immunity to all of them."

Laying her fingers against the fluttering pulse in Rhys's neck, she sighed. "Let's face it, Darius. This isn't a rescue op. It never has been. If we'd gotten to the hostages within a day or two, maybe, but now? Our objective here is to end Houtman before he endangers anyone else."

"You gonna tell *him* that?" Darius looked down at Rhys, whose unconscious face contorted into a grimace as Xolani palpated around the bite wound at his waist. Pus oozed from the seams of the inflamed flesh.

"He's going to need to get used to the realities of the world we're living in sooner or later." She bowed her head for a moment, then met Darius's eyes frankly, her gaze probing. "Which in this life means inevitably losing the people you care about."

Darius's jaw flexed at the unspoken warning. "How soon until he'll be able to travel?"

"Depends on how widespread the infection has become, how well he responds to the antibiotics. Could be days. Up to a week, perhaps."

"And exposing him to Alpha?"

She shook her head subtly. "There wasn't much point to it by now anyway. Just a precautionary measure. We'll just have to hope the exposure he's had already has done the job."

△ △ △

RHYS'S FEVER WORSENED OVERNIGHT. The clinic had no proper gurneys, so Darius and Xolani slept in chairs in the examination room with him, trying to keep him from falling off the table when he thrashed in his delirium. Xolani diluted the antibiotics in a saline IV, delivering them in a continuous feed.

As Xolani had pointed out, they didn't have any ice. If they could have managed to find a working power cell, they might have been able to rig up some sort of cooling unit, but they didn't even have that. When Rhys's temperature continued to soar, Darius broke operational security protocols to carry him outside and lay him on a blanket in the cool night air of the high desert with wet rags on his pulse points. Titus manned the infrared scanner, and Darius kept his weapon at the ready as Xolani worked to keep Rhys comfortable and medicated.

Rhys's hoarse cries sometimes split the quiet sounds of the night, calling out for his sister, for his mother, for Gabriel.

For Darius.

"The Rot . . . Is it the Rot? It's okay. Do you have to kill me now? It's okay, Darius. You can kill me."

Darius was grateful for the dark that cloaked his wince and his shudder, and the scalding sting in his eyes. If Xolani sniffled suspiciously, he pretended not to notice.

When the sun came up, they took Rhys to a mountain-fed stream that ran through town, using towels soaked in the frigid water to try to bring his temperature down. Kaleo and Gina retrieved a gurney they had found in an old ambulance the night before, and they strapped Rhys to it so his thrashing wouldn't pitch him to the ground. The rest of the squad spent the day patrolling the town to make sure there wouldn't be any more revenant attacks.

By evening, Rhys's temperature had come down some, and they moved him back to the clinic. Darius woke from a fitful sleep by Rhys's side to hear Gina and Toby, standing the second watch shift together, having a murmured conversation.

"Which one of us is going to remind Darius we still have an op to conduct, here?" Gina asked as he listened in. "We've lost two days now."

"You wanna be the one to do it?" Toby asked sharply. "You heard him: we don't leave a man behind, and I'd think twice before suggesting Cooper's not one of our men again. He's marched with us for over a month now, and frankly, he's kept up pretty damn well, considering the circumstances. Doesn't matter if he's not a Jug. He's still our brother."

"More like our mascot." Toby's silence spoke volumes, and after a moment Gina sighed. "Fine. Sorry. That was out of line. But let's be real: we don't even know if this kid's going to live yet, and I don't mean *this* infection. We still don't know if he's going to go revenant on us or if he's got Beta. This could all be for nothing. How much do we want to invest in this kid, timewise and emotionally? I mean, how do you think Joe's going to take it if we have to put a bullet in his head?"

"It'll bring up some memories for him, sure, but he probably won't take it nearly as hard as Darius. But yeah, it'll be bad. Doesn't mean it's not worth the effort." Toby's voice softened. "None of us have much worth holding on to, which makes us hold on even tighter to what we can. Joe knows that better than any of us."

Darius glanced over to see Xolani's eyes slit open on the other side of Rhys. He ignored the gentle sympathy in her gaze.

"We'll stay through tomorrow night, then we march." Something in his chest felt hollow as he made the decision. Xolani nodded, though she looked no happier about it than Darius felt. "If he's well enough to be moved, we can carry him for a day or two until he's able to walk on his own. Push him in a wheelchair or something. We can still keep up a good pace that way, maybe faster than if he were on his feet. If he can't be moved, we'll split up. Three will stay here with him, the rest will go after Houtman. I'll announce the assignments tomorrow. Whoever remains here will have to lay away provisions for the whole winter. We might not get back to base before the weather turns. We may even end up wintering separately if the party going after Houtman can't make it back here in time."

"No." They heard a dry whisper from the gurney. Xolani sprang to her feet, checking Rhys's temperature as he blinked to try to focus his bleary eyes on them. "I need to go."

"Well, you're not going anywhere tonight, so lie still." Xolani peeled up his bandage to check the wound at his side.

"Darius, please!" Rhys rasped. "I *have* to!"

"Hush, boy." Relief and dismay battled for dominance as Darius tipped a canteen up for Rhys to wet his parched mouth. "We'll talk about all that in the morning. Your best chance of being on your feet in time to march is to rest now as much as you can."

"Probably good advice for all of us." Xolani listened to Rhys's heart and lungs and nodded slowly. "Inflammation around the wound is going down, no sign of tissue necrosis. I think you just may be in the clear, kid."

Rhys smiled weakly, trying to dodge as she ruffled his sweaty hair. "Don't call me 'kid.'"

Xolani chuckled, rubbing the back of her neck as if it was stiff. "I'm gonna go bunk down with my man, get some shut-eye. If I hear you awake before third watch is over, Darius, I'll be strapping *you* to that gurney."

Joe's bass murmur came from the doorway. "Take my blanket. I'll keep an eye on him. I'm on third watch, anyway."

Darius wanted to argue, but another glance at Xolani convinced him to live to fight another day. Thanking Joe as he took the chair Xolani had abandoned, Darius settled onto Joe's bedroll in the waiting room outside.

Despite the weariness of two days with little sleep, Darius found himself staring at the block of lantern light that filled the door to the exam room where Rhys lay. He heard deep, rhythmic breaths as

Rhys dozed, but then they would catch abruptly each time he startled awake.

Just before dawn, he heard Rhys murmur, "Joe, how many days has it been?"

"This is the second night," Joe answered in a low rumble. "Try to get some more sleep."

"I've missed two days?" Rhys's voice was sharp with distress.

"Probably a few more yet to come. Don't worry about that right now. It's not likely to make any difference."

"Oh."

Silence fell, and the sky continued to lighten into the dingy gray of predawn. Darius wondered if Rhys had fallen asleep until he spoke again.

"Joe? What happened to your husband?"

"I waited too long to go look for him," Joe said. "When we got back to the States, they put us in quarantine at the CDC in Atlanta. Then the civvies outside NORAD got restless over the conditions there, so the military brought us in to quell the uprising. They didn't think that maybe none of us were all that fond of the military government, what with all they'd done to us, which meant they got a bit of a surprise. After we helped the civilians overthrow them, I went back to Milwaukee. Chip was tough. Resourceful. I knew he'd find a way to make it through. And he had. Problem was, a few weeks before I got there, another couple survivors joined his party, a mother and her little girl, and they didn't quarantine them. By the time I found him, he hadn't become catatonic yet, but he was starting to show patches of the Rot."

Darius heard Rhys swallow. He wished he were far enough away that he didn't have to listen to this. He'd heard it before, or at least a bare-bones version of it, but he'd never heard it while facing the prospect of having to do what Joe had done.

"What did you do?" Rhys asked.

"You know what I did."

"That's not what I mean."

"What, you want details?" Joe's voice grew a little harsher, and Darius heard him shift in his seat. "I made love to him, and then I killed him, just like he asked me to."

Something beneath Darius's rib cage tightened into a painful knot.

"That's not what I meant, either," Rhys whispered. "After that."

There was a slight rustle, which Darius imagined was Joe shrugging. "Went back to Delta Company. They were all I had left. My only family. Spent a lot of time drunk or high. Eventually it stopped hurting enough that when Toby came on to me, I didn't run away. We've been together five years now, I guess."

"Do you regret going back to Milwaukee to find him?" Another rustle and a soft grunt of discomfort, as if Rhys had tried to roll onto his side.

Joe hesitated. "No. Sick as it sounds, in some ways, that moment when I killed him was beautiful. He died looking at someone he loved, and his death came from someone who loved him, not some fucking virus or monster. And I never loved him more than I did in that moment. If I hadn't been there, he would have been alone with a gun in his mouth or begging a stranger to do it. Or he would have just rotted away. No." Joe's deep voice roughened. "I don't regret it. But I wouldn't recommend it, either."

A long silence, then: "Oh."

"What's on your mind, little brother?"

Rhys snorted. "Guess that's better than 'kid.'" He sighed. "Nothing. I just needed to know. I think I'll sleep now."

Darius's chest hurt, an empty ache that seemed to constrict his heart and lungs every time he tried to imagine doing for Rhys what Joe had done for his husband. It kept him lying there, wakeful, until his people began to stir for the day.

⋀ ⋀ ⋀

RHYS CONTINUED to rest and improve throughout the next day, dutifully drinking the broth Xolani made for him and napping whenever he could. Titus, Jamie, and Joe left together in the morning, saying they'd found some potentially useful supplies on the outskirts of the small desert town, and Darius and Xolani spent the day monitoring Rhys's improvement and debating whether or not they'd be able to move him tomorrow.

In the afternoon, Darius found himself by Rhys's bedside alone. He kept playing Rhys's conversation with Joe over in his head, wondering how he could possibly reassure the boy and ease his increasing fixation on his own eventual death without offering him hope that might turn out to be false.

The problem was, Darius had already succumbed to that hope. He knew it was a bad idea, knew he needed to be practical, and yet he was patently unwilling to entertain the notion that Rhys was going to die after all they had done.

Rhys's eyes were still shadowed with pain and weariness but much better than they had been two days before. "Please don't leave me behind."

"We'll come back for you, I promise."

"I need to be there with you."

"Rhys . . ." Darius gripped the side rail of the gurney. "Even if we give Houtman what he wants and bring you along, you realize there's a chance your friend might not make it. He could already be infected with Beta. Xolani isn't sure Houtman could . . . inoculate . . . all his hostages."

"I know." Rhys nodded soberly. "I still need to go."

"Why?"

"It's been over five weeks, Darius, and I'm still not a Jug. Jacob is, and he had a lot fewer chances to be infected than I did."

"Doesn't mean it couldn't still happen."

Rhys lifted his head, his eyes searching and his voice uncertain. "If I have to die, will you be the one to do it? Please?"

It took every ounce of discipline Darius possessed not to wince, not to shiver with the chill that washed through him, not to thread his fingers through Rhys's and make him promises he might not be able to keep. Instead, he gritted his teeth and nodded. "Yes. If you want me to."

"Good." Rhys gave a satisfied sigh. "It should be you."

"Why?"

"Because I matter to you."

Darius made himself smile, though Rhys's words felt like a knife in his chest. "Yeah, you do, boy. Far as most of us are concerned, this shitty life's been a bit better since you came along."

Rhys answered the smile with one of his own. "That's why I have to go with you." He fell silent and then asked, even more hesitantly, "And what if I live?"

In some ways, that question was even worse. "Well, I guess you'll have at least a few more options, won't you? You're the only one who can say what you want to do once you have a choice."

"I'm not sure I've ever had a choice before, not in my whole life." Rhys gave him a wry smile. "At least, not one that wasn't 'do this or die.'"

"You'll get used to it." Darius managed a grin. "You have to stay with us, but beyond that, well, it won't be like it is now."

"Why not?"

"Because you'll be able to choose. What you do. Who you do it with."

"What if I don't want to choose?" Rhys eyes softened, looking lost and unsure. "What if I want things to stay just the way they are?"

Jesus, but that sweet innocence of Rhys's brought out the best and worst in him. Darius caught himself thinking how he would have answered that question if Rhys were well. He'd have staked his claim again, like he'd done so many times before, and made it clear just what the situation would be if Rhys didn't choose.

That wasn't good. He couldn't count on Rhys sticking with him once he had other options. Or if he did, it might only be because freedom was too scary after being trapped for so long. The best thing Darius could do for Rhys would be to nudge him toward independence, assure him that if he thought he wanted things to remain the same, it was only because he was afraid of the unknown.

Rhys couldn't know his own mind, and if Darius were a more noble man, he wouldn't take advantage of that fact.

But he wasn't a more noble man, and if Rhys wanted things to remain the way they were until everything was settled, Darius wouldn't argue.

"Well, you don't have to decide just now."

The burring of a small engine outside the clinic rescued Darius from the battle between what he should do and what he wanted. He rose, releasing Rhys's hand. "Stay here, boy."

On the street, Jamie sat astride a two-seated four-wheel ATV, while Titus and Joe jogged to catch up with him, beaming like smug parents on Christmas morning.

"What the fuck is that?" Darius folded his arms across his chest.

"Show a little more respect, Big D." Jamie rubbed the rusty handlebars of the antique affectionately. "I spent all damn morning finding hoses and wires for this thing that hadn't been chewed apart by rats, refitting her for a power cell, and cleaning and oiling her."

"And Joe and I spent all damn morning looking for a working generator and siphoning fuel for it to charge the power cell we found." Titus wiped his mouth with a grimace, as if he could still taste gasoline or whatever they'd used. "But as long as it doesn't die, we got a way to make up some lost time moving at speed without worrying whether Cooper can keep up."

Darius glanced at Xolani, who had joined him in the doorway. "Think the boy will be strong enough tomorrow to ride on that thing?"

She grinned broadly. "I'll see to it."

27

PURSUIT

"Well, four and a half days of heavy use is more than I expected to get out of her." Jamie patted the cracked and faded vinyl seat of the smoking ATV fondly. "Especially considering her age. These things really weren't meant for long-distance journeys."

Rhys couldn't mourn the loss of the four-wheeler as much as Jamie did. Of course, he wasn't the one who'd spent so much time babying every possible mile out of the venerable thing. But after four days of jostling around behind Titus, Jamie, or Joe, his entire body ached and his butt was numb. The only good portion of riding the ATV was when, since the third day, they'd let him take turns driving, once Xolani declared him recovered enough that she was sure he wouldn't pass out and crash. It had been the first time in his life he'd driven anything, and the freedom had been exhilarating.

He'd also gained a new appreciation for the Jugs' physical stamina. They'd jogged alongside the ATV for hours on end and barely broke a sweat, making up the miles they'd lost during Rhys's illness. He felt self-conscious now that they'd have to slow their pace again for him to keep up, though Bailey and Toby were joking about how a nice stroll would be perfectly welcome after so many days of double-timing it.

"We've got another problem." Jamie dusted his hands on his

pants after pushing the ATV off the road. "I'm pretty sure we've lost the trail."

Darius frowned. "Where do you think we lost it?"

"Possibly as far back as two towns ago. We haven't seen any signs of anyone having passed through these areas all day. No footprints, no refuse, no campfires."

Rhys shrugged on his rucksack, stretching to test just how sore his wound still was. He gnawed his lip as Darius pulled out the worn map.

"You think he doubled back?"

Jamie nodded. "Yeah. We've only assumed he was heading to Boise because that's where he would have wound up if he'd continued on the most likely course by river. Now that he's going overland, he's got a lot more options."

"Fuck!" Everyone started as Kaleo dropped his rucksack and kicked it across the ground, glaring as if this latest irritating development were Jamie's doing.

"Come on, Kaleo, pipe down." Toby clapped a hand on his shoulder, and Kaleo shrugged him off.

"This is bullshit! Why don't we just chase our tails in fucking circles while that asshole laughs at us? Seems to me we'd get further."

Xolani glared at him. "Shut the fuck up, Kaleo. Unless you have any helpful suggestions, you can bitch and moan on your own time."

Rhys looked at Kaleo in alarm, glancing between him and Darius, whose jaw flexed with the fraying of his temper.

After a tactful pause, Jamie resumed his explanation. "I think he went southwest instead of southeast. After all, Nevada's been swept, too. Plenty of supplies and shelter in Reno. Maybe even Lake Tahoe or beyond if he wanted to risk the mountains."

Xolani peered around Darius's arm at the map, tracing the route from Reno into California with her finger, and shook her head. "Just him and the Donner party."

Darius shuddered. "Let's hope for his hostages' sakes they don't hit an early snowfall and come to the same end. All right, back the way we came, people. Keep an eye out for signs of passage."

RHYS SAT on his bedroll during first watch, looking between Darius and Kaleo. Kaleo sat apart from the other Jugs, meticulously cleaning an array of weapons that seemed far more extensive than what he had carried before the squad had returned to Fort Vancouver. He hadn't become any less withdrawn since that first day of futile searching up the Columbia River, and he'd only gotten worse since Darius had dressed him down for failing to scan the rear and allowing Rhys to be attacked. Now Xolani had snapped at him as well, and it didn't take particularly keen powers of observation to notice the way the whole squad was giving him a wide berth.

What happened to Jugs who went off the rails? Titus had intimated that Delta Company had ways of policing their own. If Kaleo didn't manage to pull it together, what would the others do?

Glancing at where Darius stood watch by the door, Rhys sighed and pushed himself off his bedroll, wending his way through the maze of sleeping Jugs to drop down and sit on the floor beside Kaleo.

"Shouldn't you be resting?" Kaleo asked without looking up from reassembling his assault rifle. "You're still healing."

Rhys snorted, tipping his head back to stare up at the cobweb-draped ceiling. "You'd be a lot more convincing impersonating my mother if you hadn't once threatened to fuck me while your girlfriend watched."

Kaleo barked a short, startled laugh. "Great. So now I've got to listen to sass from you as well as getting my ass handed to me by everyone else."

"It should be easier to take from me. After all, I'm cuter."

"Jesus." Kaleo stared at him, shaking his head in disbelief. "What happened to the sulking kid we dragged out of that monastery?"

Rhys shrugged. "I think he traded places with the guy who used to crack bad jokes." Kaleo scowled as Rhys picked up the freshly honed hunting knife lying out on the blanket, turning it in his hands. "It's not your fault, you know."

"Oh? What's that?"

"That Jacob became a Jug. You might have been the first to try to infect him, but you weren't the last." Rhys tested the knife's edge against his thumb. "Hell, you might as well blame Xolani. It was her crazy idea to try to infect us in the first place."

"Don't kid yourself, Cooper. Xolani blames herself plenty already for the clusterfuck this whole situation has become."

"Huh. Must be harder to tell because she's not throwing tantrums about it."

Kaleo snatched the knife out of Rhys's hand and set it down on the blanket again. "Yeah, fuck you, kid."

"Sorry, that window's closed." Rhys grinned. "Guess you're just going to have to save it for Schuyler. She seemed nice, by the way—not that I got much chance to talk with her. How long have you two been together?"

Kaleo rolled his eyes and set down his rifle. "What the fuck are you doing, Cooper?"

"I don't know." Rhys plucked at the blanket of Kaleo's bedroll. "You were pretty nice to me back there at the start, even when I didn't give you much reason to be. Seems like now maybe you could use someone being nice to you. Darius and Xolani don't really have time for it, but if you ignore the fact that I'm probably going to die soon, I've got nothing but time."

"Yeah, well, I don't need some kid patting me on the head, telling me it's going to be all right and I didn't do anything wrong." Kaleo looked away, grimacing. "Maybe there's plenty of blame to go around for making Houtman a monster, but the fact is, we did it when we should have known better. When *I* should have known better. I could tell the guy was slimy before I ever fucked him, but he was fresh meat and none of us really stopped to consider whether or not we should try to make him a Jug. That was fucking stupid. Especially after what we had to do with Charlie Company."

"You're starting to sound like Darius did that first night. There wasn't time for you to figure out if he was an okay guy." Rhys drew his knees up to his chest and rested his chin on them. "It had to be done right then, as soon as possible. If it hadn't been you, it would have been Bailey or Toby or whoever Xolani managed to convince."

"Yeah, well, Darius had a good point. You gotta understand about Charlie Company, Cooper. Those people were our brothers and sisters. I went through Basic with some of them. Took their money playing poker, went to titty bars with them, got stoned with them, learned how to function with the new abilities of a Jug with them." Kaleo shook his head. "It would have been one thing if none of the people I knew had been perpetrators. I mean, not everyone in Charlie Company was okay with what was going on, though in the end they all fought us when we attacked because their loyalty was still to their own unit first and foremost. But when it was all over, and we'd broken through their fortifications, and dozens of men and women were dead, we started interviewing the slaves they'd taken, and some of the people we thought we knew best, people we would have sworn would never be a party to such a thing, had been some of the worst offenders. Some of the things they did . . . God. If it could happen with people we thought we knew, why would we agree to give that power to strangers we couldn't vouch for?"

"Would you rather have let *me* die on the off chance I might have turned out to be crazy?"

"Yes? No? Fuck, I don't know." Kaleo groaned and began stashing his weapons so he could stretch out on his bedroll, nudging Rhys aside with his feet. "All I know is some civvies who had nothing to do with any of this shit—including *your* friend, Cooper —will probably die before this is all over, and I had a big part in making that possible."

"Yeah, I still say you're making too big a deal out of your part in it." Rhys gave him a flat look. "Come on. Everything that's going on, and you're having angst because you fucked him? Please."

Another reluctant smile parted Kaleo's lips. "Wow. Schuyler's gonna adore you when she gets to know you. There aren't many women in the Jugs, but the ones we've got are a special breed. They tell it straight, and they don't put up with much bullshit. I mean, look at Xolani and Gina."

"It'll be good to get to know her, too." Rhys refrained from pointing out how unlikely such a prospect seemed to be. He was trying to pull Kaleo out of his funk, after all. "Why doesn't she patrol with you, like Titus and Xolani?"

"Because she leads a squad of her own. Which she threw me out of." Kaleo grinned, looking a bit more like his old self. "I'm too insubordinate for her. She can't help but think it's because we're together, even though I'm the same with everyone. So I was lucky to catch her while her squad was back at base resupplying between patrols. We don't see much of each other while we're sweeping an area."

Rhys turned his head, laying his cheek on his knees to look at Kaleo. "So, back to my earlier question: how long have you been together?"

"Since we were quarantined at the CDC."

"God, that long?"

"Not quite as long as Titus and Xolani, but we do fairly well." A wince tightened Kaleo's face for a moment. "Being a Jug's a lot harder on some of the women than it is on the men. Maybe that's why they're so amazing. If one of 'em's kind enough to stick by you, you count your blessings."

The naked honesty in Kaleo's eyes was enough to make Rhys's throat ache. Strange. After watching Titus and Xolani, or Toby and Joe, it shouldn't take him by surprise to see love amongst the Jugs. It always seemed like they were too hard as a whole for anything that gentle. But then, he'd never seen Titus or Joe get that particularly sappy look before.

Rhys blinked in astonishment. God, how had he not realized it before? Kaleo wasn't like the rest. He had never developed the armor the others had, or at least not as thick as they had. That was why Jacob's betrayal had hit him so hard. In some ways, Kaleo was as fragile as Rhys himself.

Like it had when he'd witnessed moments of tenderness between Toby and Joe, seeing the way Kaleo loved Schuyler made something hurt inside Rhys. He wasn't sure why, but it did.

Maybe because it was utterly futile to hope he'd ever experience such a thing for himself. Even if Darius were capable of it, Rhys would be dead before it could ever happen.

"You okay?" Kaleo reached up, his hand falling on Rhys's arm.

"Yeah." Rhys mustered a game smile. "You're right; I should get some rest. I don't have a Jug's energy even when I'm not healing up. I'll talk to you later."

"Yeah, I'm sorry about that."

Rhys rose and brushed the dust from the floor off his pants. "About what?"

"That you were nearly rev kibble on my watch. Darius was right to call me out on that. I should have been paying more attention."

Rhys shrugged, quelling the bitterness that came with thoughts of his own impending death with the same ruthless ferocity he'd used to squash the pang of longing he'd felt just a moment before. "Don't worry about it. Not your fault I can't keep up."

He stretched out on the bedroll he'd laid out beside Darius's when they'd made camp that night. Since Rhys had healed enough to allow them to resume their pursuit of Jacob, Darius hadn't touched him. The first three nights, he'd had been too exhausted and sore from his injury and illness to mind, but now a strange restlessness set in, goaded by that envy he'd felt witnessing Kaleo's devotion to Schuyler.

Was Darius simply being considerate? Had he given up on Rhys? Did he just not want Rhys anymore, now that they were no longer trying to infect him with the Alpha strain? It hadn't seemed that way, when they'd talked that day in the clinic, but maybe Darius had changed his mind. Maybe he didn't want a scrawny weakling who slowed him down and caused more trouble than he was worth.

Rhys tried to stay awake until the first watch was over, but eventually sleep overtook him. He woke with a start when he felt a body move beside him and opened his eyes to see Darius lying on his side, facing him. His dark eyes glittered in the silvery moonlight. Hours seemed to pass as they stared at each other silently. Rhys's heart drummed anxiously in his chest, afraid of what Darius's unusual reticence might mean. Just as he began to resign himself to the inevitable rejection, though, Darius stretched his hand out, brushing Rhys's cheek.

Rhys closed his eyes, turning his face into the caress. His breath picked up, quick and shallow, as he brushed a kiss on Darius's palm with no forethought whatsoever. When his eyes fluttered open again, Darius was still staring at him.

"When this is all over, I'll have to shave you again, boy."

Rhys swallowed and wouldn't let himself think about how it would never happen. "I'd like that. Please."

The hand on Rhys's jaw slipped around the back of his neck, drawing him forward to stretch out above Darius's powerful body.

His head came up at the same moment Rhys's descended, sliding their lips together with more gentleness than Rhys had ever suspected Darius capable of. It was Rhys who made a greedy, eager sound, trying to deepen the kiss, his tongue slipping between Darius's lips.

"Shh. Easy now." Darius nuzzled at Rhys's ear. He caught the lobe lightly between his teeth, flicking it with his tongue, and Rhys went limp with a soft moan. It felt like his bones had turned to gelatin, and all he could do was slump above Darius, gripping his biceps as Darius's tongue traced the shell of his ear, his breath brushing the wet lobe.

Darius moved on from his ear down to his neck, and his hands slipped under the tail of Rhys's shirt to grip his ass, kneading. The pressure rubbed the bulges of their cocks together and without thinking, Rhys shifted his thighs apart to straddle Darius's hips, seeking more friction.

"That's it, boy. Ride me." Darius tugged on Rhys's hips, encouraging him to find a rhythm.

"Darius." Rhys gasped, seeking the right angle, the right speed. He felt strangely overwhelmed, his body more alive, more aware of each touch and brush, than it had ever been in all the ferocious couplings that had passed between them before. It was as though he had too many nerves, too much blood flushing and prickling beneath his skin, too many sensitive places alight all at once. He turned his face in wordless entreaty, seeking another kiss, and Darius obliged, this one harder, urgent. One of Darius's hands delved under Rhys's shirt to find a nipple, and Rhys cried out at just the stroke of one rough thumb followed by a gentle pinch.

He ground his cock down against Darius in mindless need, driven by instinct and wanting. His fly was an intolerable constriction, and Rhys pushed up from Darius, working his jeans and underwear down with impatient wriggles. Darius freed his own thick cock and spat into his palm, gripping them both in one hand.

"Move." He pushed up so his cock slid along Rhys's, groaning. "Move, boy."

Catching his tongue between his teeth, Rhys obeyed, a moan rising in his throat as he fucked into the firm grasp of Darius's hand. He surged alongside Darius's cock, noises escaping him with heedless disregard of the people surrounding them. It built slowly, so damn slow, the tension spooling inside him a little bit more with each thrust. It wasn't a thunderous onslaught like all the rough fucks they'd had, crashing over him all at once. No, it tugged at him, trying to tow him up and over in gradual fits and starts, until he was shaking, sweating, certain he'd burst out of his skin if he couldn't come soon. And then it was there, flashing through him in wave after wave, sending pale runners of milky fluid sliding across the dark skin of Darius's belly.

Darius gripped him tight, milking him with each stroke until Rhys cried out, oversensitized. But before he could move away, Darius seized, shaking, hot, silky spurts crossing the lines Rhys had spent.

Still panting, Darius shoved gently at him. "Taste us."

Rhys obeyed without hesitation, without shame, shimmying down Darius's thighs to slide his tongue through the salty mess on the hard ridges of Darius's abdomen. It was as bitter as he remembered from that first night in the chapel, but he didn't care. His tongue stroked until Darius drew him up for a slow, deep kiss, sharing the taste from Rhys's mouth.

Darius rolled, toppling them over onto their sides without breaking the kiss. His thigh slipped between Rhys's to press them closer together, and Rhys hooked his upper leg around the back of it to win just a few millimeters more. He couldn't say how long they lay like that. It felt like half the night might have passed, with one searching, exploratory kiss merging into another until his body was almost too limp and weary to even pull up his pants. He might have slept with them still pushed down his thighs if Darius hadn't finally broken the sticky embrace to help him right their clothing.

He fell asleep with his head on Darius's shoulder, tucked under his chin. The yearning for tenderness that had stirred within him was sated. He might never experience the sort of devotion Kaleo and Schuyler, or Titus and Xolani, or Joe and Toby had, but this was close enough for the time he had left. Darius brushed one last kiss to his forehead, a barely perceptible whisper of a caress, just enough to tip the corners of Rhys's mouth up into a smile before sleep overtook him.

⋀ ⋀ ⋀

"What're you doing, boy?"

Rhys started at the sound of Darius's voice behind him. He'd ducked around a building when they stopped for lunch and had his shirt halfway up his chest. He jerked it down, smoothing his hands over it.

He dried his palms on his jeans. "Nothing."

Darius folded his arms across his chest as he stared at Rhys for a long moment. Rhys couldn't help the way his heart began to race. It had been three nights since he and Darius had begun having sex again, and it was better than he could ever remember it being, except perhaps during those last few days at Fort Vancouver before Jacob had taken his hostages.

Maybe even better than that. Without the burden of necessity getting in the way, they could just enjoy themselves.

But now Darius looked troubled. "Go on. Take off the shirt."

Rhys hung his head and obeyed. In the distraction of everything else in the weeks since they'd left Fort Vancouver, they'd stopped doing the routine inspections, which was why he'd slipped away, trying to check himself for the bruised patches of the Rot.

He should have known Darius would notice.

Darius's blunt fingers were gentle as he laid a hand on Rhys's shoulder and lifted his arm to check underneath. First one, then the other. His fingers brushed over Rhys's skin, raising goose bumps despite his dread.

"Now the pants."

He remembered how he'd blushed in those early weeks after they'd left the monastery, each time Darius saw him nude. Now it felt completely ordinary to push his jeans and underwear down to his ankles in Darius's presence. Darius dropped to one knee in front of Rhys, gently pushing his cock and balls aside to check his groin and inner thighs, turning him to inspect beneath his buttocks.

Darius wasn't trying to be sexual in the least, and yet Rhys couldn't help but twitch in response. He closed his eyes and kept his breathing slow and steady, knowing the reaction was inevitable and strangely at peace with it.

Darius stood before Rhys made it to half-mast.

"No spots." He squeezed Rhys's shoulder, and Rhys bowed his head with a sigh of relief. Darius's hand moved from his shoulder to his neck, the touch shifting from a reassuring pat to something more caressing. Rhys turned his head in an invitation Darius didn't hesitate to accept, cupping the back of Rhys's neck and kissing him long and slow. Then he pulled back and shook himself. "Get dressed, boy. We gotta get moving."

They hadn't been on the road half an hour when the sight of buzzards in the distance led them to the mutilated corpse of a woman outside an empty house.

"Shit," Bailey muttered, looking ill. "I recognize her. She's one of the civvies we recovered when we were sweeping Portland."

Kaleo spat a bitter curse, and Rhys went cold.

"Revs got her?" Darius asked.

"Hard to tell, but I suspect so." Xolani knelt by the body, checking the various wounds. "An animal would have dragged her to someplace more sheltered to eat."

"Wanna bet Houtman's up to his old tricks?" Titus damn near growled. "Throwing someone to the wolves while he makes his getaway?"

Rhys felt a flash of fury, seeing Cady in the woman's mangled features for a split second.

Toby frowned. "He's armed to the teeth, and he's a Jug. Why didn't he just kill the revs?"

"Because he's a fucking coward." Titus spat on the dust-swept pavement and stalked away.

"Every delay puts that asshole a little farther ahead." Darius pushed himself up, away from the body. "Burn the remains, but do it quick. We need to get moving."

Rhys nodded, swallowing hard against his nausea, and began gathering up brushwood.

28

SURVIVORS

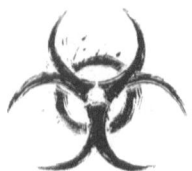

T he second week of their pursuit moved into the third, and
Darius could feel Rhys's frustration. He kept trying to push
himself harder and faster while he was still recovering from his
injury and illness, and Darius and Xolani took turns chiding Rhys
into accepting that he wasn't going to be able to match the Jug's
pace, no matter how hard he tried, and he'd only hurt himself
trying.

"You were right," he told Darius with a hangdog expression one
night in camp, sitting in a ball on his bedroll with his chin on his
knees. "I shouldn't have come along. It's just—"

"I know why you needed to come, boy. If I hadn't agreed, you
wouldn't be here."

The reassurances only went so far. What did help Rhys feel like
he wasn't holding the squad back was that he noticed a bicycle
hanging from the beams in a half-collapsed garage.

"Now why the fuck didn't I think to look for a damn bike?"
Titus looked disgusted at his oversight. Jamie located oil for the
chain and inflated the tires, which had thankfully escaped being
gnawed on by rats. The result was that they were able to pick up
their pace that day and the next, easily keeping up with Rhys as he
pedaled. The boy endured it without complaint, but he moved stiffly

that first night and gave a pained moan, flinching away, when Darius tried to touch him.

Amused, Darius treated him to a massage, during which Rhys fell sound asleep before Darius could enact the second half of his plan, which would have involved a blowjob.

The third morning after finding the bike, somewhere near the California-Oregon border, a scream split the air, shrill and feminine. It sounded eerie and out of place in the half-desert sagebrush and scrub pine ranch country they were passing through. The wind distorted the cry so they couldn't tell which direction it had come from.

Kaleo and Toby went on immediate alert, moving in circles, sweeping in all directions with the infrared scanners.

"Where is she?" Darius snapped when they had nothing to report.

"Not close enough for a signature yet." Kaleo glared at his scanner as if willing it to yield answers.

"I've got footprints here!" Jamie knelt on the shoulder of the two-lane highway. "That mailbox up ahead. I think the drive there goes to another ranch set back from the road."

With their weapons ready, they followed the trail to the long dirt drive that rose over a low hill and disappeared west of the highway. Here, the footprints were obvious for all to see.

"They made camp at the ranch overnight." Kaleo looked grim and wired, clutching his rifle far too hard. He handed his scanner off to Bailey and took point without instruction, beginning down the drive.

"Back in formation, Kaleo!" Darius barked, just as Toby shouted, "I've got signatures. Looks like two humans, straight ahead past that hill!"

Kaleo took off, leaving the rest of them to sprint after him.

A woman and a man were staggering down the long drive at a limping run. The woman cried out when she saw them, and by the time they had caught up with Kaleo, the two survivors had dropped to the ground, gasping.

"I hit him . . . I hit him . . ." She nearly sobbed for air. They were both bloodied and bruised. As Rhys caught up, Xolani examined a lump on the side of the man's scalp, from which blood trickled down the side of his face.

"Gabe? Are you okay?" Rhys asked desperately.

"Rhys?"

Dark blue eyes blinked open, and a wide smile split Rhys's face.

"We have to go!" the woman begged, bent double clutching a stitch in her side. "I don't think he'll be out long."

"Where is he?" Kaleo's tense question preempted Darius's own inquiry.

"Fall in line, Kaleo." Darius gave him a hard stare that Kaleo barely seemed to notice.

The woman took a long drink from the canteen Toby offered her. "The main house."

"What about his weapons? Does he still have ammunition?"

She nodded, her eyes huge and bulging with terror. "He's crazy. He ate Tia."

A ripple passed through the squad, followed by utter stillness.

"Say that again?" A chill prickled up the back of Darius's neck as he remembered the mangled corpse they'd found days ago.

The woman's face crumpled. "We were . . . we were going to try to escape. She was supposed to lock him in a room and then we could grab the gun, but he was too fast. He caught her and he . . ."

"He was like a revenant," Gabriel said, looking up at them. Rhys turned green. "He tore her throat out, and then he just began ripping her apart with his teeth. Like some kind of animal. He started eating, and when he was done, he just . . . stopped. Looked at us, blood all over him, completely calm again. Grabbed his gun and told us to go."

Darius looked to Xolani, whose eyes were tight at the corners. Her scar was white against her Mediterranean complexion. She shook her head, for once looking completely confounded. "I . . . have no explanation."

"Could he be a rev?"

"We've never— Revenants aren't sentient, Darius. We all know that. Their verbal and reasoning abilities shut down. They're driven purely by predatory instinct. This isn't—"

"Then what is it?"

She looked at Rhys, then met Darius's eyes again. "We were going to use the Alpha strain to give him immunity to Beta or Gamma, but what if . . . what if he got both? What if his limited exposure to Alpha wasn't sufficient to immunize him entirely against Gamma? Or perhaps continuous exposure is required to maintain immunity, or maybe it's a new mutation. *I don't know!*"

"Who the fuck cares?" Kaleo glared at them. "It doesn't matter what he is. We shoot him. He dies. Problem solved. So let's go before he gets away."

Still conscientiously keeping his distance, if not as much as protocol required, Rhys looked so pale Darius thought he might faint. "So what am I going to become?"

"Nothing." Darius snapped his head around to give Rhys a stern look. It chilled him to the bone to see just how shaken Xolani was. Of course, if Houtman had become some new sort of monster, he was a monster she had been involved in creating. But then, so had Darius, and that knowledge sat like a cold stone in his gut. "You're gonna be just fine, boy. Bailey, give Kaleo his scanner back. Kaleo, you, Xolani, and Joe, take Rhys and the others back to the highway and wait there. Find cover if you can. The rest of you, with me."

"But—" Darius saw the furious argument rise to Kaleo's lips, but he had Kaleo by the collar, slamming him back against a fence post before it could take shape. The half-rotten wood creaked and splintered with the impact.

"Whatever problems you got with your role in making Houtman what he is, you deal with them on your own time, soldier. Right now, you get your ass back in line and follow orders. Got that?"

Kaleo's eyes still burned with rage, but he gave a brusque nod, and Darius released him. Taking his weapon in one hand and the scanner in the other, he gestured the others to follow him, Xolani and Joe helping to get the exhausted and injured hostages upright.

Rhys remained where he stood, looking from Darius to Xolani and then to the hostages uncertainly. "I'm not— I can't— I shouldn't be near them."

Xolani sighed. "Don't worry, Rhys. There's no way these two

haven't already been exposed. You're no danger to them. Come on, now. Help me take care of them."

With a nod, Rhys followed her. Darius turned as his squad began moving carefully down the lane, though he knew he'd see Rhys absorbed in caring for his friend. But Rhys had stopped, falling behind the others, to stare back at Darius. His eyes were huge with fear. Darius tried for an encouraging smile, and after a moment, Rhys's lips curved in response, before he bowed his head and walked away.

⋀ ⋀ ⋀

GABE GROANED as Xolani helped him to sit at the base of a tree in the greenbelt on the opposite side of the highway from the ranch. The huge bruise on the side of his head continued to seep blood.

The sight of it worried Rhys. "What happened to him?"

"Fucker pistol-whipped him last night," the female hostage answered, slumping against another tree. "Nearly caved his skull in."

Gabe chuckled, the laugh coming out of nowhere, as if he were delirious. "He got pissed off when he couldn't get it up to rape me."

"Lucky you." The other survivor snorted.

Xolani dug in her pack and swabbed at Gabe's scalp wound with gauze pads. "He might have a concussion. I know who this guy is, but what's your name, honey?"

"Emilina Cruzado." The survivor extended her hand. "Emmy. Some of your people found me around Troutdale a few months back. I'd been sheltering in a truck stop."

Xolani shook hands with her before turning back to tend Gabe. She kept her voice mild and conversational. "You were sexually assaulted?"

Emmy shrugged, sighing. "Not much of an assault. When Jacob explained the situation, I decided it wasn't worth dying for. Tia held out, same as this stubborn *cabrón*." She jerked her head at Gabe.

Rhys gasped as if the wind had been knocked out of him. "What?"

Gabe laughed, a bitter smile twisting his bruised face. "I decided

I'd rather die than give him the satisfaction. Emmy was a lot smarter than me."

"Gabe—" Rhys's voice broke, his throat tightening. "Xolani?"

She shook her head, meeting his eyes directly. "It's been almost three weeks, Rhys. There's nothing we're going to be able to do if he's been infected."

"What about me?" Emmy asked tightly. "Am I going to go crazy and start eating people, too?"

Xolani bowed her head. "I don't know. Clearly our experiment in prophylactic immunity has encountered some unexpected variables. We're going to have to keep you under quarantine until we're sure. It's too late for you to go back to Colorado Springs with this summer's group, anyway. We'll have the winter to figure it out."

Emmy nodded, dropping her gaze. "You should probably know I'm pregnant. I was involved with another one of the survivors back in the quarantine. I had just started to suspect when we were kidnapped."

Xolani sighed, closing her eyes. "*Shit*. I'm sorry, honey. You're going to need to abort."

"*What?* Why?"

"In the best-case scenario, you're infected with Bane Alpha. The virus doesn't cross the placental barrier, which is probably a good thing if you consider the possibilities involving a fetus or infant or, God forbid, a toddler with a Jug's strength. But neither do the antibodies, and Alpha mutates to Beta when it's blood-borne and exposed to air. Childbirth involves blood. Jugs can't have children. We learned that the hard way. They're infected with the Rot the moment they're born."

Xolani's expression was sympathetic but not wounded. Either she hadn't been the Jug to learn that lesson first or it didn't bother her as much as Rhys thought it might. Who had it been? Schuyler? Gina? Maybe even Jamie? Or had it been someone he hadn't met yet?

Now Kaleo's remarks about Jug females made much more sense.

Emmy fell silent, pushing off the ground and walking away, her back to the rest of them. They let her have her privacy until she sniffed and wiped her face.

"So he's going to take that from me, too." Her eyes were bleak when she turned back to them. "Great. Just great. Well, if we're going to do it, it'll need to be soon."

"Of course." Xolani nodded. "Once we get to someplace we can camp for a few days safely so you can recuperate."

Gabe held out his hand reassuringly, and Emmy took it, squeezing back. Before anyone could say anything else, though, Kaleo's head snapped up.

"I've got a contact at the edge of the scanner's range. Can't quite determine what it is. It's large enough to rule out most wildlife, but it's low to the ground. I can't make out the shape so I'm not sure it's human. Stay down. I'm going to try to get closer and get a fix on it."

He looked to Xolani for confirmation—apparently Darius had gotten through to him—and she nodded her approval of the plan, urging Gabe and Emmy to get low near the base of the trees. Xolani, Joe, and Rhys all crouched, their weapons covering Kaleo's progress deeper into the greenbelt. Rhys wasn't certain what possessed him to move, except for the notion that it was best that they not be all clustered together in one clearing if something hostile came along. Staying low, he crept carefully to squat behind the first large tree Kaleo passed, and then the next. A glance to his left showed that Joe was making a similar covert advance on the far side of Kaleo.

Rhys barely contained a scream when a shotgun blast exploded in the silence. Kaleo's neck erupted in a fountain of blood, painting the undergrowth in a crimson spray almost to Rhys's feet. Rhys pressed his back against the trunk of the tree, covering his mouth with his hand. He tried to still his rapid breathing, hoping he hadn't been seen or heard.

"Don't move! Drop the fucking gun!" Jacob's voice was rough and hoarse, as if he'd been shouting a lot. Rhys froze, unsure whether or not he was the one being addressed, but a quick glance around the back of the tree that hid him showed Joe slowly rising, setting his gun down and lifting his hands. Joe very carefully looked anywhere but in Rhys's direction.

Shit. Ducking back into his concealed spot, Rhys glanced down to see Kaleo's infrared scanner, splattered in blood, near his feet. If Jacob came looking for it, he'd find Rhys for sure. But if Rhys tried to move it, Jacob would hear him. All he could do was stay still and hope Jacob didn't think to claim the scanner.

Closing his eyes, Rhys focused on keeping his breath quiet and steady. When he opened them, he felt like he had that day in the chapel when he'd made up his mind he was going to die. Everything around him was sharp and vibrant. Gorgeous, really. The greens of the leaves and underbrush had never been so vivid, the fallen leaves mulching the turf never so aromatic. There were so many different tones of brownish-black and gray in the bark of the trees, and the wind was crisp and clean.

Jacob's harsh voice carried through the woods. "Where's Rhys?"

"Fort Vancouver." Joe sounded calm. Unconcerned.

"Bullshit! He may be a pansy-ass faggot, but there's no way he'd stay behind with his boyfriend in danger."

"You nearly crushed his windpipe. Last I saw him, he was struggling to breathe. I think Xolani might have had to intubate him before we left. He could be dead now for all I know."

Silence fell, punctuated by Jacob's furious panting. Rhys barely dared inhale.

"I think you're lying," Jacob snarled finally. "Walk. Back the way you came. Stay in front of me like a good meat-shield."

Rhys refused to move as the sound of footsteps shuffling through the fallen leaves and undergrowth receded. Then his head thudded back against the tree, and he allowed himself to hyperventilate for a moment.

When the sounds of Joe and Jacob's passage had faded, Rhys dared to peer around the tree, listening. Of course, just because he couldn't see or hear them any longer didn't mean Jacob wasn't still close enough to pounce on him. Rhys rose and stepped around the tree, nearly tripping over his fucking gun.

Jesus. He propped the rifle against the base of the tree. He wouldn't be able to move quietly with it, and he wasn't sure he trusted himself to use it without hitting anyone else. His best hope now to help Joe and Gabe and Xolani was to sneak up behind Jacob if he could. Drawing a calming breath, he unsnapped the sheath at his hip and drew out the knife Xolani had given him, flinching at the soft *hiss* as it scraped against the leather. It seemed absurdly loud to Rhys's ears, but there was no one else near to hear it.

He inched forward, staying low, hopefully remaining out of Jacob's peripheral vision. Stopping behind a tree, he heard Jacob jeer. "Guess you weren't lying after all. Hear that, Gabe? Your little faggot boyfriend couldn't even be bothered to come after you."

He couldn't hear Gabe's answer, but knowing Gabe's mouth, Rhys was positive it would enrage Jacob. Sure enough, Jacob bellowed in response, and Rhys took the opportunity to dart to the next sheltering tree, pausing again.

"So what?" Gabe taunted when it was quiet again. "I'm dead anyway. Go ahead and shoot me."

"Or maybe I'll just drag you back to Fort Vancouver while the Rot eats away at you so that fucking pervert can watch you die!"

When Rhys dared a glance around the trunk, he could see Jacob, the barrel of his gun swinging between Xolani, Joe, and Gabe. Too far, though. Rhys had the visual but not the range. Dropping low, he crept forward again.

"He must have gone the long way around, evading scanner range!" The shout came from the road, and another voice responded. Darius and the rest of the squad. No doubt they'd heard the shotgun blast. Jacob shouldered Joe's assault rifle and fired a spray of bullets blindly into the trees, drawing alarmed yells.

"*Down! Get down!*"

"Stay back! I'll kill them!" Jacob screamed. "Keep your fucking distance!"

Jacob's shout was followed by another round of bullets, and in his mind, Rhys could see one of those blind shots finding Darius where he lay on the highway up the embankment from the greenbelt. Taking advantage of Jacob's distraction, Rhys darted forward, letting the knife slip through his fingers so that he held it by the blade. With that perfect perception, when everything was so clear, he saw Gabe's eyes widen as he caught sight of Rhys moving in behind Jacob.

Jacob saw it, too, but the knife had already left Rhys's hand before he could turn. It flipped end over end, just like he'd practiced, hurtling toward Jacob's exposed back. It was both a terrible miss and the luckiest throw Rhys had ever made. He'd been aiming for the expanse between Jacob's shoulder blades.

What he got was a kidney.

Jacob's knees buckled, and Xolani moved with inhuman speed as he completed his turn toward Rhys, his gun forgotten in his shock. The hideous *crunch* of shattering vertebrae filled the clearing, and Jacob fell to the ground, his head nearly twisted off.

"All clear!" Xolani shouted, then turned to Rhys, panting. Her eyes burned with the same primal battle fury he'd once seen in Kaleo's. And in Darius's. "Where's Kaleo?"

"Dead." Rhys slumped against a tree as the rush of adrenaline began to fade, leaving him shaking. Darius and Titus burst into the clearing, half sliding down the embankment from the road, followed by Toby, then Gina, Jamie, and Bailey. Darius's avid gaze assessed Rhys, but he didn't approach.

"Status?" he demanded instead, and the bestial rage in Xolani's eyes began to bleed away.

"Fucker got Kaleo. Everyone else is fine. The hostages are stable for now. They'll need to be quarantined away from the other civvies when we get them back to base."

"Is that really necessary where I'm concerned?" Gabe's mouth twisted in a rueful smile.

Rhys shook his head in adamant denial. "You don't know you're infected, Gabe!"

"It's okay, Rhys." Gabe gave him a pitying look. "Tia and I knew what we were doing when we refused to let him fuck us. I don't mind."

Rhys's eyes burned with tears he couldn't shed as he looked back and forth between Xolani and Darius. "Do you have to— Does it have to be— Can we—"

"We can wait." Xolani squeezed his shoulder. "Not too long or he might go catatonic. But until he starts showing symptoms. Or decides he's ready, whichever comes first."

Gabe nodded gratefully. "I wouldn't mind a few days to catch up."

"All right, people." Darius cleared his throat gruffly. "Let's lay

Kaleo to rest. We'll camp at the ranch tonight, head back to base tomorrow."

As everyone went into action, Rhys felt eyes upon him. He turned to see Joe standing there, staring at him intently. After a moment, Rhys nodded his understanding, and Joe turned away.

29

MEMORIAL

R hys watched the glow from Kaleo's funeral pyre dance on the wall while first watch secured the house and settled in. It was becoming a familiar sight. Downstairs, those who weren't on watch were toasting Kaleo, courtesy of the well-stocked liquor cabinet they'd found. Rhys had declined to join them, however. He sat with his knees drawn up to his chest in the bedroom where Xolani had settled Gabe. A stirring from the bed drew his attention from the flickering of the firelight to Gabe, who rolled over, rubbing his head as though it pained him.

"You're actually here." He blinked at Rhys. "I thought maybe I had hallucinated it."

"I'm here. For now." Rhys sniffed. "It's weird. I've been wanting to talk to you for a month and now I can't think of anything to say."

"Start by telling me why you're not one of those guys yet." Gabe flapped a hand in the direction of the door. "Back when we were on our way to Fort Vancouver, I thought that's what . . . I mean, Darius said . . ."

"Darius explained that?" Rhys was grateful for the darkness that disguised his blush.

Gabe rubbed the back of his neck. "Yeah, when I just about tried to deck him. I assumed they were doing something awful to you at night."

Instead of being mortified, Rhys found himself laughing help-lessly, rolling his head against the back of his chair. "Well, um . . ." He scratched his scalp awkwardly, unsure how to answer.

"So it hasn't worked?"

"No." He closed his eyes with a slow sigh. "I think a week or two back, I gave up hope that it would. Now I'm just waiting for the Rot to begin so I can die. And praying I don't become a monster like Jacob."

Gabe snorted bitterly. "You and me both."

"Yeah, well, we just might end up checking out together."

"Don't do that." Gabe's voice was sharp. It was filled with that same gruff, tough affection he'd used in the past to bolster Rhys's spirits back when they'd been boys together. "You've still got a chance. I don't, and that's okay. I feel like every day since I left the monastery years ago has mostly been spent waiting to die anyway. But you might still make it."

Rhys looked away. He hadn't realized it until now, but he'd spent his time at the monastery after Gabe had run away waiting to die as well, knowing that sooner or later Jacob or Father Maurice would kill him or drive him away, which would have the same effect. It wasn't until the revenants had attacked that he'd found any hope of living.

"Why did you leave?" He couldn't help the plaintive note that crept into his voice, lost and unsure, like the confused boy he'd been the day he'd learned Gabe was gone. He'd needed Gabe so damned bad back then. "I mean, you almost kissed me, and then you were gone, and I always wondered if I— If it was *me*—"

"What are you talking about?" Gabe gave a soft gasp of incredu-lous laughter. "*You* almost kissed *me*!"

Rhys stared at his shadowed profile in disbelief for a moment, echoing the laugh. "Really? Is that how you— Oh God! Is that *why* — *Was* it me?"

"No. No!" Gabe tried to push himself up on the bed, groaning in discomfort. Rhys uncurled from his chair to assist, propping pillows behind him. "It was like— I never gave it any thought, you know? You. In that way. I always assumed someday it would be Cady when she grew up, and I knew Jacob and Maurice would give me a lot of trouble over that, but that was okay. But then that day in the shed . . . suddenly there was this other possibility, and then Maurice saw us and started yelling and saying horrible things about us and all I could think was that if I stayed, we'd do it again, and it would be a hundred times worse than if I was with Cady. They would make our lives hell. They would kill us, or make us want to kill ourselves, or drive us out." He plucked at the dusty bedspread. "I couldn't think of any other way to keep that from happening, you know?"

"It was awful after you left." Rhys's eyes began burning again, and he blinked until the feeling went away. "I needed you. You were always the brave one."

"Only when it came to sticking up for others." Gabe shrugged. "I couldn't deal with all that aimed at me. I don't know. I think sometime around when the plague began, when we were just kids, everything stopped making sense and never started again."

"Guess it doesn't matter." Rhys stared at the flickering light on the wall again. "I just always wanted to know."

A long, silent moment dragged on before Gabe drew a shuddering breath. "They said my parents weren't at the monastery when they found you?"

"No." Rhys gave him an apologetic look. "They left to find you and never came back."

"What about Jeff?"

Rhys bowed his head, thinking about Gabe's quiet little brother, who'd never really recovered from the loss of his family. "I tried to look after him as much as I could. He, um, he was killed when the revs got Cady and Father Maurice."

"Are you still . . . um, with the Jugs? Are you still trying to get infected?"

"No." Rhys wished he felt as complacent about it as he sounded. "There's really no point to that anymore. Only with Darius."

"Oh?" There was an expectant lift to Gabe's voice. Rhys refused to look up.

"Yeah. He's just— He's been good about trying to help me live. They all were."

"Thought you said there's not much point to that now?"

"Well, there isn't, I mean, I'm either infected by now or I'm not. If I'm not, I'm dead, and if I am, once I'm a Jug, he won't need to . . ." He fell silent, his hands twisting in his lap.

"You know, it's okay to fall in love with someone who isn't *me*."

Rhys's head snapped up. Gabe's blue eyes twinkled, and for a moment he was the same cocky smart-ass who had always taken it upon himself to lift Rhys's spirits. Rhys shook his head, though, his smile fading.

"It was never about love. It was about self-respect. I fought it for a long time because I didn't want the only sex I ever had before I died to not mean anything, especially when it was already something I didn't have a choice in. Then it didn't feel meaningless anymore, and it was okay. Better than okay."

Gabe didn't comment, and Rhys sighed.

"I'm not sure there's much point in loving anyone in this world, the way it is." His chest ached as he thought of the tenderness with which Darius had touched him that first time after his illness, how they'd lain together and simply kissed for what felt like hours. It was better that Darius was too hard a man to fall in love. Not when he'd have to kill Rhys any day now. "It's probably better just to . . . to matter a little, until you die or they die. Just a little. Then they burn your body and go on with trying to survive."

Gabe gave him a disgusted look, anger simmering in his eyes. "If that's the best you can expect, why bother? What's the fucking point of trying to live at all?"

"I don't know if there is one. We just have to try anyway. Maybe we hope sooner or later we'll find the point."

"That's such bullshit." Gabe glared at Rhys. "I don't buy it. You wouldn't have said that four years ago when I was still at the monastery."

Rhys's eyes began to burn, and he quickly looked away, focusing on the ripples of firelight and shadow cast on the wall again. "Maybe you're right, but it's just better to look at it this way now."

"What's better about it?"

Rhys pressed the heels of his hands into his eyes until the stinging stopped. "I just— I don't want to . . . *care* about someone like that when I'm going to die in just a few days or weeks. I think I can handle dying, but not if I feel like there's something worth living for that I didn't have enough time to experience. It wouldn't be fair. And besides—"

Sympathy softened Gabe's expression. "Besides what?"

Rhys bowed his head. "I don't want Darius to have to kill me knowing I—" To his humiliation, his voice cracked, and Rhys cleared his throat. "It's just better this way."

Gabe stared at him for a long moment, then nodded slowly. "All right."

Rhys smiled bravely. Suddenly he was tired, and older than his age, and unspeakably sad. "Can we talk about something else?"

"Actually, I think I need to rest some more if we're going to get on the road again tomorrow. Do you think Xolani might have something for my headache?"

"I'll go find her and see. Do you want me to stay here with you?"

Gabe smiled and shook his head, waving him away. "No. Just send Xolani in if she's still awake, please?"

After he located Xolani, it took some searching, but Rhys found the bedroom where Darius had stowed his pack. Darius wasn't there, though. Rhys heard him somewhere in the house, talking about watch shifts with Toby. He dropped his rucksack in the corner beside Darius's and kicked off his boots, flipping over the mattress on the bed to minimize the dust before he curled up on his side to wait.

Sometime in the night, he came half-awake to feel a body behind him, lips on the back of his neck, hands pulling at his clothes. He turned blindly, seeking the kiss he knew would be there, lifting and wriggling to get free from his pants as the last remnants of sleep fled. He rolled Darius onto his back and let himself explore with hands and mouth as Darius had once encouraged him to do, and then indulged in a long-overdue lesson on sucking cock.

$$\Lambda \ \Lambda \ \Lambda$$

As they began the journey back north across the high desert of eastern Oregon, opting to return to the boats and the river rather than risk the mountain passes this close to winter, Darius continued fucking Rhys as fiercely as he had begun, as if he could compel Rhys's cells to accept the Alpha strain by force of will. As if he could drive out, with the bruising grasp of his hands and the punishing thrust of his cock, the corruption they both knew was spreading through his body.

And Rhys begged him for it, as Darius had once assured him he would. The more certain he became that he was dying, the more he craved Darius's penchant for brutality. He wanted to pack every memory he could make into the days he had left, every sensation he could feel from a life he'd barely had a chance to live.

He didn't know if Darius understood that, but even if he didn't, he still managed to deliver exactly what Rhys needed.

A week or so after they recovered Gabe and Emmy, the Jugs made camp in a high school gymnasium, where they would stay for several days while Emmy recuperated from her abortion. All the entrances were barricaded save the one they controlled, which meant he and Darius could go off to the locker room, away from the others, for a little more privacy.

The tile on the walls was cracked and chipped. The varnish on the bench Rhys bent over blistered and flaked off under his hands. Everything was covered in a decade's worth of dust and cobwebs. And everywhere else they went was the same. Crumbling, abandoned bars, abandoned offices, abandoned hotels, abandoned homes.

The haunting and haunted remnants of an abandoned world.

And in Darius's arms each night, when reason returned and they lay together, drained and weary, Rhys decided there was something inescapably beautiful about the fact that they made these memories in ruined places.

30

ENDING

They were maybe three days from the river where they had stowed the inflatable boat when Rhys emerged from the tent he shared with Darius one chilly morning to see Gabe seated by the coals of the fire, staring at something in his lap. When he looked up, Rhys could see his eyes were red and swollen.

"What is it?"

Gabe swallowed and pulled down the neck of his shirt, revealing a bruised patch of skin just below his collarbone.

"I found it yesterday." There was a rasp in his voice. He held up the plastic bag that had been lying in his lap and a large handful of pills. "I asked Xolani for these a week or so ago. She said when I was ready, I could just take the pills, put the bag over my head, and I'd go to sleep and never wake up. No pain. But . . . I couldn't do it."

Two tears spilled from Gabe's eyes and plummeted down his cheeks. Rhys's knees buckled, dropping him to the wet, cold ground. He wasn't sure how long he knelt there, shivering in the frigid morning air. Long enough for the rest of the Jugs to begin stirring from their tents.

"I guess I'll ask Xolani to help," Gabe murmured at last.

Rhys lifted his eyes to see Joe behind Gabe at the far edge of camp, where he'd been standing third watch.

"No. I'll do it." Rhys cleared his throat when his voice cracked. "I'll help you. It should be . . . it should be someone who cares."

Joe bowed his head and shuffled away.

"Today? Now?" Gabe's eyes sought his, pleading. "I don't . . . I can't make it through the day, waiting. The past couple days, I've felt my brain getting foggy, and I'm getting really tired. Xolani says I could go catatonic at any time."

"Okay." Rhys knelt there a moment longer, his legs and feet aching with the cold, and finally he turned to crawl back into the tent, grabbing the rest of his clothing: the jacket they'd scavenged for him once the weather turned cold, the belt with the knife sheath and handgun holster.

When he looked up, he saw Darius watching him.

"I can do it, boy."

Rhys shook his head. "No. It has to be me. Just have everyone start gathering wood. Please?"

Darius murmured his assent, and Rhys backed out of the tent, turning to see Emmy clinging to Gabe and crying. The other Jugs were saying their farewells to him, patting his shoulder or shaking his hand. It was polite and strange and gentle and macabre. Rhys wanted to scream at them for being so sanguine when it felt like a boulder was crushing his chest and pulverizing his ribs. How dare they just accept a world where the best gift they could hope to give someone they cared about was a swift, clean, merciful death? How dare they force him to accept it as well?

A large hand landed on Rhys's shoulder, and Joe leaned close to his ear. "There's a clearing about twenty yards that way. It's within scanner range but private. It's pretty. Take all the time you need."

Rhys nodded, feeling hollow, like someone had gouged his heart and lungs out of his chest with a rusty bayonet. It felt as if he was going to his own death. He wished he were. He would rather be Gabe, knowing it would be over soon.

He would rather be Darius, hard enough to do this without flinching.

"Do you know how you want to do it?" Rhys asked as he led Gabe to the clearing, their fingers laced together. The question felt odd and detached, especially for such a peaceful, pleasant place. The closer they got to the river, the more lush the landscape became, the scrub pines of the high desert transitioning back into a rainforest more characteristic of the Pacific Northwest.

Gabe shrugged. "I'll try to take the pills again, I guess? Maybe you could sit with me until I fall asleep. Put the bag over my head."

"Okay." Rhys ran a listless hand over the moist, mossy bark of a fallen tree trunk. His eyes burned.

How could they be speaking of this as though it were so mundane?

Gabe handed him the plastic bag and looked down at his handful of pills, staring at them as though mesmerized.

"Rhys?"

"Yeah?"

"Do you think I could have that kiss now?"

Rhys's breath left him in an explosive gasp, as if he'd been punched in the chest. His throat was so tight and dry he could barely speak, but somehow he managed a quavering whisper. "Yeah."

Gabe's lips were soft, damp, and salty beneath his. Rhys brushed his mouth across Gabe's once, then again. And then Gabe's arms snapped around him, and Gabe was sobbing into his shoulder. Rhys clung to him with every ounce of strength he possessed, trying to crush Gabe's ribs, trying to burrow into his skin. He looked up into the clear, cold sky and prayed to God—that bastard who had never once revealed Himself or His supposed mercy in all those years of hell at the monastery—to spare him this.

Finally, Gabe pulled away, wiping at his face. "Okay. I think I'm ready."

Rhys nodded, feeling hollow and cold again. Gabe sank down onto the mossy ground, kneeling, and cupped his hand to his mouth, tossing back the pills and following them with a long drink from his canteen. A moment later, he gagged loudly, falling forward. Rhys flinched as Gabe coughed and retched, spilling the pills onto the ground with a torrent of bile.

"I can't," he sobbed brokenly. "I can't make myself swallow. I can't."

"It's okay." Rhys sank down beside him, drawing Gabe to his shoulder, rocking him. "It's okay."

"What am I going to do?"

Rhys closed his eyes and shuddered, his stomach twisting. He pressed a fervent kiss to Gabe's temple. He could do this. He could do this for Gabe, who had always taken care of him.

"It's okay. I'll take care of you. Just . . . stay where you are. Keep your eyes closed. All right?"

Gabe nodded, sniffling, and Rhys stood, tipping his head back and drawing several deep breaths until his trembling stopped. Gabe knelt there almost prayerfully, his head bowed, his hands open, palms upturned on his thighs. Rhys drew his handgun out of its holster.

There. The base of the skull. He could hear Xolani coaching him. *Take out the brain stem. Death is instant and painless.*

He thought his hand would be shaking, but it was strangely steady. Gabe wasn't. He quaked visibly past the short barrel of the gun, tense and ready to flinch away.

"Hey, Gabe?"

"Yeah?"

Gabe's head came up only a fraction of an inch and, sickened with his own calculated distraction, Rhys pulled the trigger in that relaxed, trusting instant when Gabe stopped anticipating the shot.

Gabe pitched forward, and an anguished shriek echoed through the trees, like the wail of an injured animal. For a horrified moment, Rhys thought he'd missed, that he'd only wounded Gabe, and that Gabe was writhing on the ground in pain.

Then he realized the screaming was his own.

The gun fell from his numbed fingers, and arms of someone Rhys hadn't known was standing behind him seized him, turning him away from Gabe and into a hard, familiar chest.

He wished he could cry. He sobbed and screeched until he puked, but his eyes continued to burn, dry, as though the pain was too deep for tears. He thrashed and fought against those encasing arms, though, pounding his fists against Darius's chest and shoulders. Darius withstood it without so much as a grunt.

"I don't want to do this anymore." He sagged against Darius, vaguely aware of Joe and Titus lifting Gabe and carrying him away. "I can't. I can't. Please. Darius, *please*. Can't I be done now?"

"No. No!" Darius whispered fiercely, pressing his lips to Rhys's temple. His arms threatened to crush Rhys. "Not yet, boy. It ain't time. I ain't letting you go 'til I got no other choice."

Rhys did cry, then. He wept as he hadn't wept since he was twelve and Jacob had set out to make his life hell for every moment of weakness he displayed. He wept for himself, his life so soon to be cut short, and for Gabe, who he'd found only to lose, and for Darius, who would never allow himself to mourn once Rhys was gone. Scalding tears washed down his sweating face in a continuous trickle, creating tracks in the dust and smoke on his cheeks when at last he stood beside Gabe's pyre.

Then he let Darius lead him back into the tent and hold him while he cried some more.

⚔ ⚔ ⚔

THEY CAMPED in that spot another night, until Gabriel's fire had burned down to embers, and Rhys had slept like he never intended to wake again. The next morning, Darius climbed out of the tent where Rhys still slumbered bonelessly to find Xolani standing third watch, leaning against a tree and tugging on her braid as she monitored the scanner.

"How is he?" she asked as Darius came to stand beside her.

Darius gave a tired sigh and rubbed his bruised chest. "Don't know. Don't know what to do for him."

"Give him time, I guess. Which is about the most fucking useless advice I've ever given." Xolani sighed, looking exhausted. "Kid's too damn soft for this life."

"Isn't that why we wanna keep him?" Darius laughed humorlessly. "He makes us softer, and it's been too long since we had that. We miss it. Reminds us we're human."

Her mouth twisted. "Yeah, I guess you're right. And he needs us, because he's never going to be hard enough. At least I hope not."

"Oh, I dunno. That was a pretty fucking hard thing he did yesterday."

"Yeah, and it might just have broken him." She groaned. "Jesus, I'm maudlin. Get me the fuck back to base, would you? I want a blunt the size of my forearm and a ringside seat to an orgy."

Darius chuckled, this time with a little more conviction. "Wouldn't say no to some of Titus's hooch right about now." He shuffled, hanging his head. "How much longer you think he's got? It's been over eight weeks, and he's still not a Jug."

"Yeah, but he doesn't have Beta or Gamma yet, either."

"Matter of time, now, isn't it?"

"Maybe not."

Darius stiffened, staring at her sharply. "Explain."

"Eight weeks is a statistical outlier as far as the timeline for infection goes. The vast majority of infections manifest in the three-to-six-week window. The fact he's made it to this point without manifesting any of the strains might suggest he's immune to all of them."

"Keep talking." Darius heard his voice get rougher, more demanding. His fingers dug into the damp bark of the tree.

"My best guess—outside the very real possibility of another mutation—is that Houtman had a minor exposure to Gamma and limited exposure to Alpha. Neither was sufficient to confer immunity to the other, so he wound up infected with both." Darius nodded, and Xolani's braid snagged on the rough trunk of the tree as she rolled her head to the side to look at him. "Now, keeping in mind that—*again* —this is guesswork, it stands to reason that Rhys, who was the one tussling with the revs with blood all over him when we found them, had more exposure to Beta and Gamma, and combined with his massive exposure to Alpha, could get immunity to all the strains. Maybe he built up antibodies to both simultaneously so they . . . canceled each other out, for lack of a better explanation. Or maybe the continued Alpha exposure is acting as a—I don't know—a suppressant of some sort, preventing the Beta or Gamma from manifesting. We've seen that in the past with chronic viruses. Viral inhibitors could prevent outbreaks, even if they couldn't cure the infection."

"Is that really possible?" Darius stared at her, too stunned to care how urgent he sounded.

Xolani snorted. "Fucked if I know. This goddamn virus is so

erratic and unpredictable, and our knowledge of how it works so limited . . . Darius, I can't do more than make guesses based on suppositions based on radical hypotheses that would make my microbiology and immunology professors slit their wrists if they weren't already dead. Another possible explanation is that he has some sort of inherent immunity, and if he does, he is—as far as we know—quite literally one in almost five hundred million in this country alone. It's possible that survivors who haven't been found yet or who made it to Colorado Springs have the same immunity, but we'll never know because they'll never be exposed. I sure as hell hope that's the case because if it's hereditary, it means that as long as they keep growing the gene pool, a few generations down the line most of the population will be protected. Either way, my best guess, as far as Rhys is concerned, is that if he hasn't manifested any of the strains by now, he's in the clear."

Darius tightened his jaw against the ache that tried to take root in his chest, as though relief and distress were having a tug-of-war with his internal organs. "So he can go. He can go to Colorado Springs with the other civvies."

"No."

"No?"

"No." Xolani shook her head decisively. "We don't know what's living in his blood. Or what he may be shedding as an airborne pathogen, for that matter. There's a chance that he's simply asymptomatic rather than immune. If that's the case, he could still be able to transmit the disease. Ever heard of Typhoid Mary?"

"So we have to keep him away from the civilian population for the rest of his life."

Xolani nodded, smiling softly. "Lucky us."

"Jesus, Xolani. He can't stay with us. He's not a Jug. If you're right, he'll never *be* a Jug. He'll never be able to keep up. He'll never be safe with us, doing what we do."

"Who else is equipped to protect him and keep him segregated from the uninfected population? The fact that we don't want to give him up is a happy coincidence, but I'm not sure he'd be wild about leaving us, either." She sighed. "It's entirely possible we'll benefit from this a lot more than he will, but it's a pretty fucking imperfect world."

"I don't like telling him he has to stay no matter what he wants."

"Yeah? How many of us got a choice about where we ended up?" Her expression became slightly bitter at that. "Besides, he's known from the beginning that he'd be with us for the duration. I like to think maybe he wants to stay."

Darius nodded slowly. "Guess I should go find out."

She gave him a wicked grin. "Take your time. I'll oversee breaking camp."

ΛΛΛ

DARIUS SAT for some time simply watching Rhys sleep. There were still crusted tracks of salt around his eyes, and his mouth was slack. An occasional grimace hinted at troubled dreams.

Xolani was right. He was way too soft for this life. Darius wasn't sure when he'd come to need that softness, but he didn't want to give it up. The problem was, Rhys might have to stay with the Jugs, but Darius couldn't count on Rhys wanting to stay with *him*. Not when he was so young. Not when he had a whole new lease on life and so much living to explore.

Eventually, Rhys's eyes blinked open, immediately filling with a sadness that suggested he would rather have remained asleep.

Instead, his gaze slowly moved to Darius, somber and expectant.

"I'm glad you're awake." Darius hesitated a moment, though not as much as he might once have done, before covering Rhys's hand with his own and squeezing it. He could give Rhys the roughness he needed. The softness, though, that came a bit harder, but he was willing to try. Xolani had threatened to break Darius's jaw if he didn't follow Rhys to that clearing to be there to catch him after his friend died, but now he was glad he'd done it. He wouldn't trade the tears Rhys had shed in his arms, *needing* him, for all the pleasure in the world.

He'd do anything to be what this boy needed, to give him what little joy they could find in this life they were stuck with. Maybe that was twisted, but like Xolani said, it was a pretty fucking imperfect world.

"We need to get on the road?" Rhys mumbled.

"Eventually, yeah. But first, we need to talk about your future."

Wariness crept into those guileless hazel eyes. "Is something wrong? Am I . . . Does Xolani think it will be me soon?"

"Well, that's the thing. Xolani doesn't think it's gonna be you at all."

"I don't understand." Rhys's voice barely rose above a whisper. Darius suspected he might have screamed his throat raw in those first few minutes of catastrophic grief.

Taking a deep breath, Darius gave Rhys a rundown of Xolani's latest theories. Rhys took it in silently, nodding slowly, not speaking until Darius had finished.

"What will I do?"

"I suppose that's up to you," Darius fixed his eyes on a spot above Rhys's head. "You have to stay with us. Even if you never show a symptom, you might still be able to transmit the viruses, infect other people. But aside from that, you can make your own choices. You don't . . . you don't have to stay with *me*. It's not necessary anymore."

Rhys stared at him in disbelief and with something uncomfortably close to hurt. "You want me to go. Since you don't have to help me anymore."

Darius shook his head quickly. "No."

Rhys blinked and continued staring, waiting for more. But Darius couldn't put the *more* into words.

Rhys would never have the strength to be evenly matched against him. He'd never have the strength to reassure Darius that he wasn't taking unfair advantage of a weaker, more vulnerable man.

All Darius had was Rhys's determination that he knew his own mind well enough to decide.

It wasn't perfect. Not even close. Or maybe it was fine and Darius just needed to get over his hang-up about the lack of parity between them.

"I just want to make sure you have the freedom to choose what you want to do," he finally said in response to that expectant expression on Rhys's face.

"I *told* you what I wanted." Something raw swam just under the surface of Rhys's eyes. Fear, maybe. Of what, rejection? "When I was getting over that infection and I asked you what would happen if I didn't end up dying. I said I didn't want things to change. I wanted them to stay the way they were, to stay . . ." His throat bobbed visibly. "With you."

Darius sighed. It had been easy to acquiesce to that request before, when Rhys had been weak and recovering, and when it looked like the possibility of his survival was getting dimmer all the time. Now, though, Rhys had an actual future riding on the answer. And Darius wanted to agree far too much to trust whose best interest he'd be serving if he allowed himself to do so.

"I'm not sure you really knew what you were saying. You were sick. You're young, and I know you're scared of things being different just when you're starting to find your feet. What's familiar feels safe, but—"

Rhys surged up from the blanket, shoving Darius and nearly toppling him over in an assault so unexpected Darius didn't have time to brace for it. Rhys's eyes blazed with fury.

"*Fuck that*, Darius! You don't get to tell me I have a choice and then *ignore* what I say when I choose!"

Darius stared at him in disbelief and then the corners of his mouth began to twitch. "You really wanna be with me, boy?" He couldn't seem to stop grinning. "Just the way we've been, even knowing it's not needed anymore?"

Rhys nodded, then frowned, looking down. "Just you. No others."

Darius stared at him a moment, an incredulous chuckle puffing from his lips. He didn't expect his own resistance to the limitation, especially given his tendency toward possessiveness. But it had been hot, those days at the fort when he'd been directing the men who'd fucked Rhys.

"You sure about that?" He leaned in closer. "Might be different, doing it just because it feels good. Sure you don't want me to be able to decide I want to pass you around, just because you're mine and I can? To use other men as the cocks I fuck you with? Blindfold you, tie you down, then offer you up to anyone I want?"

Rhys's eyes went a little dreamy and unfocused, and it seemed to take him a moment to remember how to make words. Finally, he whispered uncertainly, "*Maybe* someday."

Darius smiled a lazy smile, shifting to grab Rhys's shoulders and drag him closer. "It's a deal."

ACKNOWLEDGMENTS

Special thanks to Anne Tenino and Rachel Haimowitz, who provided me with input on field medicine. Any mistakes are my own. And also to Angela Benedetti, who helped me brainstorm the world and scenario prior to writing.

JUGGERNAUT

A STRAIN NOVEL

They helped destroy
the world.
Now they have to survive
the new one.

AMELIA C. GORMLEY

JUGGERNAUT

A STRAIN NOVEL

They helped destroy the world. Now they have to survive the new one.

Nico Fernández has a charmed life. Working as a high-end rentboy for the agency his mother started beats the hell out of being trafficked for slave wages in some corporate brothel. And no one needs to know about his occasional side jobs, seducing political and military dignitaries and "nudging" them with mind-altering agents to swing their votes and opinions to favor his longest-standing client.

Zach Houtman's life *should* be charmed, but isn't. His father, the Reverend Maurice Houtman, has insisted Zach advise him as he pursues his political aspirations, ignoring Zach's calling to minister to the most vulnerable outcasts of society. Politics, however, are gradually turning Zach's father away from Christ and into malicious zealotry, and his campaign is courting violent fundamentalists.

When one of Nico's "special jobs" results in military approval for a weaponized virus that mutates, unleashing a deadly plague to claim billions of lives, Nico and Zach are thrown together. Each burdened by terrible guilt for their unwitting roles in the calamity, they find safety and solace in each other. But the new world is a dangerous, violent place, where the handful of survivors are willing to do anything and kill anyone to get by.

A Strain Novel
Bane
The weapon that nearly
destroyed humanity
may be their
only salvation.
Amelia C. Gormley

BANE

A STRAIN NOVEL

The weapon that nearly destroyed humanity may be their only salvation.

RHYS COOPER once thought he was a dead man. Instead, he's proven immune to the virus that nearly wiped out humanity.

Now the Clean Zone's scientists want to know why. Summoned for testing, Rhys is about to learn first-hand why his Juggernaut partner, Sergeant Darius Murrell, and the rest of his superhuman comrades in Delta Company don't trust the uninfected survivors in the Clean Zone—or the remnants of the government that unleashed the epidemic in the first place.

For a decade, Zach Houtman has yearned for his lover, Nico Fernández, but fear of infection has kept them apart. Separately they keep tabs on the last vestiges of the corrupt government, particularly the head of the Clean Zone's virus research division. Secretary Littlewood seeks to unlock the secrets of the Bane virus. But Nico knows how dangerous Littlewood will be if that ever happens.

Now Zach and Nico have the perfect bait to draw Littlewood out: Rhys. But Delta Company isn't about to let Rhys walk into hell alone. They'll take Littlewood down together, or not at all. Even if they succeed, however, for Zach and Nico one question remains: can infected and uninfected people ever be together safely?

OTHER BOOKS BY AMELIA C. GORMLEY

THE IMPULSE TRILOGY

Inertia

Acceleration

Velocity

SEASONS IN SAUGATUCK

The Field of Someone Else's Dreams

Sea Change

Risk Aware

THE STRAIN TRILOGY

Juggernaut

Strain

Bane

Player vs. Player

ABOUT THE AUTHOR

Amelia C. Gormley published her first short story in the school newspaper in the 4th grade, and since then has suffered the persistent delusion that enabling other people to hear the voices in her head might be a worthwhile endeavor. She's even convinced her hapless spouse that it could be a lucrative one as well, especially when coupled with her real-life interest in angst, kink, feminism, and pretty men.

When her husband and son aren't interacting with the back of her head as she stares at the computer, they rely on her to feed them, maintain their domicile, and keep some semblance of order in their lives (all very, very bad ideas—they really should know better by now.) She can also be found playing video games and ranting on Tumblr, seeing as how she's one of those horrid social justice warriors out to destroy free speech, gaming, geek culture, and everything else that's fun everywhere.

http://ameliacgormley.com
http://ameliacgormley.tumblr.com

facebook.com/ameliacgormley

twitter.com/ACGormley

goodreads.com/ameliacgormley